The Curia Chronicles

A Novel

The Curia Chronicles

A Novel

Jeff Durkin & Steph Nelson

ROUNDFIRE
BOOKS

London, UK
Washington, DC, USA

CollectiveInk

First published by Roundfire Books, 2025
Roundfire Books is an imprint of Collective Ink Ltd.,
Unit 11, Shepperton House, 89 Shepperton Road, London, N1 3DF
office@collectiveinkbooks.com
www.collectiveinkbooks.com
www.roundfire-books.com

For distributor details and how to order please visit the 'Ordering' section on our website.

Text copyright: Jeff Durkin Steph Nelson 2023

ISBN: 978 1 80341 680 9
978 1 80341 693 9 (ebook)
Library of Congress Control Number: 2023947151

Design: Lapiz Digital Services

UK: Printed and bound by CPI Group (UK) Ltd, Croydon, CR0 4YY
Printed in North America by CPI GPS partners

We operate a distinctive and ethical publishing philosophy in all areas of our business, from our global network of authors to production and worldwide distribution.

Chapter 1

Not my ceiling. Tessa Sinclair lay on her back, her vision coming into focus.

She was used to the water-stained ceiling of her efficiency apartment. She often found herself lying awake on her futon, staring up at the dingy stucco, her mind refusing to rest. Occasionally, she'd invite a guy over and watch that water-stained ceiling go in and out of sight as they tangled in drunken pleasure. *But this isn't my studio.* This ceiling was a grid of clean white panels and fluorescent bulbs behind a frosted plastic case. She looked to one side, then the other.

I'm in a hospital. She ran her fingers over an IV line inserted into the vein of her right hand to a saline bag hanging from a metal stand. The bed looked several decades older than 2011 – the headboard and footboard were made up of pale-green metal tubes – but was clean and not out of place with the rest of the room. A metal chair – the same institutional color as the bed – was pushed against the wall opposite the bed. She checked the bed. No call button.

Tessa sat up. Although she was a little groggy, she felt fine. *How the hell did I wind up here?* The last thing she remembered was watching the Times Square New Year's Eve Party on TV in her apartment, while working her way through a fifth of Jack Daniels. The impression of something else was lurking at the edge of her memory. *I really need to stop drinking so much.* She cradled her head. *Did someone call the cops?*

"Hello," Tessa called out to no one in particular, feeling the dryness in her throat. "Can I get some water?" She waited a minute. No response. She pulled out the IV and swung her legs off the bed. The floor was cold.

Tessa walked to the window. The glass was frosted, but she could tell it was sometime during the day. She also made out the shadows of bars crisscrossing the window. *Which hospital in Detroit has higher security and hasn't been remodeled? Could be Henry Ford.*

There were two doors. One was opposite the window. It was metal and the same vintage green color as the furniture. The other was a flimsy slab wooden door with a cheap brass knob. *Probably the bathroom.*

She opened the wooden door, turned on the light and saw a toilet, sink, mirror and her canvas Army duffle bag on the floor. She knelt on the cold tile floor and unfastened the bag. It was filled with her clothes, neatly folded and packed, as well as the black Doc Martens she wore to work as a bartender at the Blue Ox. She pulled out the boots, a pair of jeans, a plain cotton thong and sports bra, and a faded red T-shirt. She stacked the clothing neatly on the side of the sink and stripped off the hospital gown. She checked herself out in the mirror, looking for signs of injuries, but found nothing.

Fuck. Must have been alcohol poisoning. I sure know how to ring in the New Year. She stared into the reflection of her pale blue eyes for a moment. Finding a hairband on her wrist, she tied her shoulder-length, light-brown into a ponytail. She finished dressing and left the bathroom.

She approached the thick metal door and grabbed the silver handle, then hesitated. *If an ambulance rushed me to the hospital for alcohol poisoning, why is my duffle packed with every piece of clothing I own? A paramedic wouldn't do that.* She looked back at the bed. *No call button, bars on the windows, the outdated furniture.... maybe I should take this slow.*

She tried the handle. It wasn't locked. She opened the door a crack. *What the hell?* The hallway was strewn with debris and the walls were covered in graffiti. The only light came from evenly spaced work lamps. Sitting at the end of the hallway next to a work lamp was a man in a dark sweater and black tactical pants, idly flipping through a magazine. Tessa noted the pistol in a shoulder holster and the M4 Carbine propped against the wall, a familiar site from her days in the Army. She also saw a cable running from his left ear to a radio on his belt.

She carefully closed the door and sat in the chair. *Okay. I'm not in a hospital. Someone packed up all my clothing, brought me to an abandoned building, stuck an IV in me and hired a guard. Could this be some kind of alcohol-induced hallucination?* Tessa quickly ruled out the idea. She felt completely sober.

She thought back to her last memories, seeing Times Square on the TV and her bottle of Jack in hand. She heard familiar pop music coming from the TV... *was that the Backstreet Boys?* She recalled leaving early from the Blue Ox. She had the night off. A local drunk had given her a big tip, which she used to buy a bottle of Jack Daniels, her favorite whiskey, to ring in the new year. 2010 had been a rough year and she was looking forward to it being over.

Who in their right mind would kidnap me, a washed-up Army vet kicked out for bad behavior? She surveyed the room again. *Bars on the windows could be new. Tactical comms on the guard means other people nearby. Whoever did this has significant resources. I won't find answers here. I need to find a way to disarm the guard.* The only thing that she thought could be a weapon was the IV stand. *It looks pretty flimsy, but it will have to do. I'll only get one chance.*

She thrust the IV stand forward, smashing out the window. A crumbling concrete building was all that was visible. It looked familiar, but Detroit had a surplus of decaying structures. She looked down, counting floors. *I'm three stories from the ground.*

She swung open the door. "Hello, I see you down there! Can you please come tell me what the fuck is going on here?" She closed the door and waited.

She heard footsteps approaching, crunching over debris. *Finally got his attention.*

The door swung open. Tessa hit the guard across his face with all the strength she had. It was enough to break his nose.

"Owww!" He dropped the pistol in his hand, as he reflexively tried to protect his head. Although she had been out of the Army for over a year and was rusty in combatives training, the flood of adrenaline kicked in her muscle memory. She dropped the IV rod and slammed her steel-toed boot into the guard's knee. As he screamed, she landed a punch in his side and another on his jaw.

It was enough to send him sprawling on the ground. As he got to his hands and knees, Tessa kicked him in the stomach. He made a loud "oof" and collapsed. Tessa waited a moment. When he didn't move, she picked up the pistol and unclipped the radio from his belt. She slipped the earpiece in, just in time to hear a woman's voice say, "Piotr, what is happening up there? Do you need assistance?"

She left the room, shoved the pistol into the waist of her pants and grabbed the M4. It felt good to have a familiar weapon in her hands. She checked the magazine – it was fully loaded – and then took a moment to get her bearings and breath.

During her time in Iraq, she had been in a few firefights while on convoys. She knew the worst thing to do was let fear and excitement override common sense and rational thought. *Find a way out, and shoot anyone that tries to stop me.*

"I think there might be a problem," the woman on the radio said. "Oh, damn it." The radio hissed with static as the channel went dead.

There goes my SIGINT. Tessa saw a vacant window pane in a deserted office and headed over to it, hoping to get a better idea of her surroundings. She could see a row of long, deteriorating buildings, some with catwalks connecting them. *I'm in the Packard Plant.* Once, it had been viewed as the future of automobile manufacturing, a massive complex of state-of-art assembly lines. Now, it was a rotting corpse of a long-dead car company that played host to drug addicts, urban explorers and discount hookers.

Four black Chevy Tahoes were parked in front of the building she was in. *Shit. Who knows how many guards are in here.* She gripped the carbine tighter. *Make every shot count. Don't get cornered. You're only a few blocks away from people who can help.*

She stepped away from the window and went back into the hall. She heard the familiar tramp of combat boots to her left, the sound of people running up a staircase. She snapped the carbine up to her shoulder and fired a three-round burst at the first person to reach the top. The shots went wide, chewing up the wall and creating a cloud of concrete and asbestos. The man she shot at returned fire, snapping off two unaimed shots from his pistol. The slugs whizzed past Tessa's right shoulder.

Tessa heard the woman's voice echoing down the hall. "Don't shoot her! We need her alive."

At least someone doesn't want me dead. That could help me escape. Best chance of egress is a catwalk. I need to get to the roof. She fired another burst in the direction of her mysterious captors and started to run down the hall.

"Tessa!" the woman yelled. "Stop. I can explain."

Fuck you. Tessa saw a heavy steel fire door hanging from one bent hinge and ducked into the stairwell. After half a floor, the stairs going down were gone, a few strands of mangled and rusted steel rods and then nothing for 30 feet. The stairs heading up looked sound. She ran up three floors. The stairs ended at another fire door, this one intact.

Tessa tugged at the pad-lock. *Of course it's locked.*

She switched the M4 to single shot, took a few steps back and methodically shot the lock. On the fifth round it popped open. She pushed open the door. By now the sound of pounding boots was echoing up the stairwell.

Tessa could see the skyline of downtown Detroit to her south, the unmistakable cylinders of the Renaissance Center lighting up as the sun was beginning to set. The sky was pale blue and the sun seemed washed out, as cold as the winter air. She began to shake, her adrenaline mixing with shivers from the icy wind blowing off the Detroit river.

The roof was strewn with debris – stacks of rotting wood, rusting pipes and charred remnants of bonfires. She stepped on a scattered pile of frozen snow, black from pollution. Off to her left were a pair of couches, moldy and bursting. Tessa focused on the catwalk that connected her building with its neighbor. She ran toward it. *15 meters, almost there.*

"Tessa, please, stop," said the woman, emerging onto the roof.

Tessa ducked behind one of the couches and raised the M4. The woman was tall with short blonde hair and pale skin. She wore a white linen blazer and slacks and appeared unarmed. The guards were fanning out around, dressed in black with rifles aimed toward Tessa.

"Stay where you are or I'll fucking shoot you."

"It's okay, Tessa. We aren't here to hurt you." The woman turned toward the armed guards. "Lower your weapons."

The guards complied with her instructions. She turned back to Tessa. "My name is Ruth."

Tessa didn't notice that Ruth's eyes briefly looked from her tense face toward two guards who had emerged on the adjoining roof.

"I understand this is confusing. But if you put down the gun, all will be okay."

Tessa pressed her finger firmly against the trigger. "Is that what you say to all the women you kidnap?"

The men behind Tessa moved carefully and quickly. Both had tasers out and were almost in range.

Ruth stepped closer to the couch, arms up and open.

Tessa's grip tightened. "That's close enough. I want a phone, so I can call the cops. You can explain to them how all this is okay."

The men behind Tessa raised their tasers.

"I'm really sorry. It was not how I planned for this to go."

The men fired. A pair of barbed prongs leaped from each taser, trailing thin wires. Both sets easily penetrated Tessa's shirt and burrowed into her skin. As the paralyzing pain of the electrical charge rushed into her body, she squeezed the M4's trigger, firing a burst of bullets straight into Ruth's chest.

Tessa flopped onto the ground. As the surge of pain faded, she felt the prick of a needle in her neck.

"Sedative administered, ma'am," a guard said to Ruth.

Tessa's vision grew blurry, her consciousness fading as Ruth squatted beside her.

Ruth examined her shredded white blouse, unstained by blood. "Damn it, I really liked this shirt." She stroked Tessa's head, smiling. "See you when you wake up."

Chapter 2

As Tessa gained awareness, she heard the sound of aircraft engines. Her head hurt and her eyelids felt heavy, so she kept them closed. As her senses sharpened, she felt leather against her exposed skin. She couldn't smell anything, but when she breathed, the air tasted stale and cold. She felt the slight vibration of gentle turbulence beneath her.

I'm on a plane. She lifted her arms a little, testing to see if she was restrained. She wasn't. *They don't think I'm a threat. Can't really escape at 30,000 feet.*

When she opened her eyes, she was momentarily dazzled by the light. It made her headache worse. But the pain cleared away the last of her sedative-induced mental fog. When her vision adjusted, she carefully examined herself and her surroundings. She was still wearing the clothing she had changed into at the Packard Plant. A seat belt had been fastened over her jeans. Her back hurt from where she was hit by the taser, but she didn't think she was injured.

Tessa looked around the passenger cabin. It was tastefully and expensively decorated with a dozen leather chairs, personal tables made from rosewood and a wet bar against the forward fuselage. *God, I could use a drink. And some Tylenol.*

She looked out the window. As far as she could see, the surface was blue-gray water. *No land in sight, so probably an ocean. Where are they taking me?*

"Hello," Tessa said. Her throat and mouth were dry and her voice sounded rough.

"You're awake."

Tessa craned her neck around to look at the source of the response. It came from behind her. It was Ruth. She had an open laptop on her table with a stack of file folders next to it.

"How are you feeling?" Ruth asked, closing the laptop.

Tessa looked around the cabin. It was just her and Ruth, no guards. What are my options? *I could try taking her hostage. But I don't know who's in the cockpit and she clearly has resources. It's unlikely I'd be successful.* There was a door at the rear of the cabin. *There could be guards back there, waiting for me to try something. I need to play this smart. Get as much intel out of her as I can and wait for my moment.*

Her throat hurt from being parched and she decided to take care of that first. *Start with something simple. See what she is willing to give.* "I'm thirsty."

The woman nodded. "You must be. You haven't had a drink in five days. Ice or no ice?"

Five days. I must have been sedated since New Year's Eve. Maybe they weren't expecting me to wake up at the factory.

"No ice." Tessa studied Ruth as she walked to the wet bar and retrieved a bottle of water from the refrigerator. She was 5'10" with lean muscles and long limbs. She wore white slacks, a cream blouse and white heels. Her short blonde hair was cut into sporty, stylish layers, reminding Tessa of Meg Ryan back in the nineties.

Ruth handed Tessa the bottle and sat down in the facing chair.

Her steady gaze and firmly set mouth gave Tessa the impression she was being evaluated. Tessa finished half the bottle in one gulp, the cold water invigorating her. "Who are you?"

"My name is Ruth."

"Right," she finished the rest of the bottle.

"Another drink?"

I'd love a whiskey, but I have to stay focused. Tessa shook her head. "No. Where am I?"

"You're on a jet heading toward the Faroe Islands."

So we're over the Atlantic. She tried to dredge up anything she might have heard about the Faroes. *I think they are near Iceland.* "Why are you taking me there?"

"It's where our training facility is located."

Training? Is this some kind of fucked up recruitment? "Spooks or private sector?"

Ruth looked lost for a moment. "Excuse me?"

"Are you government or contractor? I assume you think my US Army intelligence background is of some use to you, unless you need my bartending skills for your fancy plane."

Ruth grinned. "Ah ... well, a little bit of both."

What intelligence could she possibly think I possess? I'm nothing special. A foreign government may want to pick my brain from my time in Iraq, but that seems unlikely. I was just your run-of-the-mill analyst trying to find terrorists.

"This might be easier if I start from the beginning," Ruth said. "What's the last thing you remember?"

Tessa thought about New Year's Eve. She started the night alone, which was nothing new. She got off work early and began drinking whiskey. *I think I went online, looking for a local hookup. That sounds like something I'd do. Did someone come over?* She could remember feeling depressed – not a new sensation since getting kicked out of the Army and returning to Detroit – but it seemed like it was more intense. Blurred memories surfaced of a man in her apartment. She saw herself unzipping his pants and kneeling down. Her mind jumped forward and she was alone again, watching the ball drop on TV in Times Square and chugging down whiskey. Then she saw herself in her tiny bathroom, looking in her medicine cabinet at a bottle of sleeping pills. She ran her tongue over the roof of her mouth, remembering a taste of chalk and bile. And then darkness. *Jesus, did I overdose?*

She fought the urge to punch Ruth. She wanted to take that ball of fear and anger expanding in her gut and lash out. *That won't help. I need information.* "What the hell happened to me?"

Ruth shrugged. "You killed yourself with alcohol and sleeping pills. Luckily, we were monitoring you and I was able to bring you back."

"Bring me back?"

"To life. You were dead for five minutes." Ruth's gaze was fixed. "If I hadn't been on site, I doubt you would be sitting here – or anywhere."

No. I wouldn't kill myself. "This is bullshit. You drugged and kidnapped me."

"Technically, that is also true. But you did commit suicide."

"Who the fuck are you?" Tessa stood up in the aisle.

"That's a bit complicated. I work for an organization called the Enochian Curia. We have a need for people like you. Normally I would have approached you in a more formal, less dramatic fashion, but circumstances being what they were, I had to act quickly." Ruth stood up. "Would you like something to drink?"

She really wanted whiskey. "No, I want answers." The two women stood in silence, the only sound the humming of the engine.

Tessa grabbed the seatback as the plane hit more turbulence. She noticed Ruth stood still, poised and balanced. *I need to understand what they do and who they do it for ... and what they want from me.*

"What is the Enochian Curia's mission?"

Ruth smiled slightly, clearly relishing the moment. "We are an ancient organization that hunts demons."

Tessa laughed, nearly doubling over. "Oh sure, like the CIA of exorcists?" She half-expected someone to jump out of the cockpit with a camera and tell her she was on a reality TV show. But the look on Ruth's face – the serious, steady gaze and firm set of her mouth – made it clear this wasn't a game. "You mean bad actors who are evil like demons?"

"No, I meant what I said. Demons. It would be easier if I showed you something." Ruth reached out and placed her hand on Tessa's arm. "Don't worry. I'm an angel."

Before Tessa could respond, her perception changed. It began with a warmth that spread through her body. Her headache disappeared, as did the lingering discomfort in her back from the taser prongs. Her fear faded, replaced by a sense of well-being that she had not felt in years. *What is happening to me?*

"Relax," Ruth said.

Tessa's vision began to change. The colors around her grew faint. It was like being in the middle of a thick gray mist. She felt a moment of panic as the fuselage vanished. But the warmth that flooded in from Ruth made that moment fleeting. Tessa closed her eyes. Nothing changed. Although everything she was experiencing was new, it seemed perfectly natural. Her eyes opened and she held up her free hand. It was surrounded by a pulsing aura of colors, a squirming, spiraling rainbow of red, green, yellow, orange, blue, indigo and violet. The hand itself was a pale, gray thing, an object with the right shape, but no details. In that instant, the aura of colors seemed more real than the flesh and blood it surrounded.

She looked at Ruth. The slender woman was gone, replaced by a glaring white light. But it wasn't just light; it was a furnace of heat that slid like a warm wave over her body. It felt so good, she wanted to drown herself in it.

"What am I seeing?"

Ruth's voice came from the light. It reverberated in Tessa's chest. "You're seeing the world the way I do. Shadows and light – and in the center of it all, you. Humans. A seething mass of wonderful and tragic emotions. Your aura."

Tessa looked back at her hand. "Not my soul?"

Ruth was silent for a moment. If Tessa had been looking with her normal vision, she would have seen a broad smile cross

Ruth's face. "No. You are seeing the basic emotional patterns that every human possesses. Fear, sadness, happiness, anger, disgust, surprise – the foundation of everything you think and do. Your soul is something ... different."

Even in her state of wonder, Tessa picked up on the hesitation in Ruth's voice. "When I look at you, all I see is a white light. Don't you have emotions?"

"I'm not human."

"You look human."

Ruth let go of Tessa's arm. Tessa's vision snapped back to normal. She shrank away from Ruth, pushing herself deep into the leather chair. The peace and joy was still there, but it no longer fully suppressed the fear.

Ruth shrugged. "As I said, I'm an angel. A servant of the Creator. An enemy of the Adversary and its agents on Earth. Demons."

This can't be real. Drugs. It has to be drugs. She thought of some of the stories interrogators had told her during her time in Iraq, of various drugs used to break down subjects' inhibitions, disorient them or keep them from sleeping. *Ruth could be doing the same thing. But why? Why pretend to be an angel? Maybe she knows I was raised Catholic and thinks this would appeal to me, but I'm agnostic now. Perhaps she doesn't know this about me. I've been taken against my will by people I don't know for reasons I don't understand. My goal is still the same. Gather intel and wait for my moment.*

"I know this is a lot to take in at once. But demons are real and they have been trying to destroy humanity for thousands of years. The Enochian Curia is all that stands between them and damnation for everyone."

Arguing with her is fruitless. Either this is the weirdest psyops I've seen, she's delusional or ... Tessa couldn't bring herself to contemplate what came after "or." "What does the Curia want from me? To be an analyst? My skills are rusty and I have no security clearance. If you've been monitoring me, you know why the Army kicked me out."

Ruth nodded. "Yes, we're aware of your background and experience. Even with the circumstances of your separation from the Army and the last year in Detroit, we believe you would make a good field operative. You would be part of a group that protects not just one country, but the entire world. How does that sound?"

Insane. She took a moment to reflect on the obvious wealth and power that Ruth wielded. *This has to be some kind of psychological test. This Enochian Curia nonsense must be a cover. Whoever is doing this has a lot of resources, so they have to be serious. I just need to figure out what they are serious about.*

"I'm sorry your recruitment has been so unique," Ruth said. "Normally, I would have arranged a meeting with you and revealed the truth over time. While this setting is more dramatic, what I have to say is the same. I can give you the opportunity to do something impactful with your life." Ruth paused. "I am not judging you. I am stating a fact. Were you living the life you wanted?"

Tessa thought about her time since being forced out of the military. The humiliation of being discharged after eight years of service over an affair with a superior officer had sent her into a downward spiral. Having nowhere to go but back to the city and toxic family she had fled after graduating high school, she buried herself in a dead-end job and numbed her nights with whiskey and meaningless sex. 2010 was a sucking morass of loneliness and self-loathing. She realized that the last 24 hours – from when she regained consciousness in the Packard Plant to this moment – was the most alive she had felt in a while.

She has a point. "No."

"I can give you the opportunity to make your life worthwhile. You used to be a part of something bigger. In the military you found purpose and belonging. Wouldn't you like to feel that again?"

Tessa looked out the window. *What's the catch?* After the disappointments and failures of the last year, she was wary. Even with the fear and anger that sat in her gut, there was a tiny part that was excited that someone was this interested in her. *Whoever is orchestrating this is very powerful. They have the kind of resources to kidnap me from Detroit and make me disappear to a remote island in the North Atlantic. Ruth is presenting this as if I have a choice, but it's not like I can get out and walk home. It's not really a choice. If I said no, what would they do to me? I've seen too much.*

Tessa looked back to Ruth, meeting her steady gaze. "Yes, I would."

"You'll give the Curia a chance?"

"I'll keep an open mind." Tessa stared at Ruth, deciding not to show her ambivalence and concern. Even as she resolved to stay vigilant and suspicious, part of her wanted the Curia. It sounded better than the life she had been leading.

"Good. Get some sleep. I'll wake you when we arrive." Ruth went back to her seat and her work.

Tessa looked out the window. As she watched the dark water pass below, she knew that wherever she was headed, her life would never be the same.

Chapter 3

Tessa was feeling better. She surprised herself by falling asleep for the rest of the flight. When she woke up, the plane was in its final descent to Vagar Airport. It was the only airport in the Faroe Islands, a single strip of concrete next to a small cluster of buildings and hangars.

The Gulfstream G650 taxied to a hangar separated from the others by a barbed-wire-topped fence. Two ground crewmen in coats and jumpsuits opened the gate and guided the plane into the hangar. Tessa noted the surroundings, debating whether to risk trying to get away. *This might be my only opportunity to escape. There's a small terminal and a highway leading to a nearby town about a kilometer away. If I can make it to the town, I could find someone and explain I've been kidnapped.*

When the plane came to a halt, Ruth retrieved a yellow parka from a closet at the rear of the cabin and handed it to Tessa. "Put this on, you'll want it for the rest of the trip."

Great, I'd be running in plain site in bright yellow. Tessa pulled on the parka, realizing her prospects of escape were slim.

Ruth led Tessa out of the plane, followed by the pilot. "I need to make a call," Ruth said. "Tessa, please wait by the helicopter."

The pilot brushed past her, heading for a Bell 407 on a landing pad next to the hangar. Ruth headed for a small office at the back of the building. The ground crew were busy securing the plane and getting the baggage out of the cargo compartment.

Tessa saw a crewman pull out her Army duffle bag, the only remnant of her former life. She looked across the wind whipped tarmac. It was early morning, the pale light of the sun pushing away the darkness. The lights of the terminal beckoned to her, promising safety and assistance.

"Hey," the pilot yelled in an accent Tessa couldn't place. "Come and give me a hand."

Tessa trudged over to him. The icy wind was brisk and invigorating. As she quietly helped him unhook the cables that kept the rotors tethered, she studied his features. Although he was wearing a heavy coat, he clearly was in good shape. His gray hair was cut short and precise. His nose bulged a bit near the bridge, evidence of it having been broken. His eyes – a light brown – were constantly scanning and there was a slight stiffness to his walk, betraying a subtle tension. Tessa had seen this before in men who had spent a lot of time in combat. *Always ready for a threat, never really relaxed. He looks like former special forces.*

"I know what you're thinking," he said, abruptly.

"Oh, what's that?"

"Maybe I should tell a crewman I've been kidnapped. But, you're too smart for that." He started to load the bags into the helicopter. "You have to assume they're our people. Now, you're checking out the distance to the fence, working out how hard it would be to get over the wire and then get to the terminal. Right?"

Tessa frowned.

He opened his coat and tapped the pistol at his hip. "I'm a good shot. Ruth needs you at the Academy alive, but not necessarily walking."

Tessa pulled the parka hood over her head as it began to drizzle. "And you put me in bright yellow, like a fucking bullseye."

"I've been doing this a long time." He held out his hand.

Tessa took it and noted the strong grip and calluses. *His hands have seen a lot.*

"My name's Uri. I'll be your combatives instructor."

Even though Tessa was worried, his gruff demeanor and no-nonsense attitude was appealing. Uri reminded her of some of the older Army sergeants she had known back at Fort Hood. *No bullshit from Uri. Someone I can rely on to tell me the truth, even if it sucks. Uri is Hebrew, I think. Could be former Mossad.*

"Where are you from?"

Uri looked up at the sky, surveying the weather. Despite having a hood, he didn't pull it on. Droplets traced down his wrinkled forehead. "Everywhere, but I grew up in Israel."

Tessa smiled to herself. Despite being rusty, she hadn't lost all of her intel analyst skills. *Likely former Mossad. I wonder if the Curia recruits from military and intelligence organizations around the world.*

Ruth joined them. "Uri, as soon as you're ready, let's go. I want to give Tessa some time to decompress before the induction ceremony."

"I'm moving as fast as I move."

"Of course. Always efficient." Ruth placed a hand on his shoulder.

Tessa thought she saw Uri's face stiffen a moment, like he was about to flinch away from Ruth. But she couldn't be sure.

Uri climbed into the pilot seat and started the helicopter. Tessa and Ruth followed, strapping into the backseat. Tessa fiddled with the harness, resigned to her fate. *Right now, I cannot escape. I need to gather as many data points as possible and stay vigilant. Ruth and Uri have not earned my trust.*

Tessa watched the rugged islands sliding below them as they lifted off.

"We are headed to Mykines," said Ruth, "the westernmost island in the Faroes. There are no people on the island who are not attached to the Curia and we don't allow visitors."

"Sounds remote." Tessa sighed. *They isolated their training academy on an island with no outsiders to prevent escape.*

"We need privacy and security," said Ruth. "Mykines gives us both."

As they approached their destination, Tessa noted the terrain. The shores were sheer walls of rock and the center of the island was divided by a spine of steep hills. The land was covered in broad patches of green and brown grass and moss.

As with Vagar, there was no tree cover. She spotted a herd of sheep on the side of the central ridgeline. After spending a year in the urban wasteland of Detroit, the raw nature of Mykines was strikingly beautiful.

The helicopter descended onto a circular concrete platform near the southern coast. It was on the outskirts of a cluster of tiny houses, the only settlement on the island. The rotorwash of the helicopter startled a group of puffins that were perched on the turf roof of a red house. They flew off in a cloud of white and black.

As Uri shut down the engine, an eerie sensation came over Tessa. She stepped out of the helicopter and got a better look at the town. It was constructed around a cove. The faded houses built up into the hillside were in disrepair. No one was walking through the narrow streets and the yards were overgrown. There was an absence of any noise, other than the whistle of wind, crash of the surf and squawks of the puffins. A dock thrust out into the dark waters of the cove. Perched at the end of the rotting finger of wood were half a dozen seals, who looked at the trio of humans with disinterest.

The village had clearly been abandoned for some time. She shivered as she passed a "Private Property, No Trespassing" sign written in multiple languages. She noted several of these signs around the town. *The signs are well maintained, the only thing not in disrepair.*

"Who used to live here?" Tessa asked.

"Sheepherders and fishermen," Ruth said as she effortlessly tossed Tessa's heavy duffle bag at her, "but no one has lived here since 1970."

Tessa donned her duffle bag, weighed down with all her belongings, and followed Ruth through the village.

Uri followed behind. "They were getting curious about our operations, so the Curia bought them out. We own the entire island now."

They reached the edge of the village. Parked next to a rundown black house was an old model Land Rover. The boxy green vehicle sat high on a modified suspension and had extra-large tires. The vehicle's sides were covered in dried mud. Seeing no roads, Tessa assumed this was their only means of transportation.

Uri climbed into the Land Rover and turned on the ignition. Tessa followed Ruth onto the backseat. The roar of the engine made further conversation difficult, so Tessa decided to focus on taking in the sights and thinking about her options. *If I want to escape, I'd have to fly or sail off this island. I don't know how to fly a helicopter and I saw no boats docked at the harbor. It's been ages since I sailed on Lake Erie, and sailing the Atlantic is very different from a lake, but I could figure it out, I think.* She surveyed the landscape as they journeyed further from the decaying remnants of civilization. Occasionally they would pass a herd of sheep, which – along with the puffins and gannets – appeared to be the only inhabitants of Mykines. *If I made a run for the village in hopes of locating a boat, I'd have to do it at night since there is zero cover.*

After an uncomfortable ride over the rocky spine of the island, they arrived at an old whitewashed stone church. It was surrounded by worn and irregularly hewn stones, driven into the ground in no discernable pattern.

"What are all these markers?" Tessa asked, walking on a path of basalt slabs toward the entrance to the church.

"It's where we bury our dead." Uri opened the door to the church. "After you."

Tessa stopped in her tracks, shaking her head. She turned to Ruth. "We are in the middle of nowhere. You're leading me into a creepy-ass church surrounded by a cemetery where it appears you have a lot of dead recruits. I need answers."

Ruth placed her hand on Tessa's shoulder. "They are hunters who lost a battle with a demon. We have been fighting for centuries, and we always bury our kind."

"If there's enough left to bury," said Uri. "Could we go inside? I'm wet and freezing my fucking balls off."

Ruth motioned toward the church. "Your answers are inside."

Despite the frigid rain, Ruth is wearing no coat and doesn't look cold. It's like 30 degrees out here, colder with the wind chill factor. Tessa walked into the church. "I don't really have a choice."

"There's always a choice," Uri said, following her, "but standing in freezing rain would be the wrong one."

The interior was cramped. There were six rows of wooden pews with a tight aisle running between them. The small windows let in a trickle of pale light, but most of the illumination came from out-of-place fluorescent lights mounted on the walls.

Electricity. But from where? She didn't hear the sound of a generator.

They approached the altar. Behind it, the front of the church was concealed by a thick red curtain. Uri pulled it aside, revealing a modern elevator built into the wall. He pressed the chunky red button and the door opened promptly.

Ruth entered the elevator. "Welcome to the Academy."

Tessa laughed, shocked and surprised. "A secret underground lair. Did you model this after a James Bond movie?"

Uri laughed. "Come on, Tessa. Time to get settled into your new home."

Chapter 4

The elevator doors slid open, revealing a hallway that was a study in blandness. The floor was a cream-colored carpet with a faint series of hexagons in a slightly paler color. The walls and ceiling were a light blue-gray. Fluorescent lights behind frosted plastic panels created a background drone. If she hadn't just taken an elevator housed in a medieval church into an underground base, Tessa would have thought she was in a generic, mid-tier hotel.

Uri pushed the elevator button again. "Looking forward to working with you, Tessa." He reboarded the elevator and disappeared.

The only colorful touches were the doors. They were a rich purplish-red, the color of a robust merlot. Each had a name placard next to it, which Tessa read as they passed. "Canton/ Reese." "Miasaki/Bao." "Al-Fadil/Gottlieb." "Shen/Sinan." "Leroux/ Sinclair."

"Here we are," Ruth said.

"What's this?" asked Tessa.

"Your quarters."

Tessa frowned. "Will I be locked inside?"

Ruth shook her head and laughed lightly. "Of course not, you are free to come and go as you please."

"Does that include off the island?"

"For the first few months, you'll be too busy training to leave, but we do have holiday breaks and field exercises. On holiday, you can go wherever you want."

"Field exercises?" asked Tessa.

"Where you'll hunt demons. I know you have many questions. I've assigned you to a second-year recruit who serves as your roommate and mentor." Ruth tapped the name plate. "Desange Leroux will be able to answer your questions."

"Good, I have a lot."

Ruth knocked on the door. "Desange," she said, as the door opened, "this is Tessa Sinclair."

Desange was tall, with broad shoulders and a tapered waist. His facial features were chiseled, the kind of strong lines found in movie stars. His coarse black hair was cut close to his head and he had a small, stylish goatee. His dark brown eyes matched the color of his skin and his full lips formed an inviting smile.

Desange held out his hand. "Hello." His English had a French accent that Tessa reflexively found enticing. "Please, come in."

Tessa shook hands and entered the room. "Okay." *Pair me with a hot guy. Not the worst recruitment plan. I wonder if this was intentional.*

"I'll leave you two to get acquainted. Desange, please answer any questions Tessa has but watch the time." Ruth then turned and walked down the hallway toward the elevator.

As Desange closed the door, Tessa checked out the living room. It was larger than her Detroit efficiency. A 55-inch TV was mounted on the far wall. Facing it was a couch. A round dining room table and four chairs were to her right, a pair of comfortable looking lounge chairs and a large, dark wood coffee table to her left. In the middle of each side wall was a door. One was open and Tessa could see a bed.

"Do you want to get rid of that?" Desange said, referring to the duffle bag slung over her shoulders.

"Yes." She dropped the bag to the ground and took off her parka.

"Would you like something to drink?"

"I want answers."

Desange nodded. "Okay. I'm going to get a drink first." He went to a small refrigerator next to the television and pulled out a bottle of Evian.

I really want a shot. Just something to take the edge off. "Have any whiskey?"

Desange frowned and shook his head. "Sorry, we don't have alcohol in our rooms. There is a lounge, but it's currently closed. I can take you there later if you'd like."

Tessa sighed. "Sure. What did Ruth mean by 'watch the time'? Is there someplace we need to be?"

Desange sat in one of the lounge chairs and motioned toward the other. "Ruth wants you to take part in the induction ceremony today."

Tessa slid into the chair. "I haven't decided to join. I don't really know what I'm being inducted into." She looked at him carefully, studying his face for a reaction.

Desange had prepared for a different recruit, a Korean woman named Kim Min-Seo. Tessa wasn't supposed to be recruited for another year, but her attempted suicide changed the plan. The last few days had been a scramble to reschedule Kim Min-Seo's induction to next year and prepare an indoctrination and training profile for Tessa.

He leaned forward for emphasis. "I know your recruitment didn't follow the normal process. From what I was told, Ruth felt like she didn't have a choice. I can answer whatever questions you might have, but all recruits have to be inducted." He sat back. "I recommend you agree to join us. If Ruth brought you here, she knows you'll make a good hunter."

Tessa laughed. "A demon hunter, right?"

Desange nodded. "You are probably thinking, *what kind of lunatics am I surrounded by?* Right?" Desange smiled.

Tessa liked his smile, easy and reassuring.

"That's a normal reaction. When I first met Ruth, I had the same doubts. Did she touch you and show you how she sees?"

Tessa nodded. "She did." Tessa opted not to tell him of her suspicions about being drugged. *Don't volunteer information. He might be hot, but he is also one of them.*

"That's what did it for me. I knew how Saint Thomas felt, doubting the risen Christ until he could feel the wounds with his own hands. After seeing Ruth's vision, I knew the supernatural was real. And I have seen a lot more since then." Desange paused. He knew that Tessa was not going to just take his word. He had read her files and understood that her background didn't lend itself to blind acceptance. "You're Catholic, right?"

"Not anymore. But I did go to Sunday School as a kid."

"Do you believe in God?"

"I don't know. I used to. But I've seen a lot since then. The idea of a loving God watching out for us is hard to accept. I'm more agnostic now."

"So the verdict's still out. You can accept the idea of physical evil, no? From your days of hunting terrorists in the Army."

Tessa nodded.

"That is who we fight. If calling them demons is uncomfortable, think of them as the worst terrorists you've ever faced. They don't fight for one political ideology or against a single country – they want to corrupt every human soul."

"And the Curia hunts them?"

"Yes. We are the world's oldest intelligence organization fighting a 2000-year-old covert war. When we were founded, we were part of the Catholic Church. You'll get more details in your training, but the Curia has protected humanity for a long time."

Tessa paid close attention to his face, looking for any tics or expressions that would indicate he was lying. *He believes what he's saying – or he's a really good liar. I should make him think I'm buying what he's selling and lighten up the mood to establish rapport.*

"Are you a priest? If we have to take vows of celibacy, that would be a deal breaker for me." Tessa gave him her best "naughty girl" smirk.

Desange laughed and shook his head. "Don't worry. The Curia broke free from the Church hundreds of years ago. There are elements of the Vatican who know about us and provide support, but we are no longer their tool."

"Good, because I'm no saint. I assume you know that since you read my file. What else did you learn about me?"

"You were a US Army sergeant and served in Iraq as an intelligence analyst. You were subsequently discharged over a sexual relationship with a superior officer, Captain Tyler Caplan. There was an investigation that dug into other things – dereliction of duty. But no charges were filed. You were raised in Detroit and have a tenuous relationship with your family, including a mother, father and two older siblings. Following high school, the Army became your way out of Detroit and a surrogate family. Since being discharged for fraternization, you got a job as a bartender at the Blue Ox and have turned to increasingly self-destructive behavior, including risky sexual encounters, alcohol abuse and an overdose that Ruth resurrected you from."

Tessa crossed her arms in reflexive defense. She didn't like the judgmental tone that crept into his voice near the end. But she didn't let it show. *The Curia has significant knowledge about my background and day-to-day actions. I can get mad, but that's not going to help me. I need to turn the conversation to him and see what I can get him to reveal.*

"I guess a super-secret demon hunting organization would have some good intelligence sources." She went over to the fridge and grabbed a bottle of water. "You seem to know a lot about me. What's your story?"

"Me? I'm not nearly as interesting." Desange smiled, attempting to defuse the tension. "I'm from Paris. I was working on a business degree when I was recruited. I was approached by Ruth in my final year and offered a position in the Curia. Much like you, I didn't believe her at first. But then she touched me and my doubts cleared up enough to see what else there was to the Curia. Hunting demons sounded more interesting than the corporate life. I came to the Academy last year." He smiled again. "And now, here I am."

"How do your family and friends feel about you being here?"

"They don't know the full story, of course. They think I am working for a government agency. It would not be much of a covert organization if we told everyone what we do, nor are they likely to believe us. I think my family would have preferred me as a businessman, but an intelligence career is good with them as well." Desange finished his water. "Most people drift through life never finding their true calling. When I told my family I found mine, they supported my decision. I had an itch, you know. I want to do something special with my life and I was always looking for that thing. I just didn't know what that was."

"The Curia scratched the itch?"

Desange stood up, tossing his bottle into the trash. "The kind of people who become hunters have a hunger to help. It may be buried deep under layers of apathy and cynicism, but it is there. They want to be part of something bigger and are willing to forgo the life of a normal person to do it."

He seems so sincere. Could this all be legit? It would mean God is real – and the Devil is real too. And that both sides are fighting a war on Earth for our souls. "Why me? You've read my file. I've led a pretty sinful life. I'm not religious or even new age spiritual. Why would I be recruited for this?"

"You've been chosen. Making mistakes, committing sins – those are things God can forgive. And there is something special about you. About all of us chosen to be hunters. Did Ruth tell you about your aura?"

Tessa nodded. "A little, I mean I saw it when she touched me."

"There is a signature in your aura only angels can see. A quality that allows you to become a hunter. You'll learn more about this after the ceremony."

She paused. "So, this induction ceremony. I assume it's not too weird. I'm not drinking blood or anything? Although I might consider an orgy, under the right circumstances."

Desange shook his head and laughed. "Sorry, no *Eyes Wide Shut* here."

"I still want an adult beverage in the lounge afterwards."

"I'm ready for more questions over cocktails."

"Good. I'm a whiskey girl."

Desange glanced at his Tag Heuer wristwatch. It was almost time for the induction ceremony. He stood up. "We should get going. The ceremony doesn't take long."

"Do I need a white robe and sandals?"

Desange chuckled. "You're fine the way you are."

Chapter 5

Tessa and Desange entered the church. The icy wind howled outside, but the interior was warmed by electric heaters along the walls. About thirty people – a mix of new recruits and their mentors – were already in the pews. Their conversations filled the confined space. Several glanced her way. She kept a neutral face, but felt a little uncomfortable. She wondered what, if anything, they knew about her.

They could have been briefed on my situation. I came in rough. It would make sense they'd be told about me. She didn't like that. It reminded her too much of her last months in Iraq where her sexual relationship with Tyler had become hot gossip among soldiers. She looked around the church for the familiar signs of whispers and knowing glances.

"This way." Desange led Tessa to an open spot. He had been told by Ruth to monitor her behavior. He didn't like having to spy – that's not how he saw his role. But he understood Tessa was in a delicate mental state and trusted Ruth's angelic guidance. When he was recruited, he had had months of meetings to prepare him for dedicating his life to the Curia. Tessa had gone from living in ignorance in Detroit to getting an icy shower of truth in the Faroe Islands. And while necessary under the circumstances, she was kidnapped instead of being a willing recruit.

Tessa continued examining the recruits. *Most of them look my age, people in their mid to late twenties. The Curia recruits hunters with some life experience, but not too old. They need us to be combat capable. There is no predominant ethnicity or sex. While some recruits have noticeable accents, like Desange, everyone speaks English. They don't look military. In fact, some don't look like they've been to the gym in years. I guess this aura signature isn't tied to physical fitness.* She smiled and shook her head. *I'm starting to think about this like it's real. Until Ruth shows me some dude in red with horns and a pitchfork, this is all an elaborate exercise in fucking with me.*

Desange saw Tessa's expression. "Are you okay?"

"I'm fine. Waiting for the show to start."

"Ah." He leaned closer to her. "Go along with whatever you are asked. It's just a ceremony. A few words. Don't do anything to stand out."

Her eyes narrowed. "What if I refuse?"

Desange shrugged. "Ruth is watching you, like she is watching all of us. You'll get more answers – all you'll need. But that won't happen in the next thirty seconds. If you press the issue now, Ruth might take that as a sign you won't be an asset to the Curia." He looked at her in a way he hoped would make the underlying meaning of the words clear.

Tessa thought about the graves surrounding the church. *How many of them were dragged into this against their will and didn't play it smart?*

Ruth emerged from the curtains. Everyone fell silent. Her heels clicked softly on the bare stone floor. She stood behind the cracked and scarred wooden altar and cleared her throat. "I am pleased to welcome you to the Enochian Curia. I hope you have had time to get yourself acquainted with our training center and bond with your mentors and fellow recruits. You will help each other during the years to come."

Tessa glanced around at the other recruits, searching their faces. Their expressions ranged from stoical to excited, and a few looked nervous.

"You are about to partake in the Ceremony of Vows. This is a tradition stretching back to the first group of hunters." Ruth paused. The only sound came from the wind blowing outside.

Hunting demons. You used to believe in things like that. God, the devil. She focused on Ruth's face, stern and serene. *Angels. But if there is a God, he hasn't shown up. Not at home or in Iraq. Not when I was kicked out and spiraling down in Detroit.* She thought about the touch. The sensation of peace and warmth that had flooded her body. The world of light and mist that Tessa glimpsed. She bit her cheek, a habit from her childhood, something she did when she felt like she had made a mistake. *Don't fall for this. Even if this isn't a test, the more likely explanation isn't demon hunters; it's a covert group indoctrinating me to kill whomever they don't like. Maybe we are assassins for hire.*

"This ceremony represents our devotion to the mission of the Enochian Curia and to each other. During your training, you will learn about our long past and come to appreciate what the ceremony represents. But the vows you take today will bind you to each other and to the Curia, past, present and future. Please stand." She lifted a dagger from the wooden altar and held it, blade up, over her head.

Tessa thought it looked odd. The handle was a flattened tube made of stainless steel. It was the blade that really caught her attention. It wasn't metal. It was clear and glittered in the fluorescent light. *Is that glass?*

"To protect the sanctity of the soul, I will give my life," said Ruth.

The recruits repeated the sentence in unison. Although this was not what Tessa had anticipated, she echoed the phrase. *What choice do I have? Desange was clear that I should just go along.* She thought about her Oath of Enlistment in the Army. She knew there was no going back once she raised her right hand and signed her paperwork. She found herself getting more nervous. *This is sounding more like a cult. One with private planes and underground bases. What the hell have I been dragged into?*

"To rid the Earth of evil, I will give my life."

"To rid the Earth of evil, I will give my life," repeated Tessa and her fellow recruits.

"To stay loyal to the Enochian Curia, I will give my life."

"To stay loyal to the Enochian Curia, I will give my life."

As the last words left the recruits' lips, Ruth stabbed the dagger into the pitted wood of the altar with a force that startled Tessa. She had a strength at odds with her svelte frame. The stones of the wall and floor vibrated from the impact.

For a moment, Ruth glared at the assembly with an unsettling intensity. Then she smiled, breaking the uncomfortable silence. "See, that was harmless."

A few people chuckled with relief, including Tessa.

"Now that you have been initiated, the Academy director has a few words. Father McKenna, the floor is yours." Ruth stepped back. A heavy-set man with a red face and fringe of white hair appeared from the shadowy rectory. Tessa thought he looked like Rod Steiger with an extra 40 pounds.

They have a priest as the director. Desange did say they had ties to the Vatican. Maybe he's their liaison? If that's a two-way communication channel to an outside organization, I might be able to use it. She took a breath. *Okay, don't get ahead of yourself. Focus. Listen. And wait.*

McKenna took a moment. He had been part of the ceremony enough times to know that many of the recruits would be uneasy. Even with the briefings and other onboarding procedures, this was a lot to digest. He placed both hands firmly on either side of the dagger and leaned in.

"Good afternoon. I want to welcome you to the Enochian Curia." He grinned. "I am sure you have questions. In the next two years, the Academy will teach you many things. But the most important lesson is that demons walk among us and you have been selected to fight them. Demons come from the depths of Hell to spread their misery and chaos. Evil manifests itself on Earth not just through the actions of men, but also through these beings. You will be trained to hunt and destroy them."

As McKenna spoke, Tessa focused on him. The Army had trained her to detect deception in an interrogation subject. While not an expert, she knew enough to be aware of the usual tells.

She listened for tonal changes. She watched his hands, eyes and posture, looking for anything in his body language that would indicate that he was lying – that this was an act for her benefit. There was nothing.

She looked at Desange, hoping that his face would betray something. Instead, he stared steadily ahead, nodding slightly as McKenna spoke. *Maybe I have been kidnapped by a cult, isolated to the point that all contact can be controlled. An esoteric belief system, branching off of mainstream Christianity.*

"You are the only ones that can stop them from corrupting more human souls," McKenna said. "A war rages both in Heaven and on Earth. It is a war between God and Satan, between angels and demons. This is an ancient struggle. The hunters of the Enochian Curia serve God, destroying Satan's agents on Earth, just as the angels destroy them in Heaven."

Tessa looked around the room and saw that everyone seemed to be buying what McKenna was saying. Her head throbbed. The cramped room felt smaller.

Desange whispered, "I know how this sounds. If you had been recruited through normal channels, this would not seem so strange. You would have been shown more. But you have a logical mind. I saw that in your file. Approach this like you would any intelligence gathering and analysis assignment. The Curia can prove everything McKenna is saying about demons."

"You have been carefully chosen by our Angelic Ambassador to Earth, Ruth, who has found you worthy to become demon hunters," McKenna said.

Tessa's eyes narrowed as she looked at Ruth. *An angelic ambassador to Earth? There is nothing logical about this.*

"I would recommend you speak to your mentors about the process. They're here to help you." McKenna motioned with his hand to three people sitting in the front pew. They stood and faced the recruits. "You can also turn to your instructors. Prior to their retirement, they were top notch hunters. They have battled many demons and will train you to survive in the field. Would you introduce yourselves?" McKenna gestured toward Uri.

"Uri Deneberg." He glanced at some of the doughy recruits. "I'll be teaching you combatives, how to fight a demon and not get killed. And just call me Uri. It's too hard to say 'Instructor Deneberg' when you're panting for air." Uri nodded at a petite, hawk-like woman standing next to him.

The way she looked at the recruits, her dark eyes sweeping the crowd, made Tessa uneasy. *Like a wolf sizing up sheep. Uri is a soldier, but this chick is a killer.*

"I am Svetlana Ivanov," she spoke with an even Russian accent. "I will be your tradecraft instructor. My friend Uri," she nodded toward him, "will teach you how to kill. I will teach you how to hunt. You will learn how to gather intelligence, infiltrate the most secure locations, track a 300-year-old demon, and most importantly, avoid blowing your cover." Her eyes narrowed. "Because you are not just fighting demons – you have an entire world that is asleep to our war."

The last of the instructors laughed. "If that doesn't send you all running for the helicopter, you are a brave bunch."

Tessa liked his voice. It was warm and deep with a Spanish accent. There was a calm confidence to his demeanor. His thick black hair was distinguished with gray streaks and his hazel eyes were commanding, but friendly.

"My name is Juan Silva. I teach demonology and the history of the Curia. While my friends Uri and Svetlana deal with the practical aspects of hunting, I'll be giving you insights into what makes the enemy tick and how your predecessors have carried out successful hunts." He grinned. "Also, being from Valencia, I host a once-a-month paella and sangria night. Attendance is mandatory."

Sangria and paella … I can't let my guard down, just because an instructor is nice, looks like Javier Bardem and offers free drinks. Be extra careful around the nice one. Uri and Ivanov put me on guard, but Silva is charming. Charming always has a cost.

"Thank you," McKenna continued as the three trainers took their seats. "As seasoned hunters, your instructors know the adjustments and sacrifices a hunter must make. They are here to help, even Instructor Ivanov, as scary as she seems."

There was a ripple of knowing laughter from the second-year recruits.

"Now that all the formalities are done, I would like to welcome you to the Enochian Curia. The next two years will be challenging, but rewarding." He smiled. "Training starts tomorrow. We've arranged a party in the lounge where you can get to know your fellow recruits a little more before the torture starts." Noticing a few grimaces among the recruits, he chuckled. "Just kidding. We don't start that until the second year."

A few of the second-year recruits, including Desange, laughed.

Tessa clenched her jaw. *I need some air. This is all too much.* "I'm going for a walk," Tessa said to Desange. "Is that okay?"

He nodded. "Sure. Don't go too far. It gets dark early this time of year."

As the rest of the people queued up for the elevator, Tessa pushed open the church door and went outside. It was cold and the sky was the color of slate. She walked around the headstones until she reached the cliff. The sea foamed below as it crashed against the dark stones. The frigid wind cut through her shirt. The clouds glowed weakly near the horizon, illuminated by the setting sun. Without warning, her heart began to race and her body shook. She was having a hard time catching her breath. She bowed her head. *I'm having a panic attack. Just breathe ... inhale ... exhale.*

It began to lightly rain again, a cold drizzle that set her teeth chattering. She lifted her head and saw a group of puffins observing her curiously. Their heads turned as one, looking at Ruth as she approached Tessa.

Ruth walked deliberately, unhurriedly. She didn't feel the slice of cold air or the sting of rain that a human would feel.

Ruth stood next to the shorter woman. "Bracing view."

Tessa focused on her breathing. "You're really an angel?"

Ruth nodded.

"Where are your wings?"

Ruth laughed, a cold sound, like ice cracking. She touched Tessa's shoulder. The warmth was there again, drowning her mounting panic attack in contentment. Her sight didn't change this time, but she knew something out of the ordinary was happening.

"That's mythology. I don't have wings, although I do have abilities that would seem supernatural to you. I am stronger and faster than any human."

Tessa recalled the last memory from the roof of the Packard Plant. *Three rounds to the chest and no reaction. Even if she had a vest on, she would have had cracked ribs.*

"I shot you."

Ruth nodded. "Yes. No weapon made by man can harm me." She smiled. "Although it did ruin my shirt, so no more shooting." The smile faded. "I also have the ability to accelerate healing. You were dead and I brought you back."

"You said I was dead for five minutes." Tessa started to shake, but not from the cold. She shook with fear and anger. "Your angelic touch resurrected me?"

"*Tactu sanitatem.* Sounds classier in Latin." Ruth hooked a finger under Tessa's chin and urged her head up until the two women were looking at each other's eyes. "Yes. I brought you back from the dead. You are precious to God and the Curia." Ruth pulled a smartphone from her pocket. "I have something to show you." She played a video for Tessa that was taken in her apartment the night she overdosed. It had been shot from a hidden camera mounted on the ceiling. The image was in shades of gray.

As she watched, Tessa's memory returned, filling in the moments before the video started. *I drank too much. Hooked up with a random guy and had shitty sex. Alone on the holidays. Looking forward to another year of insomnia and misery. Day after day.*

Tessa watched herself weaving across the tiny living room of her efficiency, bottle of Jack Daniels in hand. The view cut to a new camera, this one inside the closet-sized bathroom. Tessa saw her face in the mirror. Tears were streaming down her cheeks and she was talking. Although there was no sound, Tessa could imagine what her drunk sleep-deprived brain was saying. *Probably saying how everything is a waste ... my life is a wreck ... I'm a piece of shit.* She shook her head. *Same stuff every day.*

On the screen, she pulled open the medicine cabinet and grabbed a bottle, knocking others into the sink. She left the bathroom and the camera switched back to the living room. She watched herself take the bottle of Jack Daniels and start to down sleeping pills. Pill, drink, swallow. Pill, drink, swallow. Repeated fifteen times. Tessa wanted to close her eyes. She knew what was coming next. She looked at Ruth.

The woman's face was impassive. "Watch."

Tessa looked back at the screen. By now, her body was sprawled on the worn hardwood floor. She was convulsing. And then she vomited. It was jet black on the light gray floor. She sat up quickly, like a puppet being jerked by its strings. She vomited again and then collapsed onto her back. The video quality wasn't great, but she could make out the bubbles her fading breath was making in the blood and waste from her mouth. She felt both sick and detached. Part of her was horrified by what she saw; part was watching with the eyes of an analyst.

I must have choked on my own vomit. How long were they watching me? She thought about some of the things that had happened in her apartment over the last year. From the mundane embarrassments – going to the bathroom, dancing around drunk in her pajamas on a Sunday morning after she got a great tip at the bar – to the more intimate moments. *I hope these assholes enjoyed the show.*

After a few moments, Ruth stepped into the frame. She knelt next to Tessa's motionless form and held her wrist in one hand. She let go of the hand; it flopped to the floor. She placed her hand on Tessa's chest. A halo of light surrounded both women, growing in intensity until the screen turned white. When the image cleared, Tessa's eyes were open and darting around wildly. Ruth pulled a syringe from a satchel and injected her. The video ended as her eyes closed again.

Holy shit. For a moment, her mind tried to come up with a reasonable explanation. But unless the video was doctored, it appeared Ruth was telling the truth. *She brought me back from the dead by touching me. Who can do that?*

"You brought me back. Why?"

Ruth smiled. She slipped the phone back into her pocket. "We have great plans for you. Have faith. You will need it as you train to be a hunter. Our enemies are powerful and seductive." She slipped her arm around Tessa's shoulder.

Tessa found the gesture, the touch, reassuring. *Like a warm blanket.*

"Let's get you out of these wet clothes. Then, if you're feeling up to it, we can go to the lounge and meet your fellow recruits."

"I don't even know if I believe in God."

Ruth shrugged. "Then believe in me. I'm offering you a chance to play a part in the singular struggle of the human race. Most people live and die in ignorance. You have greatness in you, Tessa. I think it was just waiting for the right moment to come out."

"Okay," Tessa said softly, her voice lost in the wind. She wasn't sure she was okay. But she knew she wasn't going anywhere.

Chapter 6

Tessa stood in her shower. The water was hot, on the tolerable side of scalding. She was resting her head on the blue tiled wall, processing what had happened. *The Curia has resources and global reach. Neither of those things makes their claims valid. Desange seems to sincerely believe what he is telling me, having bought into the indoctrination. But I've seen that before. Half the jihadis I tracked in Iraq thought they were going to get seventy-two virgins in Heaven. That doesn't mean that the afterlife has virgin factories.*

As the water ran down her back in hot streams, she turned to the items that were harder to wrap her head around. *The ceremony was strange. It could be an act, but this is a lot to go through just to fuck with a washed-up, mid-level Army vet. This facility is too big not to be legitimate. The amount of effort needed to construct this on a remote island in the middle of the North Atlantic is substantial.*

The heat was starting to get uncomfortable. She could feel her skin tingling, approaching pain. She turned the shower off and stepped out. She stood in front of the bathroom mirror. Water pooled at her feet. She placed her hands on the sink and leaned forward, staring into her blue eyes. *Ruth is something else, but an angel? She touched me and I felt real physical changes, on the plane and on the cliff. I shot her three times with an M4 and it had no impact on her.* She closed her eyes. The black and white image of her convulsing and choking was what she saw. *And she brought me back from the dead. I was dead, she touched me, there was a light show, and I stopped being dead.* She opened her eyes, touching her chest. *She touched me and I came back. That's real.*

Tessa took a thick wool towel from the rack and wrapped it tightly around her body. She left the bathroom. Her bedroom was bare, but more comfortable than her studio in Detroit. In addition to a queen-sized bed with a firm mattress, there was a standing bureau, a three-drawer dresser, a chair and desk with a banker-style desk lamp. The green glass shade cast emerald light on the ceiling and walls. A Curia-issued iPhone was sitting on her desk. She grabbed it, feeling the urge to call someone. She noticed that her previous phone contacts had been cloned.

The only person that came to mind was Tyler Caplan, her commanding officer in Iraq. *We've been through a lot of shit together. It's been a while, and we didn't part ways under the best of circumstances, but he would listen to me. He was always a great listener, but I haven't talked to him in a year. How's he going to react when I call out of the blue and tell him I've been recruited by an angel to be a demon hunter?* Tessa laughed at how absurd that sounded. *He'll listen for about five seconds before deciding I'm the crazy ex drunk dialing him and hang up. I'll need a more believable story than that.* She dropped the phone on the bed. *Besides, it's their phone. They're probably monitoring my conversations; I would if I were them.*

She discovered that all her clothes were waiting for her. She tugged on a pair of jeans and slipped into a Ministry T-shirt. *I wonder if they sanitized the apartment? Did they erase evidence of what happened? Wrap things up with my landlord? Leave a message at the Blue Ox, telling them I quit? Tell my family that I was leaving Detroit and not coming back? Not that they would give two shits about me.*

A grim smile formed. She thought about the last time she had seen her family, an early Christmas dinner that started with alcohol and recriminations and ended with screams and slamming doors. *One positive point about being kidnapped by a cult; I never have to see my family again.*

She slipped the phone into her pocket and left her quarters. She went to the elevator and pressed the '4' button. The cafeteria, lounge and recreation center halls were wood paneled and the floor was covered with a mustard yellow carpet. The light came from soft white bulbs in wall-mounted frosted globes.

She heard conversations from down the hall and followed the sound to the lounge. It was decorated like an English pub with dark wood walls, a solidly built bar, billiard tables and enough seating for thirty. A large-screen TV mounted behind the bar was tuned to ESPN. Photographs of soccer teams from around the world hung on the walls. She grinned, thinking of her time playing soccer in high school. It was one of her few good childhood memories.

Tessa saw Desange at the bar and made her way through the crowd. He had saved a stool for her and she sat next to him.

"Feel better?"

She nodded. "Yeah. I realized I hadn't showered in a week. I must have smelled pretty bad. Thanks for not saying anything. Anyway, I wouldn't mind a drink."

A man with dark gray hair was tending the bar. Desange motioned him over with his hand. "Tessa, this is Mr Lennon."

Tessa shook his offered hand.

"You can call me Seamus," the bartender said, his voice thick with a southern Irish accent. "I'm head of support operations for the Academy and resident barman."

"Pleased to meet you. I was a bartender for a while."

Seamus smiled broadly, his whole face wrinkling. "Really? And how does your former place of employment compare to here?"

Tessa grinned. "This is better. I'm not afraid of catching hepatitis here."

"Ha! Sounds like my kind of pub. So, what can I get you?"

"How about a beer."

Seamus nodded. "Do you like porters?"

"Sure."

"I have just the thing." Seamus reached into the underbar refrigerator and pulled out a dark brown bottle. He filled a glass with the earthy liquid and placed it before her. "This is

Okkara No. 4 – Kaffistout. It is one of the finest products of these fair islands."

She took a drink. "Wow, that is good. Thanks." Tessa examined the fully stocked bar, filled with spirits from around the world. "Talisker scotch. Nice and peaty. Might have that next. How do you get all this here, on such a remote island?"

"I operate a supply ship that goes to Torshavn weekly to pick up food and beverages. The Curia gives me a generous budget and freedom to select the best meat and produce. In fact, I've got a freezer full of fresh Faroese salmon that'll be on the menu today."

A supply ship. This could be my ticket off the island. And Seamus doesn't seem to mind sharing operational details. I can work on befriending him, which involves spending some time sipping whiskey. Not a bad deal. If I need to escape, his ship might be the only way out.

"Cool. Will you take special requests?" Tessa took another sip of her porter.

"Sure, lass. What do ya fancy?" Seamus gave her a nod and smile.

Let's start with something personal and that might appeal to this guy's sensibilities. He seems like a man who sees himself as a connoisseur. I know just the thing. "There's this Japanese whiskey I've been wanting to try called Hibiki."

"I'll see what I can do for ya," he said, before heading down the bar to take care of another waiting person.

"He seems nice."

"Everyone here is," Desange said. "So, whiskey is your drink of choice?"

"Yep, I have my eye on that Talisker up there." Tessa pointed to the back shelf. "After being kidnapped by an angel and told I'm training to hunt demons, I think I deserve a few drinks."

Desange nodded. "I'm sorry your recruitment was so expedited. It's a lot to take in."

Tessa stared at him intently. She took a drink and shrugged. "Well, if you're all in some insane cult, I guess I won't be able to do much about it."

Desange swiveled in his chair, facing the room. "Look around. Do you think all these people are insane? Those who came before them? The ones buried in the cemetery?"

I think I hit a nerve. Cults can have a lot of resources and can be very persuasive. Particularly if they target vulnerable people. I'll push a little and see how he reacts. "I don't know, but people are fooled every day. Look at Jim Jones, Heaven's Gate and the Branch Dividians. A charismatic leader and a belief system that gives people an immediate purpose and a unique perspective on life can be a powerful combination."

Desange frowned.

Don't go too far. "I left my Catholic faith behind a long time ago. The Curia is saying angels and demons are real. That's not an easy thing for me to believe. I can't be the only agnostic or atheist who has been recruited, right?"

"That's true. We all come from different backgrounds. Ruth and the Curia are not asking us to take all this on faith. They just want us to have an open mind, evaluate the information they provide and accept the reality it represents."

"That we are God's soldiers, killing demons to save the souls of mankind?"

Desange laughed. "Well, when you say it like that it sounds completely mad."

She touched his elbow. *I need to soften things up.* "I appreciate your patience with me. I understand this isn't how onboarding is normally done for the Curia and that you're in a tough situation. In the Army, I had to mentor people under difficult circumstances as well. I'll keep an open mind and try not to make any trouble." *But there is more going on here than what I'm being told. I'm sure of it.*

Desange smiled. "I think that's a wise move."

"Have you seen a demon?"

"Yes, last year during my field exercise. Not up close, but it was clearly a demon."

"How do you know it was a demon?"

Desange finished his drink and signaled Seamus for a refill. "Tomorrow in Silva's class, you'll be issued glasses that allow you to see demons for what they really are."

Tessa laughed. "Magic demon detecting glasses?"

Desange shook his head. "I know, I know ... it sounds crazy. But they work." Desange took a sip from his refreshed drink. "I won't be able to convince you sitting here. That's for your training. However, from my point of view, when the preponderance of evidence points to something being true, to keep thinking it is false, just because the truth is uncomfortable is irrational. Keep an open mind and evaluate the information you're given." Desange returned Tessa's smile. "I know you were very good at that in the Army. I think you'll find that tracking down demons is a lot like looking for terrorists."

Tessa didn't want to think about the long hours spent hunting insurgents – the boredom, frustration and feeling that the task was never ending and fruitless. *A hydra, where you cut off one head and three more grow back. If demons exist, is our kill rate higher than the amount of new demons emerging on Earth? Based on the evil I've seen, it doesn't feel like the Curia is making much of a dent. Ugh, I'm starting to think this could be real.* "For the moment, let's assume demons are real. What do they look like?"

"Like us. They take the appearance of a person as their disguise. But don't mistake them for being human. They are much stronger and very cunning. They heal quickly from conventional weapons, making them hard to kill. You remember the knife that Ruth used in the ceremony?"

Tessa nodded. "Sure. It looked weird. The blade was made of some type of clear plastic."

Desange shook his head. "Not plastic. A special glass that you'll learn about when you are issued your dagger. That is the only way to kill a demon. The glasses are made from the same material."

Tessa emptied her beer and signaled Mr Lennon. "I'll switch to scotch now. The Talisker, if you don't mind. On the rocks."

The bartender laughed. "You're clearly American."

"So we're going to be given a heavenly dagger to kill demons." She tried to keep her incredulity from creeping into her voice. "If they aren't human, then I can see why weapons made out of non-earthly materials are needed. But if they look exactly like us, how do we even find them?"

"Primarily through information gathering and analysis. Being a former intel analyst, you have a leg up here."

Seamus returned with Tessa's whiskey. "Here ya go, watered down with rocks. Criminal, that is."

Tessa laughed. "Thanks." She took a sip of her whiskey, enjoying the peaty burn. "So what happens tomorrow?"

Desange pulled out a paper from his pocket and handed it to her. "Here's your class schedule. All first-year recruits have the same courses. Your first session is Introduction to Demonology with Silva. I think you'll like him. He's got great stories from his hunting days. That's also where you'll be issued your dagger and glasses."

Tessa scanned the schedule, seeing she also had Introduction to Combatives with Uri Deneberg and Introduction to Tradecraft with Svetlana Ivanov.

This is all so unreal. Tessa finished off her whiskey. "I think I'll turn in."

"Are you sure? I can introduce you around."

Tessa put her hand over her mouth, covering a yawn. *My brain is fried.* "No, I'm beat. It looks like it'll be a full day tomorrow and since we are all stuck on this island together, plenty of time to meet the other recruits."

"Do you want me to come back with you?"

"I can see my way back to our quarters. Have fun. You can walk me to my first class tomorrow if you'd like." Tessa smiled and stepped off the barstool.

"Sleep well."

She left the lounge and was soon back in her bed. She had taken off her pants and pulled the covers snugly around her. *There is a supply ship off this island, operated by a friendly bartender.* This was her last thought before falling asleep.

Chapter 7

The next morning, Tessa woke up feeling refreshed but a little confused. The unreal hours between her regaining consciousness in Detroit to her drinks with Desange in the Faroes fit comfortably into the category of a particularly vivid dream. But then she looked around. Although the room was dark, enough light filtered under the door from the living room to confirm her new reality in the Curia.

I need coffee.

Desange was sitting on the couch, typing a report on his laptop. He had made a pot of strong coffee and she gratefully poured herself a mug. She took her time showering and dressing, getting herself into the right mindset for the day. Sitting at the desk, she drank her coffee and looked over the schedule. Each day was the same: Demonology and Tradecraft in the morning, Combatives after lunch. *Daily combatives – I'm going to leave here looking like Lara Croft from Tomb Raider. All the second years have rock hard asses. Silver fucking lining.*

When she finished dressing, Desange was waiting for her. "I'll go with you to the elevator."

"Thanks." Tessa walked beside Desange down the dormitory hall.

"You're going to be exposed to a lot of information today that you'll find difficult to believe. After classes, let's meet for dinner and I'll answer any questions you have. Or we can just talk about – whatever you'd like."

Tessa nodded. "Sounds good." She placed her hand on his arm. "I'm positive I'll have a list of questions for you." The elevator doors opened and she went inside.

"I'll see you later." Desange nodded goodbye and headed back to his dorm to get ready for his Advanced Combatives training.

Tessa pressed the "2" button, the classroom level. The elevator whirred up the shaft. *Don't stand out. Listen to what they have to say and keep your skepticism to yourself. It won't help. You need intel, not pointless confrontation.*

She walked down the corridor looking for classroom C. Unlike the hotel feel of the dormitory level, Tessa thought the classroom hallway had more of an institutional look. The floors were covered in white and green speckled tiles and the walls were painted pale yellow.

She reminded herself how nervous she was stepping onto the bus headed for Boot Camp. She joined the Army after the 9/11 terrorist attacks. At the time, she was worried about what she had gotten herself into. But she committed to a new life and didn't turn back. That wasn't the kind of person she was. *I got on that bus and I survived. I have the skills and experience I need to get out of this alive. I've got this.*

The classroom was mundane, the kind you would find in any college. The front wall was covered in white boards. There was a desk and podium facing the recruits, who were seated at tables. A projector was mounted on the ceiling and bookshelves lined the other walls. Next to the podium was a table on which were stacked fourteen black plastic cases. Tessa thought they looked like pistol lockboxes. Juan Silva, the Demonology instructor, stood behind the podium.

"Saving the best for last?" Silva said.

Tessa winced. She hated being late and didn't think that she was. She checked the wall clock. It was exactly 0900, the time this class started. She sighed. *Maybe this is like being in the military, where being on time means you're late.*

"Sorry," she said, hustling to an open seat.

"Don't be sorry, you're right on time. We have a group of eager recruits this year." Silva stepped in front of the podium, addressing the class of fourteen recruits. "Welcome to Introduction to Demonology. Over the course of the year, you will learn many details about demons. For this session, we will do an overview of the seven types." He tapped one of the boxes. "I'll also be issuing your daggers and glasses."

He pressed a button on the control panel built into the top of the podium. A screen slid silently from the ceiling. When it was fully deployed, the projector turned on. The image was that of a cartoon devil with red skin, small horns and wings, a pointed tail and a pitchfork. The recruits chuckled.

Silva grinned. "If only these were your targets. Exorcisms and possession are all theatrics. Great for selling horror movies, but not how demons work." He touched another button and the image was replaced by that of a young woman. She was sitting on a park bench. Next to her was a man Tessa recognized from the news. He was the founder of a popular social media site and reputed to be one of the richest people on Earth.

"That young woman is a demon. Her name is Elodi. How old would you say she is?"

Maria, a recruit from Venezuela with thick, long black hair tied neatly into a ponytail, raised her hand. "25?"

Silva nodded. He advanced the projector. The new image was a wood carving. A woman with a ring etched around her head was standing on a platform, addressing a crowd. From the looks on the faces of the people, they were enthralled. "This woodcutting is German, from the year 1435. That is also Elodi."

Silva took a moment to let that sink in before continuing. "We have accurate reports of her presence as far back as the eighth century."

He pressed the advance button. The cafe image reappeared. "She is a demon who specializes in spreading envy." Juan advanced the image. On the screen an organization chart popped up. At the top was a box labeled "Lucifer." Below Lucifer was a layer of boxes labeled pride, gluttony, lust, anger, greed, sloth and envy.

"This is the organization of demonic orders. At the top is Lucifer, the adversary of God and man. Each order is based on one of the seven deadly sins."

He advanced the projector. The organizational chart had multiple layers added to it, a spider web of lines, boxes and names. "These are the known envy demons." He emphasized "known."

Tessa was shocked at how many there were. She thought about the handful of her fellow recruits in comparison to the hundreds of names under "Envy."

"Just as new hunters are always being recruited, new demons are being sent to Earth. We know there are many who remain undetected."

He went back to the image of Elodi at the cafe. "Demons have many powers. They are stronger and faster than humans." He pointed at the screen. "Elodi may look like a 50-kilo woman, but she could easily snap a person's neck or punch through a brick wall. Demons are also more resilient to death than we are. And they can read human auras, a manifestation of emotional states. With that ability, demons are able to tailor their temptations to each person."

Tessa glanced around and was relieved to see some of her other classmates had the same stunned look.

"In spite of all their powers, they have limits. While they are stronger than us, they do not have infinite strength. They are tougher, but they can be destroyed." He pushed back his sports coat, revealing a scabbard on his hip. He removed a knife. It was silver and highly polished. It had a long, clear blade and no hilt. "This dagger is a weapon of the angels and it is the only way to kill a demon."

"Why not make glass-tipped bullets?" Tessa interjected. "I'm a lot better with an M4 than a knife."

"That's a good question," Silva responded. "The glass interacts with the part of your aura that makes you a hunter. In keeping with the color naming convention, we call it the indigo aura. Unlike the other colors, it does not reflect an emotion. Instead, it marks you as a hunter and allows you to use the glass to detect and kill demons." Silva put his hand over his chest. "Unfortunately, you have to be very close for the glass to work. If the glass is more than around twenty centimeters from the hunter's aura, it is useless."

Silva laid the dagger across the lip of the podium and advanced the image. It showed what appeared to be a male manikin made of clear glass. He advanced the projector. The next slide showed a mound of glittering dust surrounding a football-sized glass oval.

"This is what happens when a demon is killed. Their bodies turn to glass and break apart into dust, leaving behind their heart." Silva wrote *Daemonium Vitrum* on the whiteboard and underlined it. "This is the original term for the material, Demonic Glass. But, since no one uses Latin anymore, we just call it glass. The blades of our daggers are forged from it, as well as other gear needed for your hunts."

He tapped a button, bringing Elodi's photo back on the screen. "Now you know what you are facing. Before I continue, are there any questions?"

Tessa wondered why he kept coming back to Elodi. Clearly, this demon was being monitored. She raised her hand.

"Yes, Tessa?"

"What happened to Elodi?"

He shook his head. "This photo is from last year. It was taken by a hunter in Paris. Two hours after she met with her target, the hunter returned to kill her." He frowned, looking down. "The hunter is no longer with us. Elodi is out there right now, tempting souls. She has evolved over time and now specializes in creating envy through social media. Getting people to compare their lives to one another's posts is her niche."

He picked up his dagger and slid it back into the scabbard. "But the war goes on. One day, Elodi and all her kind will be destroyed and humanity will be saved. That is our mission and our calling."

"So if they look just like us, how are we supposed to find these wankers?" asked a young Englishman, who Tessa thought looked like a younger Hugh Grant.

Good question. Glad there is another recruit who seems a bit skeptical.

"We have an extensive intelligence service that supports hunters, Patrick. Ivanov will go over in extensive detail the tactics of identifying and tracking demons in your Tradecraft class. However, the basic tool we use to detect demons are these." Silva pulled out a pair of glasses and handed them to Patrick.

He inspected the black-rimmed glasses, which looked like thin, ordinary lenses. "I wear contacts."

"Not an issue. These glasses are the only way we can directly detect a demon. Like the daggers, they are made from the glass of a demon's heart. When you wear these, you will be able to see a demon among the crowd. Your vision will become blurry, like you are severely nearsighted. However, a demon seen through these lenses will show up with perfect clarity. We use other types of intelligence to predict demonic presence down to a geographic area, but to have positive target identification, we need hunters on the ground. Try them on."

Patrick donned the glasses and looked around the room. He tolerated the nauseating blurriness for about ten seconds before removing them. "I'm happy to report there are no demons in this classroom."

"And how do you feel?" asked Silva.

"A little dizzy."

"They take some getting used to. Please, pass them around. Everyone, try them on."

Patrick passed the glasses to April, a short redhead sitting to his right. The glasses were too big for her petite face, and she removed them after a few seconds. "It's like I'm legally blind wearing these things."

"Get used to the sensation." Silva picked up one of the clear cases. "In addition to your dagger, you'll be issued a pair of glasses. These can be worn on top of contacts, LASIK or other procedures you've had done to your eyes. I would recommend practicing with them. While the unpleasant feelings will never go away, you will get used to them. And you need to; when you are on an active hunt, you'll be relying on your glasses to confirm a demon."

April handed Tessa the glasses. She hesitated for a moment, examining them. *Desange's magic glass. They look normal enough.* She slipped them on. She felt nauseous. Her vision instantly blurred and twisted. When she moved her head to look around the room, she felt like she was going to fall out of her chair. She pulled them off her face and handed them to the next recruit.

"How are we supposed to wear these all the time?" asked Tessa, rubbing her forehead.

Silva shook his head. "You're not. Even an experienced hunter like myself can only tolerate them for a few minutes at a clip." He saw the worried looks of some of the recruits. He noted that Tessa was not one of them. Once the moment of disorientation had passed, her face settled back into focused attentiveness. "Our tools are not perfect, but they are the best we have. With practice, you'll adjust to their feel and the temporary discomfort. Any additional questions I can answer before I proceed with Elodi's case?"

"One more question," Tessa said. "Are demons aware we use glasses to detect them? If they see us taking them off and on and looking in their direction, wouldn't that clue them in to being hunted?"

"Yes, it can. That is why in Tradecraft you will be practicing the art of surveillance."

Patrick raised his hand. "Can you explain what we'll be taught in this class, because it sounds like we're learning to locate, track and kill demons in the other classes."

"Demonology is a synthesis class. We will be reviewing and analyzing case studies of hunts, both successful kills," he indicated the screen, "and otherwise. Through the experiences of your fellow hunters, you will learn the best way to detect, track and kill demons." He paused for a moment. When he resumed, his voice was grave. "And the best way to survive out in the field. Never forget that these creatures are dangerous. No matter how they may look or act, they are evil. You saw the graveyard. Few hunters wind up there due to old age."

Chapter 8

When Tessa returned from her first day of classes, Desange was waiting in their dorm. She wanted to take a shower before dinner, so he left for the cafeteria, telling her he would save a table. When Tessa was done showering, she slipped on the nicest outfit she had – a pink lace skater dress with her Doc Martens – and headed downstairs.

In spite of the name, the cafeteria looked like an upscale restaurant, with four-person tables, soft lighting and pastel blue walls. It was fully occupied when she arrived. A few heads turned when she entered. She noticed the attention and felt a glow of satisfaction on her outfit choice. She crossed the room to where Desange was sitting. She checked out his plate, a steaming heap of golden curry and rice.

"That looks good. What is it?"

"Vegetarian curry. Very spicy. The chef does not believe in catering to weak palates."

Tessa laughed. "I think I'll try that." She went to the buffet and piled the fragrant curry onto her plate. *I am starving and this smells great.*

"How was your first day?" Desange asked after Tessa sat down.

"Weird, but also kind of mundane." Tessa saw his quizzical look as she finished swallowing. "I mean, we've been told demons are real, there are souls and an afterlife and that we're being trained to fight the forces of evil. But Silva treated it like he was running a training seminar on how to use PowerPoint."

"I know what you mean," Desange said. "But I trust that the Curia knows the best way to prepare us for what we have to do."

Tessa scoped a forkful of curry into her mouth, smiling at the spicy tingling. "I guess. It will take some time for me to figure out some of this stuff. Like the auras – maybe you can explain that."

"Your aura is the emotional energy that surrounds you," Desange said. "Regardless of your external expression, demons can read your emotional state as a field of colors. It is one reason they are so skilled at manipulating humans. If you are experiencing anger, demons will be able to see those impulses as a red spike in your aura. If you are sad, a blue spike or afraid, an orange spike. Humans can't perceive auras, but we can learn to regulate our emotions to avoid demonic temptation. You'll even be taught how to fake emotional states in order to influence demons."

"Even with glasses we won't see auras?" Tessa asked.

Desange shook his head. "Only angels and demons can see them."

Too bad. It would be cool to know what people are really feeling.

"Doesn't that leave us at a disadvantage?" Tessa asked. "Won't demons know we are hunters?"

"Your indigo aura is something only angels can see," Desange said. "It's not an emotion, so it is invisible to them."

"That's a relief."

Desange shrugged. "We still have to be careful. Demons are expert observers of humans and they have allies everywhere."

Tessa shook her head. "So, outnumbered, outgunned and enemies everywhere – sounds like fun."

The next morning, Tessa woke up early. Desange was already sitting on the couch, drinking coffee. He was dressed in skin tight thermal running clothes. Tessa liked the way the slick black material showed off his muscles.

"What's up?" she said, sitting next to him.

"I thought we'd go for a run. I want to show you something in the village."

"A run would be nice. I have a lot of pent-up energy." She glanced at his broad chest. *A lot of energy.* She laughed.

"What's so funny?"

Tessa shook her head. "Nothing." She stood up. "I'll get changed."

"Dress warm," Desange said, as she closed the bedroom door.

After putting on her sweatsuit, Tessa and Desange rode up the elevator to the church. Desange unlocked a metal cabinet next to the elevator and pulled out three headlamps. He handed Tessa a light. "Put this on. It will be dark for most of the run. There is a path but it is uneven."

Outside, the temperature was bitter cold. The wind was light, but enough to set Tessa's teeth chattering. The sky was bright with stars and the moon was a tiny sliver near the horizon.

"Okay, stay close," Desange said, "since it's your first run on the island, I'll set a slow pace."

Desange led Tessa along the path to the village. She found the run to be challenging, more from the cold and the need for caution on the unfamiliar terrain than from the pace. After a few minutes, the path began to angle upwards. Tessa settled into a comforting rhythm. Focusing on the run – on eating up the distance on the trail, one step at a time – was a relief after the last few weeks.

This is what I needed. Out here, I don't have to think about demons, angels, auras or mysterious organizations. I just have to keep running.

As they jogged over the spine of the island and began their descent toward the village, Tessa felt a rush of exhilaration. At first, she thought she could attribute it to the physical exertion and the bracing air. But as she looked up at the crystal-clear sky filled with unfamiliar stars, she felt something deeper.

This is what my life needed. An adventure. Maybe even finding a purpose. She grinned. *Of course, I still have to determine if these people are out of their fucking minds.*

When they entered the village, Desange led them to a house with peeling red paint and a bowed sod roof. He opened the door into the living room. Everything smelled musty and old. There were folding chairs and a metal table in the room, as well as an old footlocker next to a small propane stove.

"What's all this?" Tessa asked.

Desange started the stove and went to the footlocker. He pulled out a flask and sat on one of the chairs. "Our home away from home. It was set up years ago and then each class lets the new one know about it." He took a drink from the flask. The room was warming up, although the cold hung at the edges, waiting to flood back in once the fire was extinguished. "Don't just stand there. Sit."

Tessa sat down, the cold metal of the seat cutting through her sweatpants.

Desange held out the flask.

"Sure," she said, taking a drink. It was scotch and the alcohol burn felt good in her throat. She handed the flask back.

Desange took another drink and then screwed the cap back on. "This place is not being watched by the Curia."

"How closely do they monitor us?" Tessa asked.

"Definitely in the public areas. And our phones, of course. There are a few surveillance cameras around the village, to ensure the island remains private."

"It doesn't surprise me they're watching us. The rarity of our indigo aura makes us extremely valuable to them. We're the Curia's prize asset."

"I agree," Desange said. "This organization isn't big. Look at the size of your recruitment class. Any security breach would be disastrous."

"Do they know we are in the village?" asked Tessa.

Desange nodded. "Yes, but the cameras are pointed toward the dock and helipad. They aren't inside this building." Desange smiled. "We've checked. Ivanov has taught us well." He got up and put the flask back in the footlocker. "The only rules are to make certain the place is stocked up with spirits and don't tell anyone who might let the administration know. We don't want them closing down our clubhouse."

Tessa bent her arm, stretching in behind her head. "I wonder what causes only a small number of humans to develop the indigo aura, or is it something we are born with?"

Desange shrugged. "Who knows. I'm not even sure the Curia knows. Some think it's a genetic mutation. Father McKenna would say we are chosen by God."

"And what do you believe?" asked Tessa.

Desange extinguished the stove. The refreshing warmth was instantly obliterated by the cold. "I think God has a plan. We should head back."

Tessa stood up. Wanting to gauge the depths of Desange's belief, she said, "I was wondering – do you think we are fighting for God?"

Desange nodded. "I do." He flicked on his headlamp. Tessa's eyes gleamed in the pale light. "But even if you don't, demons are real. I've seen them. If nothing else, hold onto the knowledge that you are fighting pure evil."

She followed him out of the red house. The stars were still visible, even though the Eastern horizon was glowing orange and gold. *Fighting evil. That's something I'd like to do again. I've seen enough of it.* They started to jog out of the village. *It would be nice to make a difference in this shit world.*

Chapter 9

After a few months at the Academy, Tessa's assessment of the Curia changed. There had been no hints from Desange or any of the other recruits that they were in on an elaborate lie to manipulate her. The level of commitment required for all involved to maintain such a lie seemed highly unlikely. She decided to see how things played out, while maintaining her suspicions and vigilance. She went to her classes and followed the rules.

Uri was Tessa's favorite instructor, reminding her of some career sergeants she had served beside. An Israeli Defense Force combat vet, he had an impressive collection of scars over his torso. For the first three months, Uri had focused on basic physical fitness, which some recruits were in serious need of, and hand-to-hand combat skills combined with some knife fighting techniques. When he was satisfied with their progress, the training expanded to include small arms use and tactical problems.

Tessa joined her fellow recruits in the Hunt Room. Located on the first level of the Academy, it was the size of a football field, with a forty-foot-high ceiling. The room was filled with movable barriers, walls and catwalks, which could be easily reconfigured. It reminded her of a Shoot House she had trained in during Basic, but with the sophistication only the Curia's deep pockets could design. The Hunt Room had the capacity to simulate a large number of interior and exterior environments.

Tessa was surprised to see Uri with Desange, and three other second year recruits. They were outfitted in black tactical clothing and a harness of laser sensors. Each was armed with a G36 assault rifle, a chunky black weapon with a translucent plastic magazine. They were loaded with blanks and equipped with a laser designator.

Although she had never used that particular rifle, Tessa was familiar with the set-up. The lasers and sensors were used to judge hits during training. More sensor vests were stacked on a table next to the door and one of the arms lockers along the wall was open.

"Okay, everyone listen up," Uri said. "I am a demon and these," he motioned to the four armed recruits, "are my human goons. Your job will be to hunt me down in the maze, get past them and kill me." He walked over to the table. "Before we begin, you'll put on one of these vests. They will let me know when you inevitably are killed by one of my goons." He went to the arms locker and pulled out a Heckler and Koch USP Tactical, the standard issue pistol for the Curia. Like the rifles, this was equipped with a laser. "In addition to your training knife, you will each get a pistol with one magazine. If you waste bullets shooting at me, I will make you run the island one lap per round." He placed the pistol on the table. "Even though these are equipped with blanks, don't fuck around with them. The expelled gas jet can injure you."

He rejoined his designated goons. "We'll start with one on four. I don't expect you to get very far this time around. Just do your best and show me that the last three months haven't been a complete waste of time."

"Rules of engagement?" Tessa asked.

Uri grinned. "You can't use your opponents' weapons. Other than that, do whatever it takes to win. There are no civilian targets in there," he said, jerking his thumb at the maze of rooms and corridors that had been set up. "Try not to get too hurt. I don't need a bunch of recruits on medical call. Anyone else?"

No one said anything.

"Fine. Get your gear."

It's like OPFOR in the Army. I've got this. As Tessa strapped on her sensor vest, Desange walked over.

Tessa grinned. "You didn't tell me you were going to be a goon today."

Desange groaned. "I know. I would have preferred henchman."

Tessa had grown to appreciate Desange's sense of humor. "You have to pay your dues. Start as a goon, get promoted to lackey and then, if Uri gives you a good performance review you get to be a demon's henchman."

"Hey," one of the other opposing force recruits – a wiry woman from Tehran named Laila – shouted at Desange, "no fraternizing with the enemy."

Desange rolled his eyes. Laila had a reputation as a tough, demanding person. "I should get ready. Laila commands."

Tessa laughed. "We can fraternize over dinner, after I kick your butt."

Tessa took a pistol and holster from the arms locker. She then got one of the practice daggers. It was the same size and weight as the weapon the Curia issued her, but made from plastic. The tip was blunt and the edges dull, although being hit and stabbed with it could leave a bruise. Tessa had suffered a few of those in previous sessions.

She ran her finger along the edge of the weapon. She had done the same thing with her real dagger. With the simple handle and clear blade, it looked like a toy. But the edge was sharper than a razor and Tessa had drawn blood with it.

"Okay, recruits, let's get started," Uri said. "You'll be running the course alphabetically. When you hear the horn, go!" He motioned to his team and then entered the maze.

"How are we supposed to have any chance?" April asked Tessa.

"We're not. This is to establish a performance baseline." She pointed at the ceiling. In between the light fixtures were black globes. "See those? Cameras are behind them. They'll record everything we do and then Uri will go over it later. We'll probably run this kind of course a lot to mimic what we'll be facing in the field."

"I wish they'd send us in together," April said. She smiled broadly. "I might have a chance – you're a bigger target."

Tessa laughed. "Yeah, you are about the size of a garden gnome. If this was the Army we'd be battle buddies. But the Curia wants us to learn to fight on our own." She slipped the practice blade into its hip scabbard. "I think there are too few of us to hunt in pairs."

The exercise settled into a pattern that Tessa expected. The horn would sound. A recruit would pick one of the entrances. There would be a few minutes of silence, followed by a volley of rifle fire. Then the dejected recruit would leave the maze. Five minutes later the horn would sound and the course reset.

April exited the maze, limping up to Tessa. "That bitch Laila got me. I think she enjoyed it."

"Oh, I'm sure she did."

Tessa waited for her turn. With her last name Sinclair, she knew she'd be toward the end of the line. *Maybe that's a good thing, as Uri and the goons will have tired out some. Or it could be to my disadvantage, because they will have had more recruits to refine their skills on.*

Eventually, the horn signaled her turn. There were four entrances. While each entrance had been tried, Tessa reasoned that ones in the center would offer more options to maneuver through the maze of plastic panel halls and rooms.

Center right entrance it is. She stepped into the maze, combat ready. *It took a minimum of 30 seconds before I heard fire with the other recruits, so the goons are a little ways in. It would have been nice if Uri let us eyeball the layout. Going in blind is not how I would handle an actual field op, particularly against a demon.* She suppressed a laugh. *Why couldn't the angels invent a way to call in an airstrike versus this dagger? Not very efficient, Ruth.*

She checked each room as she passed, recalling how her instructors at Fort Benning taught her how to clear a house while moving and maximizing cover. She had learned to quickly identify areas outside of easy line of sight and never assume safety. *What was it Sergeant Osterman said? The bullet that kills you is the one you were too lazy to see. Always watch your six.*

As she crept farther into the maze she noted a doorway to one side. She stopped short and pressed against the wall. She glanced into the room. Nothing was in her field of vision. But there was part of the room that she couldn't see. If someone was on the opposite side of the wall she was pressed against, she was out of view. *Wish I had a flashbang.*

She crouched down, brought her pistol up and close to her body and leaned around the doorframe. One of the goons was waiting for her. She knew his name was Khalil, but she hadn't spoken more than a few words to him. He was against the wall and in the corner, waiting for her to pass and shoot her in the back.

"What the hell?" he said, as Tessa's head, shoulders and gun popped into view.

She fired twice and his vest beeped. "Shush ... you're dead."

Khalil frowned and sat down.

One goon down. Tessa resumed her methodical journey through the maze, glanced up at black camera globes. *I wonder if Ruth is watching me?* She fought the urge to flip off the cameras. *Don't be a rebellious child. Play the good soldier – for now.*

Up ahead, the overhead lights were off. While not dark, the hall was shadowy. She approached a turn and saw the tip of a boot sticking out. She stopped and ducked into a room. There was a doorway on the opposite wall. *That was a close call. Okay, let's see if I can flank this dude.*

She checked the corridor. Satisfied that it was clear, she proceeded in the direction that would place her behind the ambush. As she got into position, she felt exhilarated, reminding her of her better days when she was still a respected Army Sergeant. *Before Tyler. I miss sex. This adrenaline is making me horny.* She refocused her mind. *Finish the exercise. Oscar Mike.*

She looked around a corner, having determined that a goon should be there. He was. And so was Laila. She was facing Tessa, covering their rear.

Shit. Tessa fired, while Laila dropped to a knee. The vest of the other goon, an Australian aboriginal named Ngarra, registered a hit. Laila opened fire, but the laser failed to connect with one of Tessa's sensors. Tessa retreated down the corridor, putting space between her and Laila.

Down to half a clip. Laila must have alerted Desange and Uri. She saw a room ahead and ran inside. *Hopefully I can loop around her from here. Set up a good spot to take her—*

She collided with Desange, who was heading in the opposite direction, trying to cut her off. The collision knocked her pistol and his rifle from their hands.

She pulled out her dagger. "Ready when you are."

Desange took out his training weapon and settled into a fighting crouch. "Ladies first."

Tessa lunged with her dagger, not expecting to connect. She wanted to get Desange to react, then plan a more concerted effort to neutralize him. She had to act quickly; Laila might show up at any moment.

Desange side-stepped her thrust and followed with one of his own.

Tessa recalled Uri's words. *Getting in a fist fight with a demon won't end well. Every move should get you closer to putting your blade in their heart.*

She dropped into a crouch and kicked Desange's closest leg, enough to send him stumbling into the wall. *All recruits think is blade blade blade. But Desange isn't a demon, so I don't have to play by those rules.* While he tried to reset and recover, Tessa was up and running at him. She slammed into him, bouncing him off the wall again. It was enough to knock them both to the ground. Tessa was on top, straddling him.

Breathing hard, she held the blunted tip of the plastic knife against his neck. "Tell me where your boss is."

Desange grinned. "Do your worst, hunter. You'll never get me to betray my demonic master."

"Wow ... seriously cheesy."

There was a burst of gunfire that caused their vests to beep.

They looked to see Laila standing in the doorway, a sardonic look on her face.

"Did you just shoot me?" Desange asked.

"You looked like you were about to turn on us." She slung her rifle and grinned.

Uri walked into the room. "Not bad, Tessa. Three goons are dead. But I'm still alive to tempt more souls." He picked up her pistol, handing it to her.

She got off Desange and grabbed the pistol. "In the field, I would never run into a building without doing recon. If I was going to kill you," she said, tapping his chest with the point of her practice dagger, "I wouldn't run in through the front door."

Uri shrugged. "You've done impulsive things in the past."

Tessa was taken aback by the comment. She noticed that Laila and Desange looked a bit uncomfortable as well. *What the hell was that about? Fuck you, Uri. If you were a real demon, you'd see my red aura spike.*

"Okay, clear my hunt house. And you two goons, do a better job with the next one."

As Tessa navigated out of the maze, she thought about what Uri had said. *He's read my file and knows I have rushed into things without thinking. Not into a firefight. But into the bedroom and into a bottle. Even enlisting in the Army was an impulsive move.*

"How did it go?" April asked as Tessa rejoined the group.

"Laila killed me."

April sighed. "Join the club."

Chapter 10

The days grew longer and the temperature changed from chilly to mild. Tessa decided summer in the Faroes was like an Indian Summer in Michigan, and after months of enduring parkas, she was happy to switch to less bulky clothing. She spent more time outside, enjoying the rugged terrain and hearty wildlife. In addition to the ubiquitous puffins, the Curia shared Mykines with a herd of sheep, descendants of those left behind when the islanders moved away. Tessa assumed they were the reason lamb showed up often on the menu.

On a sunny day in late June, she was sitting on a flat rock near the church, watching a pair of sheep grazing along the cliff edge. The only sounds were the crash of waves against the rocks far below and the groaning squawk of puffins looking for mates.

"Hi," Desange said, approaching her.

She looked at him and gave a little wave. "Hey."

He sat next to her.

"I thought you were working on your Special Studies project."

Desange shook his head. "I needed a break. I've had enough of NGO financing for now. I know why they assigned me this, given my educational background."

Tessa looked at him with wide eyes, mouth open in mock horror. "What? The study machine has to rest?"

Desange laughed. "Even I have limits." The laugh faded and he took a deep breath. "Some days, I do feel burned out."

For a few moments, they sat silently, listening to the waves.

Desange is the closest thing to a friend I have on the island. But he's still a Curia guy. He's seen a demon. Or claims to have. Either way, until I see one with my own eyes, this is all hypothetical. She looked at him. She liked the way his lips turned up slightly, always smiling at a private joke. *I want to trust him, but I need to cultivate him to open up about things that he might already know. Build trust bonds that I can use if needed down the road.*

Tessa stood up. "Come on, let's go for a walk. Have you ever been to the lighthouse?"

Desange shook his head. "Never got around to it. Which is kind of sad, given how many months we're stuck training on this island."

"Me neither. Let's check it out," she said, holding out her hand.

Desange took it and let her pull him up.

She held on for a moment longer than necessary. "Follow me."

The sheep briefly looked up from their grazing, watching the two people walk away, before returning to eating the bright green grass and lichen.

"You haven't told me much about your family and friends," Tessa said as they walked along a rough gravel path that led to the lighthouse.

"I didn't think you'd be that interested. My family is pretty boring."

Tessa thought about her family. The alcoholic father, faithless mother, drug-addicted brother and amoral drug-dealing sister. *The Brady Bunch* as written by Charles Manson, she liked to joke.

"Boring is fine." Tessa laughed. "I wish my family had been more boring. How did your parents meet?"

"They were students at different universities in Paris. He was going to the Sorbonne for political science and she was at the Paris-Saclay Medical school. She was working in a bar to make ends meet—"

"Bartender? I like her already."

"—and that's where they met. He went to her bar with some mates, saw her and it was love at first sight."

Tessa laughed. "A real love at first sight thing? I didn't think that actually existed."

"At least, that's how they tell it. After that, they went from dating to engaged to married in months. One thing about my parents – they don't waste time. Which also explains how my older brother Claude was born a few months after the marriage."

"Ah, shotgun wedding."

Desange laughed. "My parents have had their fights and rough patches like any relationship, but overall, seeing them interact gives me hope that a deep, lasting love is possible."

Tessa thought about her childhood and how she would sometimes wish she was adopted. She had a hard time imagining what a healthy, loving relationship looked like. Her parents seemed to stay together out of destructive codependency. "Well, if demons are real, then perhaps love at first sight can happen too. But I've experienced neither."

"I read your file. Well, you know that. I'm sorry you got the parents you did."

She glanced at him. *Are you trying to gain trust and intimacy with me as leverage, or do you actually care?* "It was pretty bad. My parents don't waste time either. The problem is their addictions. My dad never met a bottle he didn't like. My mom's thing was men. I think I was about five when I figured out what all the friends from work were really about."

"Damn. I'm sorry about that."

Tessa thought he sounded sincere. *Nothing is as deceptive as sincerity.* "It inspired me to get out of Detroit as soon as I could. I talked to an Army recruiter on my eighteenth birthday and signed my papers right after graduation. The Army was a good thing for me, until Iraq. You read my file, so you know that."

"Despite all that, you've made a good impression here."

"That's because Ruth thinks I'll make a good killer. And it's slim pickings for hunters, if the indigo aura thing is as rare as Silva indicates. I wonder if indigo auras run in families. Do you have brothers and sisters?"

"One of each. Claude and Chloe. As far as I can tell, neither has been recruited to be a hunter. I think God chooses who he gives indigo auras to, but no idea why he chose me, to be honest. I'm the middle child. Claude's a lawyer with the EU and Chloe's a concert pianist."

"So, no high achievers in your family."

Desange grinned. "I'm the black sheep. I just hunt demons."

Tessa laughed. "What do they think you do?"

"I'm purposefully vague. I've told them I'm doing private security work. It seems to satisfy them, although I think they suspect there is more to the story. We're a close-knit family, so lying to them is hard. But it is necessary."

Must be nice to enjoy spending time with your family. My brother Zach is always looking for the next high and how to pay for it. She stopped herself from walking down that depressing memory lane and focused on more immediate concerns. *If Desange trusts people due to his positive upbringing, that might make him more easily swayed. If I need to do that.*

"There's the lighthouse," Desange said as they topped the last hill on the west coast of the island. "Kind of anti-climatic."

The lighthouse was a 10-meter-tall hexagonal tower topped by a rotating white light. It was painted in alternating red and white bands. A cluster of solar panels was laid out next to the tower and the entire facility was surrounded by a chain link fence.

"Agreed. I was hoping for something more romantic. The kind of place that some grizzled old sailor with a peg leg would live in with a pet dog and a case of whiskey to keep out the cold."

Desange chuckled. "That is a very specific idea you had for your lighthouse keeper."

"It's a spectacular view. Nothing but ocean from here to Iceland. And I don't think anyone comes to this end of the island." She sat down on the scrub grass. "It's nice to have a place to be alone with my thoughts. Spending too much time underground at the Academy isn't healthy."

Desange nodded. "I understand that. When I need to be alone, I go to the church."

A flock of puffins rose up above the lighthouse, landing in a black and white carpet in front of Tessa and Desange.

"When Ruth recruited you, did you leave anyone special behind?" asked Tessa.

He hesitated for a moment, deciding how much to share. "I had a girlfriend in university. I had to break up with her. I can keep my friends at a safe distance, but my girlfriend would have been more complicated. And it might not have been safe for her." He tossed a rock near the puffins. A few hopped and squawked with annoyance. "Has Ivanov given you the personal ties lecture?"

Tessa shook her head. "Not yet."

"Let me give you the spoilers; demons will manipulate and hurt those closest to you if they catch on that you are a hunter. Any close relationship can put your friends, family and partners at risk."

Tessa frowned. "The Curia can't prohibit dating and marriage. I mean, spies get to have families."

"Sure, it's not prohibited, but they warn us of what can happen if your cover's blown. Ivanov has stories that'll scare the shit out of you."

"But you haven't cut ties with your family." Tessa looked down at the grass and watched her hands run through it. When she looked up, she knew she'd hit a nerve.

Desange's face reflected discomfort. "I can't. I thought about it; but I love my parents and siblings too much to let them go. I know it's selfish..."

Tessa touched his arm. "There is nothing selfish about wanting to be with people you love. Whatever the Curia thinks, it's our devotion to each other and the people who matter to us that will keep us fighting. In the Army, I saw guys who had closed themselves off emotionally. They thought that by doing that, nothing could touch them. It didn't work. Addictions and mental illness touched them." *And me too.* There was a moment of silence. *This is getting too heavy. I need to navigate things carefully with Desange. Lighten things up.*

"So ... you're single." She grinned. "Not that I'm interested in my hot mentor." She leaned in close and lowered her voice. "But you read my file..."

Desange laughed. "Well, I'm sure Captain Caplan was something. The alliteration alone gets me going."

Tessa chucked. "I teased him about that too. Captain Caplan. Try saying that ten times fast. Captain Caplan, Captain Caplan, Captain Caplan—"

"Do you two still talk?"

She shook her head. "Not really, it's been a while. I've had other flings, but nothing serious. That's probably in my file too."

"Maybe you just haven't met the right guy."

Tessa shrugged. "Maybe there's a lust demon out there for me. We've been told they know how to push the right buttons. Silva had an interesting case study about that."

Desange's laughter stopped abruptly. He looked at her gravely. "Don't joke about things like that. If you leave yourself open to one of those creatures, it could cost you your soul."

Well, that got a reaction. "Woah, I was just kidding."

Desange's expression held for a moment. Then it softened. "Sorry. I get it's harder for you because you haven't seen a demon yet."

"Don't worry," Tessa said, "I'll make sure to have safe human sex. That's what the glasses are for, right?"

"I don't think Ruth would like her ancient devices of divine power to be used to pick out your next booty call," Desange said, attempting to maintain a serious tone for a second.

Tessa cracked up. "Nice one. Safe sex, Curia style."

Desange returned the laugh. The wind started to pick up. The flock of puffins lifted off, riding the air currents down to the water.

She looked at him. The wind blew her brown hair into her eyes. She brushed it aside. "Until I see a demon, I can't completely believe they exist. I trust you, but I need to see one for myself." *As much as I trust anyone here.*

Desange grinned and looked down.

And I really want to – I need someone on my side and you seem to be a good guy. But I have to be careful. Tessa stood up. "Come on, let's head to the lounge. We've burned enough calories to drink a pint."

The lounge was half-empty. As Tessa and Desange got drinks from the bar and slid into a booth, she noted that most of the discussions going on seemed to focus on the approaching summer break.

That reminds me, I have to think of someplace to go.

The Curia allowed the recruits two weeks in the summer to go anywhere they wanted. It was an all-expenses paid holiday, a needed break after six months of intense training.

"So," she said as they sat down, "where are you going for your break?"

"Home to Paris. And you?"

She shrugged. "Not Detroit. I've thought about just staying here. Go puffin watching. I don't know, I've thought about somewhere tropical too. When I was in the Army, I wanted to go to Fiji, but never got around to it. Maybe I'll do that." She took a drink of her stout. "As you can tell, I'm indecisive."

"Fiji sounds nice. I've never been and I imagine it would be relaxing."

"What will you be doing with your family?"

"Chloe has a concert, so I'll be attending to support. Other than that, sleeping in, meeting up with friends, hitting the clubs, enjoying some good food. Getting in some quality time with Chloe and mom."

"What about your dad and Claude?"

He shook his head. "My father is teaching in New York this summer and Claude is busy in Bosnia with a human trafficking case. Unfortunately, I won't be able to see them until Christmas. But that's okay. Chloe is a handful." Desange said.

In a few days, he'll be walking down the narrow streets of Paris, eating lunch in a quaint cafe with his mom and sister, and I'll be here, staring at puffins. That's depressing.

He saw the hint of a frown. *Maybe I should ask her to come with me,* he thought. *My family won't mind and it would be better for Tessa to not be on her own.*

"Everything okay?" Desange asked.

Tessa forced a smile. "Yeah. So, I heard Laila is taking some of the girls on a Eurorail trip. She asked if I wanted to go."

"Do you?"

"It sounds tempting ... and dangerous. The last thing I need is to spend two weeks getting drunk and laid by guys I find in pubs. Sticking around here is probably the best choice. The weather is finally perfect and I have a backlog of books. Two weeks of outdoor hikes, reading and sober living might be good for me."

"You know, you could come home with me."

The offer surprised Tessa. "Really?"

"Sure. My mother and sister would love to meet you and Paris is a lot more fun than puffins." His smile broadened. "You can play tourist; I can be your guide."

She thought about the alternatives. *Paris with Desange sounds like the perfect mix of safe and fun. Why not?* "I'd love to."

Desange smiled broadly. *"Magnifique."*

Tessa imagined herself walking down a cobblestone street in Paris, eating a fresh crepe. *It will be nice to go on a no pressure trip with a guy I like. I can behave, I think.*

Chapter 11

Tessa was unexpectedly nervous about meeting Desange's family. While she thought of herself as an outgoing person, she also knew that Desange was taking a chance inviting her home. She chewed her cheek and spent the flight alternating between trying to sleep, unsuccessfully, and probing him for information that would give her some clue as to how to act around them.

Desange took a risk inviting me back home to meet his family. I don't want to mess that up. I need to watch my drinking. I don't want to embarrass him or say anything about the Curia that he'd have to clean up. I'll stick to a two-drink limit, she decided as the plane began its descent. *I've done my fair share of interesting things I can talk to them about. I just need to leave out some of my tawdry adventures. I don't need to prove anything, I just need to be myself – within reason.* She looked over at Desange. He was reclining in his seat, eyes closed, listening to his iPod. Tessa wished she could be as relaxed as he was. She turned to the window. The Paris sprawl chased away some of her nerves.

On the taxi ride into the city, she tried to relax. Desange pointed out sights of interest and chatted amiably with the driver. Tessa wished she understood French. She stared idly out the window, losing herself in the hustle and bustle of Paris. It was different from where she grew up. Even from the back of a taxi, it had an energy that Detroit lacked. As they crossed the Seine over the Pont de la Concorde, she noted an increase in tourists. They were easy to spot with their selfie sticks and slightly lost expressions. Tessa thought about the sights she'd always wanted to see in Paris: the *Mona Lisa* at the Louvre, Moulin Rouge at night, the gargoyles of Notre Dame, and having a picnic beneath the Eiffel Tower. She knew these were all the cliched tourist destinations, but she didn't care. *No selfie stick, though. I have some standards.*

"Hey, Tessa, did you hear me?"

"Oh sorry, I was daydreaming. What did you ask?"

"Are you hungry, or would you prefer to freshen up first?" asked Desange.

"I'm too nervous to eat. Let's just get settled."

"You have nothing to be nervous about. Seriously, my family are harmless. They'll love you. Relax, okay. And remember to *faire la bise*." He smiled at a confused Tessa. "We kiss the cheeks as a greeting, but not really. It's an air kiss. Like this." He leaned into Tessa and touched his cheek to hers, making a kissing sound with his lips. He did the same on the other side.

His trimmed goatee tickled her slightly as he moved across her face, but she appreciated the effort to help her learn French customs.

The taxi took them to the 7th Arrondissement, the district containing the Eiffel Tower. The streets were crowded with midday traffic. After six months on an island, the swirl of cars, scooters and pedestrians was almost overwhelming. It reminded her of the first time she went to a busy grocery store after returning from Iraq. All her senses were heightened. The apples were vibrantly green, almost like technicolor, and a baby crying several aisles over hurt her ears. She lasted about twenty minutes before she decided to return late at night when it was quieter. It got better over time as she readjusted to civilian life.

She felt her chest tightening as she stepped onto the busy street. *It's okay, I've been living in a bunker on a desolate island. It's normal to be a little anxious. Plus, I'm meeting Desange's family.* She took a breath and followed Desange up the sidewalk.

Their destination was an exclusive apartment building on the Avenue Charles Forquet, which ran parallel to the Champs du Mars, the park that was home to the Eiffel Tower. She was impressed by the Neo-Renaissance style, a facade of Greek columns and intricate scrollwork. Over the entrance were three statues of women. Beneath the statues, chiseled into the stonework, were the words *'Liberte - Egalite - Fraternite.'* It was exactly the sort of place Tessa envisioned Desange's family living.

"Wow ... that's a beautiful building," she said as she got out of the taxi. "Liberty, Equality, Fraternity."

Desange paid the driver and got their bags out of the trunk. "See, you know a little French. That is our national motto and has its origins in the Revolution."

Desange entered a security code on the keypad next to the door and held it open for Tessa. The foyer's walls were red marble, the floor slabs of slate. A staircase curled around the metal struts of a small elevator. He slid open the accordion gate of the elevator and the two squeezed in. "We go all the way to the top," he said, closing the gate and pressing the "4" button.

"It's nice to ride an elevator above ground again." Tessa noticed that on each floor there were only two doors. "The apartments must be enormous here."

Desange nodded. "A nice change of pace from the Academy."

"You grew up here?"

The elevator came to a stop and Desange opened the gate. "For a few years. When I was younger, we lived in Aulnay-sous-Bois. That's on the other bank of the Seine. When I was twelve, a few of my parents' investments paid off and we moved. My family isn't rich, but they are comfortable."

They approached the door to apartment 5A. Desange set the bags on the floor and knocked. After a few moments, the door opened.

A young woman with dark skin and a mass of kinky curls smiled gleefully when she saw Desange. She wrapped her arms around him. *"Mon frere, ca fait longtemps, dis donc!"*

"It's good to see you too." He broke the embrace. "Tessa, this is my sister, Chloe."

Tessa put out her hand, but Chloe brushed past it and gave her a firm hug, putting her cheek to Tessa's cheek and making a light kissing sound. "It is so nice to meet you, Tessa. Do you speak any French?"

"Sorry, no." Tessa was glad Desange had prepared her for this greeting so it wasn't awkward.

Chloe grinned. "That's okay. It will give me a chance to work on my English."

Her English sounds flawless. I guess she's just being nice.

Chloe grabbed Tessa's hand and led her into the apartment. "Desange, bring in her bag. I want to show her around."

Tessa was impressed by the apartment. It had a large common room that looked out at the Eiffel Tower. Other rooms radiated off the living room, including a kitchen that was bigger than Tessa's apartment in Detroit, a small library and office – "My father's space," Chloe said. There was also a music room with a grand piano – "My favorite thing in the world" – and enough bedrooms to accommodate a small army. Decorations were minimal, mostly abstract paintings and sculptures. All the walls were cream colored and the hardwood floors a rich mahogany. In one of the bedrooms – dominated by a four-poster bed with an enthralling view of the city – Chloe said, "This is your room. I hope you like it; it used to be mine."

"It's beautiful. You don't live here?"

"I have a place closer to work." She looped her arm around Tessa. "I love my parents dearly, but there are a few things a girl wants to keep private." She gave Tessa a little nudge and led her into the living room. Desange was on the couch, a glass of wine in hand.

I wonder if it's common for Desange to bring female friends to meet his family? She probably thinks we're dating.

Chloe frowned. "Can't even wait to offer us a drink? It's a good thing mother is out. She would be shocked at your rudeness."

Desange pointed at the hardwood coffee table in front of the couch. Two glasses of red wine were waiting. "Voila."

Chloe laughed. "Ah, then all is forgiven." She handed Tessa a glass and then raised hers. "A toast – to having my big brother back home and to making a new friend."

As the three people talked, Tessa noticed that Desange was very vague about what he was doing and she followed his lead. His sister didn't press either of them for more information, seeming content with filling Desange in on her life.

After an hour of snacks and small talk, Chloe's phone chimed. She looked down at it. "Mother's finished at the hospital. She should be home soon." She slipped the phone back into her pants pocket. "So, Desange said you might want to go shopping?"

"Oh, maybe. I mean, I don't have anything really nice to wear to your concert. I thought I could pick something up." *And take advantage of the Curia's allowance.*

"That's what Desange said. Don't worry, as soon as *ma mere* gets home, we can head over to Dior."

Tessa felt an immediate case of sticker shock. The Curia provided her with an unlimited expense account, in lieu of a salary. But McKenna told them that it had to be used in a "responsible and justifiable" manner. The Curia made sure its members wanted for nothing – within reason. *I doubt an upscale Paris fashion shopping spree will be considered responsible and justifiable.* "Dior ... I'm not sure ..."

"It will be my treat, so you have to say yes. Right?" Chloe's full lips curled into a smirk.

"I guess I don't have a choice."

"*Formidable.*"

Why is she being so nice to me? She doesn't even know me. Strangers don't take someone shopping for free at Dior. For a moment, she thought this could be another Curia operation. *I only have Desange's word that these people are his family. This could be a way to tie the two of us together.* Chloe was talking excitedly about the new spring fashions. *Can a person really be this open? A family?* She felt sick. *Jesus, what is wrong with me? I meet a nice guy with a nice family and all I can think of is how this is a trap.*

"Everything okay?" Desange asked.

Tessa realized that she must have looked unsettled. She took a sip of wine and shook her head. "Sorry. Flying always tires me out." She held up the glass. "But a little more of this and some clothes shopping and I'll be back to normal."

The front door opened. Tessa heard the clack clack of heels on hardwood. She turned to see a striking woman in her mid-fifties enter the room. While Chloe had soft, full features, Desange's mother looked more like him. She had sharp cheeks and a lean frame. Her hair was straightened and cut short and her dark brown eyes sparked with intelligence. She took off the jacket of her charcoal gray Chanel suit.

"Desange, come and give your mother a kiss," she said, holding out her hands.

Tessa was surprised at how warm her voice was. It was at odds with her severe, angular features.

Desange gave her an actual peck on each cheek. "Mother, this is Tessa."

Desange's mother went right in for a hug and *faire la bise.* "Call me Lizette."

She glanced at Desange. He was smiling, like this was normal. *Maybe this is how his family acts. Or French families in general.*

"Lizette, thank you so much for welcoming me to your home. It's got an amazing view."

"Any friend of my son is welcome."

"Okay, we've exchanged greetings, can we get to the important part?" asked Chloe.

"Shopping?" Lizette said.

"Shopping," Chloe replied.

Lizette looked at Tessa warmly. "Are you ready to be my daughter's dress-up doll? She's excited to makeover an American lady for her Instagram."

"Mother," Chloe chided, before bursting into laughter. "Okay, maybe that's a little true. I have a small following on Instagram for piano stuff and fashion blogging. Would you mind if I took a before and after? It will help promote my charity concert, so it's for a good cause."

"Chloe," Desange scolded. "Tessa's here to relax from training. Not to get you hits on social media." He looked over at Tessa. "I'm sorry, I—"

"No, it's okay. I think it'll be fun actually. I like dressing up." She noticed Desange's slightly disbelieving look. "Hey, I'm not all combat boots and sports bras. I can be girly too."

"Great! Come on, let's go before the shops close. Mom, will you come too and provide your expert fashion advice?" Chloe smiled back at Desange, a look of victory in her eyes.

"You know I can't pass up a ladies shopping trip. Let me fetch my good walking flats."

Desange shrugged. "I'll sit this one out and let you ladies bond." He poured himself more wine. "I'm looking forward to seeing the finished product."

Tessa wanted to say, "Please come with us; you're the only one I really know!" But she smiled politely. *Is he testing me to see how well I can hang with his family? Or maybe he just wants some alone time to decompress.*

A complete makeover turned out to be more than Tessa had bargained for. She thought they would buy a dress and shoes. Instead, Lizette and Chloe led her on a journey through Paris that began at David Mallet's salon at Notre Dames de Victories. "It's the place to have your hair pampered," Chloe enthused as they entered.

"How would you like your hair?" asked the stylist.

"Oh, just trim off an inch at the bottom, maybe add in a few long layers." Tessa liked her current long-layered bob, and wasn't in the mood to get a radical new cut. The stylist frowned, but proceeded as Tessa instructed. *There have been enough radical changes in my life. At least I can keep my hair style.* She listened as Chloe and Lizette chatted with the stylists and felt out of place. *I should leave the salon and not stop until I'm back in Detroit, getting a 20-dollar Hair Cuttery special.*

She was handed a flute of champagne and gladly drank it. The out-of-place feeling started to fade, replaced by a giddy buzz of excitement. *Screw Detroit. This is the life I should be living and if I have to play along with the Curia, that's okay for now.* She took a sip of champagne and felt her concerns shrink, even if they didn't go away.

After the salon, the women went to Dior's flagship store on Avenue Montaigne. Tessa tried on clothes for 45 minutes, modeling them for Chloe and Lizette. She decided on an off-the-shoulder and low-cut top which flared around her waist. She paired this with sleek black slacks and black stilettos that gave her enough height to tower over Chloe and Lizette. She liked the way the clothing highlighted the hard work she had put into her body over the last six months.

Cut and sexy, she thought, when she checked herself out in the dressing room mirror.

"I have the perfect necklace at home to pair with your outfit," Lizette said, as they left the store. "But we do have one more stop."

Lizette drove her BMW F30 through the streets of Paris, with Chloe keeping up a steady stream of chatter from the back seat. It was all innocuous – vignettes of her life, interlaced with celebrity gossip, what music she was listening to and the hot places to be seen in Paris – but it made Tessa feel a little sad. *I wish I could talk to my sister like this.*

Their final destination was a small nail salon in Chaville, a suburb south of Paris. Tessa was amused to see that it was run and staffed by Asian women. *I guess that's not just an American thing.*

After the extravagance of the last few hours, this seemed like a step down. *Just like any strip mall in the States.* As if reading her thoughts, Lizette said, "Before Chloe and Desange were born, Thierry, Claude and I lived near here. He had just started his first teaching job and I was going to medical school. I know it may not seem like it, but we didn't start off with money. My one indulgence a month was to come here and have my nails done. It never hurts to treat yourself, a little self-care to get through the long days."

"Unless you max out your credit card," Chloe said.

"My daughter speaks from experience." Lizette laughed. "I like to come back here every month. It reminds me to be grateful and not forget where I came from." Lizette paused, deep in thought. "Like you, Tessa, I used to work in bars. That helped pay for medical school. I met many," she looked at Chloe, "*connard*?"

"Pricks," said Chloe.

"Yes, pricks."

"I think we may have worked in the same bar," said Tessa, grinning.

Lizette laughed. "They are all the same. So, what is your favorite drink?"

Tessa felt more relaxed. Lizette genuinely seemed interested in getting to know her and was opening up about her own experiences. *She's trying to be welcoming. Not the fake shit my mom does – she really cares.* "Whiskey sour, with a cherry."

"Ah, I agree. Always the cherry." Lizette smiled. "I made a *magnifique* dirty martini." She selected a nail polish, a bold pink, and sat down with the manicurist.

Tessa took her seat to Lizette's right, and Chloe went to a manicurist several booths over since it was the only open station.

"Would it be a cliche to ask for a French manicure?" asked Tessa.

"Yes," Lizette replied, laughing.

"I think I'll get one anyway."

"I like that about you, Tessa. You do what you want. I'm glad that Desange trusts you as well. He has good judgment in people."

"Thanks," said Tessa, taken aback by the compliment.

Chloe snapped a picture of the two ladies to post to Instagram. "I'm going to caption it 'An American getting a French manicure in France, #basicbitch.'" She laughed at her joke.

Tessa laughed back. "Fair enough."

As the afternoon wrapped up and they drove back to the city, Lizette's comment stuck with Tessa. She wondered what she had done to earn Desange's trust, but whatever it was, she wanted to keep it.

After dropping off the clothing, Desange offered to show Tessa the Eiffel Tower and the area around the Champs du Mars. Chloe begged off, saying she had had a long day and needed to be at her best for the concert. Lizette also demurred. The day had been enjoyable, but coming after an eight-hour shift at the *Hopital Necker*, it had worn her out.

"So," Desange said as they approached the Eiffel Tower, "how overwhelming was my family?"

Tessa laughed. "They've been great. I wanted to scold you for bowing out of the shopping extravaganza, but some girl time was nice. I can't believe how much they spent on me. I wish there was something I could do to thank them."

Desange gave her a little nudge on the elbow. She liked the easy familiarity. "Well, don't get used to it. I think they're making an extra effort for you. Next time you visit, it will be McDonald's and sackcloth."

"Well, I really appreciate it."

"If both my mother and sister like you, that's a good sign."

"I'm glad I passed the test. And you?"

"Me? I thought that was obvious." He dropped to one knee. "Or do I need to be more expressive, mademoiselle?"

"Okay, dork. I get it." She held out her hand.

He took it and stood up. "Why thank you." He bowed low.

Tessa shook her head. "You're cheesy."

Desange shrugged. "I'm home, so I can let my hair down."

She touched his shaved head. "So to speak."

For a moment, she left her hand on the side of his head. She stared into his dark eyes and felt herself being drawn to him. *Stop it. Don't ruin this the way you've ruined other relationships.* She pulled her hand away. "Okay let's get this tour back on track. And it better end at a cute little sidewalk cafe."

Desange smiled. "Don't you know that every day in Paris ends at a cafe? I assume you will want a baguette?"

Tessa laughed. "Yes, and I'm going to make you wear a beret for the rest of the vacation."

Chapter 12

The evening of the concert began with dinner on the apartment's terrace. Tessa, Desange and Lizette chatted leisurely, enjoying the late afternoon sun and a light meal of fruit, fresh bread and charcuterie. Chloe left before dinner to prepare for the concert. After the meal ended, Tessa changed from jeans and a tank top into the black slacks and flared top she had bought from Dior.

Lizette entered the bedroom. "You look nice, very elegant. May I suggest an accessory to complement your top?"

Tessa smiled. "I was thinking the outfit needed something else."

"I have just the thing." Lizette opened an armoire and pulled out an antique jewelry box. She removed a gold necklace from the box. Suspended from the chain was a small pendant of emeralds in the shape of a star. "This was given to my grandmother as part of her bride price in Burkina Faso. When she left, she brought it with her and passed it on to my mother. One day, I will give it to Chloe ... but tonight, you should wear it."

"Wow, I'm honored. It's beautiful." Tessa accepted graciously and finished her hair and makeup. She decided to wear her hair down, showing off her fancy haircut. When she emerged, Desange was waiting for her, wearing a perfectly fitted tuxedo.

"You clean up well." *He looks amazing. He could have been a model.*

"Thanks. You're not too bad yourself." He glanced down at her chest, the emerald pendant sparkling just above the rise of her breasts. "Mom gave you her necklace for the night?"

Tessa reflexively covered the pendant. "I hope that's not weird. I didn't want to say no."

Desange held up his hand. "No, it's fine. She likes you." He leaned close to her and whispered. "Just don't lose it."

Chloe's performance was part of a benefit concert for Doctors Without Borders. It was being held in Salle Cortot, the intimate 400-seat concert hall for the *Ecole Normale de Musique de Paris*. Chloe had arranged for her guests to occupy the seats that provided the best acoustics.

Tessa took her seat next to Desange in the concert hall. A woman, presumably the director of the charity, came to the stage and said a few words in French. Tessa found herself once again wishing she knew the language.

The spotlight shifted to Chloe, who emerged from the wing and took her seat on the piano bench. She wore a dazzling white gown that contrasted with the sleek black Steinway grand piano. She began to play Moonlight Sonata.

Tessa touched the pendant and smiled. *This is one of the best nights of my life. A year ago, I was working a crappy job, getting drunk every night and looking for the next hookup. Now, I'm in Paris wearing an outfit worth more than the rest of my wardrobe, and sitting in the best seat at an exclusive concert.* She looked at Desange. His attention was fixed on his sister's performance. *Last year, my only objective with Desange would've been how to get him into bed and then out of my apartment. Right now, I value my friendship with him more than anything.* Tessa stifled a laugh. *What a difference time makes. I'm evolving.*

The concert continued, the sound swelling as Chloe played a selection of Diabelli's variations. The music shifted from intense and mournful to light and cheerful, the latter arrangements mirroring Tessa's feelings. Although she had never taken an interest in classical music before, she found herself entranced by the sound.

She hooked her arm under Desange's and leaned close to his ear. "This is amazing. Way better than hanging out in the Faroes. Thank you."

He smiled and nodded. "You're welcome. I'm glad you're here."

Tessa watched Chloe's fingers dance over the keyboard, in awe of her talent. When Chloe completed her performance, she was rewarded with enthusiastic applause. She stood confidently on stage, beaming at the audience. Tessa caught her eye and Chloe gave a little wave. She accepted a bouquet of flowers from one of the organizers of the benefit and went backstage.

Desange, Tessa and Lizette waited in the foyer of the concert hall. A bar had been set up and they were drinking wine and chatting about the music when Chloe weaved through the crowd to them. She had changed out of her gown into a tight red mini-dress.

"How was I?" she asked.

"Magnificent," Lizette said.

"It's clear where all the musical talent in the family went," Desange added.

Tessa gave her a hug. "I've never heard anything like that before. It was amazing."

The quartet chatted and drank for a little longer. They would be repeatedly interrupted by people complimenting Chloe. Tessa noted that a few of the men were checking her out, glancing down at her chest and pendant. *That's right, guys. I can't play the piano, but I do rock Parisian fashion.*

Eventually, the crowd thinned out.

"Well, I know you have a long night of celebrating ahead of you," said Lizette, "but I have a case in the morning, so I'm going to head home."

Tessa started to take off the necklace, but Lizette stopped her. "You keep that on. It looks stunning on you. The night is still young, enjoy it."

Chloe nudged Tessa. "Let's go drinking. I know the perfect place."

A part of Tessa wanted to head back with Lizette, away from the temptations she knew she would face. However, she didn't know when she'd get an opportunity like this again. *I just need to watch myself. Two drinks, three max. And no slutting it up.* Seeing a cute man in a tux eyeing her up, she added, *flirting is fine.*

"Let's get a taxi and head over to *La Maison des Souris*," said Chloe.

Desange saw a look on Tessa's face that conveyed her lack of understanding. "That means the Mouse House. It's a little place, far away from any tourists. They are known for their cocktails and jazz bands. Very authentic."

Chloe smiled excitedly. "You'll love it, Tessa. Cozy and intimate."

Desange hailed a cab, which took them to a street near the Brassai Garden in the 13th Arrondissement. The taxi deposited Tessa, Desange and Chloe in front of an art deco tenement building from the 1920s. The severe lines of the facade and curves of the false columns were illuminated by flood lights built into the eaves.

Tessa thought the effect – strips of shadow and light bleeding into each other – was slightly sinister. *Looks like a haunted house.*

A small crowd was gathered on the sidewalk in front of a short flight of stairs leading down to a black door. A sign on the door had a white mouse etched onto it.

As they stood in line, Tessa could hear music, a soft blend of horns and piano. Desange pressed a button next to the door.

It opened and a beefy man with a thick neck and an impassive stare blocked the doorway. After a moment, he said, "Desange? *C'est vous?*"

"*Oui*, Herman."

The men shook hands and Herman stood away from the door, squeezing into a little alcove next to it. A short hallway of exposed brick ended in a black curtain. They pushed through and emerged into the bar.

Tessa thought the name was appropriate. *This place is tiny.*

The single room was divided into three distinct areas. A low stage was at the far end, occupied by a four-man jazz band.

Closest to Tessa was a corner bar only large enough for a single bartender to fit behind and an open space where a few knots of people were talking and drinking. Between the two areas were a dozen small round tables. A few were open and Desange chose one near the wall. The lighting was provided by alternating red and blue bulbs, which made the jazz club look otherworldly.

Tessa noted that everyone was well-dressed and attractive. She compared them to the shabby, broken people who frequented the Blue Ox. She couldn't help but feel a stab of depression when she thought about her wasted time in Detroit and the many customers she had served who were methodically drinking themselves to death. *Gluttony. Greed. Sloth. I bet the demons are alive and well back home.*

"What's wrong?" Desange was looking at her intently. He saw the flat line of her lips and slightly unfocused look in her eyes, like she was thinking about something far away from this Parisian jazz bar.

"Sorry. I'm in my head, thinking too much."

"You know what would help with that? Cocktails," Chloe said. "Desange, hold the table. We'll get drinks and show off a little." Chloe took Tessa's arm and led her through the crowd.

Tessa saw a pair of attractive men check them out as they passed. She looked back at them and flashed a flirtatious smile.

"My brother was right. You did look, I don't know, worried. Are you okay?"

Tessa didn't want to burden Chloe with depressing stories of her childhood, her aborted Army career or her lost year in Detroit. And she was sworn to secrecy with the Curia. She had no idea what would happen if she told outsiders, but she guessed it would not be pleasant. She decided to play things light. "It's nothing really. With my schedule, I haven't been able to get out much. I'm just taking this all in."

"How about a handsome man to sweep you off your feet for the night? Plenty of options here."

Be good, Tessa. She shook her head. "I'm just happy hanging out with you and Desange."

Chloe nodded. "What are you drinking tonight? Whiskey sour?"

"Nah, I'm in the mood for something different. How about vodka? Your choice." *Plus whiskey is my kryptonite and I'm practicing moderation.*

Chloe ordered cocktails in rapid-fire French. "You know, he likes you. I see the way he looks at you. Is there anything there?"

Tessa looked across the bar to where Desange was sitting. His shaved head glowed darkly in the blue light, nodding slightly in time to the music. "We're friends and he's been a good mentor to me." She took a sip of her cocktail, tasting ice-cold vodka and a hint of cucumber. "But I have a bad habit of getting involved with friends and messing things up."

Chloe nodded. "I respect that. Friends and lovers don't always mix."

For the next hour, Tessa listened to the band and sipped cocktails. She began to feel buzzed on her third vodka. She found herself stealing glances at Desange, picturing his shirtless torso and imagining his strong hands on her bare skin. *Down girl. The last thing you need is to have a fling with a guy you live with.*

"Well," Chloe said after the band left the stage, "this is where I bid you *bonne nuit.*"

Desange started to rise. "We can go with you."

She shook her head. "I don't need an escort. I'll get a taxi." She gave Tessa a parting hug. "Stay out, have fun. I'll see you later."

Tessa watched Chloe exit the bar, her red dress disappearing into the crowd.

"Do you want to stay here or…?" asked Desange.

Tessa held up her hands. "I've had three cocktails. If we're here any longer, you're going to have to carry me out."

"Let's walk."

Desange hailed a taxi and had the driver take them to the Seine, near the Pont de l'Archeveche, the bridge leading to Notre Dame. He guided Tessa down a flight of stairs to the walkway that ran parallel to the river. Other couples were strolling along the flagstone path. The gothic spire and towers of the cathedral loomed across the river.

"I love Notre Dame at night. It's like looking into the past." He turned to her and smiled. "A message from our ancestors, to trust in something bigger than us."

"Do you mean God ... or the Curia?"

Desange shrugged. "I suppose both. The Curia is the closest I've come to knowing God's intention for humanity." They continued strolling along the river bank. "So, have you tried using your glasses yet?"

Tessa was surprised by the question. "No. I left them in my luggage." She laughed. "I guess I was trying to forget about the whole demon thing."

Desange tapped his pocket. "You should keep them with you. Just in case."

"I'm not sure where I'd put them in this outfit," Tessa said. "Did you see a demon at the concert or jazz bar?"

Desange laughed. "No, although I did check. I'll be vigilant for both of us. And yes, that outfit. You look..."

Tessa waited a moment. "Don't leave me hanging. You start to tell a woman how she looks, you have to go all the way." She poked him with her elbow. "I would've thought a French guy would know that."

He sighed. "You look fantastic."

"Damn right I do."

They walked past a tight cluster of girls who were on their phones and jabbering excitedly, a dozen conversations at once.

Tessa, not wanting to make Desange uncomfortable, changed the topic.

"So, do you find it hard to know what's human and what's demonic?"

"Without using the glasses, yes, they look just like us." Desange said. "I've used my glasses a few times since we've been here and I've seen nothing. But on my field exercise, I saw a demon. He was the only clear object in my view. The rest of the world was a complete blur." He pulled out his glasses. "You try, tell me what you see?"

Tessa put them on, watching the cluster of girls become a blurry mass. "Nothing." She handed the glasses back to Desange. "The Curia makes us believe demons are everywhere, but that doesn't appear to be the case."

"They want us to remain cautious."

As they continued to walk, Tessa wished she had worn flats. While she thought the heels were sexy, they also were making her feet hurt. "Can we sit for a minute?"

"*Oui.*"

They sat on a stone bench by the river.

"Is everything bad a person does due to demonic influence," she asked, "or can humans be evil all on their own? And if everything bad is due to demons, then how can humans be blamed for being fuck-ups?"

Desange shook his head. "The idea that demons are responsible for everything wrong in the world is too reductive. It's comforting to think that without them we would all be kind-hearted people. But I don't believe that. I think that we are still responsible for our fate. We have freewill. The demons are good at manipulating it, but we are not their puppets."

"Good. I like being free to make bad choices, demons or not." She looked at Desange for a reaction. *I hope I'm not saying anything he'll find suspicious.* "To be honest, the training is making me a little paranoid. I try not to think too much about it, but the worldview they present is pretty bleak."

To her relief, Desange nodded. "I understand how you feel. The Curia called into question everything I believed about the world."

"Do you think the Curia is exaggerating things? Could they be trying to make the threat seem bigger than it is?"

Desange shrugged. "I don't know. Why would they?"

That's a good question. But it is reassuring to see that Desange isn't blindly accepting what the Curia is telling him. She rested her arm against his. *But he still believes. He's seen a demon – or whatever – and I haven't.* She found herself wishing she would see one; it would clear up many of her doubts.

"Let me have your glasses again."

"Okay." He pulled out the case and handed it to her. His glasses were a thin gold frame with the characteristic thin lens. She slipped them on, her world growing murky. The lights of the city seemed more intense, hammering her eyes. She watched a few blurry people pass her by. "Nope, still no demons. Just a splitting headache." She removed the glasses, handing them back to Desange.

He slipped them into his jacket. "I don't think cocktails and demonic glass mix well."

She wanted to voice some of her concerns about the structure of the Curia and how it resembled the extremist groups she had encountered in Iraq. *Is now the right time? He just opened up about some of his doubts; why can't I? I need to trust someone. And Desange has shown himself to be someone I can count on.*

"I'm worried about something else. When I was in the Army, part of my job was to provide analysis of terrorist organizations. They isolate people, train them to believe that only their group knows the truth and to trust nothing else. The Curia is doing the same thing."

Desange looked at her with concern. "You think the Curia is a terrorist group?"

Tessa shook her head. "No, but I don't know how much I can trust them." She touched his arm. "I trust you; but that's about as far as I can go. Ruth, Silva, Uri, Ivanov, McKenna — I just don't know how much of what they say is the truth. I get the feeling there are lies of omission."

"You may be right. I don't think that we are told everything. But, were you told everything when you were in the Army?"

He has a point. Any organization that deals with covert operations will have compartmentalized information, including a wealthy cult of demon hunters. She shook her head. *My life is not boring.*

Desange's look of concern softened. "I think you'll learn to trust the Curia."

"I need to see a demon for myself for the reality to sink in. Anyway, I'm looking forward to my first field exercise."

He put his arm around the small of her back. "It's okay if you're scared when you go out in the field. I know I was."

She leaned against him. She liked the feeling of his body pressed against hers.

For a few minutes they sat in silence. A dinner boat drifted by. A siren sounded. An old man passed, walking a panting pug. He looked at the couple and smiled. Tessa returned the expression.

In a few days, we go back to the weirdness, but for now ... it's nice to feel normal. She looked up. Desange was looking at her and smiling. "What?"

"You are very beautiful."

Tessa blushed. "You probably say that to all the hot demon hunters you know." *I'm not doing this. I'm not going to do this. I'm being good.*

She kissed him. He kissed her back. The press of their lips sent a pleasurable warmth spreading through her body. She wanted more. She ran her hand over his chest and felt the tip of his tongue, hot and wet, on her lips. She accepted it. For a moment, they were locked together, tangled in the night. She felt his hand on her bottom. The other went to her leg, resting on her thigh. It didn't go any higher, but the touch was enough to excite Tessa. She had the urge to straddle him right there and ride him passionately while wearing only his family's emerald star pendant.

No ... not again. Don't repeat the past. She pulled away.

Desange didn't move; he just looked at her quizzically, waiting for a cue.

"I'm sorry, it was the drinks." *Jesus, that sounds pathetic.* "And you are really attractive," she added, stating the obvious.

Desange pulled back his arm from around her and released her leg. "It's okay." He looked at his watch, a reflexive gesture.

"We should head back." He stood up, silhouetted against Notre Dame.

"This isn't going to be weird, is it?"

He grinned. "Only if you make it weird." He held out his hand and she took it, standing up. "Come on. We both have had a long night. Everything will be clearer in the morning."

They walked toward the stairs leading to the street. Tessa noticed another couple in a deep embrace and felt a tinge of sadness, knowing she had denied herself what she really wanted. *But it was the right thing to do.* She realized this would be the first of many sacrifices required by the Curia. Despite her doubts, she was starting to accept her calling as a hunter.

Chapter 13

Tessa slept in. By the time she woke up, the sun was shining brightly through the cracks in the blinds. She rolled over and buried her head in the pillows. *Don't need to get up. On vacay.* She heard a door open and close on the balcony next to her bedroom. Then what sounded like a tea kettle whistling. *I should get up. There's so much of Paris I have yet to see.*

She slid out of bed and went to the closet. She was dissatisfied with her limited wardrobe options. *Should have packed more than jeans and T-shirts.* She shrugged and repeated the thought that she was *on vacay*. She grabbed skinny jeans and a faded taupe shirt. *I want to be comfortable walking around the city today. I've got a date with the Mona Lisa and a bunch of statues.*

Tessa emerged from the bedroom and found Desange in the kitchen, pouring coffee from the French press. "*Bonjour.* Do you want some coffee?"

Tessa noticed he looked down at his coffee instead of up at her. *Is he going to make last night awkward? Maybe I should just bring it up to clear the air. He should know that I don't think our kiss was a big deal. Get us firmly back on the friends-without-benefits track.* "Yes, please."

He handed her a mug and motioned to the balcony.

Tessa followed him out, taking a seat across from him at the table. They sat in silence for a few moments, drinking coffee and watching the street below. The shrill honking of car horns reverberated off the buildings.

Say something. "Good coffee. Much better than the stuff I drank in the Army." She grinned. "Although I still like NesCafe."

Desange snorted. "Instant coffee, *dégueulasse.*"

"It's an acquired taste."

She tapped the side of her mug and listened to the sounds of traffic rushing down the Avenue de Suffren. "May I have more?"

"*Oui.*" Desange emptied the remaining French press into Tessa's cup. "Croissant?" He held up a small basket.

"Yes, please." Tessa sighed. She took a bite of her croissant. *Here goes, let's get this over with so we can move on.* "So, we kissed."

Desange looked down at his coffee, then into Tessa's eyes. "I'm ashamed of my behavior last night. I betrayed our relationship. I gave into my impulses." He frowned. "I know better. I've been up most of the night thinking about it, what I could have done differently. I was thinking it might be best if—"

"Desange, it's okay. Really, it's not a big deal." Tessa smiled, sipping her coffee.

"It's a massive deal. I've read your file, Tessa. I know what happened in Iraq with Tyler. You get involved with male authority figures. It was up to me not to get you into that kind of situation and I failed. I took advantage of my position in a moment of passion and lost my head."

Tessa slammed down her mug on the wrought iron table, louder than she intended. "What happened with Tyler has nothing to do with last night. Not everything is about my mistakes. It was a romantic night in Paris and we'd been drinking. We've been flirting with each other for months. It was bound to happen." She glared at him. "In fact, I'm the one that stopped it from going further and damn proud of myself. And don't bring up my past like it's a scarlet letter."

Tessa's anger made Desange feel worse; it also confirmed a decision he had made during his sleepless night. There was a moment of silence as he took a sip of coffee. He looked out over the city, avoiding eye contact. "When we get back, I'm going to request Ruth reassign you to another mentor. That will protect us from giving into our impulses in the future."

Tessa sighed. She took a bite of her croissant. This was not how she had pictured this morning going. *He is way over-reacting to this. Let me try again, calmer this time.* She took a deep breath. "It was no big deal. I mean that. I kissed you first. You reciprocated, but it was my fault for initiating. Like you said, you've read my file and know I can be sexually impulsive. Trust me, the fact that I stopped is progress." She smiled slightly. "You're a good friend. Can we just move on and leave that kiss by the river? You've been a great mentor to me. I don't want to lose that because of one night."

Desange had a poker face. "It's not that easy for me, Tessa."

Tessa chugged down the rest of her coffee. *This is not going anywhere useful. He just needs some time to get over last night.* "I think we need some space. Let's both take time today to think things over before we make any rash decisions. We still have a week of R&R left. We don't have to land on anything right now."

Desange nodded. "Okay, that makes sense. What do you plan to check out today?"

He's trying to bring things back to the surface, thank god. "The Louvre, I guess."

"The Louvre is a good choice. However, you might want to check out Montmartre. It has a lot of interesting little shops and galleries to see and some magnificent restaurants."

"Sounds familiar."

"It's where Moulin Rouge is located. If you decide to go, check out Espace Dalí, if you like surrealist art."

"Is that the artist with the dripping clocks?"

"Yes, he's one of my favorites."

"Cool. Maybe I'll just do Montmartre today. I'll see where the day takes me."

"Take your glasses with you."

"Good idea," Tessa said. *Stick with the job ... routine ... procedure.* "It will give me an opportunity to try them out in the field. What will you do today?"

"I've got some friends from university I could visit. They'll be happy to see me. Don't worry about me, go enjoy your day."

I hope venting to your friends will get this out of your system so we can go back to being sexually frustrated roommates. I can behave. Plus we only have six months before you graduate. Let's just be cool.

"Okay, enjoy time with your friends." Tessa rose and opened the balcony door. "I'll have my phone and glasses on me. See you later tonight."

"*Au revoir.*" Desange gave a weak wave, remaining seated.

Tessa took Desange's advice and went to Montmartre. *It'll be good to be outside. See the sights. People watch.* The weather was pleasant, with a clear sky and light breeze. *The perfect day for bumming around.*

She took a cab and spent the short trip across the Seine staring out the window. The driver's music was techno, the beat fitting her unsettled mood. The lyrics were in Arabic and for a few moments she was back in Iraq. In a Humvee, driving through the crowded streets of Amarah, head on a swivel, looking for a man with a gun or the trigger for an IED. She could taste the grit, feel the sun beating down on her.

She bit her cheek. *No, don't go back there. Those days are long gone.*

She let the memory slide from the forefront of her mind. She pulled out the small guidebook Desange had given her and read about her destination.

"...Perched on the top of a small hill in the 18th arrondissement, Montmartre is the quintessential Parisian village with winding cobblestone streets, art galleries, boutique shops and intimate cafes. Once known for its windmills, there are several left standing, including the famed Moulin Rouge. At the top of the hill sits Sacre Couer, a 19th century Romano-Byzantine style basilica dedicated to the heart of Christ. The location has served as inspiration for many artists. Van Gogh, Renoir and Picasso all took up residence in the district..."

Tessa slipped the book back in her purse. *Sounds wonderful, Desange. Maybe I should go to the church and confess my lack of memorable sins.*

After being dropped off, she decided to start her tour by taking a Promotrain. Although the train-styled tram was a little more tourist-focused than she normally would have found acceptable, she decided it would give an overview of the district. She sat by herself and watched the bohemian streets and vine-covered houses pass her by. She made a few mental notes of stores that looked interesting. She also couldn't stop herself from thinking about the tense discussion with Desange. In particular, his statements about Tyler and her past. *I wish I could see what my file says about me. Do they know every guy I've ever slept with?* Tessa laughed to herself. *That would be a long file.*

The tram rumbled down a cobblestone street. She felt the rhythm of the street in her chest. It reminded her of how she felt when a helicopter would fly low over the base, like her bones would vibrate through her skin. *Even in the mess hall. Every time a Blackhawk came in for a landing, the trays would rattle.*

For a few moments, Tessa was no longer in the Promotrain. She was no longer winding down the narrow street of a Paris neighborhood. She was sitting in the mess hall with Tyler. It was early one morning and they were having their breakfast book club. It started as a way to pass the time. He had lent her a book called *Counting Sheep* – something to help with her insomnia. After that, it kept going. *It started so harmlessly. We were friends, bonding over books. Anything to distract us from the mortars.*

A pair of glamorous young women walked past the tram. They wrinkled their noses at the tourists. Tessa didn't notice.

She was thinking about the event that started her down the road that led to Tyler. A few weeks after arriving in Iraq, Forward Operating Base Garry Owen was subjected to a mortar attack. No alarm sounded. Just three sharp explosions that knocked Tessa out of her bed. She felt her stomach turn. The tram driver was calling attention to a building made briefly famous by a poet who took residence there decades ago. Tessa didn't hear him. Instead, she heard screaming. A high-pitched wail cutting through the underwater echo of the explosions. The CHU next to her's took a direct hit. The shipping container turned housing unit was split open and smoke billowed from it. She could see herself stumbling out of her CHU in time to see her neighbor, Sergeant Nichols, walking from the shattered metal box, holding a mangled arm and screaming.

The fear was the first thing she felt. Fear of death, maiming, becoming a screaming, ruined thing. But what was worse was the thought that followed, the thought that sent her into a spiral of depression that led to Tyler.

Better him than me.

"To your left," the tour guide said, pointing at a plain building with a black sign reading *Theatre* over gray metal doors, "is the Théâtre des Béliers parisiens. For those who are looking for an intimate theater experience, it is highly recommended."

Intimate. She thought of Desange. *He takes sexual intimacy more seriously than I do. Hooking up isn't about intimacy; it's about fun. Fucking is enjoyable.* Tessa thought back to New Year's Eve with – *Marshall? Martin? Michael?* – one of many disappointing online encounters, notable only because it was the last thing before Ruth and the Curia had come into her life. *I was so frustrated with his drunk dick, and it went downhill from there. Really downhill. Alcohol and sex are not the best combo for me. With Desange, we could have gone all the way. He would have and that would have messed things up even more. We're both stuck in this demon hunter life. Throwing myself at him is a terrible way to cope with it.*

"Here is *parc des vingt chevres*. Many locals claim it is haunted by the ghost of Marie Antoinette."

That's what went wrong with Tyler. We bonded during traumatic times. Bored, lonely, terrified, stuck in a warzone. Desange and I are in a similar pattern. Trapped on an island, bonding over the intense experience of training to hunt demons. I prevented the pattern from repeating. I stopped myself from making the same mistake I made with Tyler.

She felt better. She also felt irritation toward Desange.

If he can't act like an adult and move on, fuck him. The last thing I need is a fragile man in my life.

"We are now entering the heart of Montmartre. There are many wonderful shops and restaurants here."

Wonderful shops and restaurants – let's do this. Tessa jumped down from the slow-moving tram.

The tour guide started to yell at her, but decided it was too much effort. "Here you see the place where people jump from my train in an unsafe fashion."

I need to get out of my head and take in this amazing city. She chose a random bohemian dress shop that had a French name she understood, *Kaléidoscope.* She pulled her glasses from her purse and donned them as she entered, a rainbow of colorful clothes morphing into a blotchy blur. She had the impression that there was a pattern in the swaying images, but couldn't put her finger on it. She circled around for a minute, pretending to browse. *No demons in this shop.* She took off the glasses and closed her eyes tightly. Just for a moment, until the dizziness she felt passed. When she opened them, she saw a display of scarves. She ran her hands over a sheer white scarf covered in a multicolored pastel fleur de lis pattern. The only scarves she owned were heavy wool ones needed for winter in Detroit. *I could use something fresh. This will brighten up my outfit and make a nice souvenir.* She purchased the scarf, tying it loosely around her neck.

She made her way to the museum Desange had recommended, Dali Paris, and found it underwhelming. She decided to walk to the Moulin Rouge, which was only a few blocks away. Although she knew better, she was a bit disappointed that it wasn't the decadent Disneyland from the movie. *Maybe it looks better at night.* She had a passerby take a photo of her with the facade and windmill in the background.

While deciding what to do next, she tried on her glasses. She hoped to spot a demon – and felt vaguely silly about thinking one might just be passing her by. *Nothing.* Tessa sighed. *It's early evening, I might have to wait until it gets darker.* Tessa laughed. *Why do I assume demons are creatures of the night? That's Hollywood for you.* She continued wandering, heading back into the heart of Montemarte until she found a corner cafe nestled underneath an ivy-covered building. *That's so cute. Stereotypical Parisian. Just what I need.*

By this point it was dinnertime. She was getting hungry and a jolt of caffeine wouldn't hurt.

She entered the cafe and noted it was crowded with a long line. *Hopefully that means their coffee and sandwiches are good. Let's check for demons while I'm waiting.* She put on her glasses and scanned the cafe. *All clear. Still no unholy creatures lurking about Paris.*

She approached the counter, looking at the menu. Everything was in French. *Okay, I can use my phone to help me translate.* She pulled her smartphone out.

The barista said something that Tessa assumed was "What can I get you" in rapid French. The man looked past her at the long line of customers, then back to her with obvious impatience.

"Um ... coffee and ham and cheese sandwich." Tessa bit her cheek, fumbling with her phone.

The barista rolled his eyes and said something in French that caused the closest customers to snicker. He pointed at the line.

Tessa, trying not to get flustered, started to speak haltingly. "Le jamon..."

"Excuse me, can I help you order?" asked a man, with a welcome American accent.

Tessa turned to follow the voice. A man a few places behind her smiled. "I speak fluent French."

"Oh, thank god. Yes, I'd like a coffee, just black, and a ham and cheese sandwich."

The man spoke to the barista, who nodded in understanding.

"Thanks. Can I get you something?" asked Tessa. "It's the least I can do."

"Sure. I'll take an Americano, thanks." He called out his order to the barista.

Tessa smiled. "An Americano in the heart of Paris, that's brave."

"I like to live on the edge. I'm Dylan, by the way." He held out his hand.

"Tessa." She shook his hand, feeling her heart beat slightly faster. His green eyes stood out against his olive skin and wavy black hair. He looked Greek or Italian, handsome and with a rugged vibe, like he just arrived back on shore after spending weeks at sea. *But he used sunscreen. His skin is glowing.* He wore a vintage Ramones T-shirt that was tight enough to show off the bulge in his biceps. *But not gym rat tight. Like a modern James Dean.* She half-expected him to have a motorcycle parked outside the cafe. "Are you visiting Paris?"

"Yes, I rented an apartment for the summer. I'm from Austin and needed a break. What about you?"

"I'm visiting a friend here."

The food and coffee arrived at the end of the counter. Tessa grabbed her mug and sandwich. "Well, I hope you enjoy your holiday. Thanks for helping me order." She headed outside to a table and sat down.

Dylan followed her out. "Would you like some company?" He smiled warmly, gesturing to the empty chair. "In case you need my language skills."

Oh god, yes. "Um, sure. I'd like that."

"Where are you from in America?" asked Dylan, relaxing into his chair.

"Detroit. The polar opposite of Austin." Tessa took a large bite of her sandwich.

Dylan smiled. "I like warmer weather."

"Me too. Food just tastes better in Paris, I think." Tessa reflexively ran her hands through her wavy brown hair, feeling uncharacteristically sheepish. *Are you really going to talk about your sandwich?* "Yeah, Detroit sucks. Period."

"What do you do in Detroit?"

Here we go. What is my cover? Bartender. Generic and bland. Nothing about bartending gives away demon hunting. And the best covers have a hint of truth to them, like Desange doing security work for a nondescript private company. "I mostly bartend. I can make a great whiskey sour, and I always give an extra cherry."

"Ah, can you tie the knot?" asked Dylan.

Tessa grinned. *Is that where we're going? Fine with me.* "No, but I've tried multiple times. That's a rare skill."

"I can tie it." Dylan sipped his Americano, his green eyes locking eyes with Tessa.

"Oh really? I've never had a customer successfully get the knot. Many have tried. I'm beginning to think it's a myth, to be honest."

"I can show you back at my place, if you want to see my rare talent for yourself."

This is exactly what I need. Random sex with a hot American in Paris to get me through eighteen more months at the Academy. "Seeing is believing. Shall we?" Tessa stood up, leaving her half-eaten sandwich and cooling coffee. Both her hunger and fatigue were gone, replaced by a desire that had been building up for months.

Dylan rose and took Tessa's hand. "I live a few blocks over."

As they walked down the winding cobblestone street, Dylan put his arm around Tessa's waist. She leaned into him, enjoying the anticipatory excitement of guilt free, uncomplicated passion. *Just how I like it.*

Chapter 14

They walked up the narrow marble spiral staircase that led to Dylan's fifth floor apartment.

"One more floor," Dylan said from behind Tessa as she continued climbing. She felt his hand wander down from her waist onto the back pocket of her skinny jeans, cupping her bottom. She turned to face him, and he kissed her passionately, lowering her down onto the cold marble stairs a few steps before his apartment door. He pushed her purse to the side, then traced his hand underneath her loose, taupe shirt and snaked it around to unlatch her bra.

"Oh, the athletic type." Dylan grinned, feeling Tessa's sports bra.

"Were you expecting lace?"

He pulled off her scarf, shirt and bra in one swift motion, tossing them down the stairs, and pinned Tessa against the stairs with his body. It happened so fast, Tessa found herself breathless. He pinched her nipples playfully, sending tingles over Tessa's spine.

"So you wanted to see me tie the knot," Dylan whispered into her ear, running his tongue along the edges of her earlobe.

"Not on a cherry," said Tessa. She unfastened her jeans and pulled down the zipper.

Dylan stood up. "I did promise you a drink. Come," he said, offering his hand.

"You're a fucking tease, excuse my French." Tessa grabbed his hand and he pulled her easily to her feet. His strength surprised her. She grabbed her purse and stood there topless, looking down at her clothes on the landing.

"See, you do know some French." He zipped up her pants and opened his front door. "*Apres vous.*"

"Would you kindly fetch my clothes?" asked Tessa, walking inside. Dylan's hand playfully smacked her butt.

He shook his head and motioned to a swivel stool in his kitchen. "I don't fetch. I like you half-dressed. And that drab T-shirt, sports bra, and 'I'm a tourist in Paris' scarf ... you can do better than that."

She sat down and turned the stool to look around the apartment. "The scarf came from Montemarte. It's what I can afford on a bartender's salary." Tessa heard herself getting defensive. *I don't owe this guy an explanation. I just want him to finish what he started. I'm so freakin' horny.*

She heard Dylan mixing drinks behind her. His apartment was Parisian chic. It had windows lined with blue satin curtains that stretched from floor to ceiling and opened to a balcony overlooking a romantic, winding street. There were several built-in shelves packed with books, a fireplace and a chaise lounge. The artwork was mostly vintage posters of rock bands from around the world, some of which Tessa recognized.

"Radiohead, cool poster. Have you seen them live?" asked Tessa.

"Yes, front row." Dylan handed Tessa a whiskey sour and raised his glass. "Cheers."

She clinked his glass and took a sip of her drink, pulling out the cherry with her lips. She grinned, attempting to tie the knot. After a few weird facial expressions, she pulled out her stem, still straight. "Nope, don't have the talent. Let's see what you've got. You made big promises back at the cafe."

Dylan dangled the cherry in front of Tessa. "What's my prize if I do it?"

Tessa laughed. "You can throw my jeans and panties down the steps too. I'll be completely captive, naked in your apartment. I'm sure you can think of something."

"Hmm, but I'm already going to do that." He picked her up off the barstool and carried her over his shoulder, dropping her onto her back on the chaise lounge.

Before she could think, he had pulled off her jeans and panties. The cool evening breeze from an open window crossed over her naked body. Sheer curtains peaked from behind the blue satin drapes, fluttering lightly in the wind. The distant fading sunlight formed shadows around the apartment. Tessa watched the light dance as the sun began to set, painting the sky in purple and orange hues.

Dylan pulled off his Ramones T-shirt and straddled Tessa.

His chest and abs were tight. She noted a black ink tattoo of a sparrow on his right bicep and wondered if there would be more elsewhere.

He leaned down and kissed her passionately, pushing the cherry into her mouth with his tongue. He swirled his tongue around inside her, rotating between strong, aggressive kisses and light butterfly kisses on her lips. Tessa tasted the sweet, tart cherry and swallowed it between kisses. As Dylan pulled back, he put his fingers into his mouth to wet them. He took out the stem of the cherry, knot tied, and placed it between Tessa's breasts. It rose and fell with her heavy breaths.

He slipped his fingers into her vagina and grabbed the cherry stem, using it to tickle her clit as he navigated around her G-spot.

Tessa moaned in pleasure. "Right there. Don't stop." *He's a fucking vagina whisperer.*

Dylan continued stimulating Tessa's clit and G-spot simultaneously. He bent down and kissed her neck, biting it gently. He felt Tessa begin pulsing and bit harder.

"Holy shit, oh fuck."

"Ce soir, tu m'appartiens."

Tessa came as the sun dipped below the horizon. Her entire body was shaking. "Wow." *Just wow.* She couldn't think straight.

She took a minute to let her body stop shaking and then rose, stepping outside onto the balcony naked. She watched the twilight unfold on the quiet street five floors below her.

Dylan approached from behind. He wrapped his arms around her body, warming her from the breeze. Tessa could tell he was naked now too. They stood in silence, skin on skin, as darkness fell over the city.

A full body orgasm from a hand job. Freaking incredible. Desange did me a favor by over-reacting to our kiss.

Dylan placed the cherry stem in her palm. "Well, Doubting Thomas, would you like to touch the stem again, to make sure I really did it?"

Tessa laughed. "I believe. That was quite impressive, you tied it in my mouth, while French kissing. How long did it take you to acquire that skill?"

"A few decades."

Tessa laughed. "You're not that old, either that or you have amazing genes."

Dylan grinned lasciviously. "So, what is my prize?"

"Well, I don't have any clothes left to give you." Tessa turned to face him. "What is it you want, Dylan?"

He whispered into her ear, "I want to fuck you right here on this balcony, for all of Paris to see."

Before Tessa could reply, she felt Dylan enter her from behind, filling her with his thickness. The force was intense. She gripped the wrought iron railing, her fingers curling tightly around the intricate spirals as he thrusted deep inside her.

"Ahhh," she moaned. "Fuck, ahhh."

"I'm going to make you scream." Dylan lifted Tessa up from behind and spun her around, reentering her.

She gripped her legs around him tightly. "Shit, ahhh. Harder."

"Don't let go." Dylan stepped onto a low ottoman to lift her even higher so her torso was now over the railing.

She had a moment of panic as she felt her bare bottom graze against the top ledge of the balcony. Her wavy brown hair blew in the night breeze.

"We're pretty high up..."

He thrusted fast and deep, holding her tightly against his chest. "I want them to hear you back at the cafe. My little American slut."

"Fuck, ahhh, ahhh," Tessa screamed as he pounded harder inside her body, swirling and swaying. She looked up at the night sky, watching the moon disappear behind the clouds. Her arms hugged him tightly. If she let go, she could fall backward over the railing.

Dylan guided his hand around her neck and pulled her head toward him to meet his gaze.

She stared into his deep green eyes. Then her body began shaking in ecstasy. The grip of her arms and legs loosened as she orgasmed, losing control of her muscles. She felt herself fall backward and screamed, but Dylan held her firmly in his arms. He pulled her down off the railing and carried her inside the apartment, placing her down next to the bar.

"I assume you might want to finish your drink now." He smiled.

"Fuck, wow. Yes, and water, please." Tessa wiped sweat off her brow.

He handed her a glass of cold water. Dylan proceeded to his bedroom and then returned, wearing a robe. He gave a second robe to Tessa.

"Thanks. You didn't come that time." Tessa knotted the robe around her waist and then sat on the barstool.

Dylan smiled. "I'm saving it for later. Does that bother you?"

Tessa laughed. "No, I'm a satisfied lady. I have an IUD, by the way, in case you were wondering."

"I know, I could feel it."

Tessa laughed, choking on her whiskey sour. "Bullshit."

"No really, I felt the string."

Tessa shook her head. "Okay sure. Your dick's so big it can feel my IUD." *Maybe he could feel it. He was really deep inside me. And he's big, maybe eight inches? That was seriously intense. My pussy is throbbing.*

"I want you to answer three questions, honestly." Dylan stood across from her, the counter between them.

"Okay. I'll probably never see you after tonight, so fuck it." Tessa took another sip of water. "What do you wanna know?"

"On a scale of one to ten, with ten being the best orgasm you've ever had, how good was your orgasm?"

Tessa laughed. "Nine. Do you really need the ego stroke? You know you're good at this."

"Hmm, your body was saying something different."

"Fine ... nine point five." *I can't give him a ten, that would go to his head.*

Dylan grinned. "Okay, I'll take it. Second question, what's your favorite band?"

Tessa looked around his apartment, eyeing tastefully framed band posters from different decades. She noticed a large bookcase stacked with hundreds of CDs. *Music must be his hobby.*

"I don't know, I can't really say I have one favorite band. I have a favorite decade – definitely the nineties."

"What's a song you played over and over again? First one that comes to mind."

"Hmm, as a teen, I really liked that song 'One Headlight.' Who did that?"

"Ah, the Wallflowers." Dylan went over to his bookcase and within seconds, found the right CD. He handed it to Tessa. *"Bringing Down the Horse*. 1996. You know the lead singer is Bob Dylan's son, one of the greatest musicians of all time."

"You think? I mean, Bob Dylan has amazing lyrics but his vocals are kinda meh. It's impressive you found that random CD so quickly. You must have close to a thousand CDs."

"Pretty close. Music is a passion of mine." Dylan laughed and popped the CD into his stereo system. "Let's check out your song and see why it spoke to you."

Tessa took a sip of her whiskey sour as she listened to the familiar tune. It had been a long time since she had heard it. *Why did I choose that song out of the cobwebs of my brain? No idea, my mind is mush tonight.*

"It's dark, lyrically," said Dylan. "*Well they said she died easy of a broken heart disease, as I listened through the cemetery trees.*"

"Yeah, well I was an angsty nineties teen. And it's not all dark. She's driving, even if her car has a broken headlight, she's still got one light going for her."

"*She hit the end, it's just her window ledge.* What was your window ledge? Your way out of Detroit and your broken home."

Tessa paused. "My broken home?"

"Come on, Tessa." Dylan sang along with the lyrics. "*Well it smells of cheap wine and cigarettes, This place is always such a mess, Sometimes I think I'd like to watch it burn.*"

Tessa laughed awkwardly, biting her cheek. "I really don't want to ruin a great night talking about my childhood."

"Fair enough, I don't mean to pry. It's just such an interesting song choice."

Tessa took a big drink of her whiskey sour, finishing the glass. *I need to shift the focus.* "What's your favorite band or song?"

"I'm the one asking questions. I want to understand you tonight. I get to remain the sexy man of mystery you met at a cafe."

Fine, anything to get him off my broken childhood. "Okay, ask your final question. Make it good."

"What do you really do? You aren't a bartender working in Detroit."

"Yes, I can make you a drink to—"

Dylan came around the counter and lifted Tessa up toward him, kissing her passionately. When their lips parted, he locked eyes with her.

She found it hard to look away. His eyes were so intense, deep emeralds peering inside of her, desiring to know her more intimately.

"I read body language well. Your eyes shifted when you said that at the cafe."

"Umm ... okay." *Wow, I'm impressed he read through my bullshit so quickly. Most guys who want to fuck me wouldn't care or take the time to really see me. Let's see if I can get him to believe this version of reality instead.* "I used to be in the Army. After I got out, I bartended in Detroit at this shithole dive bar. I was drinking too much and just in a dark place. So I'm working on finding myself again by traveling around and figuring myself out, which brought me to Paris." *It's the core truth, minus the demon hunting bit.*

Dylan paused, taking a slow sip of his drink.

Tessa bit her cheek. *Shit, he probably noticed that if he reads body language. Did he buy it? I can't tell, he's such a tease. He is more perceptive than your average one-night stand guy.*

"What was the name of the dive bar?" asked Dylan.

"The Blue Ox. It smells like beer and fries all the time. And they have a miniature replica of Joe Louis' fist they proudly display. Super tacky."

"I enjoy a good dive bar. I'll check it out if I ever pass through Detroit."

"It's really not worth it, but suit yourself. You won't find me there."

Dylan locked eyes with her again. "You're done with that life." He pulled her in closer, stroking her hair.

He said those last words with a strength of conviction that comforted Tessa. *He sees me. I am done with that life.* She leaned into him, finding comfort in his words and body.

Dylan kissed her softly and loosened her robe, running his hands over her breasts. He picked her up, cradling her in his arms and carried her into the bedroom. Then he pressed her down against the satin duvet and slid off her robe.

He entered deep inside her as he stared into her eyes. He moved gently but firmly, knowing exactly how to touch her and navigate inside of her. As the Wallflowers album played on in the background, their bodies moved in a harmonic rhythm. She felt open to him, surrendering completely to his touch. Her nerves felt more sensitive, tingling as he ran his fingers along her arms. He didn't have to say anything, he just moved with her energy until she came, pulsing even harder than before. Her entire body shook as he came inside her, full and warm. He stayed inside her until he felt her stop pulsing, then gently pulled out.

"Elle a touche la fin, en fait c'est juste son rebord de fenêtre." He kissed her goodnight and lay on his side, cuddling Tessa and stroking her hair.

She didn't know what it meant, and she decided whatever it was, it was best left untranslated. She fell asleep in his arms, wet and naked, listening to the sounds of the city.

Tessa awoke the next day, finding herself in an empty bed. She heard music coming from the kitchen. *Radiohead.*

She put on her robe and walked over to the bar. On a plate were an assortment of fresh pastries.

"Coffee?" asked Dylan. He was over by the stove, cooking.

"Yes, please. What are you making?"

"Crepes. I figured I'd send you off into the world with a proper French breakfast."

"Wow, thanks. Last night was … awesome. And before you ask, I'm giving you a 10."

Dylan laughed. "Damn, I didn't need to do the crepes after all to pad my performance review." He handed Tessa a mug. "I recall from your order yesterday, you like it black."

"Yep, that's the only way to drink coffee, in my opinion."

"We agree on this point."

Tessa saw her shirt and bra lying on the chaise. "Oh, so you do fetch sometimes." She walked over and put them on.

"In my own time and certainly not on command when my goal is to get your clothes off."

She went to the bedroom to get her jeans, panties and purse. After dressing, she checked the time on her phone. 9:27am. *I slept late. Good sex has that effect. I feel so refreshed. This is exactly what I needed.* She checked her texts. Five missed text messages from Desange, two missed calls, and a voicemail. *Ugh. Crap. I should have checked in.* The last message read, *Are you mad at me? Just let me know you are okay please.*

"Hey, Dylan. I'm sorry, but I need to head out. My friend is worried because I didn't come home last night. Gonna have to pass on the crepe." Tessa grabbed a pastry. "Can I take this to go?"

Dylan looked a little disappointed. "It will be ready soon. Just call your friend and let her know you're on your way. I can drop you off if you'd like."

That would be super awkward. "Um, no, my friend seems pissed. I think it's better if I just head out."

"Okay, well I hope you find what you are looking for on your travels. I'll remember last night years from now. It was … magical."

"It was amazing, like we knew each other in a past life or something." *He's not exaggerating. This was some of the best sex I've ever had. Three full body orgasms in one night. I don't even believe in past lives.*

Dylan gave Tessa a hug and kissed her passionately. "Take care of yourself out there."

"I will. Goodbye." Tessa walked out of the apartment and down the winding stairs.

Outside, she beamed with joy as she walked toward a crowded street of people gathering at a farmers' market. *Regardless of the crap Desange gives me, it was a great night. Those memories will keep me warm on cold, blustery days in the Faroes.*

As she entered the outdoor market, she put on her glasses, scanning the crowd. Everything grew blurry, but she could still smell the fresh flowers and produce.

"Tessa, wait!" She turned, hearing Dylan's voice. "You forgot your scarf."

She stood frozen, as Dylan approached, holding up her scarf. She could see his features clearly – his dark wavy hair, faded Ramones T-shirt, olive skin, and now, his green eyes.

Shit. Holy shit. She was paralyzed in fear, a statue as the crowd parted around her.

Dylan tied the scarf around her neck. "It's a nice excuse to kiss you one more time."

He could snap my neck in an instant. Does he know I'm a hunter? Was he fucking with me last night when asking questions? If he knew, he would have killed me. He doesn't know. Breathe. He reads auras. That's how he could tell I was lying. Fuck.

"Are you okay?" He kissed her, touching her glasses as he ran his hands through her hair.

Suddenly, she felt the scarf choking her, tightening around her neck. Dylan yanked it forcibly back. He removed his lips, as she gasped for air.

"Hunter." He stared into her eyes and yanked the scarf again, tearing it into pieces. He ran past her and disappeared into the crowd, faster than Tessa could think.

Tessa turned and sprinted in the other direction. She had no idea where she was running to, but she ran until she found herself hopelessly lost in the city of Paris. She knelt down in a side alley and took several deep breaths, trying to calm down her panic attack. Her whole body was shaking, now from fear. As she shook, she remembered how her body felt last night. *I slept with a demon. Demons exist. And now I'm a target.*

Chapter 15

Desange looked at his phone for the tenth time since waking up. Still no message from Tessa. He placed the phone back on the glass topped table and took a drink from the steaming mug of coffee he was trying to enjoy. "Trying" because he was concerned about Tessa.

She's an adult. She can take care of herself.

That sounded good as he thought it. But, he couldn't get rid of the feeling that something was wrong.

Even if she is okay, she should have checked in just to let me know.

The part of him that was concerned, however, was countered by a sense of relief that he had some time to himself. Although he enjoyed Tessa's company, he was worried they were getting too close. He was attracted to her and didn't want to get involved with another recruit. He knew that it couldn't go anywhere – once they were out of the Academy and in the field, there was little chance they'd see each other. And he respected her too much to just engage in casual sex. Also, after a day of being ruthlessly interrogated by his sister about Tessa and their "relationship" he didn't want to have to go through that for real.

In a few months, you'll be out of the Academy. Tessa won't be an issue any longer. He looked at the phone again. *Although I wish she would call.*

He didn't hear the front door open or Tessa come in. She felt frantic. The entire trip back to the apartment had taken longer than it should have. She didn't know if she was being followed and went by the most roundabout way she could think of. Now that she was in a safe spot, the pent-up anxiety was about to burst out.

"Desange?" she said as she entered the living room. She saw the curtains covering the open balcony door billowing and went straight there.

Desange felt relief when she walked onto the balcony and sat heavily across the table from him.

"I need a drink," she said.

He tapped his mug. "There's coffee in the kitchen."

"No ... a drink."

He frowned. It was still fairly early; but, he decided not to say anything. She was clearly agitated. "Of course." He went into the apartment, poured a tumbler of scotch and sat it in front of her.

Tessa drank half the contents in one gulp. "Fuck. Better."

"What's wrong?"

Tessa hesitated. She didn't want to blurt out "I just had sex with a demon and he knows I'm a hunter. We both might be fucked." She bit her cheek. "I had an ... encounter with a demon."

Desange stiffened. "What? Where?"

"I'm not sure. Somewhere in Montmartre."

"Did you see it in a crowd?"

I have to tell him. He needs to know everything so we can decide what to do next.

"Not exactly." She finished the scotch. "Can I have a little more?"

Desange was sympathetic. *This is the first time she has seen a demon. No wonder she's shaken up.*

When he returned with her refilled glass, she took a sip and a deep breath.

"Yesterday, I was in a cafe. I met a guy. I didn't know he was a demon at the time. We hit it off and ... well ... I slept with him."

Desange felt a flash of anger, a mix of jealousy and disappointment. *She's gone for a few hours and has sex with the first man she meets. What the hell is wrong with her?* But his sense of self-preservation and his training overrode the impulse to respond in a way that reflected his thoughts. "When did you find out he was a demon?"

Tessa was relieved that Desange was focusing on the problem and not getting judgmental. "This morning. When I was leaving his apartment. I was checking out the area with my glasses and saw him for what he is."

"You didn't check him out before you ... went with him...?"

Tessa noticed the catch in Desange's voice. *Maybe he is mad. If he is, this isn't the time to talk about it.* "No. I had been using my glasses, but when I met him ... I don't know." she shrugged. "He seemed nice. I didn't really think about it."

Desange shook his head. "Tessa, whenever you are in an..." She heard the catch again "...intimate situation, you need to be certain about who you are with."

"I know, I know. I was just having a good day and I wanted to feel normal."

By fucking the first man who looks your way, Desange thought.

"Did he know you were a hunter?"

Tessa shook her head. "No. I mean, not until this morning. When I had my glasses on, he touched them."

Desange nodded. "Of course. They can sense the items made from their hearts." Desange leaned forward. "Why didn't he kill you? If he knew you were a hunter, he should have torn you apart."

Tessa shuddered. When Desange said that, the fear she had felt in that moment flooded back, a wave of prickly cold. "There were other people around. I think he didn't want to get caught. He just said 'Hunter' and left."

"When you were with him, did you say anything that could betray the Curia?"

Tessa snorted. "What the hell would I say? 'Hey, I don't know you, but I'm training to hunt demons. Oh, you are one? Glad we had sex before I found out.'" She took a drink. "I made a mistake. I should have used the glasses on him first. But I'm not an idiot."

"Did you mention me or my family?"

"No. I just said I was visiting Paris with friends. I also took precautions coming back here to make certain I wasn't followed." She hoped that would reassure him a little. "Should we alert the Curia? There must be hunters here. Won't they want to look for him? I can give a good description."

"I'm sure you can. This sounds like a chance encounter. Otherwise, you'd be dead." He stood up. "But we are going to need to leave. The Curia will want us back at the Academy for debriefing. When they ask you what happened, be completely honest." He started to walk inside, but stopped. "Except for one thing. Please, don't tell them about what happened between us."

"I didn't realize it was against regulations for adults to kiss."

"It's not ... but I don't want the Curia or Ruth thinking our relationship is more problematic than it is."

"And telling her about having sex with a demon won't be a problem?"

"It may be. I don't know what Ruth will do." He continued into the apartment. "Come on, let's pack. I need to contact my mother and tell her we have to leave."

"I don't like running."

"We're not running; we're being prudent. And right now, prudence is getting as far away from my family as possible. If you're right, the demon doesn't know about them and I want to keep it that way."

He's right. I don't want to be here anyway. That ... thing ... knows me.

While Tessa packed, Desange contacted his mother and told her they were being called away on urgent business. He promised to explain later. He went to his room and started stuffing his clothes into his bag.

Damn, he thought, *I never really thought about how dangerous this could be to my family. What if I'm in the field and get identified? What would they do to my parents ... my siblings? It's not her fault they might be in danger; it's mine, for picking this life.*

"Stop second guessing yourself," he said out loud. "You're careful and the Curia will watch out for your family. They've been protecting the families of hunters for hundreds of years."

Saying it made him feel better, making the sentiment more real than thinking about it. He used his secure phone to contact the Curia support division, requesting tickets on the next plane to the Faroes. He also sent an alert to the Academy that he and Tessa were coming back and needed an immediate debriefing after a demon encounter. Doing these things made him feel better. Once in the process of handling the crisis he found himself in, his concerns faded. But he couldn't completely quiet them. Even when he saw a demon on his first-year field exercise, there was a distance he felt. He was an observer, watching a thing that was not completely real. This was different. Tessa showed him how easy it was for a moment of weakness to make a hunter vulnerable to the creatures that they hunted.

Tessa knocked on his door. "Come in."

She opened the door. She was holding her duffle bag and looked anxious. "I'm ready to go."

"Good. I contacted the Curia. Tickets will be waiting for us at the airport. I also contacted the Academy. Ruth will be there to debrief us. While we're traveling, work on your report. Every detail will be helpful."

"Should we contact the local cell? They may be able to find the demon."

Desange shook his head. "I doubt it is going to go back to its apartment. It must realize that even if you weren't able to kill it, other hunters will be alerted. But if the Curia wants to mobilize the Paris cell, they will. Our only concern is to get back to the Academy."

Tessa bristled at the comment about her not being able to kill it. She was unarmed; even if she wanted to, she was powerless to hurt a demon. She let it slide, however; she knew Desange was trying to adapt to a situation he had not expected.

"Desange, I'm sorry I wasn't more careful. I wasn't trying to make things difficult."

"I understand," Desange said, shouldering his bag, "but Ruth is the person you need to convince." He smiled, hoping to be reassuring, "Ruth has been dealing with us flawed humans for two thousand years. I'm sure you are not the first recruit to end up in this situation."

Tessa felt a little better, although a part of her wondered what the angel might do.

The Curia makes it clear that we are not the focus – winning the war is. If Ruth thinks I'm a security risk, would she hesitate to put me six feet under?

She didn't know the answer – but she knew she'd find out soon.

Chapter 16

Tessa sat by herself at a table in O'Toole's, an Irish pub at Copenhagen Airport. The dark wood and brass interior reminded her of the bar she worked at in Detroit, although this place was considerably cleaner.

Every time I went into the Blue Ox, I worried about getting hepatitis. She took a bite from the bacon burger she'd ordered. *This place is great.*

Desange had demurred. He was tired; Tessa left him slumped and snoring in a seat at their gate. *That's fine. He's been shit company since we left anyway.* Other than informing her that the hunter cell in Paris was alerted and waiting for her description, he hadn't said anything that was more than perfunctory. *He's probably worried that my mistake will look bad on his record.*

"Or that I might have gotten his family killed. Fuck." She took a drink of her beer and spent a few moments watching the flow of travelers.

They have no idea what is going on. She thought about putting on her glasses. *Forget it. I don't want to know.*

Two women in US Army fatigues walked by. Her eyes followed them as they disappeared into the flow. *That should be me. Heading to the next post. Maybe on leave. My life mapped out. I liked being in the Army. And I screwed it up.*

She thought about her time in Iraq. There, digging through endless mountains of photos, videos, reports from units in the field or the intel agencies that worked their shadowy magic. Everyone she saw or read about seemed the same. Men and women she would pass on the street, never knowing they were part of a terrorist organization, dreaming up new ways to kill people like her.

How do I live, not knowing who to trust? Jesus, I sleep with one guy and he's the enemy. Is that what being a hunter is? A paranoid, lonely killer. Burning out, getting maimed or getting killed.

She finished her beer. She swirled the sudsy dregs around the bottom of the glass.

I could just disappear. I have my passport. I'm at an airport. I'm in Europe. I could head out and never look back. She laughed, mirthlessly. *And then Ruth would hunt me down. I know too much.*

She sighed. *I'm committed to this path. I need someone to talk to. I need to get out of my own head.* She pulled out her phone. *But who?* Her current contacts list was superficial friends or hookups that she hadn't talked to since Detroit. There was Zach, her brother. *But he's so damaged, probably high on drugs right now. He can't help. Family ... sucks. None of them would have any idea of what I'm going through, even if I told them a sanitized version.*

She tapped the black glass screen. One name came through the noise. *Tyler. I could call Tyler. He'd understand.*

She pressed his name "Tyler Caplan" and dialed. *Captain Caplan. Not anymore.* She checked the time. *Thirteen hundred here ... that's oh-seven hundred in New York. At least it's not the middle of the night.*

"Hello?" The voice on the phone was the one she remembered from Iraq; deep and firm. One that sounded good giving orders and offering advice.

"Hi, Tyler."

There was a pause. She wondered if he was going to hang up. *It's been months since I contacted him. What if he doesn't want to...*

"Hey, Tessa. I was just making coffee."

"Still super-strong with too much sugar?"

Tyler laughed. She really liked his laugh, a soft chuckle. "Still. I need it to face the office. So, what can I do for you?"

"I just needed someone to talk to. If you don't have the time—"

"Oh, I have time. I am the boss, after all."

Tessa knew he was running his family's foundation. After the two had parted company at Fort Hood, she would Google him. Once in a while, his name showed up in the New York press, always connected to the Caplan Foundation and a project it was funding.

"Right. How's life as the head of a non-profit? Saved the world yet?"

Tyler laughed again. "Not quite – but we are doing some good work. In fact, I'm meeting today with a research oncologist who needs funding for bleeding edge gene therapy."

"That's great. It sounds like you've found a good niche."

There was another pause. "I'm doing okay. I still have some fallout from Iraq I'm dealing with. But I haven't had a panic attack in, oh, at least 36 hours. So … progress." More silence.

Damn, it sounds like his PTSD is still bad. I should ask about it … but this is about me. Next time.

"One day at a time – that's my motto," said Tessa.

"As mottos go, that one works. So, you wanted to run something past me?"

She wanted to tell him everything. She also knew he would think she had lost her mind. *Keep it vague. Make it sound more mundane.*

"I'm not in Detroit any more. In fact, I'm sitting in an airport in Denmark."

"Huh. Decided to take a European vacation?"

"No. I got a job. But, I'm not sure if I should keep it."

"What kind of job?"

"Security work."

"Putting the skills Uncle Sam paid for to use? That's great. You are a really good analyst. I always thought you were one of the best members of my team."

Tessa couldn't help herself. "I'm sure there were other parts of my skill set you liked more."

He chuckled. "Yeah ... but I don't think the Army taught you those."

Tessa joined him in laughing. It felt good. Normal. She missed his laugh.

"Anyway, what's wrong with the job? Pay? Or are they going to send you to some place with bad memories?"

"I'm concerned about the agenda of the group. But, more immediately, I fucked up OPSEC recently and I'm worried about the repercussions."

"Was anyone hurt? And were you negligent?"

"No one was hurt. And I wasn't really negligent. Just ... a little careless."

"Other than this, have you been performing?"

"Yeah, I think so. The feedback I'm getting is good."

"Okay. Is your boss a leader or a manager?"

Tessa had to think about that for a minute. *Leaders take charge and understand how to use – and modify – the system they are in to get the best out of people. Managers know how to function within the system. They may be really good at their job; but they have a vested interest in process over people. But Ruth is the system. She founded the Enochian Curia and has been running it for 2000 years. I guess that makes her a leader.*

"A leader."

"Well, then I wouldn't worry too much. I know you. You're an asset anywhere you go, anything you do. Just stick to the facts, explain what you did wrong and how you'll take steps to not do it again. And be confident, not defensive. Your boss will want people who own their mistakes, not whine about them."

He's probably right. I am an asset. Heck, since I'm one of the few people who can kill demons, I'm critical to the war.

"So ... does that help?"

"It really does. Thanks."

"No worries. You know, I have been thinking about you."

Tessa perked up. "Oh? Something good, I hope."

"Mixed. I've been seeing a therapist for my PTSD. The sessions bring up a lot of memories, good and bad. I've thought about the intensity of Iraq. I miss that."

Tessa laughed. "You miss mortar rounds and camel spiders in your tent? You are weird." But she knew exactly what he meant. What they had was intense. The type of desperate romance that could only metastasize in a warzone.

"Ha ha … it's just that everything seems to be in slow motion now. Washed out. I don't miss all of it, of course. I've gotten to the point where I can go to a Starbucks and not worry about a jihadist showing up with a bomb vest. But there was more than just fear."

"I get it. When I was in Detroit, the days all merged into one long slog." She never thought of herself as an action junkie; but life outside the military was both boring and disorganized.

That's why you need the Curia. To give you structure and a cause worth fighting for. That's why you can't run away. And that's why you need to convince Ruth that you can handle yourself. That this was a lapse, not a pattern.

"It made what we had more intense too," Tyler said.

Up until her night with Dylan, sex with Tyler had been the most satisfying and exciting she had ever had. The place, the circumstances, the secret nature of it – everything combined to make her crave it even now.

"You're right. But that's the past."

"That's what we agreed on." Tyler's voice sounded perfunctory. He knew that was what she wanted to hear. "You know, the offer I made in Killeen still stands."

She remembered the last time they were together. They were being processed out of the military in Fort Hood. They met at the 1st Armored Division Museum. The day was cold. Tyler was there first, leaning against an olive drab Pershing tank. The discussion was short. There wasn't much to say.

They had agreed that their relationship was over, although that seemed more of a formality to Tessa. They hadn't seen each other in months, having been sent to different commands while their case was examined and punishment meted out. Before she walked off, Tyler told her that she could come to New York with him. That he would help get her started in a new life. Tessa said no. She sometimes wondered if that was a mistake.

"I'm going to be okay. I might come for a visit, though. Once I get through my thing here."

"That would be great. I'd love to show you New York."

Tessa noticed that Desange was approaching the pub. "Hey, I need to go and you probably should head out and save the world from cancer."

"Okay," Tyler said. "It was nice hearing your voice. Don't wait so long to call again."

Tessa smiled. That was an ego boost she needed. "I won't. It was great talking to you."

There was a moment of silence. Desange was in the bar, approaching the table. Tessa didn't want to hang up. "I do need to go. Bye."

"Talk to you later."

Tessa hung up just as Desange sat down.

"Who was that?"

"A friend."

Desange frowned. He thought about pressing her, but decided to let it go for now. *She deserves some privacy. And the Curia is listening anyway. If she says anything compromising security, they can deal with her.*

"Okay," he motioned over a waiter and ordered a coffee. "I was called by Ruth. She'll be at the Academy when we arrive."

"What did you tell her?"

He shrugged. "Not much. Just that you encountered a demon and that I decided to pull us back to the Academy. They'll be a formal debriefing and she should hear what happened straight from you, not filtered through me."

"Thanks."

"Of course. I don't want this to be a black mark on your record."

Or yours. "I've finished my report. Do you want to read over it?" asked Tessa.

Desange shook his head. "You were there, I wasn't. I assume this is similar to the kind of reports you wrote in the Army."

Sure, I wrote about getting fucked by demons all the time. "I think the Curia will find it's complete."

For a few moments they sat in silence, Tessa taking a bite from her burger and Desange drinking his coffee.

I should reduce the tension, Desange thought. *Tessa is going to have a tough time with Ruth; she shouldn't have one with me.* "So," he said, leaning forward, "what was it like?"

"What was what like?"

"You know ... sex with a demon."

Tessa looked up from her burger and saw Desange grinning. While still concerned about Ruth and the Curia, she felt some relief. She returned his smile.

"How much time do we have?"

"About four hours."

"That should be just about enough."

Chapter 17

The lurching of the Land Rover over the spine of Mykines was something that Tessa had not missed. Desange was sitting in the front with Uri. The taciturn instructor had said little on the flight from the airport to the island. Tessa wondered how much Ruth told him.

It doesn't matter. I don't have to explain myself to him. Just her.

"You know," Uri said as he swerved to avoid a flock of stubborn puffins, "I had to cut short a yomp with some friends from the Regiment to chauffeur you sorry fucks around."

"What the hell is a yomp?" Tessa asked.

"Overland march with a full pack."

"On vacation you go on a ruck march? And you're mad that you got called away from that?"

"Yeah, my life choices are the ones that need examining," said Uri.

Desange laughed. "Sorry."

Tessa punched his shoulder lightly. "Hey, he's pissed at you too."

"That's right. You two are on my list of practice dummies in combatives." The Land Rover thudded over a rock. "So, why are you back anyway? Get too drunk in Paris and need to get pulled out before the gendarmes toss you in *La Santé*."

"Tessa had an … engagement … with a demon."

Uri craned his head around to look at her. "No shit? And you're still alive?"

"Apparently."

"I see why Ruth wants to talk to you."

Uri pulled up to the chapel. "Head in. I want to park this in the shed. Storm's coming tonight."

Desange and Tessa shouldered their bags and headed into the chapel. As they approached the altar, Desange said, "Wait a minute," and sank to his knees. He said a silent prayer and stood up.

"What was that for?"

"I thought we might need some divine intervention."

Tessa snorted. "That's reassuring."

Desange shrugged. "Nothing wrong with making an appeal to the CEO."

When the elevator doors opened on the dorm level, Ruth was waiting, dressed in a crisp white suit, arms behind her back.

"Please," Tessa said, "tell me you've been standing here for an hour for the intimidation effect."

Ruth cocked her head to one side. "We have cameras everywhere. Desange, you're up first. Tessa, please wait in your room."

"Right, mom," Tessa muttered as she brushed past Ruth.

Tessa tossed her bag on the couch and stripped as she walked to the shower. It felt good to have hot water running down her body, wiping away some of the fatigue from a day spent in transit.

When Desange returned from his debriefing, Tessa was sitting on the couch. CNN was on, but she wasn't paying attention. Instead, she was thinking about what to say to Ruth. *I need to be clear that there was no reason to suspect that I was with a demon and that I didn't say anything that could be used against the Curia. All he knows is that I'm a hunter.*

"Anything interesting?" Desange said.

Tessa was shaken from her introspection. She glanced at the TV and then at Desange. "World's slowly committing suicide. So, nothing unusual. How did it go?"

Desange sat down next to her. "Okay. She asked about why you were off on your own and your demeanor when you got back."

"What did you tell her?"

"That you wanted to see Paris and give me some time with my family. As for your demeanor, I said you seemed concerned, but still mission-focused."

"And about us?"

"She didn't ask and I didn't volunteer anything."

"A lie of omission?"

He shrugged. "No one is perfect."

She stood up. "I guess I'm up. Wish me luck."

"You'll be fine. Ruth isn't our enemy. She just wants what's best for the Curia."

That's what I'm afraid of. "I know. So do I."

Tessa went to Ruth's office and knocked.

"Enter."

Tessa had not been in the office before. It was austere, like Ruth. A single painting hung on the wall behind her head. It looked like a Van Gogh, a passionate swirl of reds, yellows and blues – a field of flowers with a blonde woman in white in the center. The desk, chairs and bookcase were institutional, metal and plastic in bland, functional shapes.

Ruth was looking over Tessa's report. "Please, sit down."

Tessa settled into an uncomfortable plastic chair and waited. Ruth had already read the report twice, but made a show of skimming it again. She wanted to give Tessa a few moments to become less comfortable and likely to color her report in an attempt to make herself look better. When she looked up, however, she was surprised to see Tessa looking at her with an even, confident gaze.

"Tessa, I'm very concerned. On your first trip away from the Academy, you put yourself into a dangerous and compromising position. You violated field protocol and common sense. And, you demonstrated the same impulsive behavior that resulted in your being separated from the US Army. Am I wrong about any of these assessments?"

"No," Tessa said, "but it is not that simple."

Ruth drummed her fingers. Her nails clicked gratingly on the metal desktop. "What makes it more complex?"

"Ruth, I had no reason to think I would randomly encounter a demon and that he would approach me. Clearly, he didn't know I worked for the Curia. Otherwise, as Desange made it clear, I wouldn't be alive. If this was an attempt to gather intel or to capture me, it failed. But, it wasn't," she said, making certain to keep her voice calm and firm, "that should be clear from my report."

Ruth flipped open the report. "You talked about music and the bar you worked in. Correct?"

Tessa nodded.

"What did you learn about him? Anything not in the report?"

Tessa shrugged. "He seemed to know a lot about older bands. I thought it was just small talk. Someone who was as interested in music as I am. But since he's a demon, he may have been speaking from experience. I included what I could remember, but that could be a way to determine who he is. Know any demons in the music industry?"

Ruth sighed. "Too many." She scribbled a note in the report. "I'll make it clear to Analysis to keep your suspicion in mind."

"He didn't —" Tessa started, but then grew silent.

"He didn't what?"

Tessa shifted in her seat. Ruth could see her aura change, reflecting a growing unease, one that had not been there when she sat down.

"I guess, I expected demons to seem more ... evil. Or inhuman. Something. He seemed like a man. Like any man." *Except for being phenomenal in bed ... but I'll keep that to myself.*

Ruth nodded. "Of course he did. If demons showed up looking like monsters, dripping bile from their mouths, they wouldn't do a good job of tempting humans."

Tessa grinned. "I guess not."

"And that is why you have to be more careful when getting close to anyone." Ruth leaned back in her chair. "The Curia doesn't discourage personal relationships to be cruel. We do it because of what you experienced; demons are just like you. In some ways, they are better than humans."

Tessa nodded. "He was very strong."

Ruth waved her hand dismissively. "I don't mean physically. By reading your aura, this demon was able to tailor every word and action to appeal to you. To get you to do what it wanted. Even the most perceptive, manipulative human is like someone who is deaf, mute and blind compared to a demon."

"Or an angel," Tessa added.

Ruth's expression didn't change. "Yes, of course."

Tessa thought she detected some irritation in her voice. *She hasn't made it any secret that she can read our auras. That's how she finds hunters. Is she mad that I compared her to a demon?*

Ruth continued. "This is why you have to treat every person you will be close to in any way as a potential demon. And if you are going to be intimate with someone, you have to be even more careful. You in particular."

"What does that mean?"

"Please, Tessa, don't be obtuse. You have a problem with sex."

Tessa felt her stomach knot. "Just because I like sex doesn't make me a risk to the Curia."

Ruth didn't react to Tessa's angry tone. "Your inability to control your impulses led to the end of your military career. And based on our surveillance in Detroit, your relationships were a central part of your self-destructive behavior." She steepled the fingers of her hands, her eyes boring into Tessa's. "That flaw could be fatal. A demon like the one you slept with could use its abilities to manipulate you into any agenda it wished." Her gaze grew more intense, so much so that Tessa looked down at her lap. "I've seen it happen before. I do not want that to happen to you."

The silence that followed was only a few seconds, but it seemed longer to Tessa. *She's right. I wasn't thinking – when it comes to sex, I can get carried away. But I don't like having her fucking scold me.*

"You know," Tessa said, looking up, forcing a little grin, "that's the worst safe-sex talk I've heard."

Ruth was impassive for a moment. Then, her thin lips curled up. "Granted. You understand my concern, however?"

Tessa nodded. She was relieved that Ruth went along with her attempt to lighten the mood. "I know I made a mistake. It won't happen again. You can read my aura. Am I lying? Or do you see how committed I am to being a member of the Curia?"

"I think you have learned a valuable lesson," Ruth said. "I also think you know how close you came to death. If not for the circumstances, when it discovered who you were, it wouldn't have hesitated to kill you."

Tessa nodded. "I know. I got lucky."

"You did." Ruth closed Tessa's report. "I think we are done. Analysis may have other questions for you. But I am satisfied that Curia security wasn't harmed." She folded her hands on the desk. "And I believe you will be more careful. I know you have an important part to play in the war. As long as you stay focused." She nodded to the door, indicating the debriefing was over.

Tessa stood up. She looked at the painting, the mass of color, the white figure.

"Is that you?"

Ruth's voice betrayed a hint of surprise. "Yes. It was painted by Van Gogh. Just for me."

"Vanity?"

Ruth smiled. "No. Just history. You've had a long day. Get some rest."

Chapter 18

"Why did this hunter fail?"

Svetlana Ivanov was sitting behind her desk, conducting a review session for her Introduction to Tradecraft class. The recruits had just returned from their summer break, and she wanted to get their minds focused back on demon hunting. To do so, she selected a case study of a hunt from 1985 that ended disastrously. An envy demon was located in Toronto, a hunter dispatched, the demon cornered ... and then everything went wrong. It ended with the hunter dead and the demon free. She found the case was a good overview of what not to do and put into stark relief the importance of the lessons she had taught over the previous six months.

"He failed to detect the second demon," April said.

"Correct. The hunter had been operating for four years. He had multiple kills and a spotless record, but he became too accustomed to success. He located his target and, rather than conducting further surveillance, assumed that it was alone. It was not."

Tradecraft was Tessa's favorite class. While she enjoyed the physicality of Uri's combatives sessions, she loved the information that Ivanov imparted. Tessa learned that in addition to being a hunter, she served with the KGB in the waning years of the Soviet Union. If someone said that Ivanov could kill with her pinkie, Tessa would believe it.

However, the Tradecraft course was not about fighting. It was about observation and analysis. From the beginning, Ivanov stressed the importance of preparation.

Ivanov said little about her time as a hunter and even less about when she was an agent. Tessa paid attention to the crumbs she did provide, asked some discreet questions and pieced together a tentative biography. As a hunter, Ivanov focused on demons who infiltrated governments, using her intelligence training and contacts to ferret them out. After fifteen years in the field, she was badly hurt by a demon working within the Chinese government, losing her left leg below the knee. Although still fit, the prosthetic caused her to limp and forced her to transfer to training duties, becoming the Tradecraft instructor.

Tessa admired her no-nonsense attitude. She could also tell how much Ivanov missed being in the field. When she talked about a hunter operation, Tessa saw a glint in her eye and a hint of a smile.

I hope someday I can carry myself like that.

"You should all know this by now. What are the three things a surveillance mission depends on?" asked Ivanov.

"Functioning equipment," Tessa said.

"Correct. I've been on operations that have failed because someone forgot to replace a battery. Before any operation, double check everything."

"Attentive personnel," Patrick said.

Ivanov nodded. "Yes. Remember, most surveillance operations involve hours of sitting and waiting. The moment you relax or let your attention drift, it is almost guaranteed that the subject will make an appearance. What is the third mission critical thing?" There was silence in the room. "Come on, did you lose your brains on break?"

"A demon," said Tessa.

"Correct." She nodded at Tessa. "Operations often fail because there is nothing worth finding. Get used to long hours and regular disappointment."

Ivanov liked to focus on her, since she was the only other person in this class with an intelligence background. *Pride. That was this guy's problem. He spent three weeks finding his target and less than a day surveilling him. He missed the second demon because he was impatient. Because he had never failed before. He got sloppy, forgot to use his glasses. Just like I did with Dylan.*

"Now that I have determined you remember some of what I taught you, back to our case. Tessa, what would you have done differently?"

Although Tessa was sometimes reluctant to speak up in Silva's class – due to her feeling out of her depth – she had no such qualms with Ivanov.

"First, I would have set up a comprehensive surveillance program. Learnt where the target went, what he did and who he saw. He worked in an advertising firm. If the hunter had been more thorough, he might have seen the second demon meeting with the target in his office. Second, I would have asked for a tap on his phone. Post-op analysis showed that the target was in regular contact with a number of known and suspected demons. Third, I would have contacted the Surveillance and Analysis Directorate and asked for regular sweeps of the city."

"Wouldn't that have taken a significant amount of time?" Ivanov said, clearly playing devil's advocate.

"Yes, but it would have saved his life." She smirked, intuiting what Ivanov wanted to hear.

Ivanov nodded. "Exactly. Your job is tough enough. You are outnumbered by an enemy that is almost invulnerable. They are physically superior to you. Don't make your life harder by rushing into a fight. You are a hunter; think like one. Get to know your prey. Stalk them. Learn their weaknesses. The war against demons has gone on for centuries; you're not going to win it, so don't be in a hurry."

Ivanov saw some despondent looks in response to her last statement. She shook her head. "What's wrong? You think because the war will go on after you are dead and buried that it is not worth fighting? During World War Two, my countrymen died by the millions to slow down and then stop the Germans. They would go into battle without guns and pick up the rifles of their fallen comrades. Their fight was hopeless, but the war wasn't. Each hopeless individual battle led to the Red Flag flying over Berlin. One day, the war will end and the Curia will be victorious." She shrugged. "None of us will be there to see it, but it will happen."

That has to be the most depressing pep talk I've ever heard.

"This hunter did not understand his target. He had destroyed enough demons that he made the mistake of assuming that the image he had up here," she tapped her forehead, "was more real than what he could learn from careful observation and analysis."

Tessa understood what Ivanov was getting at. *I've seen firsthand the difficulty the Army had adapting to insurgent warfare in urban battlespaces, where each person could be an insurgent, a sympathizer or an innocent. Fighting demons will be a lot like trying to find the insurgents. They're moving in a civilian population, some of whom are supporters. Collateral damage has to be avoided. And we have to keep a low profile. People would lose their shit if they realized demons were manipulating our planet.*

"So when do you know you have enough information to stop watching and start slaying?" asked April, bringing Tessa out of her introspection.

"There is no easy answer to that. I can train you, but you need to develop a feel for the hunt on your own." She looked from one recruit to the next with an even, unemotional gaze. "There is a balance each of you must find between recklessness and paralysis. If you cannot do that there's always more room in the graveyard."

After Ivanov's class ended, Tessa headed back to her dorm room. Desange was there. He was sitting at the dining table, tapping on the keyboard of his laptop. He glanced up when she entered, smiled, then returned to work.

Tessa dropped her satchel next to the door and sat on the couch. She picked up a copy of *The Economist* – Desange read it religiously – and flipped idly through the pages. She wasn't reading the articles, but she wanted to give her hands something to do. Her mind was focused on Desange. Since returning from Paris, he had been a bit withdrawn, quieter and more focused on his own work. She was worried that their make-out session bothered him and he wasn't being forthcoming about it.

She looked at him, diligently typing. "Hey, you've been pretty quiet the last few days. Anything wrong?"

Desange didn't look up. "I've just been busy. My Special Studies coursework is heavy. When I deploy to West Africa, it's going to be tough balancing hunting and maintaining my cover job. I also am a little worried about fitting in there. I've never been to that part of Africa and the Ivory Coast just ended a civil war." Desange stretched. "I'm used to Paris, not a warzone."

Tessa thought about her own experience. When she first learned she was being deployed to Iraq, it had led to a mix of fear and excitement. She was looking forward to putting her training and experience to the test. She wanted to do a good job for her fellow soldiers and "get into the shit." But this anticipation was balanced by a clear understanding of what Iraq was like. She had lost friends there and in Afghanistan. People killed by IEDs or in firefights. Others were wounded, some permanently. That part of the deployment had worried her.

And when she arrived, it was nothing like she imagined. *It won't be for him either. You can't know what going to war is like until you're in the middle of it – when it's too late.*

"You're going to be fine. With the training they give us and your own natural charm—"

"Ah, my charm is natural? Why thank you."

"—you'll be fine. Everyone likes you for a reason, Desange. You're a great guy." Tessa smiled. "Now that I've massaged your ego, I'm thinking of going for a run. Want to join me?"

Desange was tempted, but reluctantly shook his head. "I should get back to this. But I'll be ready for a dinner break when you get back."

Tessa sighed. "Fine, but I think you don't want me to beat you," she teased.

She went into her bedroom and changed into her running gear. After slipping on her shoes, she re-entered the common room. "Okay, I'll see you in a while." She punched him playfully on the arm. "No slacking."

Desange smiled. "If Ivanov ever retires, you'd make a good successor."

"Now that is a compliment. See ya."

Chapter 19

Tessa was excited. It was finally time for her first field observation exercise, a final exam that recruits had been training for all year. She was looking forward to getting off the island and being able to shadow an actual demon hunter. She hoped that her tradecraft, combatives and analyst skills would be put to use. She was also looking forward to spending more time with Desange outside the confines of the Academy.

But strictly friendzone.

Before being sent on their assignment, Ivanov briefed every pair of recruits. Tessa and Desange sat at the work table closest to the front of her classroom. An image of an attractive, petite dark-haired woman sitting at an outdoor cafe was projected onto the screen. Her eyes were lost in shadows, an effect that Tessa found disturbing.

She sighed softly. *It's just a low-quality image, but she looks so human. A monster wearing a human shell.*

"This is Marit," Ivanov said, motioning toward the screen with a chop of her hand. "She is a gluttony demon who has been operating on Earth for over 300 years. Her first confirmed appearance was in 1683." The image changed to an illustration of a woman standing in front of a blue and red conical tent. Men in armor were lined up, waiting for their turn to enter. "During the Ottoman siege of Vienna, she ran a brothel and hashish business. That set the tone for her subsequent activities. She no longer is involved in the sex trade; as a gluttony demon, she is here to prey on our other weaknesses, drugs and alcohol." The image changed back to the original photo. "Marit runs a drug distribution operation specializing in synthetics, mainly party drugs. When she is conducting business, it is primarily in nightclubs, bars and other high-traffic locations. We've had leads on her from time to time, but she has been very adept at evading our hunters."

"Where was this photo taken?" Tessa asked.

"Amsterdam, last June. It was taken by Arno Wollman, an experienced hunter with a strong kill record," said Ivanov.

"Why wasn't he able to kill her in Amsterdam?" asked Desange.

"She stays in crowds, so it's hard to isolate her. She has a keen sense of when she's being tracked and knows how to vanish. Arno recently re-acquired her in Berlin and our surveillance analysts were able to tag her. She is in Copenhagen now. If she follows past behavior, she will be working the nightclub circuit."

"Do we think Marit knows she was spotted?" Tessa asked.

"Possibly, but we have no reason to believe Arno's identity has been compromised. Her past behavior indicates that she goes completely off-the-grid when spotted, which is what happened in Amsterdam. However, she is also highly mobile. Many demons focus on one area, but Marit regularly moves around Europe." Ivanov shrugged. "It is also possible that Marit decided it was time to move on, to throw us off, if we were watching. In either case, assume that she will be wary."

Tessa felt her heart quicken with excitement. *Mission Impossible, demonic-style. Tracking a monster through an old European city, sleuthing around trendy nightclubs and getting rid of a drug dealer. Marit is the kind of monster that ruined my family. I can't save them, but I can help protect others from downward spiraling into addiction. This is what I signed up for.*

"Can you elaborate on the intel around her drug-dealing behaviors?" Desange asked.

"She mainly deals MDMA in nightclubs and music festivals. Our assets in Interpol have provided information linking her to the Russian cartel, although the nature of her connection is not clear."

Desange was taking notes on his iPad. "Anything else that would be helpful for us to know? Does she have associates with her? Demonic or human?"

"We believe that she operates a number of small-scale labs across Europe, but she is on her own when dealing. There is no reason to think this behavior has changed." She leaned back against her desk. She had been standing all day and her prosthetic was starting to irritate the stump of her leg.

"We'll be shadowing Arno?" asked Desange.

"Correct, he will be your operational command for this exercise. Follow his directives," Ivanov said. "Remember, hunting demons is an exercise in patience and perseverance. They are skilled at covert operations and evasion. It is rare that a recruit gets to see a kill, but in the event you do get close enough and Arno decides to fight Marit, it's very important you follow his lead. Understood?"

Tessa and Desange nodded.

"Marit may not look like a threat, but don't let her features fool you. You have been taught how dangerous demons are."

Tessa glanced at the metal and plastic leg sticking out from Ivanov's mid-length skirt.

"Believe those lessons. Marit has killed many, both hunters and civilians. She is fast and brutal. If you do encounter her, she will show no mercy."

Desange had been through this before. He knew that Ivanov was done with her briefing. He rose from his seat. "Thank you."

Tessa followed.

"Good hunting," said Ivanov, as they exited her classroom.

"What do you think?" Desange asked.

"I'm ready to get into the field and kick some ass."

Desange laughed at Tessa's enthusiasm. "I like your attitude, but don't get carried away. Be prepared for some long, tedious days."

Tessa bumped Desange's arm with her elbow. "Don't worry. I won't embarrass you out there."

They entered the elevator.

"I just want you to be careful," Desange said, pressing the button for their floor. "And if I were you, I'd buy a large container of NesCafe when we land in Copenhagen. You'll need it."

Tessa grinned. "You read my mind."

Chapter 20

Tessa, Desange and Arno Wollman sat in the back of a white BMW Sprinter cargo van. It was parked near the Kobenhavn K, a park in the center of Copenhagen. The neighborhood was thick with bars, restaurants and nightclubs.

The boxy vehicle looked innocuous, the kind you could pass without noticing a dozen times a day. However, the interior was filled with state-of-the art surveillance and communication gear. Tessa was familiar with the electronics lining the walls from her time in the military and Ivanov's training sessions. The exacting Russian repeatedly stressed the need for comprehensive surveillance and information gathering. "Remember the three Ps: Patience, Persistence, Perspiration," had become a refrain in her Tradecraft class.

Arno wasn't thrilled about their presence. He understood the importance of field exercises; but he had been on Marit's trail for a while. He felt she was close, that he had finally learned her patterns and would confront her soon. He wanted to focus on cornering and killing Marit, not shepherding two recruits.

For the first few days, he said little to them. As the week was drawing to a close, however, the late nights and long hours led to a grudging acceptance of Desange and Tessa's presence. He saw they were diligent and attentive. He thought they would make good hunters, even as he wished they had been assigned to someone else.

"Okay, tonight is Desange's turn to accompany me," said Arno. "Tessa, you'll be monitoring comms and conducting exterior surveillance."

As Desange and Arno climbed out of the van, Tessa said, "Hey, when you're done with the first club, maybe you could bring me something to eat that doesn't come out of a bag. Or a cocktail ... a whiskey sour would be nice."

Desange grinned. "I'll see what I can do."

Arno pointed to the binoculars with lenses made from demonic glass sitting at Tessa's workstation. "Just keep an eye on the entrance."

"Roger that, sir," Tessa said.

Arno didn't pick up the mocking tone. He nodded and slid the back doors closed.

He's a lot of fun.

In spite of his sour attitude, Tessa preferred to shadow Arno when he went into the nightclubs to perform eyes-on reconnaissance. Although using the glasses for any length of time was headache-inducing, it was better than eight hours in the back of the van. Last night, she had been able to mingle with the locals while looking for Marit. Arno, however, wanted to give the recruits equal time in the van and shadowing him. That meant she would spend the night on an uncomfortable stool with her mug of NesCafe. She took a sip. The familiar taste was comforting, a reminder that she was back on mission. Tessa recalled her small electric kettle and container of NesCafe she kept on hand in Iraq. Many days in the Tactical Operations Center were fueled by mug after mug of strong black coffee. When she wasn't able to leave her desk, her instant coffee and kettle were at the ready.

Finding a demon was not an easy task. For a hunter, it involved using lenses made from the heart of a demon and trying to catch a glimpse of them. In Ivanov's class, she made the recruits wear them until their heads pounded. During the first extended wear exercise, Tessa had thrown up, along with almost half the class. Ivanov was unperturbed.

"The glasses are only one of our tools," Ivanov had said, while the recruits wiped up the remains of their lunch. "And it is an imperfect one that interacts with the human mind and body in unpredictable ways." She stopped in front of Tessa and touched the bucket she was using with the toe of her shoe. "As you have seen. Over time, the glass deteriorates from use."

Since Paris, Tessa had practiced wearing her glasses more and had begun to adjust to them. While the visual effect was like extreme nearsightedness, the physical effect was harder to describe. The closest sensation she could think of was when she had been caught in a riptide and pulled a hundred meters from shore. Although she had quickly gotten control of the situation, there was a moment when she felt the yawning darkness tugging her down into the ocean's depths. Now she only felt a dull, throbbing headache when she wore them. However, the feeling of an ancient darkness pulling at her when she looked through the lenses never went away.

As Arno and Desange crossed the street to the *Greone Bier* Bar, Tessa ran through her equipment checks. Desange had done a thorough job of preparing everything after last night's surveillance. The external cameras were all operational, audio and visual recorders were running and the communications gear was set to keep her in touch with Arno and Desange. She knew that even with all the sophisticated equipment, the only way to see a demon was a hunter using glasses. She sighed at the thought of eight hours of staring out the one-way glass panel in the side of the van and looking through the binoculars.

She scanned the crowd in front of the bar and felt the growing throb behind her eyes. She took another drink of coffee and flicked her comms channel to Desange's earpiece. "Are you having fun in there? Drinking enough for both of us?"

There was a brief hiss of static and then his voice. "*Oui.* This place is really happening. Too bad you're stuck in the van."

"Haha … hey, don't forget you owe me a drink."

"Arno is finishing up his sweep. Have you seen anything out there?"

Tessa sat back from the binocular mount and rubbed her aching eyes. "Nothing. Just getting a migraine."

"What did you say when I complained about that last night?"

Tessa laughed. "I believe my exact words were 'Suck it up.'"

"Exactly. Okay, Arno's approaching. We're going to the next club. I'll see if I can sneak something past our dour taskmaster."

"10-4."

After two more bars, Arno and Desange returned to the van to check in. Tessa was disappointed that Desange came bearing only a falafel wrap, not the drink she half-hoped he would try to smuggle out. The three sat in the van, Tessa eating. Arno and Desange drank coffee and swapped out their radios for ones with fresh charges.

"Maybe our demon decided to take the week off. Or our intel is wrong," said Tessa around a mouthful of falafel and pita.

"The Curia's analysts are the best in the world. And I know the demon is here. I've been tracking Marit long enough to understand her." Arno tapped the binoculars. "Don't slack off. I need your eyes on target." He finished his coffee and slipped into the driver's seat. As he drove to the next location, Desange and Tessa shared a knowing look.

He thinks this guy is a dick too. Arno's treating us like we're kids.

As if reading her mind, Desange gave her a half-smile. "Almost done," he whispered. "We'll be back at the Academy soon. Then you're off to Fiji for winter holiday."

Tessa nodded. She was looking forward to finally going on her Fiji vacation. That Desange would also be graduating, with no guarantee when they would see each other again, was a painful realization. She pushed it aside and replaced it with thoughts of palm trees and over-water bungalows.

Arno parked the van near the next target, the nightclub *Rod Aften*. He climbed out, then opened the back doors. "Let's go."

Tessa sighed, watching the two men walk toward the throbbing club. She pulled up the floorplan on one of her monitors. A narrow corridor led to a large dance floor. A stage was at the far end. Behind it were offices and storerooms. There was a fire exit to an alley that could be used as an escape route. Tessa notified Arno of this option.

"Understood," he said.

She looked at the half-eaten wrap and mug of cold coffee on the workstation desk. *Another hour of sitting here. Wonderful.*

She alternated between checking the line outside the club door and massaging her aching temples. She heated up more water and made another mug of coffee. After forty-five minutes, she was about to call Arno and recommend they try someplace else, when her headset crackled.

"I have a possible hit," Arno's clipped German voice came over her headset. "I'm moving to confirm and engage. Desange will remain in a backup position."

Tessa put down her mug. "Arno, shouldn't we establish a trace and wait until the target gets to a more secluded area?"

"I'm not going to risk losing her again. Arno out."

Tessa wanted to argue the point, but decided against it. *He's a veteran hunter. He knows what he's doing.*

She contacted Desange. "Can you report on what's happening?"

"Arno's on the dance floor. He's approaching a woman near the stage. It's blurry with these glasses on and the club is packed, but I think I see spots of clarity as she moves. Could be a demon."

Damn it. I wish I could see what's happening. She sat waiting in anticipation. She didn't want to break protocol and head inside. She was about to contact Desange again, when his voice blared in her ears. "Arno just attacked her. I think he's down! Everyone is panicking."

She saw people surging out of the front entrance of the nightclub.

"Fuck! Arno, do you copy? Arno?" She switched frequencies. "Desange, what the hell is going on?"

"Arno is down! I'm going to engage."

"Get the hell out of there before you get killed!" Tessa felt her heart quicken as adrenaline surged through her body. She was not going to sit back and let Desange fight that thing alone. *Why the fuck did Arno engage the target inside a nightclub?* She slipped on her glasses and pulled her dagger out of its hip sheath. She depressed the stud on the handle. The thin, razor-edged blade popped out. She was about to leave, when she decided she needed more than the dagger. She retracted the blade, put the dagger back into its sheath, grabbed a pistol from the van's weapon locker and exited. People were still streaming out of the entrance. She would never get in that way. *That's not the only entrance.*

Tessa ran into the alley behind the building. It was quiet. No one had gone through the fire exit. She tried the metal door and found it unlocked. She took a deep breath to steady her sparking nerves and entered the club. She was in a service corridor lit by bare fluorescent tubes. The deep bass of dance music vibrated her chest. Pistol up and at the ready, she carefully made her way to the door leading to the dance floor and opened it.

The scene was chaotic. There were still people trying to push their way out through the front door. Two heavily built men were on the ground. She assumed they were bouncers who had tried to intervene. One was moving slightly. The other's head was twisted in an unnatural position. Desange was leaning against the bar, cradling his arm. Tessa couldn't see Arno from her vantage point.

The demon was sauntering toward Desange. Marit was a lithe woman with short dark hair and pale skin. She was wearing a tight scarlet halter top and matching miniskirt. She approached Desange with confidence, moving in for the kill.

Although Tessa knew bullets would not harm the demon, she thought they would distract Marit and slow her down. She fired, the loud bangs lost in the ear-splitting music. She could see the bullets tear into the demon's exposed back. The flesh parted as the bullets entered and then almost instantly closed, leaving no evidence of anything having happened.

Marit turned, a look of annoyance on her face, and headed for Tessa. She didn't say anything – not that she could have been heard over the music – but she did point at Tessa with one long, manicured nail. She wagged it at her, like she was scolding a misbehaving child.

Shit. Tessa dropped the gun and pulled out the dagger. She settled into a fighting stance, crouching slightly and putting her free arm in front of her face. She held her dagger near her side, ready to stab the demon. The thin, smiling woman didn't look like a threat, but Tessa knew that demonic strength had nothing to do with how they looked. *Don't panic, don't panic, don't panic.*

The demon led with a right hook. Tessa ducked out of the way. She jabbed with the knife, missed and followed that up with a kick to the stomach. She hit as hard as she could. Marit was knocked off balance and stumbled backward a few feet.

Tessa saw Arno running toward them, dagger ready. Marit followed her gaze with a jerk of her head. Tessa saw a look of concern cross over Marit's icy blue eyes.

The demon rushed past Tessa toward the emergency exit, moving faster than any person could. She was unprepared for Marit's speed. The demon backhanded her in the chest, before she had time to react. She could feel an explosion of pain as one of her ribs cracked. Tessa dropped to her knees and for a moment was doubled over, catching her breath.

When she looked up Marit was gone and Arno was standing over her, screaming,

"You fucking idiot! I had her!"

By now Desange had struggled to his feet and shuffled over to Arno and Tessa. His arm was broken and he was trying to hold it motionless.

Arno looked at him, shaking his head in disgust. "You two, get back to the van." He then dashed toward the exit, hoping to catch the demon.

Desange held out his good arm, helping Tessa to her feet. He was in too much pain to say anything; he just nodded toward the exit. Tessa retrieved her dagger and gun and the two hobbled out of the nightclub, into the crisp night air.

Although breathing hurt, the cold air gave Tessa a boost. "Are you okay?" she asked, the dance music now muffled by concrete.

Desange nodded. "My arm. I think it is broken."

"What happened?"

"Arno tried to stab her and she tossed him aside. When I tried to help, she snapped my arm like it was a dry twig. I've never seen anything with that kind of speed and strength."

As they approached the van, she heard Desange groan. It was soft, but only because he was doing everything he could to control his reaction to the pain.

I had to help. If I hadn't engaged, Desange wouldn't just be hurt – he'd be dead. I'm not going to let another friend die. Not on my watch. Images of herself back in Iraq flashed through her mind, the screams and the mangled bodies in the remains of the TOC. She pushed back the memory. *Not on my watch.*

Tessa helped Desange into the back of the van, then slid into the driver's seat. There was a shooting pain as she closed the door. She waited for it to subside, then slipped on her headset. "Arno, do you copy?"

There was a moment of silence. Then Arno's voice, angry and out of breath. "I lost her. I'm near the *Ved Classens Have*. Get the goddamn van over here and pick me up. Assuming you can do that right. Arno out."

Sure. Fuck you too.

"Tessa," Desange said, voice strained. He was listening to the police band radio. "I have incoming police. We need to go now."

"I know, I know. Arno needs a pick up. Hold on and we'll get you help."

As she drove to the public garden that Arno had specified, Tessa braced herself for what was to come. *Did I make a mistake? Did I help a demon escape? Or did I save Desange? I do nothing, people die. I do something, a demon escapes ... and people die.*

She saw Arno waiting in a shadowy bus stop near the garden, his hoodie pulled low over his forehead. As she pulled up, he stepped out of the darkness, his face seething with anger.

He got into the passenger side and slammed the door. "Sinclair, you fucked this up. I'm going to make certain Ruth knows. Now, get us out of here before we're arrested."

Tessa held her tongue. But she felt a falling sensation. She was back in the riptide, being pulled into darkness.

Chapter 21

"How is she?" Father McKenna asked. He was talking to Ruth. The two were in McKenna's office, discussing the return of Tessa and Desange. Although her face was impassive, McKenna could sense a tension in her posture and voice. She had returned from a recruiting mission in Tokyo and was not happy to have another Tessa Sinclair problem waiting for her.

"A cracked rib and some bruises, but otherwise fine. Desange has a broken arm, but it's only a hairline fracture. Uri thinks he'll be able to use it in a few weeks."

"You opted not to heal them?"

Ruth nodded. "If the injuries were more serious, I would have. In this case, the recovery will serve as a lesson about the dangers of fighting a demon. Pain is a valuable training tool."

McKenna knew arguing with Ruth would not work. Her mind was made up. "I've read Arno's report. He is blaming Tessa for Marit's escape." He glanced over at the monitor on his desk. "Willful disobedience of orders," he read. "Failure to follow operational instructions. Use of firearms in a public location..." he looked back to Ruth. "What do you think?"

"I have no reason to doubt Arno's assessment. He is a seasoned hunter and has a high rate of success. However, I plan to debrief Tessa when I am done here and gather more details. She may have a good reason for what she did."

McKenna detected a slight downward curl at the corner of her lips. "And if the reason isn't to your satisfaction?"

Ruth's voice was ice. "We need hunters we can trust. She was told to follow Arno's commands. This is the second time she's behaved impulsively with a demon. We may need to reevaluate her role in the Curia."

McKenna knew that could mean a lot of things. While recruits rarely had to repeat a year, it had happened. Or, she could be sent into support services, working as an analyst. While hunters were a rare and valuable asset, McKenna had seen recruits who couldn't cut it get other jobs. "I spoke to Tessa when she returned. I don't think Arno is telling the full story about what happened in Copenhagen."

Ruth grinned, tight and mirthless. "Humans never do, even if they mean to. They don't have full access to their unconscious motivations. After I am done here, I plan to visit Arno. He should never have lost control of the situation. Confronting Marit in a public venue," she shook her head, "that's sloppy and makes it difficult for us to fashion a strong cover story."

"At least the number of witnesses was limited. Most of the people in the club were more concerned with getting out. I think we can pass this off as a drug deal gone bad."

"We can't take any chances. We will have to move Arno to another region, at least for now. He's been compromised. Our contacts in the Danish government are monitoring the investigation and will undertake mitigation efforts. Those will be more successful if he is not in the country." She was silent for a moment, making a decision. "We need more coverage in the Balkans. He will be reassigned to Bosnia. He can be re-evaluated later. If he doesn't show better judgment, other actions will have to be taken."

"He's still a good hunter."

Ruth stared at McKenna, her gaze icier than usual. "We'll see."

It was clear to McKenna that Ruth was finished with the topic of Arno. "So ... Tessa..."

"Yes. Tessa. I knew she was going to be a challenge, but I thought she might be worth the effort. Now..." Ruth shrugged. Her feeling about Tessa was intuitive. Nothing was unique about her in particular. Like all humans, her aura was a kaleidoscope of emotion, along with the indigo signature of a potential hunter. But there was something else she saw in Tessa.

A streak of independence, unlike the desire to serve found in most humans who were recruited by the Curia. After 2000 years of leading the fight against demons, Ruth had learned to trust her instincts; they told her that Tessa could be an asset to the Curia. "I'll reserve judgment until I've spoken to her."

"I'd like to accompany you and get a sense for myself of how she is doing."

Ruth stood up. She found his request annoying – she liked to conduct the field observation exercise debriefs herself. She saw humans as getting in the way of what she was able to do more efficiently and effectively. But there was nothing in Curia regulations that prevented McKenna or any other director from attending. "Of course. I'm sure she'll be happy to see you."

McKenna followed Ruth to Tessa's room. Uri, who had previous experience as a combat medic, had taped Tessa's ribs and recommended bed rest for a few days. When Ruth and McKenna arrived, Tessa was stretched out on the couch. She was wearing a loose track suit and watching *Parks and Recreation*.

She waved them in. "Sorry I can't get up. It's taken me an hour to find a comfortable position. I'm not giving that up, even for an angel."

"That's all right," McKenna said. He and Ruth brought chairs from the dining table and sat them in front of the couch. "We just wanted to ask a few questions about the exercise."

"I already filed my AAR."

Ruth nodded. "I still have questions."

"Okay."

"You didn't have a full picture of the situation inside the nightclub. Arno told you to remain in place." Ruth leaned forward, her gaze hard and steady. "You decided to disobey a direct order and enter the club. Why?"

"The report I received from Desange indicated they were in trouble. I wasn't going to sit back and listen to my friend get torn apart."

"You understand that we tell you to listen to the senior hunter for a reason. They have the experience to judge a situation better than a recruit, particularly one who is not directly engaged. Arno's report indicates that you interfered with a certain kill."

Tessa felt her blood begin to boil. She tried to keep her voice even, but there was a quiver of anger. "He's wrong. When I arrived on scene, the demon was about to kill Desange and Arno was down. He did not have control of the situation."

Ruth saw Tessa's aura flare red. She could tell pushing her further on this would not be productive.

"Let's set your decision to intervene aside. When you first engaged Marit, you used a handgun. Why? You know that guns are ineffective against demons."

"I thought it would distract her, maybe slow her down and buy me a few seconds. She was advancing on Desange and he was in no shape to defend himself."

Ruth leaned in a little. "So, you wanted to draw Marit's attention, rather than using the opening that was provided."

"Opening? What do you mean?"

"While Marit was occupied with Desange, you could have approached from behind and killed her."

Tessa couldn't believe what she was hearing. "You mean while she was killing Desange."

Tessa's aura glowed a vibrant red, like metal on the verge of melting. The light washed over her, hot and rippling. "Your best chance of neutralizing the demon was using the cover of music and her attention on Desange to your advantage. You didn't."

"I'm not about to let a hunter get killed just to gain a momentary advantage."

"You would have been able to kill Marit. That is the mission." Ruth paused. "Preferring to protect the one person you care about instead of the many nameless humans who will be harmed in the future by your choice to let Marit go is a very human decision. As you learn to think more like a hunter, you will see the bigger picture over time. Do you consider Desange your friend?"

"Yes."

"That friendship caused you to act impulsively and fail to take advantage of a vulnerability. This is why we emphasize the solitary nature of a hunter. We know that people will form connections; but the mission comes before everything. Family … friends … our lives … these are all secondary to the mission."

Tessa felt a tightness in her chest, exacerbated by the ache from her cracked ribs. "You talk about our lives, but you're not risking your life. We're doing your dirty work. Can you even die? Or do you just go back to Heaven?" She saw a sour look flash across Ruth's face, before it settled back into its normal inscrutability. When Ruth failed to answer, Tessa continued, "I had a limited window to act. Desange needed help. You're right, I didn't know what was going on in the club; but it sounded bad and I went with my gut."

"Tessa, the creatures you fight are powerful. Finding them vulnerable is a rare opportunity. There may be a time that you have to sacrifice a hunter in order to kill your target. That is always going to be your priority. The war can only be won by destroying the enemy." Ruth nodded. "And to answer your question, yes, I can die. Only God is eternal."

"We understand why you took the actions you did," said McKenna. "We are trying to impress on you what your priorities have to be."

Tessa noted the look Ruth gave McKenna, a sideways glance that reflected an apparent irritation with his presence.

Ruth looked back at Tessa. "I'm going to Rome next month. Instead of your planned holiday in Fiji, you will accompany me. I have a special assignment for you."

Tessa forced herself to sit up, even though it was painful. "I don't need a time out."

Ruth shrugged. "I disagree. I want to personally see how you operate in the field." She looked at McKenna. "Father, please coordinate the change of plans. Now, I think we should leave Tessa to recover." Ruth stood up and patted Tessa's shoulder. "Take a few days to rest. And think about what I said. You are a valuable member of the Curia. But you are not more important than our mission."

"If you need anything, don't hesitate to ask," McKenna added, as he scurried to follow Ruth out.

Once they were in the hall and the door was closed, McKenna looked at Ruth quizzically, his eyes narrowing. "Are you sure taking her to Rome is wise?"

Ruth looked at McKenna, like he was an annoying insect. "I have been recruiting hunters for thousands of years. They need to be able to balance initiative with a respect for the chain of command."

"Because you are the chain of command," McKenna replied, a strong emphasis on "you."

Although he meant it as a rebuke, Ruth took it as a statement of fact. "Yes. Directors come and go, but I am the constant in the Curia."

"God is the constant."

"Of course, Father. I merely meant that I am God's agent on Earth."

McKenna had seen this side of Ruth before. Long ago, he came to the conclusion that she saw humans in a more abstract fashion, as tools to be used in the holiest of wars. All she cared about was winning the war.

"Father, I've seen what happens when hunters are left with too much initiative. Most will do the right thing. Others," she shook her head, remembering the pogroms, inquisitions, witch trials and sectarian massacres instigated by over-zealous hunters, "they will allow their anger and passion to spill out.

When they do, people suffer and demons thrive in the chaos sin creates."

"I'm sure you're right. Your insights are greater than mine."

Ruth nodded. "You still have doubts, don't you?"

"I do."

"I value your views. And I am not arrogant enough to think I'm infallible. Only God is infallible." Ruth smiled. They entered the elevator. "But I know things you don't. And I have been observing people for centuries. My assessment is correct. She will accompany me to Rome, and I will make a decision about her disposition after directly observing her."

"And if you don't like what you see?"

Ruth stared at him for a moment, eyes boring in. He couldn't hold her gaze, looking down at the mirror polish on his shoes.

"Then there will be a final disposition." She touched McKenna's shoulder.

He flinched slightly.

"But I'm sure she'll perform to my satisfaction."

There was a finality to the statement that signaled an end to the conversation.

Chapter 22

The *Magna Domus* was buried deep beneath the teeming streets of Rome, under the Chapel of Columba of Rieti. The tiny church, built in the late seventeenth century, was dedicated to an obscure saint. However, it had a more important purpose. The construction served as a cover for the excavation of a warren of underground tunnels and chambers. For centuries, it was the Curia's headquarters, training center and base of operations for hunters, earning its name of "Great House." The location – a few hundred meters from the Apostolic Palace, the Pope's residence in the Vatican – facilitated communications between the Church and the Curia. With the evolution of the Curia into a global organization, hunters expanded their battleground beyond Europe and the Levant. The Academy moved to Mykines. The *Magna Domus* narrowed its scope. By the dawn of the twenty-first century, it was home to the analysts of the Surveillance and Analysis Directorate and the Sphere.

Hours after arriving in Rome, Tessa stood just inside the entrance to the Sphere room, a massive cavern whose ceiling was lost in darkness. On the flight from the Faroes, her thoughts had mostly been on what this mission with Ruth meant. Between her encounter in Paris and the fiasco in Copenhagen, she knew she was on thin ice. Ruth was clear that this trip was an evaluation. Tessa hated having people second guess her decisions. But, she wanted to get through this and make a good impression on Ruth.

In spite of her feelings, she was looking forward to seeing the *Magna Domus* and the Sphere. *This is like something out of Indiana Jones.* She knew it was a device used to track demons, but that was all. She was surprised by how massive it was. Although Ivanov described it in one session, her words failed to convey its true size. The device was a 30-foot diameter globe, supported by an iron and brass framework. The surface was covered by a mosaic of demonic glass shards set in the shape of the continents. Across the surface rippled the colors of the rainbow, the merging of billions of auras. In some places, it was a shimmering haze; in others, it danced in jagged peaks and valleys. A web of wireless cameras surrounded the Sphere recording every undulation for later analysis. A row of workstations was near the entrance, manned 24 hours a day by monitoring teams.

As she watched, one of the men at the monitor station stood up and walked over to Tessa. He was a doughy, middle-aged man with thinning white-blonde hair and watery blue eyes.

"Hi," he said, holding out a hand. "Lars Olsen."

Tessa shook his hand. "Tessa Sinclair."

"You're here with Ruth."

Tessa nodded.

"Training to be an analyst?"

Tessa shook her head. "Nope. Hunter."

Lars laughed. "Probably a good thing. After a while in the pit, we all start looking like moles." He turned toward the Sphere. The dancing lights reflected in his eyes. "Impressive, yes?"

Tessa nodded. "I was told about it in the Academy, but seeing it in person – it's amazing."

"The entire surface of our world, replicated in the glass hearts retrieved from hundreds of demons that you hunters have killed. Before 1950, it was surrounded by scaffolds. Monitoring staff would be seated on the scaffolds, watching specific locations of the Sphere. Thankfully, we were an early adopter of TV cameras. That makes our job easier."

Tessa imagined what that must have been like. She pictured monks bent close to the shimmering Sphere, the cavern lit by glowing candles and the cold fire of the Sphere. Even as she let her imagination wander, she felt pressure building behind her eyes. It wasn't painful, but it reminded her of the feeling she got when looking through the glasses. She rubbed her eyes.

Lars noticed. "Getting a headache?"

"No, not really."

"It's because you've been using the glasses. After a while, you become attuned to the field it generates. All the glass in the Sphere is reaching out to you."

She glanced at him, wondering if he was joking. The set of his face reflected his seriousness. "Are you affected?"

"Yes, but not as severely. We minimize our time in the Sphere room. Otherwise—" he pantomimed throwing up. "Mankind wasn't meant to be around the divine or the infernal."

"That's not reassuring, given what I'm training to do," Tessa said.

Lars smiled, his cheeks puffed up like a deep-sea fish. "Sorry. Just a flourish."

"Lars," one of the men at the monitor station said, waving him over, "it looks like Romeo-191."

"Want to see this?" Lars asked Tessa.

She nodded and followed him over. He slipped into his chair and pointed at one of the three computer monitors at his workstation. It showed a blur of shimmering color, overlaying a map that Tessa recognized as Tokyo. Lars tapped a key and the image froze. He intensely scrutinized it. Tessa couldn't make out anything other than a smear of rainbow colors flowing like waves in an ocean.

"Got you," Lars said, a note of triumph in his voice. He used his mouse to select an area of the map and zoom in. What had seemed to Tessa to be just another blob of color resolved itself into colored spikes, mostly red, orange and green, around a small black spot. Lars looked up at her. "Say hello to an anger demon." He clicked on a menu. "Romeo-191 to be exact."

"How can you tell?" asked Tessa.

"You get used to seeing the patterns." He pointed to the screen. "A spiking of human auras indicates a skewing of emotional states. In any random sampling, the auras stay relatively flat in a blur of colors — orange for fear, green for disgust, yellow for happiness, etcetera. Sometimes one emotion will spike, and if it's a low spike, we don't worry. But when the auras really start swelling, like a tsunami, you look for this," his finger moved to the tiny dark spot. "That's a demon."

Tessa nodded. "But how do you know which one? An anger demon could cause a variety of emotional states."

"Ah ... magic."

Tessa frowned at him.

"Kidding, of course." He pointed to the screen. "All demons have a spiritual signature. A fingerprint. That's how we can differentiate between individual demons. We go through special training to learn how to analyze these signatures. Of course, we still need to fill in the blanks. What they look like, how they operate, who their favorite targets are. That kind of intel depends on hunters and intelligence gathering." Lars clicked his mouse, revealing a more detailed file. "We don't have a name for Romeo-191, but we have a description from a hunter," he indicated a sketch of a man with a narrow face and a mop of black hair. "From analysis of emotional states and actions in the area, we think that he is working with the yakuza, encouraging violence among the criminals of Tokyo. Clearly, operating in a target rich environment."

Tessa admired the work that was being done here by the monitors and analysts. Outnumbered as they were, she knew every scrap of information was critical for the hunters. "This is pretty cool."

Lars nodded. "Yeah, well if you get sick of stabbing demons, you could always transfer here. It's safer at least."

Tessa laughed. "And risk becoming a mole girl?"

Lars grinned. "There's Vitamin D pills for that."

Tessa thought about Dylan. She wondered how much the analysts knew about him. *Ruth must have forwarded my report.*

Could they find him? He knows me. My name, what I look like. If I can find him, maybe I can do something.

"Lars, do you keep a record of prior scans?"

He patted the monitor. "Sure. We don't forget anything."

"Would it be possible to check for a demon in Paris from your July 15th scan?"

"Sure, I could," he said, "but you're not a hunter, yet. If Ruth, McKenna or a hunter approved it..."

"Never mind." Tessa wasn't surprised. *Of course the Curia's security wouldn't let anyone access this information. Let's see if this guy is susceptible to flirting.* She brushed her hip against his arm and leaned against the desk. She folded her arms under her breasts, pushing them up a bit. Although he tried not to look, Tessa caught Lars' eyes going from her's to her chest. "It's just, I saw a demon when I was there last summer. You know, I'm just a recruit, so I couldn't do anything." She moved a little closer and leaned in, conspiratorially. "It's kind of dumb, but I just thought I'd feel better if I knew he wasn't near me. And you seem like the kind of guy who's helpful." She smiled.

Lars swallowed. "Well," he said, "I guess it couldn't hurt. But it will take some time. Without a priority order, I'll have to wait until my shift is over."

Tessa smiled and placed her hand on his shoulder. "Anything you can do would be great. And there's no rush. I'm not going anywhere for a couple of weeks."

"When and where?"

Tessa felt a twinge of sexual desire. Not for Lars; but for the demon. That was replaced by a stronger desire – to see the demon turn to glass, her dagger buried in his chest.

"Paris. July 15th. Montmartre. It was in the evening."

Lars nodded. Then he looked past Tessa. "Our boss is here."

Tessa looked at Ruth. "She looks ready to go. Nice meeting you, Lars."

"You too."

Tessa followed Ruth out of the Sphere room. Unlike the raw rock of the cavernous space, the halls of the Great House were lined with marble, the floors scuffed and worn from centuries of use.

"Did you get what you needed?" Tessa asked.

Ruth nodded. "Analysis has located several new recruits, and as luck would have it, one is in Italy, narrowed down to Tibburtino IV. Unfortunately, the neighborhood has a large number of apartment buildings. It will take time to locate the right aura. Analysis has been able to discern a number of repetitive travel patterns and we'll be staking those out."

That sounds boring as hell. This is a punishment, after all. "You're an angel, do you really believe in luck?"

Ruth laughed. "I have adopted some of your sayings over the centuries, but no, it is as God ordains it to be."

They walked up the spiral staircase that led into the chapel's crypt. As soon as they exited out the service entrance, Tessa was hit by the noise of the city. Although she wished she was in Fiji, she decided there were worse places to be than Rome at Christmas Time. *If only I can get away from my chaperone.*

Ruth had not been talkative during either the flight to Rome or since they landed. Tessa noted that Ruth seemed exceptionally alert. *Is she seeing demons? Is Rome a focal point for them? It makes sense. Demons would have to know that the Curia's based here. Plus, corrupting the Church would fit with their plans for the human race. Would she tell me if she saw one?*

As they walked down the *Via Sant'Agatone Papa* to where their rental was parked, Tessa felt the glasses case in her leather jacket. She was tempted to slip them on and see for herself. *No, follow Ruth's lead. She wants me to be an obedient soldier. I can do that.*

When they arrived at the car, Ruth slipped into the driver's seat. Tessa got in and Ruth sped off, deftly weaving through the car-choked streets.

"Before we begin our surveillance, I want to show you something," Ruth said.

"Hopefully, a nice little cafe where we can have expensive pastries and tiny cups of strong coffee."

"Not exactly," Ruth said, "but I think you'll find this interesting."

Chapter 23

Tessa looked out the window at the passing city, so unlike her hometown.

Rome is so amazing. There are buildings that have been around for hundreds, even thousands of years. These streets have been walked on by millions of people going back before Christ. Being here is like being half in the past, half in the present. How many demons have prowled these streets, making life miserable for everyone?

She remembered how pleasurable the night with Dylan had been and the terror that followed the next morning.

That's how they are. Insidious. Showing us what we desire, but only to tempt us. Eventually, I need to find him and glass him. Like all of the demons, he's a threat to everyone. She allowed herself a hint of a smile. *Even if he is great in bed.*

The traffic slowed to a crawl. The sidewalks were crammed with people. The urge to slip on her glasses crept back. She looked at Ruth; she seemed to be lost in thought.

Why not? She pulled out the high impact case and put on the glasses. The city became a throbbing blur that turned the lingering remnants of the pressure she felt in the Sphere into a sharp spike of pain. She saw none of the tell-tale clarity that would indicate a demon. She put the glasses away.

"What were you doing?"

Tessa massaged her temples. The action helped push the pain away. "Just curious. You seem distracted and I was wondering why."

"You thought we were surrounded by demons?"

Tessa shrugged. "Maybe. Silva said they're attracted to big cities. More prey. It's logical they'd be in Rome."

"I'm sure there's a few out there," Ruth said, "but I've had other things on my mind."

Other things? Care to share? Tessa examined Ruth's face. The cold gaze and firm lips made it clear that wasn't going to happen. *I guess it's a need-to-know situation.*

They crossed the Tiber river and left the crush of downtown Rome. They soon were in the suburban neighborhoods to the southeast. They were heading to the *Parco Regionale Appia Antica*, a 16-kilometer long finger of green that pointed to the heart of Rome. It followed the Appian Way, one of the great roads of the Roman Empire, and encompassed the relics and ruins of Italy's past.

Ruth's destination was on the outskirts of the park. Nestled in a copse of trees off the Via Ardeatina was a nondescript corrugated metal building surrounded by a tall fence. Ruth pulled up to the gate. She entered a code into a pole-mounted keypad and the gate slid open. Ruth parked in the small gravel lot next to the building.

"What's this?"

"Someplace special," Ruth said, getting out of the car.

Tessa hesitated a moment. *This is creepy; but if Ruth wanted to do something to me, she could have just tossed me off a cliff back at the Academy. She needs me, I have to remember that. Hunters are rare.*

Ruth took a few steps, then turned and looked at Tessa. She didn't make any other motion; just stared.

Fine. Let's do this James Bond shit. Tessa got out of the car and closed the door with just enough force to make it clear she was getting fed up.

Ruth either didn't notice or didn't care. She walked to the shed, her white leather boots crunching the gravel. Tessa trailed after her, hoping that what Ruth had to show her was worth her enigmatic behavior.

There was another keypad next to the door. Ruth punched in a lengthy number sequence and entered. Tessa followed, the door closing behind her with a loud clack of the lock sliding into place. The interior was empty except for a marble sepulcher in the exact center. A weathered cross over the doorway was the only adornment. The entrance was covered by a metal gate. Ruth opened it and entered.

Tessa poked her head in. She was only slightly surprised to see a flight of stone stairs leading into the earth. Ruth was standing next to the opening in the ground, holding a flashlight. Tessa noticed a charging station with three more flashlights against the wall.

"Take one," Ruth said, "and follow me." She started down the stairs.

"Sure," Tessa muttered, "Why not follow you into another underground lair."

Tessa focused the light on the stairs. They were narrow and worn. Tessa wanted to make certain she didn't slip on the way down. Ruth was waiting for her at the bottom, in a tunnel of raw rock.

"What is this place?"

"This is part of the Catacombs of Saint Domitilla. If you walk far enough, you'll find a metal gate. Beyond that gate is the part of this complex that the public knows about. This side … this is for the Enochian Curia."

She started to walk down the tunnel. Tessa followed. As she shone her flashlight over the walls, she saw there were shelves carved into them. She was not surprised to see bones on the shelves. She knew that people had used catacombs for burial.

"Are these hunters?"

"Yes."

The tunnel widened into a large room. The floor was covered by a mosaic that Tessa could only partially make out. Tiles were arranged in the form of leering demons, valiant hunters and winged angels in Heaven looking down on a world at war.

"This is where I started the Curia." Ruth faced Tessa. "When I came to Earth, I wandered. Alexandria, Jerusalem, Byzantium,

Athens ... I hunted demons, fighting the war alone. But when I arrived in Rome, I found the early Christians. They were still a cult, hounded by the pagans and existing in secret, even when they held positions of power. I knew this was the place to recruit hunters from among people who had faith and understood the need for secrecy."

Ruth focused her light on a long, narrow slot in the wall. "That's where I slept for years. This place was the center of the war. A few of us, hiding from the authorities, hunting demons."

She sounds wistful. "Why am I here?"

"I wanted to share this with you. This place is important to me. No matter where I travel, part of me will always be here, living in the shadows of the past." Her gaze hardened. "I have been fighting this war a long time. I need you to understand your role. You're important. But you are also mortal. The only question about your death is when it will happen."

"You give shitty pep talks."

"Tessa, why do you think I brought you here?"

Tessa sighed. "Because I didn't sit in the van while Arno and Desange got killed."

Tessa was surprised when Ruth shook her head. "No. I read your report and Arno's. His actions were questionable and his assessment of your role was wrong. I'm dealing with him." Ruth looked down at the mosaic. She focused her light on a winged figure wearing a silver breastplate and wielding a flaming sword. "You know, that's supposed to be me. I never had a flaming sword."

Tessa laughed. "Well, that's disappointing. No wings either."

Ruth squatted down and touched the chipped tile likeness of her face. "History crushes us all. We stop being who we are and start being what we did."

Tessa thought she sounded sad. *What is going on in her head? She's been fighting for centuries. I was in Iraq for less than a year and it stressed me out. What is it like to fight a 2000-year-long war?*

Ruth straightened up. "You can't understand the stakes of what we are doing. Not really."

"I thought we were fighting to save souls."

Ruth nodded. "You are. But there is more than that."

Tessa studied Ruth's face. The cold eyes seemed to look past her, at some point in distant space. "Tell me."

For a long moment, there was silence. Tessa grew certain that Ruth was going to remain quiet, to keep her thoughts to herself.

Ruth nodded. "If we lose, the world won't just become more sinful. It will become Hell. Mankind was meant to exist in balance, the good and evil impulses countering each other. If you were nothing but your virtues, the world would be sterile. Dead. That won't do. That's not what creation is for." She pointed at the demon made from bits of tile. "If they win, however, the world won't be sterile. It will be every nightmare your race has conceived of. Every genocide and torture chamber. Every rape and murder. Every atrocity from the worst moments of your history. That's the future if we lose."

Tessa took a moment to let that sink in. The Curia's indoctrination focused on the spiritual stakes of the war. Although she knew that demons spread misery, she had never thought of the consequences in such apocalyptic terms. The question that followed was reflexive, a residue of her Catholic upbringing.

"But God won't let that happen, right? He won't let the Devil win. That would be ... evil."

"God is beyond those things. His plan is unknowable. If God didn't want there to be a war, there wouldn't be one." Ruth took a step toward Tessa and leaned close. "Do you really want to gamble that your sense of right and wrong is the same as God's? Or, do you want to fight for your future?"

Tessa bristled at the question. "You know I want to fight."

Ruth straightened. "Good ... but to be effective you need to change. You're here because you are impulsive. You have shown poor judgment at crucial times. Your affair with Tyler and your drug overdose are only two examples of a lifetime of poor choices. It's a pattern that is bigger than your mistakes in Paris and Copenhagen."

Tessa started to defend herself, but Ruth held up her hand. Tessa's response died unspoken.

Ruth saw her aura flash red and violet, showing anger and surprise. "Don't bother to make excuses. I have heard them all." Seeing Tessa's aura calm down and a look on her face that indicated she was ready to listen, Ruth lowered her hand and continued. "The Curia has survived because hunters adapt. You made your decision in Copenhagen for reasons you felt were valid. But that's the problem. You *felt* they were valid. It is the same impulsiveness that led you to value pleasure over prudence in Paris."

Ruth turned abruptly and walked over to her former sleeping cubby. She could remember nights spent in the dark, wrapped in the fetid air of unwashed bodies, oily smoke and decaying corpses. She remembered each sensation with perfect clarity. Every experience was as vivid as the moment it happened. She envied humanity's ability to forget.

She heard the click of Tessa's heels as she walked up behind her.

"I know I've made shitty calls," Tessa said. "My relationship with Tyler, the overdose, getting sloppy in Paris ... but I don't think Copenhagen was a bad call. I don't want to lie to you just to tell you what you want to hear."

"You went in because you were afraid that Desange was going to die. Once engaged, you made a tactical decision based on that same fear." She closed her eyes. The faces of every hunter for the past two thousand years cascaded across her memory. "Have you seen anyone die?"

Tessa felt her chest tighten as she remembered the dead in Iraq. Her friend Martinez, his shredded and crushed body in the ruins of the TOC. Even now, she remembered vividly how he stopped looking real after he was blown up. *Like a doll.* "Yes."

Ruth turned to face Tessa. "Let me show you something." She reached out and took Tessa's hand. The shift in vision came faster than it had the first time on the cliff in Mykines. The shadows of the crypt were impenetrable darkness. Tessa wanted to wrap the warm light of Ruth around her. An arm of blazing white light pointed. "Look."

Tessa turned her head. In the center of the room was a man-shaped hole in space. She felt like she was being drawn to the void, a nauseating feeling of emptiness. As she stared, she realized that there was more than just darkness to the shape. She saw threads of orange light squirming in the nullity, like worms in a corpse.

"What is it?"

"On November second, in the year 438, Lucius Atticus died here. He died in fear, as many humans do. He was a hunter. He died when a demon shattered his ribs. Friends of the Curia brought him here, hoping I could heal him. But I was out finding new hunters, new soldiers for the war. By the time I returned, he was already dead. I see them all. Where they died. This remnant of their lives lasts forever. The part of the aura that gives you the ability to be a hunter imprints itself in space. Wherever I go, they're waiting. The ones who fought for me, and the ones who died without knowing the abilities they possessed."

"That must be hard to live with," Tessa said. She wanted Ruth to let go of her, for the vision to fade. She also felt grateful that Ruth was sharing this part of herself. "To see ghosts wherever you go."

Ruth released Tessa. The black shape faded, as her vision returned to normal.

"Ghosts ... I suppose they are. When I see them, I know what their last moments were like. What they felt and thought while they were dying."

Tessa felt sorry for Ruth. *How can anyone deal with that? Even an angel must have limits.* "How do you live with seeing these things?"

When Ruth replied, Tessa detected a stiffness, like she was saying something that was a rote answer and not a reflection of her true feelings. "I've been here for 2000 years. I've seen millions of people die, in every way possible. I am the only thing in this world that does not end." She paused.

The silence pressed in on Tessa, until it became an uncomfortable, suffocating weight. *Is that what she really thinks? She must be so lonely.* She wanted to help Ruth, but didn't know how. *Just reach out.* "You're not alone. You have us. We follow you because we believe in your mission."

When Ruth replied, her voice was soft and low. "I know you think I'm cold. Hunters always do. It's because I have to be. And so do you. It is the only way to win the war. Demons are skilled tempters who prey on emotion. The second you show them your true feelings, they will use them to their advantage."

"I thought you didn't want robots. Emotions make us human."

Ruth placed her hand back on Tessa's shoulder. She tensed up; but Ruth did not allow Tessa to see through her eyes. Instead, she squeezed.

"I want thoughtful, dedicated warriors. I do not want someone who leads with their heart. That's what you do."

Tessa found Ruth's grip becoming uncomfortable. She tried to shrug it off, but Ruth didn't let go.

"You could be a proficient hunter. You could save more of your kind than you'll ever know." The grip tightened a little more. "But that won't happen if you let your heart overrule your head. Was it smart to get involved with Tyler?"

"No."

"Was it smart to turn to drugs and alcohol to solve your problems? To be led into danger by your desire for physical pleasure?"

"No."

"And was it smart for you to let your feelings for Desange lead you to lose focus on the mission, which is to kill demons?"

Tessa paused. "Yes, because by saving Desange, he will go on to kill many more demons in his career as a hunter. I know it. He's very loyal to the mission."

Ruth let go of Tessa's shoulder. She stepped back. "In time, you will come around to my way of thinking. Marit is out there, tempting more souls. Who knows when she'll resurface again and be in a vulnerable enough position for a hunter to take her out."

Tessa rubbed her shoulder. "And if I don't?"

Ruth smiled. It was thin and sharp and not comforting. "These crypts are filled with hunters who fought with passion and bravery and died far too soon." The smile faded, submerged by her default placidity. "But I have faith in you. You'll come around."

Tessa didn't say anything. The two women looked at each other, eyes glowing in the harsh light, then lost in the shadowy gloom. For a moment, Tessa felt the same unease that struck her when Marit had looked at her. *It's like I'm not really here to her. I'm an expendable pawn.*

Ruth motioned toward the tunnel with a nod. "It's getting late. Let's find someplace for dinner and then go to our hotel. We can start our surveillance operations in the morning."

Tessa led the way back to the stairs. She saw grinning skulls and heaped bones out of the corner of her eyes. She felt the presence of Ruth behind her, something cold, ancient and alien.

A sudden, inexplicable fear gripped her. *If I turn around, I'll see something horrible lurking in the darkness.* She shook the feeling off. *Ruth is being a hardass because she wants me to be an effective hunter, and I can respect that. I have a bias toward action, for better or worse. Ruth thinks that could get me killed. I think that might protect me. The only way to know for certain is to start hunting.*

Tessa sat on the tiny balcony of the apartment she shared with Ruth. It was a few days after her trip to the catacombs. She accompanied Ruth every day on her reconnaissance and surveillance operation. In the evening, Ruth left her to her own devices. Tessa located a few nice restaurants and bars in the area. She kept her excursions to the latter under control. An after-dinner drink, some light flirting and then back to the apartment. Ruth was merciless when it came to getting up in the morning.

She was sipping a cordial glass of port, a digestif before turning in. *Not exactly the booze and fuck fest I had planned. I feel like a nun.* She smiled at the weight of the dagger on her hip. *A heavily armed nun.*

Her phone chimed. She thought it was going to be Ruth and was surprised when she saw an unknown but secure number. *Huh ... maybe Desange.*

"Hello?"

"Hi, Tessa. This is Lars."

She had almost written off her request for information on Dylan. *I thought he got cold feet. I guess I haven't lost my charm.*

"Lars. How are things going in the mole hole?"

"Okay. I took a look at the surveillance records for Paris. Given what you told me, I think I have your demon."

"Great. Were you able to track him?"

There was silence. For a moment, Tessa thought the call might have been dropped. When Lars spoke, his voice was uneven, worried. "No. At least, I'm not going to."

"Why not?"

"Someone put a lock on his file. I've never seen that before."

"Someone," Tessa said. "Ruth."

"It has to be. Look, I don't know what's going on. I don't want to know. Please, don't contact me again."

Lars hung up. Tessa stared at the blank screen for a moment, then slipped the phone into her pocket.

Why would Ruth do that? Is she trying to protect me? Or is there something else going on? She sighed and finished her port. *Well, I'm not going to learn anything else tonight. And whatever Ruth has going on in her head, I know one thing – she'll be getting me up at oh-dark-thirty. I'll sleep on this and see what happens.*

Chapter 24

Tessa stood in the center of Desange's empty bedroom. It looked like her room had when she arrived: bare walls, a neatly made bed, an empty desk and chair. All of his personal touches were gone – the photo of his family that he kept on his desk and his stack of *The Economist* magazines that he faithfully read.

It's not going to be the same without him. He's really my only close friend at the Academy. Tessa kept most people at a distance. In her deeper moments of introspection, she realized her upbringing had not predisposed her to trust that people genuinely cared. With Desange, she knew he cared and hoped he realized the feeling was mutual. *I risked my life fighting a demon for him. Would I have done the same for another recruit?*

Feeling lonely, she went back into the living room and sat at the dining table, shifting her mind to more practical matters. She still had to review the information packet for her recruit. Although she had access to it before her assignment in Rome, she only gave it a cursory glance prior to leaving. Being under the watchful eye of an angel over the holiday hadn't allowed her enough mental energy to really sit and think about how she was going to mentor a new recruit. *I need to stop procrastinating.* She opened the packet.

Kim Min-Seo, South Korean, 22, Orphan, Atheist. Detected by the Surveillance and Analysis Directorate in 2010. Studying physics at Sungkyunkwan University. Scheduled for entry in 2011, but delayed for one year due to immediate intervention needed for another recruit. Tessa realized she was the recruit that had taken Kim Min-Seo's place. *Shit. Does she know? Why would Ruth assign her to me?*

She thought about asking to have Min reassigned, but dismissed the idea. *This is one of Ruth's tests. I should have known that shadowing her in Rome wouldn't be the end. This is another way to push me and see how I respond.*

She looked at the enclosed photo. It showed a young woman with a narrow face and intense eyes, framed by long layers. Her lips hinted at a smile, one that was at odds with the keen gaze.

Should I tell her? It may not even be a problem. It wasn't my decision to delay her entry. I can't be faulted for that.

Tessa flashed back to her bleak days in Detroit a year ago. She saw herself wiping down the bar at the Blue Ox at 2am in the dead of winter. As the memory grew more vivid, she could smell the cheap beer and cigarettes on her last call customers. She wondered what this recruit had been doing in South Korea at the same time she was in Detroit. *She was packing and eager to come to the Academy, while I was overdosing.*

She closed the folder, coming back to the present. *Once I feel her out, I'll decide whether to inform her or not.*

She had her training schedule for the year. She read through it, focusing on the session titles and instructors. *Advanced Demonology – Juan Silva, Advanced Combatives – Uri Deneberg, Advanced Tradecraft – Svetlana Ivanov.* The final entry read *Special Studies – Father Ian McKenna.* Desange told her that in the second year, she would be given specific training in the skills she would need to function in her area of responsibility. She'd also find out in this class what region she'd be assigned to as a hunter.

Tessa was not looking forward to spending time with McKenna. He repeatedly made subtle attempts to get her to embrace her Catholic roots, something she had no interest in revisiting. She had grown to find the priest's manner disingenuous. What she first thought was a natural warmth and charisma eventually seemed more calculated. She realized that every interaction with him was like talking to a used car salesman. She preferred the directness of Ruth, a personality trait she was beginning to understand better.

I might be short with people too if the responsibility for winning the war between good and evil rested primarily on my shoulders.

Tessa hadn't forgotten Ruth's implication that she was the only angelic ambassador on Earth for hundreds of years. *If the war is so critical to Heaven, shouldn't God send more angels to help fight this battle? Ruth never said there weren't other angels, but she has only talked about her time on Earth. Silva indicated other angels lived in Heaven, but never mentioned their involvement on Earth. There's a huge information gap here. This year, I'm going to get some answers. I've earned that much.*

The next morning, Tessa was sitting in the cafeteria with Laila and April, trading stories of their vacations over eggs benedict. Tessa shared the details of her fight with Marit. She didn't want rumors to start, having experienced their corrosive effect in the Army. She also wanted to make it clear that she did not think what she did was wrong. But opening up to her fellow recruits had caused them to ask more detailed questions about her time in Rome with Ruth, and that was something Tessa felt uneasy about.

There is a difference between telling the recruits about the details of my fight in Copenhagen and what Ruth shared with me in confidence in Rome. The former was her business. It let her fellow hunters know what her priorities were and, by telling them of the mistakes as well, could help them do better in the field. While a few looked at her with apparent unease – judging her for the perceived failure – the rest seemed to accept what she did. Laila and April were two of those who understood and supported her actions.

After telling the two ladies her diluted version of Rome, she asked how their holidays went. April launched into a lively tale of her backpacking trip in the Rocky Mountains with her brothers. Tessa was only half listening.

I've had enough of sleeping in tents. She felt anxious, biting her cheek. *I should tell them about Rome. Everything. They deserve to know how high the stakes really are. But Ruth must have a reason for telling me and not them. I just wish I knew what it is.*

"And then the bear stole our box of Hot Pockets. I really wanted to kick its ass. But, you know, bear."

Laila laughed at April's story. Tessa realized she had been so lost in thought that she'd missed most of it, but laughed anyway.

"Okay, how about you, Laila?" asked Tessa. "Any exciting tales of debauchery?"

Laila had gone to Athens with a couple of other recruits and Tessa was interested in hearing how the trip had gone. However, before she could start, Ruth approached the table.

"Sorry to interrupt," she said, not sounding sorry at all, "but I need to speak to Tessa. Come with me."

Tessa pushed back from the table. "Let's meet up later in the lounge. I'll introduce Min-Seo to you."

She followed Ruth out of the cafeteria and down the hall to the elevator. They rode in silence to her second-floor office.

"I'm pleased with your performance in Rome. This coming year will be very important for you, both as a hunter and mentor. I know that you will do a good job."

"Thank you." *Wow, a compliment from Ruth. I guess I'm freed from timeout.*

"I do have one concern." Ruth smiled slightly. It was not comforting. "Will this year include further communication with Tyler Caplan?"

Where did this come from? "He's my friend. You've read my psych profile. I don't have many of those. Throw me a bone, Ruth. I'm not violating OPSEC."

"It matters who you are connected to outside the Curia." She opened the MacBook on her desk. "You haven't said or written anything that breaches security. However, you've toed the line a few times. I am concerned that your relationship with Mr Caplan could result in a security breach. When under the stressors of an active hunt, slip-ups can happen."

They've been monitoring my comms? Of course they have. They pay the phone bills. "I understand the top-secret nature of our work." She shrugged. "Besides, if I told him I'm training to hunt demons, he'd think I was delusional."

"He's a loose end." Ruth closed the laptop. "I do not like loose ends."

"Are you ordering me to stop talking to him?"

Ruth stared at her. She shook her head, a sharp, clipped motion. "Not at the moment, but I would hate to have an accidental security breach. It would be unpleasant for everyone." The uncomfortable smile returned. "You understand."

"I won't do or say anything to compromise our mission. You have my word."

"Good. Your loyalty is important to the long-term success of our operations on Earth. Now go prepare for Ms Kim's arrival."

Tessa rose stiffly and left. When she got back to her room, she slumped onto the couch. *I need to be careful with anyone outside the Curia. The safest thing to do would be to let Tyler go.* She saw his kind brown eyes, staring at her inquisitively from across the dusty DFAC table as they analyzed the latest book she was reading. *If only it were that easy. He's my only tie left to the old, normal world.*

She looked at her iPhone and saw that it was almost time for Min-Seo to arrive. *Right now, she's landing in the abandoned village. She'll be walking through the doors to our dormitory soon, expecting me to help her transition into the Curia. I need to get my head straight. I mentored people in Iraq. They depended on me, just like Min-Seo will. Just like I depended on Desange. I'll have time to worry about Tyler later.*

She grabbed a mango juice out of the refrigerator and returned to reading Min-Seo's file. She was still bothered that the Curia paired her with the woman she replaced. Combined with Ruth's barely veiled threat, it made Tessa's effort to focus difficult.

The door opened and Ruth entered. A petite woman followed her in. "Tessa, this is Kim Min-Seo, your new roommate. I trust you will mentor her well." Ruth turned to Min-Seo. "Tessa will help you settle in and show you around, as well as guide you through your first year of training."

Ruth left, closing the door behind her. Min-Seo smiled nervously.

She must feel the way I did. Confused, wondering how real this is. Desange held my hand. I need to hold Min-Seo's.

"Hi, you can call me Min." The girl smiled, extending her hand. Her voice was soft and her English had a distinct accent.

Tessa shook her hand. "Let me show you around first."

She helped Min with her bags, then took her to the classroom level. "This is where you'll spend most of your time. Once the weather is nicer, Uri likes to hold combatives training outside."

"I see," Min said. "This is not what I expected."

"Oh? Not impressed?"

Min laughed. "Nothing like that. It just seems so..."

"Ordinary."

Min nodded. "In my head, I thought it would be like a Christian monastery or a high-tech base. Or maybe Hogwarts."

Tessa laughed. "I know the feeling. It all seems so mysterious when you fly in, land in a ghost town and then go through the chapel, especially that confessional booth elevator – very James Bond. But once you're here, it's institutional."

"What's the library like? Ruth said we have access to the Curia's archives."

"That's right," Tessa said, "but the main archives are in Rome."

Min looked at Tessa sharply. "Really?"

Tessa thought the look odd, although since she had just met Min she couldn't guess why. "Yes. The Curia's primary operations and intelligence center is located there. You'll learn all about that in Ivanov's class."

"I see." For a moment, Min looked downcast. Then she perked up. "Well, I look forward to seeing what they have.

I'm something of a history buff; the Curia's library must be fascinating."

"I've only used it to write papers for class. Can't say I've spent much time there beyond that to fully appreciate its offerings. I can show it to you on the tour. It's on the same floor as the classrooms."

As they entered the elevator, Min said, "Ruth told me you fought a demon."

Here we go. At least Ruth left out that I fucked a demon. "That's true."

"What was it like?"

"Terrifying." She thought for a moment. "And exciting. Did Ruth tell you how it turned out?"

Min shook her head.

"My mentor and I were injured and the demon escaped."

"I see." Min exited the elevator, studying her surroundings.

Tessa thought she detected a judgmental tone in Min's voice. *Just wait until you face one of those things.* "You'll be taught about how dangerous demons are; the reality is worse. I shot the demon a dozen times and she barely reacted. It was like the bullets were absorbed. The speed was incredible. And the strength," she frowned, thinking about the pain she had felt for weeks, "it was like getting hit by a truck."

"When you shot the creature, did you notice any odd effects? Any optical distortions?"

That's a weird question. "Not that I recall. Why?"

"Oh, just curious." She smiled, a tight, thin curl of the lips.

She doesn't want to share what is on her mind. I can't blame her. I wasn't very trusting when I arrived either.

"I've been wondering about something. Since you are my mentor, do you know why I was delayed entry for a year? I asked Ruth, but she didn't answer. Since she is the only member of the Curia I've met before today, I had nowhere else to turn for information. Could you find out for me?"

Great. I might as well get this over with. "Let's go to the lounge."

The lounge was empty and the bar was closed. However, soft drinks and snacks had been left out, as usual. Tessa grabbed a couple of Cokes from a tub of ice and a bag of chips. She led Min to a booth and then slid in.

"Okay." She paused for a moment, hoping that Min wouldn't resent her. "I'm the reason your entry was delayed."

Min didn't react, other than to cock her head to one side. "What do you mean?"

Tessa sighed. "It's a long story." She spent the next hour filling Min in on her year in Detroit. She knew it was a lot to share with a person she had just met, but Tessa wanted to start her relationship off right with Min. *The Curia has enough secrets as it is.*

She described how Ruth saved her life, her trip to the Academy, and gave an overview of the first year, leaving out her moonlight embrace with Desange and her sexual encounter with Dylan. *Not necessary details.* By the time she was done, Min, who said little, was slumped in the booth, a grin lighting up her face.

"Wow," she said. "I understand why the Curia saw you as a priority." She straightened up. "You don't know me, but you just shared a lot. And you could have kept the truth to yourself. Many people would have to spare themselves embarrassment. Thank you for being honest."

Tessa felt better. "Once I found out who you were, I felt guilty as hell."

"It wasn't your decision. And it gave me the chance to finish my degree." She sipped her Coke. "It doesn't look like they have any traditional educational programs here."

Tessa shook her head. "No, it's all demons, knife fighting and surveillance. Some psychology too."

"See, it all worked out," Min said. Her smile broadened, this time with a devilish glint in her eyes. "Of course, I reserve the right to throw it in your face if I'm feeling bitchy."

Tessa laughed. "Understood. You fight dirty."

Min grinned. "Is there another way to fight?"

Tessa felt some of her unease dissipate. *She seems pretty cool.* "I've arranged to have you meet some other recruits at dinner. Would you like to get some rest or do you have any other questions?"

"I have many questions, but I wouldn't mind settling in and getting my room in order." She reached across the table, touching the hand that Tessa had on her drink. "I'm really looking forward to getting to know you and everyone here. This is going to be an adventure."

Chapter 25

Tessa was in the lounge. It was late – after last call – and she was drinking a cup of black coffee and reading *Priest*, a South Korea *manhwa* that Min had recommended. The black and white comic dealt with a struggle between mankind and fallen angels. Although Tessa had never been into comic books, she found the theme and art to be reflective of the battle she was training for against the demons.

Her phone rang. It was Desange. This was the first call she'd gotten from him since his assignment to the African cell. He had mentioned in an earlier text that he would try to call her today around this time. The lounge at 2am was about as private as the island got, outside of the abandoned village.

"Hi," she said.

"Tessa, it's great to hear your voice. How are you doing?"

"Good. You were right about the course work getting harder in the second year. Everything is turned up to ten. But at least I know where I'm getting assigned now."

"Oh, where's that?"

"Los Angeles. They have me working on film production in my Special Studies class. Back-end stuff. Right now, I'm focusing on the business side, although McKenna said I'd be learning some filmmaking as well. I bet Hollywood is riddled with demons."

Desange laughed. "They sure know how to make money from it. *The Exorcist, Rosemary's Baby, Insidious*."

"All those demons are grotesque." Tessa flashed back to Dylan – his dark wavy hair, captivating green eyes and faded Ramones T-shirt, fitted just enough to accentuate his biceps. *Dylan looked like a Mediterranean model.*

"The demons working in the film industry have played into our stereotypes. Keeps their true intentions under the radar. You'll be a busy hunter once you get out there."

"Yeah, I've never been to California. Hopefully I'll get some time to relax at the beach. Who knows, maybe I'll take up surfing. Might as well show off my combatives body."

Desange sighed. "I'm a little envious. LA is a lot nicer than here."

"Are you still in the Ivory Coast?" Tessa worried about Desange. The West African region that he primarily operated in was not particularly safe, even without demons. A civil war was being fought in Mali and another had recently ended in Ivory Coast.

"Yeah, for now. A demon stirred up shit here."

"What's it like out in the field?" asked Tessa.

"Like Ivanov told us, it's a lot of surveillance work, often without a payoff."

"So, no demon kills yet?"

There was a moment of silence. "I never said that."

Tessa perked up. "Seriously? You got one?"

"Yes, there is one less greed demon in the world."

"Wow," Tessa said, genuinely impressed, "that's great to hear. I can't wait to get out there and rack up some kills."

Desange's voice hardened. "Tessa, this is serious business. The things I have seen … the misery these creatures spread. It's not a game of scoring points."

That was insensitive. He may be a little traumatized. He came from business school in Paris and a healthy upper-middle class family. "Don't worry, I'll keep my head on straight. Do you think you can take a break, just to relax a bit? Go to Morocco? I hear they have some nice resorts."

Desange, realizing how harsh he sounded, was grateful to change the topic. "That's a good idea, I'll look into it. I found a gym near my apartment and I'm using that to destress. You should see me now, I'm in better shape than I was in the Academy."

She laughed. "Oh, please send me a pic, from the pool in Morocco. Seriously, I know you can be a bit of a workaholic. You don't want to burn out your first year in the field. Take a break."

Desange laughed. "Yes, ma'am. You're right, but you'll see when you get into the field and connect with your cell leader. There are so many demons and so few of us to fight them. The sense of responsibility will weigh on you, especially when you see just how many people they are influencing."

"What type of demons are operating in your region?"

"Oh, Africa has it all, but lots of greed and anger. There is plenty of work for us."

"The only boring part of demon hunting is running surveillance. Remember those long nights with Arno in Copenhagen?" asked Tessa.

"That turned me off NesCafe for life."

"It's an acquired taste." Tessa looked down at her empty coffee mug and contemplated a refill. She decided she'd need to get to sleep at some point soon so resisted the urge.

"How is your recruit doing?" Desange asked.

Tessa assumed Desange knew that she had replaced Min. She decided to bring it up, not wanting there to be anything hanging between her and Desange. "I know my unusual recruitment is what bumped her to the next class. We talked about it and she understands. She said she appreciated my transparency."

There was a pause on the other end of the phone. "Well, that's good."

"Yeah. It would have been helpful to mention this to me, but whatever. I dealt with it." Tessa could tell she was sounding more irritable than she had meant to. *I assume he was ordered to remain quiet by Ruth.*

"Tessa, I'm tired. I just came off an active hunt. Why are you picking a fight? If you want the truth, I had been preparing to receive Min-Seo for weeks and you were dropped on me at the last minute. It was hard on me at first, but you ended up being the best thing that happened to me at the Academy. We were meant to train together and Min was meant to be with you. God has a reason for how things played out."

"Sorry, I'm getting tired. And I really miss you. It's hard not being able to hang out with my best friend."

"I miss you too," Desange said. *There is nothing more to say about this,* he thought. *Separation from the people you care about comes with the job.* He decided to refocus the conversation on something tangible. "How is Min settling into her studies?"

"Pretty good. She's smart, but she sucks at combatives. Uri has asked me to do extra sessions with her to get her up to speed."

"She's in good hands."

"I don't know about that. I fucked up with Marit."

"Fighting demons is hard work. Go easy on yourself. You held your own in Copenhagen. You are a strong fighter. Others would have been killed by Marit given the same situation. You break the mold, Tessa."

Tessa laughed. "I tend to think that I just break things." She paused. "You're in my thoughts too. I wish I could be there to help." She felt a sad longing beginning to rise. *I don't want to feel like that. Not about him.* "So, how is your family?"

"I was told by my mother that you need to visit. Apparently, you made a great impression."

"Maybe we can coordinate a vacation this summer?" Tessa smiled, happy at the thought of spending time with Desange and his family again. "I need to meet your dad and brother."

"I know, they'd love to meet you. You'll have to watch out for my brother though. He's something of a … player, is that the right word?"

"Yes, sounds like my kind of guy." Tessa laughed.

"You're incorrigible."

"At least we know your brother's a human."

"Well, he has that going for him. I hope you are using your glasses more now."

"Yes, I'm practicing safe sex, Enochian Curia style. I mean, not that I'm getting any here. Too much potential for drama." Tessa yawned. "Sorry, I'm getting punchy. I'm fading. My extra training for Min starts early."

"No problem, I have to go anyway. We should make this a regular thing. Texting is fine, but this is more personal. It's great to hear your voice."

"I'd like that. It was nice catching up. Be careful, okay? And save a few demons for me to slay."

"Will do. Goodnight, Tessa."

"Goodnight."

She placed the phone on the table. Talking to Desange felt comfortable – natural. Her happiness was tinged with sadness; she knew any relationship with him would be tenuous, negotiated over phones and emails, with only occasional time together. While her suggestion of Morocco was well-intentioned, she imagined vacations were few and far between for an active hunter. But she trusted him more than anyone else in the Curia, and she needed that kind of friend. Desange was mission-focused, but he was loyal too. She'd like to think that if he had been in her shoes in Copenhagen, he would have also chosen to save her over killing Marit. She couldn't be certain, but something told her he had her back, no matter what.

***

"Uri hates me." Min dropped her gym bag on the floor and sat heavily on one of the lounge chairs. She looked deflated.

Tessa was lying on the couch, reading a report on a multi-cell surveillance and combat mission from 1989 that Ivanov handed out as homework. As the Berlin Wall was falling, hunters on three continents killed a dozen demons in a series of coordinated strikes. The operation had been a success, but Ivanov thought it could have been managed better. The assignment was to locate the flaws and present a revised plan. This was the kind of exercise Tessa loved. It highlighted her strengths of analysis and planning.

"Uri doesn't hate you." Tessa closed the report folder. She walked over to Min and sat in the other chair. She noticed that Min had a black eye forming, but didn't point it out.

"Every class, he uses me as an example of what not to do. Whenever he wants to demonstrate a fighting technique, I'm the one he calls on." She jabbed a finger at her bruised eye. "Evidence."

Tessa could sympathize, but she knew that Min didn't need hand-holding. "Uri is trying to give you the tools to survive in the field. That's it. He's a former IDF soldier, so he isn't the most touchy-feely guy. He is focused on you because you're not very good at fighting and he doesn't want you to get killed by a demon."

Min sighed. "I see. I'm beginning to think I'd make a better analyst than a hunter. I mean, there are some things that just aren't fixable. I'm petite; I can barely fight a person. What if this is the best— "

Tessa raised a hand to stop her. "You'll get better. You just need to work at it and play on your strengths. Being small can be an advantage. Remember, all you need is one good stab with the dagger. You're smart. There are lots of clever ways to catch a demon off guard."

"If I went up against a demon today, it would tear me apart." Min tried to maintain her defeatist attitude, but the logic of Tessa's statement eventually won out. After a few moments

8

she smirked. "Maybe we should have another sparring session tonight after dinner?"

"Definitely. How are your other classes going?"

"Really good. I like Silva. He provides useful information about the Curia and demons that are lacking in the other classes."

From her personnel file, Tessa knew Min was an atheist. She wondered how her beliefs were affected by what the Curia was teaching her. She decided to gently probe her and see if she wanted to talk about it. "It is a lot to take in, to find out that there is a war between angels and demons on Earth for our souls. It doesn't fit neatly with any one religion or lack of one, does it?"

"I'm not convinced that the spiritual explanation is correct. In fact, the revelation that no organized religion is correct indicates some other conclusion."

"How so?"

"If there is a God with a specific set of goals who can send emissaries to Earth, why wouldn't those emissaries create a religion that directly reflects its values? And if there is a God that resembles the Christian idea, why allow demons to come to Earth in the first place? The religious explanation raises more questions than it answers."

"I've had similar questions. But I've seen demons up close. We've both interacted with an angel. That does indicate—"

"It indicates that there are creatures on Earth that identify themselves as angels and demons. Nothing more." She smiled mischievously. "Unless you know something I don't."

"I grew up Catholic, but I'm not sure what I believe anymore. Other than the fact that demons and angels are real and they're using Earth as their battleground." She held up her hand when Min started to object. "What I'm calling angels and demons."

Min rubbed her temple. She rose to get an ice pack from the fridge. "I don't denigrate people for being religious. You read my file, so you know I was raised in a Presbyterian orphanage. I was impressed by their kindness, even if their beliefs didn't make sense." She shrugged. "Maybe there is something bigger out there, but ultimately, any entity resembling a God would be unknowable to us. Ever read Lovecraft?"

Tessa shook her head.

"You should check some out. Start with the *Call of Cthulhu*." She smiled. "If there is a God, it's probably like that. But I don't think there is. This is all just marketing."

Tessa returned the smile and nodded. She was not as certain in her beliefs but could appreciate her skeptical attitude. "Hey, I have a question. When we met, you asked if there was a visual effect when I shot Marit. Why?"

"You described a rapid change in molecular structure when you shot her." Seeing Tessa's quizzical look, Min said, "When the bullets hit the body, you described the impact wounds as rapidly closing. That would require energy, which should have manifested as a heat pulse or a photon burst. That neither of these happened indicates something else. And, before you ask, I don't know what … yet." Min stood up. "Anyway, I'm going to take a shower and put some ice on my eye. Want to grab dinner with me later?"

"Sure," Tessa said.

Min went into her room, leaving Tessa to her thoughts. She never fully accepted the Curia's explanation for the war. Part of this stemmed from her natural suspicion of people and the world in general, the rest from the absence of proof for many of the Curia's assertions. That demons were dangerous and hostile seemed true. But why there were thousands of demons on Earth but only one angel they knew of was a mystery. And what happened to a soul after death still had to be taken on faith. *Desange believes in God, but it seems more cultural than deeply felt. He is Catholic because his family is Catholic.* Tessa's beliefs were closer to Min's, although she described herself as an "agnostic with Catholic tendencies," not an atheist. Part of her hoped it was true and that at the end of life, something better was waiting.

Tessa returned to her Advanced Tradecraft studies, but the thoughts about faith, God and the true nature of the war kept surfacing. She knew if she voiced her doubts to the staff, they would either give her the party line — that God was real and took an active interest in the souls of humanity — or, in the case of Ivanov, would chide her for wasting time on existential musings when there was a war to fight. *Maybe Ivanov's right. Does it really matter if the high-level stuff is known? I've seen what the enemy can do; I should just focus on that.*

Feeling she had settled her mind for the moment, she got back to work. The mental exercise of dissecting the operation and finding the holes helped push her philosophical thoughts to the background. But that hint of something wrong, something she was missing, refused to fully go away.

Chapter 26

"You're dead." Tessa jabbed her practice dagger into Min's left side. "That's the third time in a row today. Are you okay, you seem distracted?"

Min wiped sweat off her brow, panting. "I need to get some water. Can we take a break?"

Tessa nodded, pointing to a set of empty bleachers. It was early in the morning, and they were the only ones in the gym. For the last hour, Tessa had been helping Min practice her hand-to-hand combat skills. The exercise was fairly simple. Whoever got a lethal hit with the dagger first lost the round. While Min's reflexes weren't as fast as Tessa's, today she was even more off than normal.

"I am distracted. I didn't sleep well last night. I stayed up reading some materials I found in the archives. I already suck at combatives so add on top of that four hours of sleep and you're gonna kill me every round. Sorry. I just can't stop thinking about the Curia – there are too many facts that just don't add up. I have a few questions for you."

Tessa grabbed her scuffed-up Nalgene water bottle, unscrewed the cap and took a long sip to calm her rising irritation. *This girl's questions never let up.* Min was constantly asking Tessa about the Curia and the nature of angels and demons. When Tessa would respond based on the information she had learned, Min would point out inconsistencies or knowledge gaps, refusing to take anything she was told at face value. Tessa could relate to some of Min's suspicions. She too felt there was "more to the story," but to Tessa, Min seemed driven by something else, a gremlin inside her mind that wouldn't sleep until it achieved its goal. *She's a scientist with a degree in physics. I'm not surprised that she needs to understand how everything works. But it's exhausting. And none of that matters if she gets killed by a demon in the field. It's my responsibility to help her become a better fighter.*

Min pulled apart her messy ponytail and combed her fingers through her long, dark hair. She began fidgeting with her scrunchy. "Do you think the amount of demonic influence is as great as we are told? The narrative they tell us has inherent contradictions."

This should be good. "Such as?"

Min grinned. "Glad you asked. For example, Silva said that demons have infiltrated social media so deeply that even individual posts should be questioned." She collected her hair, re-doing her ponytail. "If they are so pervasive, how can the Curia fight them? Based on the size of each class and an estimated average of 20 years' service for active hunters, the number of hunters in the field can't be more than 300. It's probably less than that, based on reasonable attrition rates from death or permanent injury."

"Not all hunts are successful, which is why improving your fighting skills is so critical." *Someone needs to tell her this. If she's this clumsy in the field, she'll end up in the graveyard above us.*

"I know, I know. Unless there are other training centers, the Curia can't be larger than a few hundred hunters and a thousand support personnel. The information we've been given implies the minimum number of demons is in the tens of thousands. And if Silva's theory of near universal infiltration is correct, that number has more weight."

Tessa nodded. "That tracks with what I've learned."

"Doesn't that seem like a completely hopeless battle? At this stage, there is no human society left, right? We live in a hybrid human-demonic world. At least, culturally and socially. Also, why are there no other angels? As far as I've been able to determine, Ruth is the only one who has been on Earth. Ever."

"I mean there's Gabriel, Michael, those dudes from Sodom and Gomorrah." Tessa laughed. "See I remember stuff from Sunday School."

"Stories with no credible data to support their actual existence." Min took a sip of her water.

Tessa leaned back into the bleachers, stretching her arms. "There could be other angels in the field that we don't know about."

Min pursed her lips. "I don't think so. I've been digging through the archives and the only angel mentioned is Ruth. And I've read a lot, hence my late nights. I know it's messing with my concentration in our morning combatives sessions, but this is important stuff."

Tessa screwed on her bottle cap. "You really haven't found any other angels mentioned in the archives?"

"There are stories of others, but the archives indicate these are myths or more commonly, demons mistaken for angels."

"That's interesting. So let's say you're right. What's your conclusion?"

Min shrugged. "I don't have a conclusion. But I know you have suspicions of the Curia too and what they've told us about the war. Something is not adding up and it's keeping me up at night. We've got to get to the bottom of this."

"The Truth is Out There." Tessa laughed, humming *The X-Files* theme song.

Min laughed. "I'm clearly Scully, just saying. You can be Mulder."

"I guess in this case, I'm the believer. It helps that I've actually encountered a demon. I've felt their strength. It's not natural, not human." Tessa reflexively massaged her neck, flashing back to Dylan choking her with the scarf – how quickly he shredded it to pieces on the busy Parisian street. And how fast he bolted through the crowd, disappearing in seconds. *He almost killed me. He could have, easily. He chose not to.*

"I'm going to keep digging, I have to know what I'm dedicating my life to. What the real story is behind the Curia."

Tessa leaned in and lowered her voice. "I'm supportive, and frankly, I agree there is more to the story. But be careful. The Curia is powerful. If they are keeping information compartmentalized, it might be for our own protection."

Min chugged her water, biting into an ice cube. "When I was a child growing up, I became obsessed about who my parents were. In my head, I had built up all these different scenarios about how I ended up in the orphanage and who my mom and dad could possibly be. I was restless. I searched through thousands of birth records in Seoul, hoping to find a clue. There was a part of me that was missing and if I could just find out who my parents were, it would all make sense. I keep searching, even in college."

"Did you ever find out who they were?"

"No. It was a – how do you say it – needle in a stack of hay. The staff at the orphanage had no idea, I was dropped on their doorstep bundled up in a bassinet. No note. I sequenced my genetics and looked through databases to see if I could find a match, but the closest I got was a fourth cousin. Then, Ruth came and recruited me at university. Suddenly, this quest to find my birth parents seemed so silly in the grand scheme of things. But my restless energy, my need to know the truth and understand what it all means to me, that remains."

"I can't relate to not knowing who my parents are, but I know what it's like to feel like you don't have a family. Growing up, my parents felt like strangers to me. I sometimes wondered if I was adopted. Was it hard growing up in an orphanage?"

Min fished out another ice cube. She felt her face and neck grow warm and rubbed the melting ice over her skin. "Being an orphan is different, like you're in a separate class of people. It marks you as an outsider in Korean society, someone without family honor. While there is no legal discrimination, being without a family makes life much harder. The orphanage I grew up in was very good, however. Many children without families live on the streets and have little future. I was lucky. The Presbyterians who ran the orphanage raised me to believe in their God, but it clearly didn't stick."

"Clearly."

"God's an unnecessary appendage of human existence, an atavistic remnant of the pre-scientific age. That's what I told my caretakers at the orphanage."

"They must have loved that."

"Oh, they did … after they looked up atavistic." Min grinned.

"Well, I don't think I'd say that to Ruth."

Min laughed. "No, I suppose not. Anyway, they were very kind to me. I learned English and they helped me get into university. I don't share their beliefs, but they'll always have my gratitude. And they put up with all my questions. They used to call me Detective Min."

Tessa glanced at the clock on the wall. "Sorry, I have to go. Father McKenna and Special Studies await." Tessa stood up and grabbed her bag. "I'll see you tonight. And please, get some rest. All the sleuthing in the world won't save you if you can't fight a demon."

"That is fair. Okay, I will do better. Have a good day." Min waved as Tessa walked off.

McKenna was waiting for Tessa in the classroom. With him was a middle-aged man wearing a black turtleneck and jeans. The two were engaged in a conversation that stopped when Tessa entered the room.

"Tessa, allow me to introduce Mike Barrington," Father McKenna said, indicating the man who was sitting on the edge of the desk. "Mike has been involved in the production end of the film industry for 20 years."

Mike gave Tessa a lopsided smile and held out his hand. "That's probably longer than you've been alive. Father McKenna, your recruits keep getting younger."

McKenna sighed. "I think we're just getting older, Mike. And I recall you being an eager young recruit once. Now I'm showing my age, I mean experience." He laughed lightly.

Tessa shook hands with Mike. "You're a hunter?"

"Was," Mike said. "Retired. I used to be assigned to the European cell." He tapped his left leg; it made a hollow, plastic sound. "A sloth demon took this off me about ten years ago. Ripped it out with his bare hands. I was already in the British film industry as my cover, so I just kept working there since I was well-networked. My position allows me to continue providing vital information to the Curia, even though I'm out of commission from hunting."

"It is a lifelong vow we take," said McKenna. "There are many ways to stay loyal to the Curia."

Mike nodded solemnly. "Yes, many ways."

It bothered Tessa that McKenna grouped himself among the hunters. He had not taken the same vow as them. She understood he served the Curia faithfully as a priest and administrator, but he was never a field operative. *Not like me or the others. He doesn't have to risk his life. He can never know what it means to be a hunter.*

"So, ready to get started? Father McKenna wants me to go over the exciting world of film financing with you today."

Tessa crossed her arms. "Exciting?"

"Well only if you run out of money." Mike smiled and motioned to a chair.

Tessa settled into her seat, taking notes as the former hunter provided an overview of various aspects of raising money for a movie and the different types of accounting that were used. While some Special Studies sessions involved equipment and practice of techniques, this was a straight-up lecture by Mike.

She paid attention, although by the end of the first thirty minutes, it had become an effort to sustain her interest.

There's no way to make accounting interesting, even in Hollywood. Most people accept you when they hear a bit of jargon, so it's good I'm learning it. But this is more involved, he's teaching me practical work knowledge. I wonder what my cover is going to end up being? Production assistant? Wardrobe? Lighting? Clearly, I'm not going to become a leading lady. My acting skills peaked at playing a tree in Ms Trotter's third grade play.

"So, think you're ready to become the next Steven Spielberg?" Mike asked as he wrapped up his lecture.

"Maybe his accountant."

Mike grinned. "I know this is deathly boring, but the key to being a good hunter is the ability to move through as many social circles as possible. Demons are in all walks of life and it can take time to get close to them. They have worked to develop their own surveillance network to identify and track hunters. The greater the efforts you take to blend in and not blow your cover, the safer you'll be." He patted his prosthetic leg. "You don't want to end up like me."

Tessa thought about Ivanov, with her replacement limb. She had felt the power demons possessed when she fought Marit. *Is that what's in store for me? Death? Maiming?* She thought about the soldiers who had lost limbs in Iraq. Tessa didn't want to be like them. She didn't want to be like Mike.

"Tessa?"

She realized that McKenna had been calling her name.

"Is everything okay?"

Is everything okay? Are you out of your mind? I've met two former hunters with missing limbs now. "Oh, yeah. Just processing."

McKenna nodded. "Mike, I need to talk to you before you head back. Tessa, do you have any additional questions?"

She shook her head. "No, I think my brain is full for today. It was nice meeting you, Mike."

"Same here."

Tessa left the classroom. The pleasant facade on her face faded, replaced by a tight frown. She went into the nearest bathroom and sat in a stall. *It's going to be okay. You can get killed crossing a street. You're not going to wind up crippled. You're going to kill a shitload of demons and die in a blaze of glory.*

She thought about Sergeant Nichols, his mangled arm, his terrified eyes. She thought of her friends in the TOC, limbs torn off, bodies shredded. She thought of the vets she would see in Detroit, hooks for hands, stuck in wheelchairs, bodies ruined by war.

Not me. Not me. She repeated this to herself until she almost believed it.

Chapter 27

Tessa stepped over a puffin who sat in the way of her path, looking at her with beady, defiant eyes. It refused to move, letting out a sharp squawk. She was walking on the trail to the village, which topped the hills that made up the spine of the island. The abandoned town clung to the shore below. The walls were starting to feel like they were closing in on her, and after hours going over a case study Silva had given her for homework, she needed some fresh air. Summer was approaching, so the weather on the surface of Mykines was at least tolerable.

She entered the ghost town. Even in the pale sunlight, the town seemed darker, like it was shrouded in a fragment of night. She chalked this up to the bare gray wood of the decaying buildings, the bowing turf roofs and the overgrown footpaths. The windows were broken and the doors were pulled ajar by years of wind and rain. She listened to the hollow sound of the wind slipping through the empty homes and took a few deep breaths.

She made her way to the red house with the peeling paint. Despite its dilapidated state, the sod roof remained intact. She was relieved to see no other recruits had decided to go there that day. She pulled out a flask from the footlocker and took a large swig of whiskey. Then she climbed the stairs and entered one of the bedrooms. The room was empty, except for a cot and a heavy wool blanket, left by some previous recruit.

She took off her light jacket and boots and curled up beneath the blanket. The alcohol warmth was spreading, as she cocooned inside the thick wool. She took another sip from the flask and yawned. She was getting sleepy.

In the last few months, she had been dreaming about Paris. Sometimes the dreams were good, with her in bed with Dylan, feeling him inside her. Sometimes they were bad, with her standing on the sidewalk, staring into his dead eyes while he choked the life out of her.

As she felt her eyes getting heavy, she thought of the good dreams. The two of them on the balcony. How his erection felt against her ass, hot and hard. Dylan pushing inside of her, fucking her relentlessly. In his bedroom, coming inside of her. How her body shook while his strong arms enveloped her, spooning her from behind.

If I didn't have an IUD, could his sperm impregnate me? Demonic sperm. She laughed at the absurdity of it all, picturing little tadpole-like sperm with horns. She closed her eyes. *I hope I don't dream about having demon babies.* She felt herself fading into unconsciousness.

She didn't. Instead, she found herself back in Iraq, walking away from the Tactical Operations Center where she worked, Captain Tyler Caplan by her side. The sun was setting, a vast orange ball on the horizon. The *maghrib* – the Muslim call to prayer – was booming from loudspeakers across the city, mingling with the *thump thump thump* of helicopter blades and the growl of engines from a line of Humvees preparing to roll out on an evening patrol.

"Sir, I read somewhere that we should perform integrity checks on the bunkers every month. Shall we perform a quick inspection?" asked Tessa, approaching a dusty, concrete slab topped with sandbags and set into the ground. She glanced around Forward Operating Base Garry Owen. No one was in the immediate area.

Tessa slipped into the dark bunker. It smelled like diesel fuel and sweat. She turned on a battery-powered lamp hanging from the ceiling. There was a wooden bench in the center of the dugout and a first aid kit propped in a corner.

Tyler followed her inside, letting out a long breath. His deep brown eyes stared intently at Tessa. He removed her patrol cap and tucked back a loose strand of hair that had escaped from her military-style bun.

Her heart skipped, excitement building as she removed her body armor.

He doffed his patrol cap, revealing his sun-kissed dirty blond hair. Then he removed his body armor. "No need for this in a bunker, I suppose."

Tessa laughed. "It's awfully hot in here." She looked at him and unzipped her camouflage jacket, dropping the mottled tan and gray garment to the ground.

He followed her lead, pulling off his jacket and shirt. His abs were sweaty and cut, hardened by hours spent in the gym to kill time. "We can't be gone long."

She pulled off her tan shirt and bra, sitting down on the wooden bench inside the bunker. She leaned back, feeling the concrete cladding chaff her bare skin.

Tyler unbuttoned his pants and pulled out his erection.

She smiled in satisfaction. Tessa pulled down her pants and panties, spreading her legs.

He bent down and slipped two fingers into her, eliciting a groan of pleasure.

"I fucking need this." She reached up and wrapped her hand around his erection. "Good to see you're at attention, Captain."

"Yes, ma'am," Tyler said, withdrawing his fingers. He picked her up and pushed her body against the bunker wall.

Braced between his warm, sweat-slicked body and the cool, rough concrete, Tessa linked her legs around Tyler as he thrust his penis inside her. She let out a satisfied sigh, gripping his shoulders tightly. "Fuck me hard."

Tyler obliged, starting with slow, powerful strokes. He gripped her thighs tightly and kissed her neck, tender and reddened from the sun. He moved to her lips, working his tongue in and out in rhythm with his thrusts.

She heard the whoosh of rotary wings from a nearby helicopter and felt the wall vibrate as it lifted off. Tessa let out a breathy moan and started pulsing. The sensations were too much. She felt her orgasm building, a much-needed release only a few moments away. She unlocked her legs, relaxing into the sensations, but Tyler's strength still kept her firmly in the air, pinned against the wall.

Tyler pounded harder.

Tessa looked into his brown eyes. There was a focus and intensity she had not seen before as he approached climax.

A familiar alarm sounded – a loud, rhythmic, screeching klaxon.

"Fuck!" Tyler pulled out and dropped Tessa, her back scraping painfully against the concrete as she regained her footing in the sand.

Tessa felt a tightness in her stomach, an anticipation of what was going to happen next. "Incoming!" screamed an approaching soldier.

Tyler ejaculated on Tessa's stomach as a loud boom shook the ground beneath the bunker.

Three soldiers ran into the bunker while Tessa scrambled for her clothes, pulling her tan shirt over her wet, sticky abdomen.

Tyler's penis was still out and glistening in the harsh light of the lamp.

"Shit, sir." A soldier turned his eyes away. "Sorry, sir."

"The TOC's been hit!" Colonel Ortiz shouted, running into the bunker. He cast a disapproving stare in Tessa and Tyler's direction as they continued dressing. "As soon as we get the all clear, we need to get over there."

"Yes, sir," mumbled Tyler.

Colonel Ortiz glared at Tessa, but didn't say anything.

She pressed herself into a corner and tried not to look at anyone, fading into the wall. Time slowed. She could hear her heart beating over the distant screams.

The all-clear klaxon blared over the base speakers. The men and women in the bunker raced outside. When Tessa emerged, she saw that the TOC had taken a direct hit. She joined the cluster of soldiers pulling at the debris, looking for survivors. Four mortar rounds had landed directly on the operations room, where all of her friends and colleagues were working. Panic rose in her throat, but she pushed those feelings aside and focused on the immediate concern – to rescue the living.

After a few minutes of sifting through the wreckage, she found Specialist Martinez under a shattered desk, his eyes and mouth wide open. He was missing his legs. Tessa backed away.

"Medic," she shouted, voice cracking.

Then she vomited. Someone grabbed her shoulders and led her away.

Tessa turned to see who had taken her hand. Tyler's deep brown eyes were staring at her. She looked around. They were no longer in Iraq. They were outside the Third Cavalry Museum in Fort Hood. The grounds in front of the red brick building were crowded with armored vehicles from America's wars. The sweltering desert sun shifted to a chilly Texas winter. Tessa fidgeted impatiently, tugging her jacket tighter.

Tyler stopped in front of an M1 Abrams, painted desert tan. "Saw too many of these in my life."

Tessa nodded, wondering where Tyler was going with this.

"I'm heading back to New York, for now at least."

"The Caplan family business?" asked Tessa.

"Something like that. My parents..." He shook his head. "There was a lot of pressure. They had my whole life laid out for me. All this," he patted the loaming metal of the tank, "was not part of their plan for the eldest son of the Caplan dynasty." His eyes looked distant, like he was seeing into the past.

"Well, at least you've got your family fortune, so you'll be fine," said Tessa. "Once I burn through my savings, I'm fucked."

Tyler placed his hand on her shoulder. "I'm sorry about that." He smiled slightly. "Who knows? Maybe my parents will disown me. We can both be baristas."

She walked a few steps from him, leaving his hand hovering in the air for a moment.

Tyler dropped his hand. "What will you do?"

"Well, with no GI Bill, forget college. And this discharge will kill my security clearance." She felt herself getting angry. "I'll head back to Detroit, figure something out."

"Look, I have an idea." He paused. "You could come with me to New York."

She had rolled her eyes. "Right. I can be ... what ... your fuck buddy? We can get drunk, have sex, and eventually come to a mutual agreement that we aren't right for each other. Let's be honest, I'm not the girl you take home to your parents." She paused. "I need space to work on myself." She reached out and grabbed his hand, squeezing tight. "I know you mean well, but running away with you would be a bad idea for both of us. We screwed up our lives getting kicked out of the Army; we need to fix them first."

Tyler nodded.

Tessa forced a smile and released his hand. "I'm not going to forget you. Even if we did all this to ourselves, you helped me through some rough times. I'll always appreciate you for that. Don't worry about me, I'll be fine." She said the last sentence without any conviction, knowing it was what Tyler needed to hear.

"I won't forget you either, Tessa. And I don't want this to be the end. I think that what we shared means something."

"You have my number and I have yours." She felt the anger and despair fade away, replaced by a crushing fatigue. She didn't want to talk anymore. She just wanted to be somewhere else, by herself, with people who didn't care if she was good or bad, alive or dead. "Look, I have to finish packing my gear. I have a flight to Detroit tonight."

Tyler gave a half-smile. "Goodbye, Tessa."

"Goodbye."

There was more to say. She turned away. She felt him watching her. She wanted to look back. She wanted to feel him wrapped around her, but she kept walking. He didn't call her. She didn't turn back. The two were left on their own, feeling the chill of the crisp air sink into them.

Tessa awoke in the abandoned village, shivering. Her blanket lay crinkled on the floor. She was drenched in sweat. She stood up from the cot, searching for her flask. She picked up the blanket, finding the flask resting underneath.

Tessa wrapped herself in the blanket and took a long swig of whiskey. *I should call Tyler. I should tell him what I wanted to say that day at Fort Hood.* She began to cry and slumped against the wall, cupping her hands over her face.

It had been months since her last nightmare about Tyler. It occurred on repeat, vividly replaying the fateful events the day she was caught having sex with her superior officer in the bunker. Then, it moved forward to the final day she saw Tyler, the day she said "No" to his offer to move to New York City.

"Fuck," she said, hearing her voice echo. She was so cold. She took another sip, emptying the flask. The warmth raced down her throat and spread over her chest.

She gathered herself together and walked down the stairs, returning to the footlocker. She opened the large bottle of Jack and refilled her flask, spilling a little in the process.

Tessa pulled out her phone, bringing up her contacts – Tyler Caplan. *He was trying to help me, and I just pushed him away. I didn't say what I wanted to say. I was a fucking coward.* Tessa took another long drink of whiskey and then pressed Tyler's number. She had no idea what time it was in New York, and she didn't care.

After a few rings, he picked up. "Hello, Tessa?"

"Hi, Tyler. How are you?"

"I'm fine. How are you?"

Tessa took a deep breath. "I'm ... I'm ... not great." She fought back tears. "I just dreamed about us in the bunker and I just wanted to say, I'm so sorry. For everything. I was the one that tempted you that day to leave our duty station. I got our friends killed. I was distracted. I wasn't focused on the intel and I missed the tell-tale signs of an attack. I'm so sorry for fucking up your life. I should have said yes, I should have moved to New York with you so we could have worked through things together. But I was a fucking coward. And now I'm stuck alone on this island having nightmares and...." Tessa paused to catch her breath, sobbing lowly. "I just wanted you to know how sorry I am. I know you wanted to carve your own path in the Army and not be beholden to your parents' money and I'm the one that fucked that up for you. I wish I knew how to make things right between us."

There was a long pause on the other end of the line. "Tessa, it's not your fault. I'm responsible for my choices too. Have you considered seeing a therapist?"

Tessa shook her head. "There's no therapist where I am. I don't have anyone I can talk to about this."

"You're on an island?" asked Tyler, sounding confused.

Shit. OPSEC. "Yeah, umm ... a therapist can't help me. I just don't want to live my life with regrets. Maybe I could come visit you in New York, and we can talk in person. I miss you."

"Umm ... sure, just let me know when you want to come, okay. I'm busy with the Foundation, so give me a heads up so we can coordinate schedules. Sometimes I'm out of town for work and family obligations."

"Okay." Tessa wiped her eyes, taking another drink.

"Okay." Tyler paused.

She could hear voices in the background now, like he had opened the door and was walking through a crowded Manhattan street.

"I have to go. I'm running late for a meeting in Midtown. Let's catch up soon."

"Okay. Goodbye."

"Goodbye."

Tessa stared at the black screen on her phone for several minutes. Then she returned the flask to the storage locker and headed up the hill, walking the winding path back toward the Academy.

Chapter 28

Min was hard at work studying the latest demonology files provided by Silva. They were all related to how sloth demons functioned. The older material was in hard copy, thick bound folders of flimsy paper. The rest were on the Academy's intranet and she accessed them through her laptop. At first, Min assumed sloth demons weren't as dangerous as the other types. *Sure*, she thought, *they might promote junk food or binge-watching shows, but they don't start wars.* But as she delved into the case studies, she was surprised to learn how insidious they were. She was particularly disturbed by how they had penetrated education systems and popular culture around the globe, promoting intellectual laziness and superficial pursuits. *A lazy mind is more important to demons than a lazy body.*

Silva's class was her favorite. His material was data driven and focused, dissecting one demon at a time. Her current case study focused on a demon named Harry. The Curia believed he had been on Earth for a short time, a decade at most. Before being killed by a hunter late last year, he had created a popular YouTube channel, "Harry's EasterEggs." It was a video game streaming channel, with video after video of the demon playing the popular game of the moment. While not in the upper echelons of online gamers, he had 200,000 followers when the Curia killed him. He would mainly give tips on how to unlock parts of the game, with some videos having over a million hits.

Harry is dead, but how many other sloth demons are still out there? Their actions aren't as spectacular as anger or pride demons, but that might make them more effective.

She closed the Curia's archived copy of Harry's channel. Although the information was fascinating, it had been four hours since her last break. She rubbed her eyes and looked longingly at her Xbox. Whenever she felt stressed or tired, video games were her go-to stimulant.

Taking a break doesn't make me slothful. It makes me tired. She was about to head to the couch when Tessa entered the room. She had a broad smile on her face.

"What are you so happy about?"

Tessa sank into one of the recliners, sitting her backpack on the end table between them. "I am done with entertainment law."

For the last four weeks, Tessa's Special Studies course had focused on the laws that governed the film and TV industry in the US and Europe. Min knew this because Tessa had complained about it constantly.

"That's great, because I don't know if I could take another night of you bitching about contracts," Min said.

Tessa nodded. "I know, I know. I've been a pain in the ass. I just have a hard time seeing how I'm ever going to use any of this. It's like learning calculus in high school. Who uses that?"

Min held up her hand. "Me."

Tessa laughed. "Nerd." She noticed the stack of homework. "Ready for a break?"

"Yeah, I was just thinking of playing Call of Duty before getting back to the gripping case of Harry the sloth demon and his defunct YouTube channel."

"I have a better idea." She opened up her backpack and pulled out a bottle of whiskey. "Have a drink with me."

"We're not allowed to have alcohol in our rooms."

Tessa nodded mischievously. "Seamus went out of his way to get this for me. Just came in on the supply ship this week — Hibiki, a premium Japanese blended whiskey. Come on, we're celebrating no more entertainment law!"

Min sighed. "Okay, but I need to warn you, I'm a total lightweight. One drink and I'll be intoxicated."

"Great, cheap date. Grab two glasses."

Tessa filled the water glasses Min brought over, then held up her glass. "Cheers."

"*Geonbae.*" Min took a sip.

Tessa took a drink. "Ahh ... that's nice. Rich." Tessa paused, looking into Min's eyes. "I'm sorry, I've been so focused on my work. I've kinda sucked as a mentor lately."

Min shook her head. "Not at all. Your tutoring in combatives has been of immense help. With all those extra morning practices we've put in, I think I might almost be competent."

"You're better than competent. And with more practice, you will kick some serious ass."

Min blushed. "I doubt I'll ever do that. But thanks to you, I will be able to protect myself."

"Well, I would want you watching my back in a fight."

Min bowed slightly. "*Daedanhi gamsahabnida.*"

"You're welcome." She took another drink. "Okay, no more shop talk. Let's talk about something else. Something fun, like boys."

Tessa had been thinking a lot about Tyler since her drunk phone call to him back in the village. He had texted her a few times afterwards to check in on her. She could tell it had obviously worried him, and that he genuinely cared.

"Did you leave anyone behind? I mean, someone special?" asked Tessa.

Min thought about how to answer. *Should I tell her?* She studied Tessa's face. *She seems pretty open-minded.*

"I did," she hesitated. "I had a girlfriend in university."

"Oh sorry, I didn't mean when I said boys to exclude—"

"It's okay. I'm bi. I like having options." Min smiled. "Her name was...is...Hyo-joo. We were very close and it hurt to leave her. I made a clean break; I knew that I couldn't maintain a relationship while in the Curia. But it wasn't easy."

"What was she like?"

Min felt a flood of relief. Being gay or bi in Korea was frowned on and something Min had to work to keep hidden and compartmentalized from the rest of her life. "She was brilliant. She was studying to be a physician. By the time I'm out hunting, she'll be saving lives." For a moment, she grew quiet, remembering how Hyo-joo's oval face looked when she grinned, the way her brown eyes would shine when she saw Min walk into a room. "We were together for a year. We had to be careful. Being found out could have led to social and professional ostracization. We were never affectionate in public, but we did enjoy going out to the clubs and dancing. We both loved EDM."

Tessa thought about her own secret relationship with Tyler. While not the same — the main problem she faced was professional sanction — she did have a sense of what Min had gone through. "How did you meet her?"

Min shrugged. "I was sitting in a cafe on campus and reading *Attack on Titan*. She saw it and sat down. She talked to me about it, like we were old friends. That was how she was. I was attracted to her immediately. We started hanging out and getting to know each other. But I didn't say anything for months. I was afraid that she would reject me. That she wouldn't feel the same way." Min took a drink. "Besides, Ruth had already recruited me and I knew I would be leaving for the Academy soon. Why take the chance when I would be gone?"

"And then Ruth came back, delaying your entry."

Min nodded. "I was upset. At that moment, I didn't know what to think. I wondered how I messed up, even though Ruth assured me it was nothing I had done. I was feeling really down. Hyo-joo knew I was waiting for something. I had hinted it was an acceptance at an American university for graduate studies, but had been purposely vague. The night Ruth notified me, we went out drinking. We had a lot of soju. A lot. We went back to her place, and I told her I was attracted to her. I took a chance."

She smiled sheepishly. "She felt the same. She had been working up the courage to say something as long as I had." Tears misted Min's eyes. She sniffed. "We had a great year together. We had to be careful in public, but in private, we were ourselves."

Tessa felt choked up as well. "That's pretty awesome."

Min nodded. "Yes, it was." She finished the whiskey and indicated with her glass that she wanted more. As Tessa filled it up, she continued, "The end came as I knew it would. Ruth contacted me again and said I was back on track. I told Hyo-joo that I was leaving Korea and might never return. She didn't understand. She said she would wait for me, that she would even look into transferring to the school I was going to." Min shook her head sadly. "I told her it wasn't possible. I couldn't tell her why though. The last I saw of her she was standing in her apartment crying."

Tessa put down her glass, stood up and went to Min. She bent over and gave her a hug. "I'm so sorry."

Min felt the warmth of Tessa's caring and acceptance. She let out a soft sob.

Tessa decided to lighten the mood a little. "So, do you find anyone here attractive? I've seen you and Francisco flirting with one another. Any girls?"

Min shook her head. "I like Sushmia," she said, referring to one of her classmates, a curvy young woman from Mumbai, "but I get the impression that she's not into girls. Please, don't tell her I think she's hot."

"Aw ... someone's shy about her secret crush." Tessa grinned and was happy that Min followed suit. "Don't worry. Anything you tell me stays between us."

"Thanks, so what about you? Any boys, or girls, that you like?"

Tessa sighed. "It's complicated, of course. I haven't told you about Tyler, have I?"

"Only that you served with him in Iraq and that he was part of the reason you left the Army."

"Yeah, that's the G-rated version. We were in a relationship. Very intense. The kind of intense that happens when every day might be your last. And it went bad."

"I see." Min didn't understand exactly what Tessa was getting at, but she didn't want to interrupt with a question.

"We were having sex when we should have been on duty. Some people died, people that were in my Army family." Tessa took another sip of whiskey. "We're still friends, but it's tricky. Whenever I think of him, part of me wants to fuck him, part of me wants to tell him to fuck off. I know that whatever we had died in Iraq. I've been clinging to that corpse for a while. But I'm sure he's moved on. He's got a nice life in New York City running his rich family's foundation that's trying to cure cancer."

Min paused, looking Tessa in the eyes. "He's not a corpse."

Tessa was surprised by the statement. "What do you mean?"

"I can tell he still has a heartbeat to you. We make so few real connections, we should cherish the ones we find, even if they're not perfect. You liked being with Tyler for a reason, right?"

"Yes."

"Has that reason changed?" asked Min.

"I don't know."

"Then maybe you should answer that question first."

Tessa grinned. "That's pretty wise."

Min shrugged. "I read a lot of romance *manhwa* in the orphanage. They are surprisingly deep."

"I called him recently, when I was drunk and not in the best frame of mind because I had just had a nightmare."

Min cringed. "Oh, how did that play out?"

"Well, I apologized for what happened between us. And then I said I should have taken him up on his offer to move to

New York when we got kicked out of the Army. And then kind of invited myself to New York. He was nice about it, but he seemed non-committal."

"Has he contacted you since the drunk call?" asked Min.

"Yes, several times by text, checking in on me."

"Well then, he obviously still has feelings for you. He would be ghosting you if he didn't. It sounds like you both went through a traumatic experience together, and those bonds can be intense. Hard to break."

Tessa nodded. "Yes, intense, but our relationship in Iraq was toxic. It went to flirting at breakfast over the book club we started, to private hookah nights in his tent where I sucked on more than just a hookah pipe and well, more private nights in his tent where I went to borrow books." Tessa made air quotes with her hands. "We got addicted to the taboo of it all. He was my commanding officer. I'd salute him during the day and bend over for him at night. Our encounters got riskier. The danger of getting caught caused this massive adrenaline rush that heightened the whole experience, plus the adrenaline of being in a warzone and hyped up on caffeine with little sleep. We had sex in an armored vehicle and in the wide open, under the desert stars. And the bunker ... it was toxic."

"It went through a toxic period, but it doesn't mean the core of your chemistry was bad. You were friends first, right?"

"Yes. It started out so harmlessly. He loaned me a book to read to help with my insomnia, *Counting Sheep*. And then we just started talking about the book and I commented on some of the other books he had on his shelf. He likes history, especially nineteenth-century American history, so he loaned me some other books and that's how our breakfast book club began." Tessa grinned, remembering. "He was a big nerd. He comes from old money. His family made a fortune in the railroads, so he'd collect all these fancy antiques from the Victorian era and show me pictures of them, totally geeking out on these artifacts.

We joked about going antiquing together back in the States. It never happened, of course. But it was nice to dream. Anything to get away from thinking about being a sitting duck on a FOB in Iraq, waiting for the next mortar to hit."

Min smiled. "I think you're still in love with him."

Tessa paused. "I … I cared about him a lot. But love, that's a strong word. I fucked up his life, Min. He never wanted to be locked in his family's golden handcuffs. That's why he enlisted in the Army and put himself through school. He didn't want to be a trust fund baby with all the expectations that come with that. His family actually cut him off from his trust fund when they found out he enlisted in the Army. But now, he's back in their good graces because he's doing exactly what they want him to do. The model son who's running the Caplan Cancer Foundation. That's not the life we wanted."

Min shrugged. "I call it like I see it. Speaking of love, I convinced Seamus to make *jjamppong*. It's a Korean spicy seafood stew that I love. Perfect comfort food. Are you hungry?"

Tessa gave Min an impromptu hug.

"What was that for?"

"Because you're my friend." She let Min go. "Come on, let's go eat. I'm looking forward to the stew."

Chapter 29

Tessa shifted her balance from one foot to the other. She was facing off against April in Advanced Combatives. Over the past year and a half, she had sparred with the diminutive redhead numerous times. Tessa respected her as a cunning and unpredictable opponent. In this session she had already landed more crippling and killing blows with her practice dagger than Tessa.

Uri had threatened that the losers of today's drills would run laps around the island, but Tessa had other plans. Min had found something in her research and wanted to meet Tessa later for a debriefing.

April was grinning, knowing she was getting the better of Tessa. Their matches were close to fifty-fifty and she was looking forward to winning. She had plans later with Patrick and preferred a more horizontal exercise to running laps. April feinted left and brought her plastic blade up in an arc meant to connect with Tessa's abdomen.

Tessa spun out of the way and landed a kick on April's side. It was off balance and weak, but enough to send April into retreat.

April took a few steps back. "Nice. But you're going down, bitch."

Tessa smirked. "Is that what you say to Patrick?" She lunged, tagging April's arm with her blade.

"Hit," Uri said. "Minor damage."

Tessa circled April. *She likes those feints. Watch her eyes, watch her shoulders. Watch her eyes, watch her shoulders.*

The other members of Tessa's class were spread around the padded sparring area of the gym, watching the two women and good naturedly urging on their favorites. After spending so much time together, the fourteen members of Tessa's class had formed strong bonds of camaraderie. While there were personality clashes, these were offset by the intensity of the shared experience.

Tessa shifted her weight and exploded into a flurry of jabs and slashes. April avoided most of them, but did receive a painful jab to her left shoulder. She winced and danced out of the way.

It had been drilled into everyone's head that when they were training, they couldn't hold back. And none of them did. They understood the seriousness of the exercises and lessons. Uri was teaching them to survive, even if the lessons he taught were often painful.

When April next attacked, she led with the knife, an obvious thrust toward Tessa's midsection. Tessa saw her posture and readied herself for the real attack, an uppercut aimed at her jaw. Tessa bounced to the right.

April's punch went wide. "Fuck!"

Tessa brought her blade up and into April's chest. It knocked the wind out of her and she lost balance. Tessa hit her again, slashing across her abdomen.

"Two hits, one kill, one cripple," Uri said. Tessa and April were strong fighters. He enjoyed watching them, admiring the passion and artistry they brought to combatives. He thought Tessa would come out the worse in this session, but she found her second wind.

The match continued for another few minutes, but Tessa had gotten into a lethal rhythm. When it was over, both were bruised and sweating. They stood panting, waiting for Uri's final score.

"Close, but the match goes to Tessa."

"Damnit," April muttered.

Tessa gave her a playful nudge. "Looks like Patrick will have to wait. Unless you want me to keep him company."

"Touch him and die," April growled, before the two women burst into laughter.

"Okay, that's it for today. Losers, head up to the surface and start in. I want three laps, and I'll be watching and counting. Winners, the evening is yours. Have fun."

Tessa returned to her room. Min was waiting for her, playing Call of Duty on their Xbox. A tote bag stuffed with food and drinks was on the dining table. She paused the game. "Are you ready to go?"

Tessa groaned. "I need to take a shower. Go back to your game. I'll be ready in a few."

To the sound of electronic mayhem, she went into her room and undressed. She checked out her latest welt from one of April's kicks and shook her head. *I'm going to leave here with the body of an MMA fighter.*

She stepped into the shower and pressed her forehead against the wall as hot water soothed her sore body. She was looking forward to the end of her time at the Academy. She was getting restless and was ready to start hunting.

Tessa dried off and dressed, slipping into jeans, a T-shirt and a light jacket. June in the Faroe Islands was pleasant with a temperature like Michigan in the fall. *All I need is a cider farm and a Red Wings game.*

Min was mowing down video game terrorists and making little squeaks every time she was shot.

Tessa picked up the tote bag. "I'm ready."

Min saved her game, threw on a jacket and trailed after Tessa. "How was class?"

"Painful. I was up against April."

"Ouch." Min knew that the two women didn't hold back when they fought. She practiced with both of them as part of her combatives tutoring. Tessa wanted her to have experience with different types of fighters.

"At least I won. Uri is having the losers run the island, so let's ditch the village."

Min nodded in understanding.

They reached the surface and headed outside. It was a clear day and the sky was a pale blue. It would remain this way until late in the night. At this time of year, it never got very dark, with the day stretching for almost twenty hours before fading into a gray twilight. Tessa led the way to the edge of the cliff, scaring off a few puffins. The waters of the North Atlantic churned against the rocks. *One day, they'll eat the island, wear it down to nothing. The chapel, the graves, the Academy, it will all be gone.*

Min pulled out sandwiches, a thermos of coffee and a bag of sour cream and onion potato chips. She handed Tessa a sandwich, tuna fish on rye.

Tessa sat on the moist grass. "Thanks. So, you had something you wanted to tell me?"

Min squeezed a packet of mustard onto her sandwich. "I wanted to tell you what I've found in the archives." She grew quiet. A look passed over her face like she was about to make a monumental decision. "I've found references to something that I think is key to understanding what's really going on here."

Tessa leaned in. "What did you find?"

"As you know, we have part of the Curia's historical archive here. The sources available are from hunters and are used for case studies. I decided to start with those. I wanted to see if there may have been some anomalous information. Last night, I found my anomaly."

Min pulled out a leather-bound notebook. She opened it and said, "This is from the journal of Sir Reginald of Cornwall. He was a hunter and English knight in the twelfth century. Thankfully, he wrote in Latin."

"You read Latin?"

Min nodded. "The orphanage believed in a classical education. Anyway, his last entry was apparently written just before he died. Based on the description of symptoms, I believe he was dying from tuberculosis."

"You translated his journal and diagnosed his illness?" Tessa said, grinning.

"I believe in being thorough. Now, do you want to hear what he wrote?"

Tessa held up her hands. "Sorry, Professor Min. Please, continue."

Min cleared her throat.

"I write this as my vision grows dim. I will soon be with my Lord, in Heaven. I have done His work and sent many demons back to their just punishment. My weakness, however, prevents me from carrying out one last task in His service. I hope that whoever reads this is able to complete this task."

"I was approached in my bedchamber by Joseph of Alexandria, a good and faithful friend of the Enochian Curia. For many years, he has informed me of the comings and goings of our infernal foes. He came in search of me with information that may be vital to our Holy War. Joseph came to me, bearing a piece of pottery and a fantastic story. He obtained the pottery from a merchant traveling from the south. He told Joseph of a place where demons emerge from a gate of the Pit. They come forth from a disk of fire, like a shield of burning metal in the sky. These demons are worshiped by the lost souls of the land, celebrated in revels and debaucheries. Joseph did not know where this place was, although he believes the pottery might hold the information of its location."

"Joseph has left me to spend my last moments in prayer. I will do so. I will pray that another true Son or Daughter of Christ will find this gate and close it. Perhaps then, the Lord's Kingdom on Earth will come to be."

Min looked up. "Well?"

Tessa shrugged, "Kind of weak, isn't it? A dying hunter gets a broken plate and a story about a gate to Hell. Doesn't sound like much to go on."

Min pursed her lips. "I agree that it's not conclusive. But I have found no other mention of a gate that demons use to come to Earth."

"Okay, assuming this is something, what do you think it means?"

"Are you familiar with an Einstein–Rosen bridge?"

"Yeah, a wormhole, right?"

Min nodded. "Right. Theoretically, a wormhole could connect two parts of spacetime. It could allow instant travel across vast distances. A race with sufficient knowledge and technology could use wormholes to move from world to world." She tapped the journal, leaving a smudge of mustard on the cover. "Technology like this would seem like magic – but it is more plausible than a gate to Hell. Or the Curia's story of angels and demons."

"Have any other journals you've read from hunters mentioned this gate or anything like it?"

Min took another bite of her sandwich, letting the pause linger while she chewed. "No, it's an anomaly. That's why it stuck out. I checked the archive's online log to see when it was cataloged by the Surveillance and Analysis Directorate, and it's a new addition that came into Rome only a few months ago. It's the first real clue we have that we can follow up on and confirm if there's anything to this idea of a gate."

Tessa opened the thermos of coffee, watching the steam swirl upwards. "How exactly can we follow up?"

"In the archive log, it lists the name of the antiques dealer, Zala Kebede, who sold the journal to a shell company of the Curia, the Mannerheim Group. It also lists a few other artifacts for sale from Sir Reginald's crypt, including a piece of pottery. But there's no record that the Mannerheim Group purchased anything besides the journal. Her business is in New York City." Min grinned, a twinkle in her eye. "Since your friend Tyler lives in New York City and we have summer holiday coming up, I thought it might be time for you to visit. I'd go myself, but I already planned to go to Ibiza with Francisco and it would look odd for me to back out so close to summer holiday."

Tessa took a long sip of coffee. "I did talk to Tyler recently and he seemed open to the idea of me visiting New York. If I can find Zala and she still has the pottery shard, I'm sure an artifact like that would be expensive. I can't exactly pay for that on the Curia's travel card without arousing suspicion."

"Isn't Tyler loaded – old money, trust fund, all that?" asked Min.

"Well, yes, but keep in mind I haven't seen Tyler since Fort Hood, like early 2010. I can't just show up, bat my eyelashes and expect him to pay for an expensive artifact for me. Don't get your hopes up. But I could at least ask to see it and confirm its existence."

"So you'll do it?" Min said.

"Yes, I'll go to New York on the 'quest for the shard,'" Tessa said, with dramatic flair. She began humming the theme music to Indiana Jones.

Min laughed. "It's an adventure, plus I think you and Tyler have some unfinished business. I hope I didn't ruin your current plans. Did you have any?"

"Well, I was thinking of going to Paris to see Desange and his family, but he told me recently he's on a hunt and can't coordinate his schedule with mine, so the Paris thing was kind of up in the air." *And it's probably best I stay away from Paris in the event Dylan is still lurking around Montmartre. Tyler might be complicated, but at least he's human.*

"See, it was meant to be. You're going to be quite useful in helping me uncover the truth about this whole operation." Min squeezed out mustard onto a chip.

"Ugh, mustard with chips? So weird." Tessa shook her head. "So, I'm not just useful for teaching you how to stab things?"

Tessa took a little bow with her head. "Just happy to be of service to my super-smart friend."

"It's delicious! Ketchup and mayonnaise are way overrated." Min ate another mustard-covered chip.

"Have you found out anything more about demons? Like what they really are?" asked Tessa.

Min leaned back on her elbows. "There is no evidence of a spiritual world or entities. I include angels and demons in that." She gave a little shrug. "Whatever they are ... I think it's something else. Aliens is my working theory."

"I can tell you from experience that they aren't like us. I mean, they are super-strong, lightning fast. Could they be some type of genetically engineered human?"

Min was silent for a moment. "Possibly." She gazed at the churning ocean and clear sky. "I don't know what they are and the lack of information is frustrating."

Tessa sighed. "I get it. It's like when I was in Iraq. Trying to track down targets with little information, never enough time and the knowledge that if you fuck up, people die."

Min didn't look away from the ocean. "Extraterrestrials are a possibility. So are entities from another dimension, the next step in human evolution, or a government black ops team with bootstrapped DNA." She laughed. "Maybe they are a shared delusion and this is an asylum."

Tessa chuckled. "That I believe."

"I don't have enough information to offer a reasonable hypothesis, but the explanation that they are spiritual creatures is the least plausible."

She's really struggling with this. Trying to fit something that seems supernatural into a box that conforms to natural laws. I don't know what I can do to help.

"Look," Tessa said, "I agree that the Curia hides information from us. We just need to proceed carefully. I don't want you getting in trouble with Ruth."

For a few moments, Min sat silently. Then she grinned. It was only a faint one, but it was enough to encourage Tessa. "I know how to be sneaky."

Tessa heard the thud of feet as the losers from the fight ran over the spine of the island, heading for the chapel. She changed the topic to something lighter. "So I saw you in the lounge with that hot Brazilian recruit ... Francisco. Ibiza should be a good time."

Min started to tell Tessa about the flirtatious relationship Francisco had struck up with her. But Tessa's attention was still focused on what Min had said about the portal. *Could there be any truth to this old reference? It's one entry in the journal of a long-dead hunter. If Min had found multiple references to a portal from hunters across centuries, it would be a pattern and have more credibility, a lead worth following up on. But it's a newly discovered journal so maybe the secrets of this portal died with Sir Reginald. There could be other references in Rome's archives, but we'd have to be there to dig through original source materials.* Tessa recalled the volume of intelligence she had received as an Army analyst, most of which was unsubstantiated noise. She needed patterns, like putting together the notes in a song. *Min only has one note.*

"...he does have great eyes. And he's a good cook!"

I should encourage her to keep investigating. Min might be the best hope I have of getting more answers, as long as she's careful.

"I'm hoping we can hook up in Ibiza. I know it complicates things, having a fling with a fellow recruit, but I've got needs."

"I think it's fine, as long as both of you know what it is," Tessa said. *At least he's not your mentor.* "He seems like a nice guy. And if nothing else, I bet he's good in bed."

Min nodded. "He's good at combatives, if there's any correlation."

"You should do it. Go spend two weeks on the beach, have some hot sex and tell me all the details. I can live vicariously through you while I'm hunting for pottery shards in New York."

Tessa's iPhone buzzed. She looked at the screen. It was a text from Chloe: *Have you talked to Desange? Haven't heard from him in a couple of weeks.*

Tessa hadn't heard from him either. The last few times she had tried, she was routed straight to his voicemail. She didn't find that too odd; if he was on an active hunt, he probably would go dark. *But I can't tell Chloe that.* She typed back, *Not in a little while. I'll see what I can find out and get back to you.*

Thanks! Chloe responded, *Are you coming to France this summer? I have a whole list of new nightclubs to check out.*

No, I'm going back to the States this year. Thanks so much for the invite, I hope we can plan another time to get together.

Chloe's response was a smiling emoji. Tessa put the phone down.

I hope Desange is okay, Tessa thought. *I haven't heard from him in over a month. He's a workaholic. I'm sure it's nothing to stress about. He's got demons to kill.*

"You seem lost in thought. You okay?" asked Min.

Tessa looked up, watching nearby grass blow in the breeze. "Yeah, just thinking about how I can get in touch with Desange." She held up her phone. "That was his sister. She was asking for him, but I'm pretty sure he's on a hunt."

"You've left messages?"

Tessa nodded.

Min shrugged. "One of the drawbacks of being a hunter, I guess."

"Particularly when you have a family that cares. You and I don't have to worry about that." She immediately felt bad about saying that, knowing Min's background. "Shit. Sorry, I didn't mean to—"

"It's okay. I've been an orphan since I was a baby. It is what it is."

Tessa nodded. "We've got each other. Sherlock and Watson, Mulder and Scully. The Truth is Out There."

Min's smile broadened, "Only a lot hotter. And don't forget, I'm Scully."

Tessa laughed. "I'm not sure about that, you are the one talking about aliens. 'I don't know, therefore Aliens,'" said Tessa, laughing as she quoted a popular meme.

Min chuckled hysterically. "Ancient Aliens."

"But seriously, if anyone can find out the truth about the Curia, it's you."

"I'm glad you think so." There was silence for a few moments, except for the wind in the grass and the soft trilling of puffins. "I'm really happy to have you as a friend."

Tessa took Min's hand and gently squeezed it. "Me too."

Chapter 30

Tessa awoke, having fallen asleep when her flight lifted off from Heathrow. When she looked out the window, the Manhattan skyline loomed in the distance. She was excited, looking forward to seeing both Tyler and New York. This was her first time in the city, one she always wanted to visit. That she had a mission to perform didn't detract from her anticipation.

It will be nice to have some downtime. The last six months have been tough. I bet Tyler knows all the best clubs and restaurants and New York seems like the kind of place that is great to wander around in. I'll run Min's errand and then I can have some fun. She flashed back to having sex with Dylan on his balcony at twilight. She could still feel the cold, wrought iron metal against her bare bottom as he lifted her higher over the streets of Paris. *Safe fun, with a human. Not like last summer.*

"Hello, this is your captain. We are beginning our descent into La Guardia. The cabin crew will be passing through to collect service items. Have a great day and thanks for flying British Airways."

A slight smile creased Tessa's lips. She thought about how Tyler sounded when she asked about visiting. Not that he was demonstrative about his feelings. Someone who didn't know him as well as she did would think he sounded disinterested. But that was just his personality. In Iraq, even in the most stressful situations, he was calm and commanding. She liked that about him. She knew several other officers who either got too "chummy" with their subordinates – which struck her as forced – or who were from the "shout orders and pretend you're Patton" school of command. Neither style impressed her. Steady and in-charge was what Tessa wanted in a leader; Tyler fitted that model perfectly.

As she got to know him, however, she saw cracks in that calm facade. When they spoke about books they liked or when he'd open up about his past deployments, little bits of passion or frustration would leak through. These glimpses inside were fleeting; but she grew to recognize them. Those moments when he was inside of her, his face showing the intensity of his desire. And in the ruins of the TOC, the shock and pain plain on his face, mirroring the black spike of anguish piercing her chest.

Her smile faded as she thought about the wisps of smoke rising from the mound of timber, metal and sandbags. Men scurried over the wreckage, pulling out bodies and parts of bodies. The moment she saw the remains of Specialist Martinez. A thick silence that wrapped around her head.

The silence of the dead. She shook her head, pushing those dark memories back into the recesses of her mind.

I'm not going to be depressed. This is a vacation. I get to see a friend who I haven't been with in years and tour a city that I've wanted to visit my whole life. And, I get to do it with an open-ended expense account. Leave the past where it belongs.

After deplaning and collecting her luggage – her OD green duffle bag – she headed into a bathroom stall. She opened the bag and pulled out her dagger. After the events of last year, she wasn't going to leave the island without it. She hiked up her long skirt and strapped the scabbard to her thigh. The press of the leather case against her skin was reassuring.

She took a taxi to her hotel. It was a pricey boutique inn located in the heart of Little Italy. Tyler offered a room in his Greenwich Village brownstone, but Tessa didn't want there to be any misunderstandings. She was concerned that things might get intimate if they were staying together. She was there as Tyler's friend, not a fling.

She unpacked her clothing and stretched out on the king-sized bed. *If I find some hot guy, it'll be nice to have someplace to take him that I'm not sharing with my ex.*

"You're a bad girl, Tessa," she said, laughing. "Remember to use your glasses."

Her phone rang. "Tyler."

"Hey there," Tessa said.

"Hi, Tessa. How was your flight?"

"Great. I slept most of the way."

"Nice. So, I just finished up with my last meeting for the day. I know a place near your hotel. Meet for dinner?"

"That sounds wonderful. What time?" asked Tessa.

"Half an hour? I can meet you in your lobby."

"I'll see you then. Bye."

Tessa stripped and showered, the hot water giving her a little boost of energy for the evening. She slipped on loose slacks and a light blouse – it was a hot and sticky July evening and she wanted to be comfortable. She stuffed her dagger and glasses into her purse. *You never know when you'll encounter a demon.*

She checked herself out in the mirror, gave her hair a spritz to keep it under control – humidity was not a friend to her wispy brown strands – and headed downstairs.

Emerging from the elevator, Tessa saw Tyler first. He was dressed in a light gray suit that fitted his athletic body like a glove. She noted that he was standing ramrod straight, like he was at attention. His dark brown eyes were focused on his phone.

He looks good. Really good. But you are not going to throw yourself at him. Sometimes, being the adult in the room sucks.

"Hey," she said, "I hope you're not going to be on your phone all night."

Tyler looked up, smiling. Tessa felt a part of her melt. *It would be so easy to drag him upstairs and have him fuck my brains out.*

"Wow, you look great."

Tessa smiled. "You too. Please, keep the compliments coming."

The two hugged. Tessa felt the solid muscles of his chest and arms. *He's still in shape.*

"Will do," he said. "Are you hungry?"

"Starving."

"There's a great little Italian place a few blocks from here. Family style, amazing food, massive portions."

"You know I like my food massive."

Tyler offered her his arm and they left the hotel. The sidewalks were crowded. Tessa almost pulled out her glasses, a reflexive action.

Not tonight. Tonight it's just me and Tyler. No demons, no angels, no Curia. A normal, simple night.

The restaurant was a walk up, a small room filled with the heady aroma of basil and garlic. They sat next to one of the windows, looking down on Grand Street. Tessa couldn't stop grinning.

"What's up?" asked Tyler.

She shrugged. "Nothing. I just feel so – normal."

Tyler laughed. "Do you usually feel abnormal?"

Tessa shook her head. "Sorry. The last year has been pretty nuts. Mostly training in a secure location and when I've been in the field, it's strictly business."

"Well, while you are in New York, you don't have to think about whatever alphabet agency you work for. I just want to show you a good time."

"Thanks." She felt some of the weight of the war lift from her shoulders. "Well, I do have to bring up business for one minute, then I'm done. Promise. Did you get an appointment with Zala Kebede?"

Tyler nodded. "Yes. Tomorrow at 2pm. Just to warn you, she's a little eccentric, but she's always been fair with me and knows her industry well." He ordered a bottle of Chianti and the *prix fixe* menu. "I was a little surprised that you wanted to see an antique dealer. Starting to come over to my side of the fence?"

"Oh, don't get your hopes up that I'm gonna start collecting old teacups or something. This is for a friend. I think you'd like her. She's very into history."

"I should have known. You always were a today-and-tomorrow type of person."

"When you have my past, looking backward sucks."

The wine arrived and the server filled their glasses.

Tyler raised his glass. "Here's to today and tomorrow."

Over dinner, they caught up. Tessa was circumspect about what she did, never giving away more than vagaries. She let Tyler think she was CIA or working for a private military contractor. She wanted to tell him more – it would have felt good to unload on someone not in the Curia — but knew it wouldn't go anywhere productive. She didn't mind the conclusion that he jumped to and subtly played into it. Over mouthfuls of mushroom and sausage risotto, she gave him a highly sanitized and skewed overview of her last year and a half.

"But what about you?" she asked, as she finished.

Tyler shrugged. "Just living the life of a trust fund baby."

Tessa frowned. "Come on. There's more than that."

"Nothing you haven't heard. I go to work, try to keep the Foundation functioning smoothly, see my therapist regularly and keep my nose clean. I find that if I stick to a full schedule, life is easier. Stay busy and out of trouble." He poked at the food on his plate. "When I returned home, things were harder. Too much free time. I had some bad days. Weeks." He shrugged. "Okay, months."

"I know what you mean. Before I was recruited ... well, you know. I drank too much."

"It looks like we each found something to give us a purpose." He grinned. "But your's sounds a lot cooler."

"It has its moments," Tessa said.

"Oh, I took off the whole week, so I'm around as much or as little as you want."

She smiled. "Thanks. I might want a day or two to wander around by myself. See what kind of trouble I can get into. Otherwise, I'm all yours."

"All mine – I like the sound of that." Tyler grinned, locking eyes with Tessa.

She remembered how it felt to have him inside her, the insistent thrusting, his rough hands on her skin, the intensity of his chocolate brown eyes as he looked into hers. She shuddered with anticipation, then felt bad about it.

Stop. We're just friends and I'm going to respect boundaries.

"I wanted to ask you something," she said, changing the topic. "Why are you so into antiques? I mean, I'm happy you know the person I need to talk to. But I always wondered what it was about collecting old stuff that appealed to you?"

"Collecting old stuff? Wow ... thanks for reducing my careful, thoughtful curation of an amazing collection of nineteenth-century Americana to 'old stuff.'"

Tessa laughed. "Sorry – but antiques are both old and stuff, right?"

"Ugh," Tyler groaned, "philistine."

"Hey, I like PBR with my PBJ ... I'm a simple girl," she said, laughing, "Really, what is it?"

"I've always been fascinated by history; but there is something different about being able to hold a thing you've only read about. I can almost feel the people who made and used it."

Tessa sensed Tyler hesitating. *Something else is going on.* "Hey, if it's too personal..."

Tyler shook his head. "I've told you about my family. My parents. How they didn't approve of my choices starting with going into the Army. I don't think I mentioned my grandfather, though."

Tessa shook her head. Tyler was typically reserved when talking about his family.

"When I was a kid, I would spend summers with him. He had retired from the business and was living on a ranch in Colorado. After dinner, we'd go out on the porch. He'd have a big glass of whiskey and ice. We'd watch the sun go down and the stars come out and he'd tell me the family history. During the nineteenth century, the Caplans built things. Railroads. Factories. They helped build America. They started out working with their hands and then with their brains and bank accounts. But at the end of the day, they left a legacy that's part of the foundation of our country."

Tessa saw a look cross his face, one she had never seen before. A hint of wistfulness, a longing to recapture the glory days of old. It was hard for her to relate. Growing up in Detroit, she survived by dreaming up a better future, far away from her toxic family and generational trauma. Her grandfathers both worked in factories, drinking themselves into an early grave.

"Now, we just move piles of money around. Our fortune is made of nothing."

"What about the Foundation? It does good work, right?"

Tyler frowned. "You sound like my parents. Sure, some of the research we fund is useful. But we could be doing a lot more. And we aren't building anything. I want to be like my ancestors and make something that lasts. Even if that meant going my own way and having a career in the military." He finished his wine, leaving a crimson film in the glass.

Tessa felt a pit rise in her stomach. *The career I fucked up for you.* "I'm sorry things didn't work out in the Army. I wish—"

Tyler grabbed her hand, squeezing it. "No, don't go there. Not tonight." Tyler released her hand. "When I find something from those days, when the Caplan family wasn't just about holding onto money and power, I feel like I'm part of a tapestry from that time." He smiled. "Weird, huh?"

Tessa shook her head. "We all want to find a purpose. You can still find yours."

"Like you did?"

Tessa nodded. "I guess so."

"I'm happy for you. And I hope you're right about me."

Tessa felt empathy for Tyler. Seeing him adrift and not being able to do anything about it made her sad. She mustered a smile. "Of course I'm right." She took her wine, pouring some Chianti into Tyler's empty glass. Then she raised her glass. "To today and tomorrow."

"To today and tomorrow," said Tyler, clinking her glass.

Chapter 31

Tyler picked Tessa up from the hotel in his black BMW 6 Series convertible. Tessa realized that this single vehicle probably cost more than every car she ever owned. She wondered what it would have been like, growing up in wealth and privilege. *I should tell him I get to fly on a private jet with an angel. I bet he hasn't done that.*

The antique dealer's store was in the Bay Ridge area of Brooklyn. It was a hot day, but having the top down helped. As they drove, Tyler spoke a bit about the Foundation. Tessa only partially listened. She was too busy thinking about what the artifact might mean. If Min was right and there was a hidden history of the Curia, this could be the first part of the puzzle.

I'm finally feeling like part of the Curia and then Min comes up with her theories about something suspicious going on. The Curia is asking us to devote our lives to their war. We should know if there is another agenda besides saving souls. What if there is a secret that Ruth hasn't told us? She confided in me, but I'm not naive enough to think that an angel might not tell a mortal everything about her mission.

When Tyler parked, Tessa looked around, a little disappointed. She anticipated an old curiosity shop with knick knacks behind age-discolored glass and an ornate sign hanging over the door. The kind of place where you might find a worthless trinket or a priceless treasure. The building didn't look like a store; it was a warehouse. There were no windows, only bare brick walls and a metal door. A small sign next to the door read "Zebede Antiquities – By Appointment Only."

"This is it?" asked Tessa.

"Yeah. Not exactly like going into a junk shop, right? Ms Zedebe deals exclusively with high-end clientele. No weekend antiquers looking for a rusty Happy Days lunch box."

"I feel honored," Tessa paused by the front door. "I have a big favor to ask you."

"What is it?"

"If she has what I'm looking for, could you pay for it?" Before he could respond, Tessa hastened to add, "I can pay you back right away in cash. I just need to keep this off-book."

"Ah. Spy stuff."

Tessa shrugged. *Technically, it's me sneaking around behind the back of an angel and her army of demon hunters. But I can't exactly say that.*

"Sure," Tyler said. "I'm not exactly hurting for money."

Tessa breathed a sigh of relief. "Thanks."

He pressed the buzzer next to the door. There was a whir and click as it unlocked. Tyler opened the door and waved Tessa in with a flourish. "After you, m'lady."

Tessa thought the interior was as opulent and unique as the exterior was bland and cookie cutter. "Wow," she said.

The room they entered was large, the width of the building. It was two-stories tall, with metal circular staircases leading to a wide walkway that encompassed the entire room. The ceiling was lined with bright spotlights that cast dramatic pools of light and shadow. The showroom floor was a maze of paintings on easels, statues, furniture of every type and display cases for smaller objects from the past.

"Is that a mummy case?" Tessa whispered, pointing to a gilded sarcophagus lurking in a shadowy corner.

"Probably," Tyler whispered back. "We're not in a museum. You don't have to whisper."

Tessa laughed. "Sorry. It's just – this place is amazing."

A voice answered, one that was rich, deep and warm. "Thank you."

Tessa turned to look at the source of the voice. A woman emerged from the shadows. Tessa thought she looked striking.

Her flawless skin was a deep chocolate brown. When she smiled, her dark eyes sparkled. Her slender body was encased in a matching red silk blouse and skirt. She gave Tyler an air kiss on his cheeks.

"Tyler, darling. It's been too long." She turned to Tessa. "And who is this enchanting young woman?"

"Zala, Tessa Sinclair. Tessa, Zala Kebede."

Tessa held out her hand. Zala brushed it away and gave Tessa a hug and air kisses. "Any friend of Tyler is my friend," she said.

"Particularly if they want to buy something," Tyler added.

Zala laughed. "That doesn't hurt. So, Tyler says you are looking for something specific. An artifact from a Crusader tomb."

"Yes," Tessa responded. She let Zala guide her through the maze of antiquities. "It's for a friend. She thinks it was in a lot that you sold last year to the Mannerheim Group, but they only wanted some of the artifacts. She's hoping you might still have the remaining pieces in the lot."

"What is this wayward rarity?"

"A piece of pottery."

"It's possible. I've sold numerous items to the Mannerheim Group, but usually books. They have an interest in the scribblings of monks and knights." She tilted her head to one side and smiled slightly. "I need to go into my office and consult my inventory. I'm sure you and Tyler can amuse yourselves for a few minutes." She glided into an office and closed the door behind her.

Tessa turned to Tyler. "I hope she has it. It would be disappointing to come all this way for nothing."

Tyler rolled his eyes. "Oh, so now I'm nothing?"

Tessa laughed. "You know what I mean."

The door to Zala's office swept open. "I have located your pottery, my dear. It's upstairs. Come with me."

Zala led Tessa and Tyler up one of the spiral staircases and onto the walkway. Halfway around the perimeter, she stopped at a glass case, lit from within. She unlocked the door and slid it open. She snapped on a latex glove and pulled out a jagged shard of pottery.

"Here it is," she said. "Although, to be honest, it doesn't look like much."

Tessa agreed. The pottery was thick and the edges looked crumbly. It was slightly curved. Tessa assumed it had been from the body of a pitcher or jar. One side was glazed red. The other was covered in faded paint. It depicted a skeletal white figure emerging from a pale-yellow disk. Brown stick figures knelt in front of the white entity, whether out of homage or fear, Tessa couldn't tell. There was writing below the scene, although Tessa didn't recognize the language.

"Do you know what the inscription says?"

Zala shrugged. "Not my area of expertise. I do know some people who could translate it for you, if you wish."

"No," Tessa said, "I think I can handle that."

Zala shrugged and nodded toward the stairs. "Let's put this into a lovely box, fill out the paperwork and take care of the financial details." She breezed past Tessa.

Tessa and Tyler descended the stairs and waited for Zala to package the shard.

"Thanks again. This is going to be very helpful."

Tyler's head shook slightly. "Some day, you'll have to tell me what this is really all about."

I wish I could. "I will."

Zala returned, carrying a small box, a certificate of provenance and a bill.

"I'll take the bill," Tyler said.

Zala handed it to him. "I wish I had more friends like you, my dear. Rich and generous." She then handed Tessa a business card. "If you change your mind about the translation or if you need anything else, please let me know."

A few minutes later, they emerged into the muggy afternoon. Tessa said, "Thanks for paying for this. I'll get you the money."

Tyler waved his hand. "No worries. Let's call it a gift."

"Really? Thank you."

"But, you have to come to my place for a drink on the roof."

"Oh, twist my arm," Tessa said, grinning.

***

"Welcome to Chez Caplan, Greenwich Village Annex."

Tyler ushered Tessa into his brownstone on West 10th Street and into the first-floor living room. The furnishings were tasteful American Empire style. Everything looked sturdy and comfortable. His walls were decorated with a mix of period paintings that fitted the furnishings – men heading off to hunt in dark colonial forests, women in bonnets standing in wheat fields, and rustic landscapes of the American frontier. A display case held original nineteenth-century advertisements for the railroads his family had built. The only modern touches were a fifty-inch TV on one wall and a Bose sound system in a glass cabinet underneath it.

"Nice. Very homey."

"It works for me."

"So, woodfired stove in the kitchen?"

Tyler laughed. "Try Viking range. My love of the past only goes so far. Why don't we head upstairs. It should be about time for martinis."

Tyler led her to the roof. It had a small flower and herb garden in pots and a wrought iron table and chairs. "Have a seat. I'll be right back with the drinks."

Tessa walked to the edge of the roof and looked down. She saw a few people on the sidewalks, heading home from work, looking for someplace to eat, or going to meet friends for drinks. The normal flow of life. She pulled out her glasses and put them on. The world grew blurry and indistinct. She felt like she was sinking into the waters of a gray ocean. She swept her gaze up and down the street. There were no islands of clarity. *Good. No demons on 10th Street. Probably pulling overtime on Wall Street.*

She put the glasses back in her purse and sat down. The sun was sinking toward the horizon. The air was heavy. She felt her cotton skirt cling to her legs. The scabbard on her thigh was poking her. *I did my job for Min. The rest of this time is for me. I need to leave my glasses and dagger in a safe and pretend to be a normal woman on a normal vacation. To let go, relax and have fun with an old friend.*

"Drinks have arrived."

Tyler placed a pitcher of martinis and two glasses on the table.

"You know," Tessa said, "if we start drinking, this might lead to something."

"Oh," Tyler responded as he filled her glass. "What's that?"

"I might have to go clubbing. Dancing. And you might have to come with me."

Tyler groaned. "I do not like dancing."

Tessa grinned mischievously. "You did say you were going to show me a good time."

"Yes," Tyler said, "I guess I did." He held out his glass. "Here's to drinking and dancing the night away."

Chapter 32

After the pitcher of martinis, Tessa was hungry. Tyler took her to one of his local favorites, a dive bar with great pizza. She ate half a greasy, delicious thin crust pepperoni, while downing a couple of Red Bulls. The food and caffeine counteracted some of the alcohol, just enough to feel ready to party all night.

"Okay, time to get my dance on. Are you ready, Captain Caplan?" she asked, slamming down her last Red Bull.

Tyler nodded and forced a smile, but he was uneasy. He was not looking forward to being in the close confines of a crowded nightclub. However, he found her enthusiasm impossible to deny. *Besides,* he thought, *it might be therapeutic. Exposure therapy.*

He took her to a nearby dance club, *Z-Bar.* The walls were painted in splotchy white and black stripes, the black glowing purple in the light of the ultraviolet tubes that covered the ceiling. A DJ played House music – a thudding bass that sounded like a 120 decibel heartbeat. Strobe lights behind the stage fired with each beat. The floor was packed with sweaty, colliding bodies. It reminded Tessa of the clubs in Copenhagen, before the demon nearly killed her.

Perfect. Tessa grabbed Tyler's hand and dragged him onto the dancefloor. She pushed her way into the center of the throbbing mass of bodies. When they were in the center, she turned around and draped her arms over Tyler's shoulders.

Tyler felt panic rising. His heart rate was increasing. His stomach twisted. His shirt grew damp with cold sweat. He closed his eyes, fighting the urge to leave, to run into the sweltering night and find someplace to hide. *No,* he thought, *I'm not going to do this. I'm going to move through the past and leave it behind. To today and tomorrow.*

Although the panic didn't go away, it did recede. He knew it would be back, stalking him. But, for now, for this night, this moment, Tyler was in control. He took a deep breath and opened his eyes. He focused on Tessa's swaying hips, her wild smile, and the animal blaze in her eyes. She looked the way she had when they were in the bunker. For the first time in years, he thought of that moment and did not feel sick. He felt aroused. He placed his hands on her waist.

Tessa let herself be drawn closer to Tyler. She could see sweat beading on his forehead, running down his cheeks.

Tyler felt Tessa's legs against his. Each contact sent a surge of warmth through him. He slid one hand down her back and cupped her ass.

Tessa's smile broadened. *Yes. That's what I want. Touch me like you want me.*

The music reverberated through them, a tremble from one to the other. Their skins glistened in the blasts of the strobes. They were buffeted by other dancers, but only vaguely aware of anyone else on the floor.

Tessa pulled Tyler's mouth to hers. They kissed, hard and desperate. For only a moment. Then Tessa felt the scabbard dig into her thigh as Tyler's leg pressed against it.

What the fuck am I doing? She pulled away. "I have to go to the bathroom," she shouted, barely audible over the music. She knifed through the crowd, leaving Tyler behind.

The panic that had been replaced by lust came back, a cold wave that crashed over his head. Tyler headed off the dancefloor, hoping to find some refuge.

Tessa was nauseated by her actions. *You idiot. You cannot do this. Not again.*

She pushed through a door labeled "Restrooms" and into a dark corridor. A few people were hanging out there. It was marginally less noisy. As she wove to the bathroom, she felt a hand on her shoulder. She turned, expecting it to be Tyler.

"Hey, babe." The man who grabbed her was muscular, young and bleary eyed.

High, drunk and horny. Not what I need.

"I saw you on the floor," he said, words slurring, "That guy you're with is a piece of shit. How about you and me party?"

Tessa shook her head.

The man kept smiling. "Aw, don't say that 'til you see what I got." He grabbed her waist and started to pull her to him.

Tessa reacted, the months of training and background hum of paranoia and fear bursting out as reflex. She punched his throat. His eyes bugged out. She grabbed the arm holding her and smashed the elbow with her fist. It shattered.

The other people in the hall started to notice. Tessa didn't see them. Her vision was narrow, a red tunnel focused on the man.

She brought her foot up, kicking the side of his head. He smashed into the wall, face first, flattening his nose and knocking him out. Her right hand went to her leg, ready to pull out the dagger and slice him open.

As he slumped to the floor, Tessa looked around. She realized where she was and what she was doing. The other people looked at her with a mix of fear and surprise.

The lingering effects of the martinis were wiped away, replaced by ice-cold sobriety. She looked back at the wreckage of the man on the floor. He was moving sluggishly. She felt a spark of relief. *At least I didn't kill him.*

Tessa could see that some of the bystanders were shaking off their shock.

I need to get out of here. I can't deal with cops or this asshole's friends. She ran past them, back across the dance floor, through the thrashing arms and legs, heart-beat music pushing her on. She burst from the crowd of dancers. Tyler was standing near the bar, drinking a glass of water. She grabbed him.

"Hey," he shouted, "I think I've had enough dancing."

"Me too," Tessa shouted back, pulling him through the door and out onto the sweltering midnight street.

"Are you okay?" asked Tyler.

Tessa shook her head. *I fucked that guy up without even thinking about it. I treated him like a demon. I was going to kill him.* She was horrified.

She was also elated. *Maybe he deserved it. That asshole could've raped me. Or some other woman. Why is it only demons deserve to suffer?*

She looked up into Tyler's eyes. The ones that looked at her years ago with desire. The ones that still looked at her that way. *Why not?* "Let's go back to your place."

"Are you sure that's a good idea?"

"No, but it's what I want to do."

As they ran down the street, Tessa felt like her body was on fire. She imagined her aura was a blaze of red and yellow. *Anger. Happiness. That's what I feel. That's what the Curia wants to harness in me. Violence and lust. All for their war.*

They tumbled into the brownstone. "Tessa," Tyler said, as Tessa pushed him against the foyer wall. She cut off the rest of his protests with her lips.

She broke away. "Let's fuck. We can deal with the fallout tomorrow. Or never."

She dropped to her knees and unzipped his pants. She reached in and tugged down his underwear. Then she wrapped her fingers around his erection and pulled it out.

Tyler let out a satisfied groan as Tessa ran her tongue over his shaft, before putting him in her mouth. For a few moments, there was only the sound of Tyler's heavy breathing and the honking, grumbling traffic on the street.

Tyler looked down. He saw blood on Tessa's knuckles. "Hey, are you okay?"

Tessa pulled away from him. "What?"

"Your hand."

She looked, seeing the smear of blood. "It's nothing." She wanted to be someplace else. Someplace that reminded her of the balcony in Paris. Of the demon taking her while the whole city watched. "Let's go to the roof."

She stood up and pushed him toward the stairs. As she followed, she pulled off her scabbard and dropped it along with her panties on the couch.

On the roof, she bent over the table and pulled up her skirt. She looked back at him. "Come on. I know you want me. No one gets hurt."

Tyler hesitated for a moment. He thought of the wrecked TOC. His dead men. Tessa's writhing body against his. The dull thump of explosions. The smell of sweat and diesel. The sand grit rubbing into his palms. The metal stench of blood. The wild look in her eyes when he fucked her.

He was behind her, inside her without realizing it. He wasn't slow or gentle. He grabbed her shoulders and thrust himself fully into her. He thought about his stunted life, taking it out on Tessa's body.

"Yes," she moaned. This was what she wanted. To bring one man to the edge of life and then get fucked by another who was desperate for her. She felt power swelling inside, harder and more pleasurable than the cock that was bringing her closer and closer to climaxing.

This is what the demons feel like. What Ruth feels like. What a hunter feels like when she's killing one of those fuckers. I'm above everything ... everyone.

The edge of the table pressed into her thighs. She gripped the edge with her hands. She looked at them, seeing the blood and bruising. She thought about the way the crack of bones could be heard over the pounding music and the look of terror when the man realized what was happening to him. She saw the fear on the faces of the bystanders, as they watched Tessa take him apart. She pushed back, wanting Tyler to make her feel anger and lust.

Tyler dug his fingers into her shoulders as he increased the fervor of his thrusts.

Tessa was panting. Her orgasm was welling up. Her legs trembled. Her hands ached. Her body seemed to tighten in anticipation of the release to come.

Tyler pushed in one last time. "Oh fuck," he said as he orgasmed.

Tessa knew that Tyler was done. She was almost there. "Not yet, not yet."

Tyler pulled out of her and dropped to his knees. He put his tongue to work on her sensitive clit. It only took a few moments for the orgasm that had been building up to burst.

Tessa sighed as months of pent-up tension softened and dissipated. Her knuckles stung. Her blouse clung to her back. Her breasts ached from being pressed into the swirls of iron on the surface of the table. Her legs trembled with the after effects of her orgasm. Her breath came slow and easy as she came down from her high.

I'll regret this in the morning. But it's not morning.

Chapter 33

Tyler was standing next to Tessa's bed, a hotel towel wrapped around his dripping body. He looked down at her. She was nude and curled up. That's how she liked to sleep – in a ball, with her back to Tyler. He would wrap around her, feeling her warmth in the night. It was comforting. He would miss it, just like he'd miss her company and energy. After the night on the roof, Tyler played tour guide by day. At night, they explored their mutual passion that had started in Iraq.

He felt a twinge of sadness. She was leaving today. *She's going back to her real life,* he thought. *This was a vacation for her, a break from who she is now.*

He wanted to touch her, to take her in his arms and ask her to stay. Or to walk away, to get dressed, head out the door and not look back. But he couldn't move. Either action would mean commitment and he was afraid of her reaction.

Tessa woke up and uncurled. She stretched her arms and legs, groaning as her joints popped. "Getting old at twenty-eight," she said.

"I made some coffee."

"Mmm ... high end hotel java. Please, get me a cup."

He handed her a steaming mug and sat on the bed. He placed a hand on her bare thigh.

She smiled. She glanced at the clock and saw that she had a few hours before she needed to head to the airport. *Plenty of time.* "Feel like one last round before I go?"

Tyler shook his head. "I'm going to need a couple of week's rest."

"Yeah," said Tessa, laughing, "you might want to limber up for my next visit."

Tyler smiled, feeling hopeful. "Next visit?"

Tessa shrugged. "Why not? I had a great time." She glanced at the bruises on her knuckles. They were already fading, a sprinkle of light purple splotches. She no longer felt bad about what she did to the man in the club. She didn't feel much of anything about the incident. He sexually harassed her and paid the price; she was finding it easier to move on from things that would have stuck with her before.

Is that my training kicking in? Is everyone going to be a victim, a bystander or a target? Ivanov would say that's the best way to look at people, that it helps you stick them into emotional compartments and get on with the mission. But I've never been that person. I don't know if I want to be.

"I hope I'm more than just a sports fuck," Tyler said.

Tessa gently kicked his back. "Sure. You also have a great car."

"Ha ha ha," Tyler deadpanned. "I'm serious. Is this going someplace?"

She sat up, propping her back against the headboard. "I don't have the luxury of planning that kind of stuff out. Not now. But I care about you. I don't want whatever it is we have to fade away. I wish I had a better answer for you, but my job, it's complicated."

Tyler nodded. "I guess it has to be." He stood up and let the towel drop. Tessa grinned at the sight of his rising erection.

***

Tessa reclined in her seat. The afterglow of her time with Tyler lingered. She ordered a vodka tonic and looked out the window. The Atlantic slid blackly beneath the plane. It reminded her of that fateful day eighteen months ago, flying with Ruth to the Academy. *If I knew then what I do now, would I still have gone through with everything?*

She thought of Min and Desange, and the sense of purpose the Curia gave her. Her life was spiraling into a blackness infinitely darker than the water below. She knew that it would eventually have consumed her. The Curia saved her from herself. *I would have drunk myself into the grave. Or finished the job of killing myself.*

The comfort she felt was balanced by the new threats she faced, not least the danger she might represent to Tyler.

Ruth warned me about Tyler, she said he was a loose end. But I care about him. I don't know where this is going, but I want to find out. He thinks I'm doing intel work and knows enough not to press me about it. That should satisfy the Curia.

He's a fantasy. The guy who I can't really have. I know this can't last. The life of a hunter is not compatible with Tyler's. Besides, beyond the sex and a brief, dark part of my past, what do we have? Our attraction was always in part about how illicit it was. Without that, would I even want a relationship with him?

She looked out the window. The sun was behind the plane, reflecting off the wings, making them look like they were on fire.

The reality of my life is that Tyler has no place in it.

She found the bright glow unpleasant and slid the shade down.

And what about Ruth? If she finds out I went to New York and rekindled things with Tyler what will she do? I was careful about comms, but she could have had me followed. New York has hunters. Tessa sighed. *It doesn't matter, I did nothing wrong. At least I didn't have sex with a demon on my R&R. That's an improvement.*

It was fun to pretend to be like everyone else for a few days. And the sex was pretty good ... but not Dylan good.

The last thought bothered her. Prior to having sex with Tyler, she had been able to focus on the fear that encountering the demon had generated. But now, she couldn't help but compare the two. And Tyler, for all his passion, failed to measure up to what the demon did to her.

Dylan was bred for sexual pleasure. He read my aura and saw how I responded to what he was doing. And it's all he does – tempt people with physical pleasure. Charm, use and manipulate them. A slight smile formed. *Fuck them in ways they've never been fucked before.*

Her drink arrived. She took a sip and turned her thoughts to other things.

Mission accomplished, I got the pottery shard. Hopefully, Min can translate the writing and make some headway with her theory. Although what we do about it, I have no idea. What if she's right? If these are aliens...oh shit, I fucked ET. Well, he did know how to use his magic finger. She couldn't help laughing out loud. The woman sitting next to her looked over.

"Sorry, private joke."

If this war is a fight between two alien races what's with the temptation stuff? Why would aliens want to have sex with people? Or get them to eat too much junk food? Min might have part of the answer; but I think her focus on aliens is going to miss some important details.

She finished her drink and decided not to order another one. The fatigue she felt from lack of sleep and reunion sex was intensified by the vodka. She yawned and snuggled against the bulkhead, the light turbulence rocking her to sleep.

Chapter 34

It was a cold and windy day in late October. Tessa and Min were making their way from the Academy to the abandoned coastal town. They would soon be assigned a mission for Min's first field observation exercise. This was also the final step in Tessa's training before graduation. She could see that Min was nervous about the possibility of facing a demon. Most weren't as dramatic as Tessa's, but Min questioned her ability to survive if the worst happened.

Tessa hoped that this excursion would take Min's mind off that prospect. She pulled the hood of her jacket up and fastened it in place. Although the sun was high in the sky, its pale light carried no warmth.

"I'm not looking forward to winter," said Min, stepping around a patch of purple-colored marsh thistle. The tough little plants were scattered around the island, bursts of color among the dominant greens and browns.

"At least you've got winter break coming and you can go any place you'd like," Tessa said. "Maybe you and Francisco can enjoy a romantic adventure somewhere tropical?"

Min hugged herself to keep warm. The thought of a sunny beach and gentle sea breeze sounded appealing. She let out a sigh. "That would be nice. But I've already made plans – winter break in Rome, doing research. I'm hoping I can find more references to portals in the Curia's archives there."

"At least you won't have Ruth play chaperon. Did you get the green light to enter the archives?"

Min nodded. "I told them that I was coming up with a new, data-driven metric for rating hunter scenarios for training purposes and needed a larger data set than is available here."

Tessa smiled. "Good cover. Ivanov has taught you well. Any luck determining the language on the pottery shard and where it originated from?"

"Yes, it looks Coptic, so likely from Northeast Africa. When I'm in Rome, I'm going to find someone who can help me interpret this. I've identified a few leads through the Vatican that can read Coptic."

Tessa admired Min's devotion to her side project. Finding the secrets of the Curia would provide both of them with a fuller picture of the organization they were devoting their lives to. She hoped Min would contact her after Rome with information that might shed light on its shadowy aspects. She looked at her friend, bundled up against the biting wind. *She needs to be careful. She has a good sense of self-preservation, but the stakes are high.*

"I'm excited to hear about what you find. Ruth is well-connected in Rome and I imagine has eyes around, so watch your six, okay?"

Min rolled her eyes. "Yes, mother."

Tessa laughed. "I know, I know I'm being paranoid. Product of my time in the Army. So how are things with you and Francisco?"

Min spent the next few minutes talking excitedly about her budding relationship with the handsome *carioca*, a native of Rio de Janeiro. Although Min remained focused on her studies, both formal and otherwise, Tessa had noted a few times when the two slipped away together. A hike to the village. An overnight in their dorm, when Tessa had made it a point to linger late in the 24-hour lounge. She had also noted Ruth's blandly disapproving looks when the two were sitting together in the cafeteria or lounge. *I bet they will get assigned to different cells.*

"I'm happy for you," Tessa said as Min took a break from enthusiastically talking about Francisco. She thought about her own, complicated relationship with Desange and how hard it was to deal with him being gone.

Over the months, he had dropped off comms a few times. After the first instance, she had gotten somewhat used to it. She would field calls from his family, telling them he was working on a vaguely defined assignment. When she had mentioned this to him after the first incident, Desange had offered to tell his family not to contact her. She declined; she didn't mind assuaging his family's concerns. She found it sweet that they cared so much, a very different attitude from her own family.

Since leaving Detroit, she had received minimal texts and emails from her family. Her mother had sent an email a week after she arrived at the Academy, asking if she was okay. She tried a few more times in the months that followed. Her father and brother Zach never tried to reach her. The last contact she received from anyone in the Sinclair clan had been a text from her sister Carrie. She wanted to know if she was going to show for the holidays and make the family dinner "a hilarious shitshow." Tessa didn't bother to reply. She was busy on her field observation exercise in Copenhagen and had bigger problems to deal with.

As they trudged across the broken ground, she thought about her first-year summer break in France with Desange. *That's what a family should be like. People who care about each other, who lift each other up.*

"You should be careful," Tessa said, hiking up a hill.

"About what?"

"Francisco. When you get your field assignments, you might never see him again."

"I know, like you and Desange. Being a hunter means we have to sacrifice connections for the mission." Min shrugged. "That's more important than relationships. I guess."

Tessa felt the cold cut through her jacket. "Hunters still get to see their friends and family, But being a hunter imposes limits you wouldn't have in a normal life. Let's warm up." Tessa led Min to the red building with the stove. She started a fire and set a kettle of water on a small propane burner. "I want to talk about what's coming up."

"The field observation exercise."

Tessa nodded. "Exactly. I know you're worried about it."

"You almost died on yours and you're a much stronger fighter than me."

"That's not how they usually go. When Desange went on his first one, he spent a week in a cafe. Some demons take months to successfully hunt. The idea isn't to kill a demon. It's to see how a hunt works. The steps that a hunter goes through, the precautions they take and how everything you've been taught is put to use."

"You still almost died. I think demons, or aliens, are a legitimate thing to be afraid of."

Was I afraid? My adrenaline was surging. But I've seen people die. My definition of fear has shifted. She hasn't been to war. She came straight from a university. I'm the anomaly here. She made hot cocoa and handed one steaming mug to Min. "Good. You should be. It's normal to be afraid."

Min raised an eyebrow. "Were you afraid?"

"Yes." *This is a good lie. The truth is too complicated.* "Fear keeps you from getting complacent. We got in trouble because our hunter was sloppy. He should never have engaged our target in a nightclub. He should have tagged her and tracked her." She saw the look on Min's face changing, becoming more reassured. "A healthy amount of fear makes you smarter. You avoid mistakes like the one Arno made."

"I hadn't thought of it like that."

Tessa grinned. "That's what I'm here for, to share my boundless wisdom."

"Do you know where we'll be going?"

Tessa shook her head. "Not yet. McKenna told me we will get our briefing this week. I'll find out at the same time as you." The wind set the plastic stretched over the windows humming. "Hopefully somewhere nicer than here."

Min nodded and took a sip of her cocoa. "And warmer."

Tessa got up from her camp chair and warmed her hands by the stove. In the Faroes, even the chilliest day had a clean crispness about it. While bundled up against the cold, she also felt invigorated by each freezing gust of wind. She thought about how different the cold felt in Mykines compared to Detroit. During Detroit winters, it was a numbing blanket that settled over everything, making time slow to a crawl. The gray sky and dirty snow seemed to last forever. There were times when Tessa thought the cold and gloom were working into her, freezing her insides.

"Can I ask you about something?" asked Min.

Tessa sat down again. "Sure."

"You don't talk about your family much. Why is that?"

Min was right; Tessa hadn't said much in the last year about her family. When she opened up about Detroit and how it led to being in the Curia, she had glossed over her family history. That was not too hard, given the tenuous contact she had with them; but she also opted not to tell Min about her upbringing. She described her relationship with them as "complicated" – a word she thought sufficiently vague to cover a host of interpretations, including the correct one.

"My family is a disaster. I have toxic parents, a sociopathic sister, and a drug-addicted brother. It's the kind of family you wouldn't wish on your worst enemy."

"Wow, that's a lot. I'm sorry."

"I left them a long time ago and I'm better for it. I think I left them even before I went into the Army. I knew that the only reason they were my family was an accident of birth and social conventions." She opened up the cooler and pulled out the quarter bottle of vodka inside. "Drink?"

Min wrinkled her nose and shook her head.

Tessa opened the bottle and poured a shot into her mug. She drank it and smiled at the spreading warmth. She put the bottle away; she didn't want to get drunk – she just needed that burn to continue.

"I make my own family. I thought the Army would be it, but I fucked that up. I want the Curia..." she stopped, shaking her head. "No, not the Curia. The people in the Curia. You and Desange ... you guys are my family. I hope that doesn't sound too fucked up."

Min reached out and took Tessa's hand. "You're talking to an orphan. I don't think that sounds messed up at all."

"Thanks." Tessa listened to the thrumming plastic for a moment.

Chapter 35

"Tessa, can I talk to you in private for a moment?" asked Ruth.

Do I really have a choice? Tessa and Min had just been briefed by Ivanov and given their field observation exercise assignment. They would be going to Iceland and shadowing Arno Wollman again, who was still pursuing Marit. Sphere analysts had reliable information that she would be attending Northern Lights, a large music festival in Reykjavik. It was a prime location for her to deal party drugs. Ruth had been present during the briefing, which Tessa found odd. *She wasn't present during my Copenhagen briefing.* "Sure."

Ruth glanced at Ivanov. "Can you escort Min-Seo out?"

Min looked disconcerted, but didn't say anything. She exited the room with Ivanov.

Ruth closed the door behind them and turned off the projector, leaning against Ivanov's desk. "I want you to do a favor for me."

What can I do for Ruth that she can't do herself? "Of course ... if I can help, I will."

"This is a delicate matter, which is why I asked Min-Seo and Svetlana to leave. Arno's fitness reports have been slipping since Copenhagen. He lost track of Marit and then failed to close out three hunts."

"We're told that hunters lose their targets regularly," Tessa said. "Silva profiled several hunts that took years to complete. Maybe it's just a bad streak."

Ruth nodded. "If it were just that, I wouldn't be concerned. But he has dropped off comms with his cell leader for extended periods of time as well. As you know, that is a violation of field protocol."

"Can that happen in deep cover?"

Ruth shook her head, a clipped motion that made Tessa feel like she should stop interjecting. "Occasionally, but these were not deep cover assignments. We also have indications Arno has been drinking heavily."

"There's no rule against drinking in the Curia. What do you want me to do, spy on Arno and pull him out of the bar after a three-drink limit? I'm here for Min, not him."

"You are here for the Curia," Ruth said, her eyes narrowing. "Drinking on your own time is your business. Doing it on an active hunt is a problem. And he has been. I've had our psych team in Rome look at his performance over the last year and there are concerning patterns. It appears losing Marit in Copenhagen was the beginning of a downward spiral for him. It broke his confidence. You will be in a good position to monitor him and report back on how he performs." She approached Tessa, placing a hand on her shoulder.

The grip was firm. Tessa noticed that whenever Ruth touched her, she seemed to squeeze just a little too hard, like she was unfamiliar with her own strength. *Or she likes demonstrating it.* "Okay. Should I do anything if there is a problem?"

Ruth released her shoulder. "No. Just report back to me. Not to McKenna or anyone else. I'll handle Arno."

Tessa couldn't read the look on her face. It was back to the impassive stare, the lack of emotion. *Handle Arno ... what does that mean? Is there a hunter rehab? Or an unmarked grave?*

"That's all. You can go. Uri will fly you and Min-Seo to Torshavn in the morning. Your tickets, hotel rooms and festival passes are in your briefing packets. Good luck."

Tessa raised an eyebrow. "No God bless?"

Ruth smiled slightly. "That too."

Chapter 36

There were no direct flights from the Faroe Islands to Iceland. Tessa and Min spent hours in transit between Vagar Airport to Oslo and then Copenhagen, before finally boarding an Airbus A330 for the final leg to Keflavik.

Tessa squeezed into her coach window seat. *Demon hunting on a budget. This really is like working for the government.*

"I'm looking forward to Iceland," Min said excitedly, taking her seat next to Tessa. "Even if we're going there on..." she hesitated, "business, it will still be neat to see a new country. I've always wanted to check out the hot springs. Maybe we can stop at the Blue Lagoon? It's on the way from the airport."

"That would be fun..." She thought about her own attitude in Copenhagen, and how little time there had been during the week-long exercise to play tourist. "But this isn't a vacation."

Min sighed. "I know. It was just a thought."

I handled that well. Tessa fidgeted in her seat. She wanted to set a good example, but she was not looking forward to seeing Arno again and the thought of having to fight Marit frightened her. *If Ruth's report is accurate, he's behaving in an impulsive, unpredictable manner. It must be bad if she's asking a recruit to babysit a seasoned hunter. What if he acts rashly and tries to engage her in a crowded music festival?*

"Are you okay?" asked Min. "You seem a bit on edge."

Tessa smiled, pulling up her window shade to look outside. "I'm fine, a little restless. I was like this before an operation in Iraq. Wired. I'll be better once we land and get settled into our hotel."

"I see." Min wasn't sure she believed Tessa, but decided not to press her.

Tessa gave Min a friendly pat on the shoulder. "Hey, don't worry about it. I'll figure out a way to get us some free time.

I've never been to Iceland either." She leaned close to Min, conspiratorially lowering her voice. "I'm sure we can go out dancing one night. I know you like EDM. Check out the line up and let me know if there's a DJ you really want to see."

Min smiled, making Tessa feel better. "Awesome, thanks."

Tessa settled back in her seat and went over a mental checklist as the plane took off. *Arrive, rent a car, head to Reykjavik and meet Arno at our hotel. Our gear should be in our rooms. Arno provides us with mission parameters and I make sure Min is clear about the role Arno has for us. Then we hunt Marit, in a city with thousands of music festival attendees, in a country I've never been to, all while keeping an eye on Arno, Min and any random demons that might be there. Piece of cake.*

The only equipment she had brought, her dagger and glasses, were in her carry on, the former stored inside a hidden compartment in her laptop. She had learned from Ivanov that the dagger didn't show up on any type of scanners, including x-rays. It wasn't made of metal, although it appeared to be. "The only thing that can detect a dagger are your eyes," Ivanov had said.

Min had spent time trying to understand how this metaphysical weapon could work from a scientific perspective. She attempted to explain her theory to Tessa one night over drinks at the lounge. *Something about higher dimensional vibrations and the holographic universe. However it works, it kills demons.*

Tessa wished she had been able to keep the dagger on her. However, she knew that if airport security found it, they would turn her over to law enforcement. When she boarded, she had put on her glasses briefly and been rewarded with blurry vision and a throbbing head. However, she felt better knowing there were no demons on the flight.

She looked at Min, who was watching a Korean soap opera on her iPad. *I've read the briefing material. I have two years of training under my belt. I've survived a fight with a demon.*

We've got this.

Tessa had a few hours to kill and wanted something to distract herself. She pulled out her latest mystery novel, *The Willow Home*, and lost herself in the story of a crime-solving Guatemalan immigrant working as a housekeeper.

After reading her book for a while, Tessa decided to pull out the briefing packet. One of her main concerns was the size of the music festival. With venues spread over the city and thousands of attendees, the task of hunting Marit seemed daunting.

She did have some information to build on. She knew what Marit looked like. She could still see those icy blue eyes and well-manicured nails wagging at her. She also knew the gluttony demon sold party drugs and followed the music scene. The analysts believed she would be dealing at the festival, taking advantage of the permissive environment to engage in widespread temptation. They also were confident she was unaware that the Curia was on her tail. Tessa wasn't so sure. *If it's true what Ruth said – that Arno has gotten sloppy – it's likely she's aware of the hunt. Even if she isn't, we should proceed as if she is. Arno will focus our efforts on the best places to spot a drug dealer. With three of us in the field scanning stages and crowds with our glasses, and with a little luck, we'll find Marit.* She hoped that Arno would fall back on his decade's worth of experience as a hunter and that Ruth's concern was exaggerated.

She glanced at her watch. There was still an hour until the plane landed. She had lost interest in her book, and Min seemed to be enjoying herself in the world of household drama.

Maybe I should get some rack time. This is going to be a long week. She slid the window shade down and laid her head against the bulkhead. She closed her eyes and was soon asleep.

She was in Paris. Instead of Desange, she was there with Dylan. They were standing on the observation deck at the top of the Eiffel Tower. It was dark and the city spread out at her feet, a million lights burning away the night. They were sharing a bottle of blood red wine. The lights of the city grew brighter, a field of suns, washing out Dylan's face. She wanted to see him. She put on her glasses. The world went blurry, a smear of green, blue and yellow. She tried focusing on the empty bottle of wine, but it was an amorphous scarlet blob. She turned to Dylan for comfort. His image was clear. Every line on his face popped out. The color of his green eyes was so intense, it made Tessa squint. *Shit, he's a demon.* She pulled out her dagger and slit his throat. He fell to the metal deck, his body turning to glass and shattering on impact, leaving behind a pile of sparkling dust. All except for his beating heart, a wet hunk of throbbing muscle.

Tessa awoke abruptly.

"Ladies and gentlemen, we are beginning our descent into Keflavik Airport and should land in thirty minutes."

She pulled her window shade back up. It was still light out.

Min took off her headphones. "Did you have a bad dream?"

"Yes, about Iraq. I get them from time to time." *She is already nervous about this mission, no need to tell her I had a bad dream about a demon. Especially one I slept with. That is a secret Desange and I share.*

Tessa and Min disembarked into a claustrophobia-inducing mass. Planes full of festival goers and tourists were forming a steady stream of people slowly filtering through customs. Everyone was crushed together, wanting to get out of the airport. Tessa could feel tension hanging in the air.

It reminded her of a street market in Iraq. The *souk* near her FOB was always crowded. She heard the din of shouting children, braying parents, and merchants in their stalls calling out their wares. The sound hung over the market like a noisome cloud. Standing in line at Keflavik Airport customs, she could remember the smell of sweat, rubber and burning meat. And there was so much dust, it caked her throat. She hated that dust.

"Everything okay?"

Min was poking her. Tessa realized she had stopped and a gap had opened up in line. She glanced behind her and saw the faces of annoyed people, glaring at her.

"Sorry." She picked up her bag and moved forward.

Customs went smoothly – ten seconds of perfunctory questions followed by a "Welcome to Iceland" from a bored-looking agent. Tessa and Min shuffled through the airport to baggage pickup. They found their luggage. Tessa bought coffee from a Dunkin Donuts near the entrance and stepped outside. The scrum of people waiting for buses and taxis made her thankful that the Curia rented them a car. She pulled on her thick parka. The temperature was hovering around freezing and a stiff breeze from the west made it even worse. *At least it's not snowing.*

Min had a grin on her face, clearly enchanted by the stark, rugged terrain. "I can see why science fiction movies are filmed here. This looks extraterrestrial."

The rental agency the Curia used was called *Gildi*, Icelandic for "value." An older-model Land Rover was assigned to them. While they waited for the boxy vehicle to be brought up, the sky turned from pale white to dark gray. *Orange?* Tessa thought when she saw the Land Rover. *Not great from an espionage standpoint. Maybe the Curia thinks we may have to do some off-road hunting and this is all they have available. Arno probably has a van anyway.* Almost as soon as they got to the Land Rover, heavy, wet snowflakes splattered the windshield.

"It's like being back in Michigan."

"And Seoul. We have weather coming down from Siberia."

"After we meet Arno, let's find a good coffee shop. I'll buy you a hot chocolate. Come on, I'll drive." Tessa hoisted herself into the vehicle.

"Great, I'll DJ." Min reached for the radio and found an EDM station, featuring the bands playing at the festival. "You like?"

Tessa nodded, drumming her fingers on the steering wheel in time to the thumping synthesizers. She had to fight the urge to drive the way the music inspired: fast and reckless. It had been a while since she was behind the wheel of a car. She missed speeding down a lonely highway, music blaring. *That would be a bad way to start a field exercise – traffic accident.*

The trip from Keflavik to Reykjavik was uneventful. Due to the festival traffic, the single road between the two cities was filled with buses and cars. Tessa focused on driving, while Min took in the sights.

Min was impressed with the stark landscape of the country. To the west, the gray waters of the Atlantic churned. Around her, the broken volcanic terrain of weathered rocks was slowly being buried under a layer of fresh snow. She made a mental note of the turnoff for the Blue Lagoon. Entering the outskirts of Reykjavik, she was surprised at how generic much of the city felt, a jarring contrast to the otherworldly sensation of the countryside. Most of the buildings were of the steel, glass and concrete box variety.

Tessa was wondering how another week with Arno would play out. Although she understood Ruth's point of view, she didn't relish reporting on the hunter. *Arno is one of us. If I ever fell on hard times, I'd like to think the Curia would show some compassion and not send someone to spy on me.* The more she learned about the Curia, however, the less she thought that was possible. Deviance would not be tolerated, especially if Ruth thought it would impact the mission. *Security is the primary concern of the Curia. The privacy of hunters is clearly secondary. Besides if he really is slipping, it would be better for everyone to get him out of the field before he becomes compromised.*

The Land Rover zoomed past a sign with an enormous pink pig on it. Tessa immediately thought of eggs and bacon, realizing how hungry she was. *I should have grabbed something at the airport.* An unexpected sensation overcame her. Her life at the Academy had become regimented. The handful of vacations and brief excursions to the abandoned village didn't make up for that fact. *Soon I'll be hunting in Los Angeles on my own.* She took a deep breath, relishing the freedom that awaited her after graduation.

When Tessa and Min entered Reykjavik proper, the buildings became more varied and colorful. They cruised past the Hallgrimskirkja cathedral. The gray spire was lost in a fog of snow. Their hotel, the Traveler's Inn, was nearby. It was a five-star, boutique hotel in the heart of Reykjavik. Tessa thought it would be the perfect location to operate from, close to the festival's venues and many of the bars and clubs frequented by tourists. *This is a fertile hunting ground for demons. Drunk, high and horny tourists. It's a buffet of temptation and sin.*

After parking in the attached garage and making their way through check in, Min and Tessa went to their rooms. Tessa dropped her luggage on the floor and stretched out face down on the king-sized bed. She had work to do, but the firm mattress and silky sheets enticed her. She gave herself five minutes to decompress from her journey. She felt herself getting sleepy.

No naps. I have to check all my gear and contact Arno. With a wistful sigh, she got up and laid out her surveillance equipment on the bed. Remote cameras and microphones, night vision with demon glass snap-down lens, a police scanner tuned to the local channel, a secure satellite phone and a laptop in a milspec case. She checked the small infiltration kit – a glass cutter, lock pick kit and specialized electronic lock decoder – and, finally, laid out her glasses and dagger. She took off her jeans and strapped the small, thin dagger on her left thigh. The subtle weight and pressure inspired a feeling of security.

She opened up the laptop and established a VPN connection to the Curia's communication network. She clicked on the messenger application and typed in a simple message: *On site.*

She then sent a text to Arno through the Curia's encrypted app: *At the hotel. Time and place to meet?*

In less than a minute the reply came: *Hotel bar 20 min.*

Tessa stowed her gear and changed into a long wool skirt. She stuffed her glasses in an across-the-shoulder travel purse and reflexively patted her thigh. She could feel the straps and sheath, the bulge of the dagger within.

Min was waiting for Tessa in the hallway, looking out the window at Faxafloi Bay. The sun was already dipping below the horizon. Although it was only 3:30, the days were short this time of year and the water glimmered in the dwindling sunlight.

"Great view, huh?" Tessa said.

"It really is. It can almost make me forget why I'm here."

"Well, come on. We're supposed to meet Arno downstairs in a few minutes. Besides, I owe you a hot chocolate."

The two women went to the hotel bar. It was mostly empty. There was a table of women near the picture window in tight dresses and high heels, talking loudly in Russian. Tessa led Min to the bar and the two sat on the high-backed stools. Tessa ordered Min a hot chocolate with Bailey's and a whiskey sour for herself.

"Are you sure we should be drinking before meeting Arno?" Min asked.

Tessa laughed to herself. *I'm sure Arno won't mind.* "Meeting here was his suggestion. To blend in, we should do what people do at a bar."

Min laughed. "No complaints here." She took a drink of the rich chocolate and made a happy yummy noise.

Tessa nodded toward the door. "Arno just walked in."

The hunter was wearing his glasses. He scanned the room. Satisfied there were no demons, he took them off and walked over to Tessa and Min. The look on his face was not a happy one. It was not even the same annoyed look he had last year in Copenhagen.

He looks pissed. "Mr Wollman," Tessa said, holding out her hand.

He stared at it for a moment, then reluctantly took it. "Ms Sinclair, Ms Kim. Welcome to Iceland, the most pointless nation on Earth." He sat down and ordered a vodka tonic. "Is all your equipment here and ready?"

Tessa nodded. "Roger, it's all accounted for."

"Good," Arno said. "Plan on going off mission this time?"

Don't engage, don't engage, don't engage. Oh fuck it. He's being a jerk. "No, sir, unless I have to save your ass again."

Arno glared at her, downing half his drink in one gulp. "Just stay out of my way." He paused, nodding to himself as he made a decision. "When we begin the exercise, leave your daggers behind." He finished his drink and ordered another. "Kim, you know what's expected of you?"

"I'm here to observe you and learn about field operations."

"Good." He smiled. It was not a friendly expression.

"Arno, I think we should keep our daggers on us at all times. If the situation goes kinetic, they could come in handy." Tessa took a long sip of her whiskey sour and waited for the fallout.

"I don't need you thinking you're hunters and making me lose a kill. If you have your daggers, you are not welcome on my hunt. That's my rule, take it or leave it." Arno looked expectant, hoping Tessa would opt to stay behind.

Min was afraid the two were going to start throwing punches. *He's handicapping our capabilities out in the field. This isn't good. Fighting is not my strong suit, and without a dagger...*

"Your hunt, your rules," said Tessa.

Arno's face grew sour. He finished his drink, threw a couple of kroner notes on the bar and stood up. "Use tonight to start scouting out the festival locations and this part of the city. I'll send Sinclair the mission outline. We can meet tomorrow morning and start at 9am sharp."

Tessa nodded. "We'll see you in the morning."

"And no daggers." Arno stalked out of the bar.

"Wow, there is some serious bad blood," Min said. "I agree with you about the daggers. Should we report this to Ruth?"

"It's up to him how we conduct the exercise. If he wants us without daggers, then we have to follow his directive. Or sit this out." She took a drink and placed the glass back on the bar with exaggerated care. "Which is what he wants, for me to fail." She looked at Min. "But we're not going to do what he wants." She looked away. "We just have to put up with him for a week. It'll be okay."

Min's face reflected her concern. The nervousness she had experienced before the field observation exercise, which had faded thanks to Tessa's reassurances, returned in full force. "So what's your call on the daggers?"

Tessa laid a hand on her shoulder. "When we're with him, we play by his rules." She grinned. "Otherwise, we take the initiative and go out armed."

Chapter 37

Tessa and Min were in a small Thai noodle shop on Laugavegur street, making their plans for the evening over dinner. The Northern Lights festival was spread out across central Reykjavik, with bands playing at a dozen venues.

"Since we're conducting a preliminary recon, let's stick together and try to hit as many places as possible," Tessa said, perusing the festival schedule on her iPhone app.

Arno's mission outline had a comprehensive schedule of when and where they would be over the next four days. While she hated his attitude, she liked his detailed plans.

"I'm glad you let me have my dagger," said Min, stuffing noodles into her mouth.

"Yeah, well tonight, it's just us recruits."

Min shook her head. "Why would he want to leave us defenseless against a demon? All because of his ego?"

Tessa frowned, biting her cheek. "I'm not sure, but if I sense that he is endangering us, I'll stand up to him. I hope he has learned his lesson after Copenhagen. If we find Marit and he follows protocol, he will try to get her into a confined location away from civilians. Without our daggers, we'll have to stay back." She shrugged. "We'll probably be on surveillance duty all week. Which is fine – it's safer that way. Just prepare yourself for a lot of caffeine."

Min sighed. "I appreciate that. I'm fine watching the attack from a safe distance. This hunter is different than I imagined. Did it seem like he was intoxicated when he met us?"

Tessa debated her answer as she savored her green curry. *Should I disclose my concerns to her fully about Arno, increasing her anxiety, or should I temper her worries and make excuses for his behavior?* She thought back to her transparency with Min about her delayed entry into the Academy. *She thanked me for my authenticity. Go with honesty here.* "Yes, I'm concerned that his years hunting demons have caused him to lose his nerve. I saw it happen in the Army. Soldiers who were fine one day stopped being able to function the next. They had just had enough." She snapped her fingers. "Like a switch. Maybe he's trying to self-medicate with alcohol." *I hope that's not my future – fight demons until I burn out and crawl inside a bottle.* Tessa reflexively shook her head. *It won't be. I have more self-control.*

"Should we report this to the Curia?" Min asked. "I don't want to get him in trouble, and if it was just the drinking, I might let it go. I mean…" She caught herself. She was almost going to say, "you drink," but realized that wouldn't help. "…this dagger thing has me worried."

"Let me worry about that part. I promise, I'll do everything I can to ensure Arno's behavior does not endanger us. Okay?"

Min scooped up the last of her drunken noodles. "Okay. I trust you." She refocused on the mission at hand and pointed to Tessa's iPhone. "Where should we start tonight?"

"Let's try this band … *Dödskatt vill ha en kaka.*"

"What does that mean?" Min asked.

"No idea, but they start in twenty minutes and they are on the next block."

"Enough time for me to go back and change?" Min looked at Tessa hopefully.

"Change?"

Min grinned mischievously. "Yeah, if I'm going to go clubbing I want to dress for it."

After returning to the hotel, Tessa went to the bar while Min scampered up to her room. She ordered a Jack Daniels on the rocks. She slowly sipped the drink and thought about her next steps. *Tomorrow I will contact Ruth and let her know my concerns about his drinking. And I'll mention his no-dagger policy and get her thoughts. Ruth was right to question Arno. Something is off with him.*

After fifteen minutes, Min crept up behind Tessa and tapped her shoulder. "Ta da."

Tessa turned around and laughed with surprise. Min normally dressed casually, wearing jeans and blouses, with a minimum amount of makeup or hair styling. The woman standing behind her was a completely different creature.

Her dark hair was pulled into open-ended pigtails. Her deep brown eyes popped due to the heavy blue eyeshadow surrounding them and her lips were a firecracker red. She wore a midriff-baring black T-shirt that showed off her tight abs, a product of Uri's training and Tessa's extra combatives practices. A cartoon cat was on the shirt, its big, white eyes pushed out by her breasts. On her back was a tiny red backpack, barely larger than a purse. A black miniskirt, fishnet stockings and black platform shoes completed the ensemble.

"Wow. Who are you and what have you done with Min?"

Min laughed. "This is my clubbing look. You didn't think I was all sweat pants and physics books, did you?"

Tessa shrugged. "Kind of."

"Loser. I was raised in an orphanage, not a convent." She slipped on a black leather jacket. "Ready when you are."

"You'll freeze your ass off in that outfit."

"Siberian winters, remember? I have a jacket on. Besides, I checked out the schedule. We're going to be hopping from one club to the other. That'll keep me warm."

"Where is your dagger?" asked Tessa.

Min half-turned. "Backpack. Glasses too."

"Good." She finished her whiskey and got off the stool. "Let's go."

The two women walked to the first venue. Although it was only two blocks away, Min was regretting some of her fashion choices halfway there. *Okay*, she thought, *Tessa was right. Tomorrow I wear more than half a shirt and a flimsy jacket. But I look amazing.* She smiled to herself, remembering her clubbing days in Seoul with her girlfriend.

The first destination was *Jokull*, a nightclub with a single, cavernous dance floor and bar occupying an old cannery on the waterfront. One wall was painted with a mural featuring the bar's namesake, a blue-white iceberg, populated by cartoon animals and a handful of recognizable faces from films, music and TV. The band, a Swedish dubstep group from Stockholm, was already pummeling the ears of the crowd when Tessa and Min arrived. Tessa checked her parka at the entrance and made a beeline for the bar, while Min headed onto the packed dance floor.

At dinner, they had decided they would alternate conducting a visual sweep of each club with their glasses. Tessa reasoned that swapping this role would help stave off the inevitable headaches, and she volunteered to take the first club. After ordering a beer she wove through the swaying crowd to a spot on the wall. She took a drink and slipped on her glasses. The mass of people and strobing-colored lights were replaced by a vertigo-inducing blur. She reached back and steadied herself on the wall, then swept the room. After a minute, she was satisfied there was none of the tell-tale visual clarity that a demon's presence would create in the blur. She slipped the glasses back into her purse and finished her beer.

Tessa thought the band was okay, although dubstep wasn't her thing. She saw Min bouncing happily on the dance floor, sandwiched between two attractive men who seemed more than happy to be bouncing along with her. *Well, that's one way to get warm. I like this side of Min. Normally she's so studious and focused; it's good to see her cut loose.* Tessa found herself smiling, a little sadly though. *I'm going to miss her.*

Min looked over and picked Tessa out of the flashing darkness. She waved happily and bounced through the crowd toward her.

"Hey," she said, squeezing tight against Tessa. "Anything?"

Tessa shook her head. "All clear. You want to stay for a bit?" Tessa nodded toward the two men Min had been dancing with. Both were looking expectantly across the dance floor at the women. "I think you made some friends."

Min shook her head. "There'll always be more boys and girls. We have a job, right?" She hooked her arm through Tessa's. "Let's get going. I get to check out your dance moves now."

For the next few hours, Tessa and Min went from one club to another. Each would spend a few minutes searching the crowd for demons. Not seeing any they would move on. However, the amount of time they would spend between finishing their sweep and leaving the club grew longer. By the time they went to the third club – a basement bar called Landlocked, whose walls vibrated from the deep bass of the music the DJ was playing – they were both on the dance floor.

Tessa was regretting her skirt. The wool provided ample protection from the cold, but was a heat trap in the confines of the bar. She decided to wear something a little looser and more comfortable the next day.

Min was bouncing up and down as much as possible, her pigtails flapping wildly. Whenever she was coming down, her skirt lifted enough to give anyone looking a peek at her underwear. Tessa felt tired watching her. *How many Red Bulls has she had?*

"I need to take a break," she shouted at Min. She left the dance floor and went to the bar. She asked for water and watched the DJ as she sipped her drink. The ice-cold water felt good sliding down her throat.

An attractive young man wearing an artfully torn Magnetic Man T-shirt took up a spot next to her and shouted, "Want a drink? I mean, another drink?"

Tessa gave him an appraising look. *Nice eyes, nice hair, great lips. Lean body. A bit Skarsgardian. Why not?* She nodded. "Whiskey Sour."

He pressed against her, not too hard, but enough to be clear that it wasn't an accident.

Tessa gave him her best bedroom eyes. *I should be good and stay Oscar Mike. But it doesn't hurt to flirt.* She took a drink and noticed Min was approaching.

"Hey! Who's your friend?" Min asked between panted breaths. She eyed Magnetic Man warily and brought her mouth up to Tessa's ear. "Everything okay?"

Tessa nodded.

"Should I take off?"

Part of Tessa wanted to say "yes." She wanted those lean muscles of Magnetic Man wrapped around her, to forget about demons for a moment and have recreational sex in her hotel room. *But that would be shitty to do to Min.* "No. Let's hit the next club."

She handed Magnetic Man her half-finished drink. "Sorry," she shouted, "maybe in another life."

She retrieved her coat and the two women left the club. Snow pelted their bare faces. The wind snaked around their legs. Min scurried along the snowy sidewalk, moving as fast as her platform shoes would allow.

Tessa, feeling invigorated by the cold, trailed after her. Her hands were tingling from the contrast of the sweltering nightclub and the frozen exterior. She stuck out her tongue and caught a snowflake, feeling the cold crystal dissolve on her warm skin.

Chapter 37

This is a good night. Arno hasn't bothered us. Min seems more confident or at least more relaxed and we have a better lay of the land. I got hit on by a hot guy and heard a bunch of different music. She smiled from ear-to-ear as she hurried to catch up with Min. *Even if Arno's off the rails, I can handle myself. I am ready to be a hunter.*

Chapter 38

Arno was pissed. He stalked through the streets of Reykjavik, hands thrust into the pockets of his jacket, face red, eyes staring hard ahead. Seeing Tessa had reminded him of Copenhagen, a hunt he tried very hard to forget. The fallout from his decision to engage Marit in a crowded club led to him being reassigned to the Balkans. While reassignments around a cell weren't uncommon, he knew this was a punishment. And it caused personal hardship. During his time in Copenhagen, he had formed a relationship with a local woman, Anna. They dated for two years and he proposed just before his field observation exercise with Desange and Tessa. She said yes, one of the happiest moments of his life.

Being reassigned ended everything. After attempting a long-distance relationship for three months, Anna broke off their engagement. She wanted someone who would be with her, not living in another country with no idea of when he'd return. As his loneliness and anger increased, so did his drinking. He had tried to prepare himself for his meeting with Tessa, but seeing her sitting at the bar had set him off.

I have a limited window to catch Marit during this festival. This is a chance to prove myself again. Then I can get out of Bosnia and back to Denmark. I can get Anna back. I can get my life back. Of all the recruits they could have paired me with, why the fuck did they give me Tessa again? Ruth is testing me. Desange and I had Marit under control. Tessa was just supposed to watch. She violated protocol when she ran into the nightclub. She should have stayed in the van. How hard is it to follow a simple order?

When he found out that Tessa was to be part of his team for the Marit hunt, he had asked for a new pair of recruits. Ruth denied his request.

That angel bitch. I know she was behind my reassignment. She complains about my methods, that I'm too impulsive, but who had the most kills three years ago in Europe? Arno Fucking Wollman! Sometimes you have to strike while the iron is hot and accept some collateral damage. Better to have a dead demon.

He impulsively ducked into the first bar he came across and ordered a beer. He took his drink and found an empty table. The sound system was playing American pop songs from a few years ago.

Tessa Sinclair. She ruined everything for me. Another stupid American, thinking with a gun. I don't need her or Kim getting in my way. I'm going to kill Marit and get assigned back up North where I belong.

He finished one beer and got another.

Stuck in Bosnia. Shitty food, shitty booze. Even the demons are second rate. Lust demons acting like 10 Euro hookers turning tricks. Gluttony demons selling moonshine to drunks. Nothing worth putting my blade into. Killing Marit is my ticket out of that hellhole.

He finished two more beers before paying his tab and leaving. It was dark and cold. The snow was falling in heavy sheets. He turned up the collar of his coat and trudged down the sidewalk. He wasn't even sure where he was going. Just wandering, getting a feel for his hunting ground, learning the streets, back alleys, open spaces and dead ends.

Getting cold, he entered another bar. He didn't notice the name or the decor. He didn't care. He shook the snow off of his coat, stamped his boots and went to get a drink.

"Vodka."

He drank the shot, ordered a beer, then searched for a seat. He found one on a window bench that looked out to the street. He sat down heavily, his scowl warning people off. He continued drinking, watching the falling snow.

I had a bad year. A few demons evaded me. I was forced to relocate to Bosnia. I got dumped by my fiancé. He looked at the glass. *Just a shitty fucking year.*

He took a drink and glanced around the room. He pulled out his glasses. *Why not? Maybe some luck will come my way. I'm overdue for it.* He looked at the clear lens in the silver wire frame. He wished he could use them to see auras like the angels and demons could with their naked eyes – to know a person's true feelings.

He put on the glasses. The room dissolved into a blur.

Except where it didn't. Sitting at a table on the opposite side of the bar was a figure. The light was dim and the glasses did nothing to enhance it. The features were lost in the poor light of the bar, but the clarity was unmistakable.

He took off the glasses and slammed the rest of his drink. *A demon.* Arno set his cup down on the bench. He took a moment to steady himself. *I need to get closer and confirm this is Marit.* The demon was sitting with other people. He could see it was a woman. He saw her body convulse in laughter and the people subtly arch toward her.

Those idiots. They have no idea what is sitting with them, laughing with them. Tempting them. They don't understand that war is being waged over their souls. I'm the only thing that stands between them and damnation.

Arno stood up. He put his glasses back on and briefly picked up a menu, pretending he needed them for reading. After thirty seconds, he casually walked past the demon's table.

Identity confirmed. He recognized Marit immediately – her short dark hair, slim body, well-defined cheekbones, full lips, and icy blue eyes that had led countless souls astray. She was wearing a crimson coat, fringed with fur. *Don't fuck this up.*

He went to the bathroom and into a stall. He pulled out his phone and opened his contacts. *I should let Tessa and Min know I've found Marit. But if I kill Marit now, I can redeem myself and not have to worry about Tessa getting in the way. I need to do this kill on my own.*

He put the phone back into his pocket. His knife was in a sheath at the small of his back. He pulled it out and pressed the stud at the base of the handle. The blade slid out. He stared at it for a moment. The dirty yellow light of the bar bathroom glinted weakly along the razor edge of the blade. *I haven't needed anyone for years. I don't need help now.*

He left the bathroom, blade in his coat pocket. *I'll take Marit in a rush and knife her before she knows what's happening.*

But she was gone, the table empty. Arno looked around frantically. *No. I can't miss my chance again.* He darted out the front door. He looked up and down the street. He saw the crimson coat in the yellow light of the street lamps. She appeared to be alone.

He followed her to the waterfront, maintaining enough distance so she wouldn't become suspicious. It was a broad sidewalk, broken up by abstract sculptures, almost hidden in the snowfall and night. *Where is she going?* He noticed that she twirled along the walkway, arms flung out. *What the hell is she doing?*

Suddenly, she stopped, facing him. She leaped to the top of an abstract sculpture of a Viking longboat, metal points gleaming in the city lights. "Looking for me, hunter?"

Shit. Arno pulled out his knife and extended the blade.

"You have no idea how fucked you are." Marit jumped off the sculpture, landing a few meters in front of Arno. She was smiling.

Arno braced himself into a fighting stance. He bent his knees a little and kept his arms up, but loose. He knew that tensing up would leave him vulnerable to the speed of a demon.

"I saw you watching me. But that's what you hunters do – watch us. Watch us free mankind from their shackles." She crouched, like a predator, ready to spring on her prey. "Poor little humans, fighting a war you don't understand. What has Ruth told you? That you fight for God? What God would send you to me?"

Arno backpedaled. His eyes gleamed red and yellow in the city lights. *I'm a hunter. I fear nothing. I am God's strong right arm.* "I will send you back to Hell, demon."

Marit laughed, the sound mingling with the slicing wind off the bay. "Good luck." She shrugged off her coat. She was wearing a tight black cocktail dress. Her pale skin and blue eyes stood out in the night. Snow clung to her short hair, but she took no notice.

Arno held up his dagger, a shield against the demon approaching him.

Marit didn't stop smiling. She turned in a lazy pirouette, then stopped, laughing. "No hope for you. Will anyone mourn you when you are gone, hunter?"

He chose not to respond. *I can't let her get to me.*

"Time to die!" Marit darted to the left, slashing out with her fist, striking Arno in the side.

He felt a rib crack and stumbled back into a bench.

Marit didn't follow up the attack. She just watched and waited. The snow stopped for a moment. The sky cleared and the moon shone fat and bright among the stars.

Arno charged Marit, hoping to take her off guard with an aggressive attack.

She evaded the thrust of his knife with ease, twirling away from him. When she sensed he had expended his adrenaline surge, she grabbed his arm holding the dagger and bent it backward. He screamed as the bones shattered.

"It's okay," Marit said. "You've done your job. Played your part. Spread your blood on the snow." She punched him in the face with her free hand.

Arno's nose caved in and his orbital sockets exploded, blasts of bone shrapnel shredding his eyes. He made a wet, grunting sound and dropped to his knees. His knife fell from senseless fingers. Marit yanked his arm free of its socket, the sound of cracking bone and tearing flesh carried away by the moaning wind.

Arno fell back onto the snow-slick pavement. The pain had forced his mind into a tiny box, a safe place where none of this was happening. He was in Copenhagen, living with Anna, not lying on the freezing ground, his life hemorrhaging out of him.

"Not much of a challenge." Marit tossed the arm into the black water of the bay. She lifted his spasming body off the ground. She looked into his ruined eyes, searching for a sign that he was alive and aware. "Are you here?"

Arno opened his mouth, ready to say his final, defiant words, but he could not speak.

"Still here." She grabbed his head and yanked it to the side, snapping his neck. Arno went limp. She threw his body into the water and watched as it sank out of sight.

Smiling, she retrieved her coat and walked back to the clubs and bars, throbbing with life.

Chapter 39

Tessa and Min waited in the hotel restaurant for most of the morning, becoming increasingly concerned when Arno didn't show at 9 am. While they ate breakfast, Tessa left a string of voice and text messages.

"He's probably hung over," said Tessa.

"I hope he didn't run into Marit," Min said, sipping a kale and orange smoothie.

"That's unlikely. Hunting demons takes time. You saw how much he was drinking. Hell, he's probably still hammered."

Min checked the time on her phone. "It's 10:30, he's more than a little late."

"He's been hunting demons for ten years. Don't worry, even with the drinking, he can handle himself." *She has to stay focused on the mission. Let me be the one to worry about Arno.* "Finish up. I'll head upstairs and contact the Curia. He may have reported in. If he hasn't, we have his operational plan. I'm going to recommend that we proceed with it."

She saw that Min looked concerned, but she nodded in agreement.

Tessa found herself getting frustrated. She wanted Min to have a good field observation exercise and as her mentor, Tessa knew she'd be judged for how the exercise went. *Maybe Arno and Ruth are working together on this to try and test me after what happened in Copenhagen. His whole thing about being a drunk, washed-up hunter could be an act. It doesn't matter. Just keep mission-focused and we'll be fine. Show Min how a professional hunter behaves under these circumstances.*

Tessa went back to her room and removed the satellite phone from the case. She punched in her access code and waited. When she received the connection tone, she entered Ruth's number.

"Yes, Tessa."

Tessa was surprised the angel picked up the phone. She assumed she would have to leave a message. "Ruth, we have a problem here. Arno missed a meeting this morning and isn't responding to my calls. He's ninety minutes past his check-in time. Has he contacted his cell leader or been on secure chat?"

"Wait a moment." Ruth put her on hold. Tessa stared out the window at the overcast sky. *Come on, just tell me he checked in.* When Ruth came back on, Tessa detected exasperation in her voice. "No, nothing. The last report he filed was yesterday. I confirmed with his cell leader. He indicated Arno was going to meet you and Min. Did that happen?"

"Yes. He was pretty hostile and showed up intoxicated. He even told us to leave our daggers behind when we shadowed him."

There was a long enough pause that Tessa thought they had lost connection. "Ruth, are you there?"

"Yes. I was thinking. Although that is his prerogative, what was his rationale?"

"He said he didn't want us to interfere in his hunt. It was clear he had a problem with me because of Copenhagen."

"I'm disappointed but not surprised. I wanted to see if he could work past his problems with you and do his job. We've given him a year. At this point, we may have to pull him from the field and provide him with additional therapy."

"Therapy? That's it?"

Ruth laughed. "Of course. Don't you think he needs rehabilitation?"

I thought you'd kill him. He's compromised. Tessa immediately felt guilty for thinking Ruth would behave in such a cold manner, void of compassion. *She's an angel. Of course she would try to help him.*

"Yes, he does." Tessa paused. "What should Min and I do?"

"In a few weeks, you'll be a hunter. What's your assessment of the situation? Do you want to be pulled out or continue the exercise?"

Tessa thought about the meaning beneath the question. *If Ruth is giving me the choice, she wouldn't want me to pick the weaker option. She's giving me an opportunity to be a hunter.*

"We have his mission plan and I have my surveillance package. I think we can proceed with the hunt without Arno. If he resurfaces, I will contact you."

"I concur. However, I only want you running surveillance and reconnaissance operations. If you find Marit or any other demon, report it immediately. Do not engage the target. Make this clear to Min-Seo as well."

"I will."

"Keep me apprised of the situation. We'll try to locate Arno. If he checks in, I'll contact you. Anything else?"

"No, that's it."

"Good hunting." Ruth hung up.

Tessa returned to the restaurant. Min was drinking tea and playing Candy Crush on her iPad. She looked up expectantly.

Tessa shook her head and sat down. "He hasn't reported in. Ruth is going to try and track him down, but our job is to continue with the mission. We have everything we need."

"What if we find Marit? I don't feel comfortable confronting a demon without a hunter. You've seen me in combatives. I've improved, but I'm not there yet."

"If we find her, we pull back. Ruth doesn't want us engaging the target."

Min looked more at ease. "Okay, that's good."

"We'll use the equipment I have and trade off field and monitoring roles. This is the kind of improvisation we have to expect once we're hunters, right? If I learned one thing in Iraq, it's that no plan survives contact with the enemy."

***

"Good hunting." Ruth hung up the phone with Tessa. She left her office and went to McKenna's. He was on his computer, working on the next year's budget request.

He leaned back in his seat. "Please say you've brought me something interesting. Finances are enough to drive me to drink."

Ruth had no time for banter. "Arno Wollman is dark."

"Dark ... how long?"

"At least 16 hours."

"Well, this isn't the first time—"

"It's not. But it is the first time he's done this with recruits. Tessa said he was drinking and ordered them to leave their daggers behind."

"What?" McKenna sat up straight. "I told you he was becoming unstable."

"Yes, that's why I told Tessa to watch him and report his behavior."

McKenna's normally placid tone was replaced by a harder one. "And you didn't tell me?"

Ruth leaned on his desk, a menacing shadow passing over her face. She raised her voice. "I have been fighting this war for 2000 years. I know what is best for the Curia."

McKenna sighed loudly.

"What's wrong?" asked Ruth. She stared at McKenna for a moment.

"What's wrong is we have invested a lot of time and money training Arno. You were the one who wanted to reassign him to Bosnia. I preferred that he stay in Copenhagen."

Ruth maintained her composure. "You run the Academy, not Operations. His romantic attachment only complicated his job."

McKenna shook his head. "Not every hunter can be alone. You should know that. Humans need connection and you broke that. Your decision to move him ended his relationship. A few years ago, he was one of our top hunters in Europe. Moving him due to one mistake was an overreaction. Let's not forget that Tessa also had a role to play in the Copenhagen failure. Your decision with Arno was too harsh."

"You're entitled to your opinion." Ruth started to exit McKenna's office.

"Wait! What about Tessa and Min?" he asked.

"They will remain in Iceland, with Tessa taking the lead until we can locate Arno. Once the exercise is over, I'm recommending that Arno be pulled from the field for an evaluation."

"If they find Marit?" asked McKenna.

"If they find anything, they will report it to me. I made that very clear to Tessa. I'm not going to put them in unwarranted danger. This will give Min-Seo a chance to learn surveillance operations, something Tessa excels at. I'll keep you informed about Arno." As she left, she added. "As I see fit."

***

Over the next three days, Tessa and Min settled into a routine. Tessa would contact the Curia for news of Arno and update Ruth on their hunt. Tessa then provided a formal briefing to Min about the plan for the day, reinforcing the need to treat field missions in a structured fashion. After the briefing, the recruits would proceed to the venues from Arno's operational plan. Tessa thought it was methodical and well thought out, despite her overall low opinion of Arno.

Once at the surveillance locations, one would go inside and scan for demons while the other maintained a support position. Tessa wanted Min to get a feel for all aspects of the hunt, including the long, boring days of no demon detection. Tessa was pleased with Min's performance and planned to give her a glowing evaluation. She remained worried about Arno, but trusted that Ruth would tell her if anything bad happened to him.

Three more days and we're done, Tessa thought on the evening of the fourth day as she lay in bed. It had been another eight hours of going from one noisy, crowded bar to another, courting a headache from the glasses and searching in vain for Marit. *Three more days, then we'll travel back home.* She grinned when she realized she thought of the Academy as home.

Chapter 40

Tessa sat at the small desk in her hotel room. Heavy, wind-driven snow thudded against the window. It was nine in the morning, but the dense cloud cover, inclement weather and lingering night made it gloomy. The sun wouldn't rise for another hour and would set again at four.

She signed into the Curia's secure network, checking her emails and voice messages. There were no updates about Arno or the mission. She filed her report on the previous day's surveillance and added a few words of praise for Min. The snow turned to sleet, the heavy thuds drumming against the window. Tessa let out a resigned sigh at the thought of going out in the cold. *At least this is almost over. Min's learned a lot. I think her confidence has improved and I'm glad Arno isn't here to wear down her spirit.*

She thought of the German hunter, seeing his ruddy, angry face telling her to leave her dagger behind. *I hope he's okay, but he would have done more harm than good if he had stuck around. When I write my AAR, I'm going to suggest future field exercises that focus on mentors and mentees planning and running their own ops. This has been a much better experience for me than Copenhagen.*

She made herself a strong cup of coffee and opened up Marit's file. Although she had read through it multiple times, she thought she might have missed something. *Sometimes repetition leads to inspiration.* She laughed. *Great, inner Tessa is starting to sound like Ivanov.*

She found herself coming back to the three photos in the packet. The first two were from the same encounter. A hunter in 1982 took photos of a dark-haired woman with delicate features backstage at a Rolling Stones concert. Keith Richards and Mick Jagger were laughing at a lost joke. Behind them was a crowd of groupies. She was among them, her face hard to make out. Analysts confirmed it was her – she traveled in the band's entourage during their 1982 European tour – but even blown up, there were few useful details. The most recent image was the one she had seen prior to Copenhagen – the black and white surveillance photo of Marit sitting in a cafe. Even though she had fought Marit, she didn't get a good look at her. All she clearly recalled was her short, dark hair and slender body. She traced the outline of Marit's face with her fingertip. *Over 300 years of tempting souls and all we have are a few low-quality photos. She's good at avoiding detection. I guess you have to be to survive for centuries.*

She felt heat rise through her body, remembering the alcohol-fueled shouting matches between her parents, glass breaking on the kitchen tile floor. *Marit and other demons like her have ruined the lives of millions.*

Tessa closed the folder. *She goes after the music and party scene. A good source of customers for her drugs. We should keep focusing our search efforts on the venues where DJs are playing.* She let out a sigh of resignation. *Which is what we have been doing. Every club in Reykjavik is swamped by ravers.*

Tessa looked at her phone. It was almost ten. Min would be knocking soon, ready to start the day's surveillance. Moments later, the knock came. Tessa opened the door and gave her a half-smile. "Good morning."

"*Joh-eun achim.*"

As the two walked to the elevator, Min said, "We're almost done. In a few weeks you'll be off to LA."

"Did I tell you that the Curia already picked out my place?"

Min shook her head. "No. Where are you living?" She grabbed her arm. "Oh, tell me it's someplace famous, like Beverly Hills."

Tessa laughed. "Try Culver City. Looks nice though. Some little garden-style buildings from the Sixties. Probably has a lot of character."

"But no movie stars?"

"Doubt it."

They entered the small cafe attached to the hotel and sat down to order breakfast.

"Have you talked to your cell leader yet?" asked Min

Tessa shook her head. "Not yet. All I know is that it's a guy named George. He'll get in touch with me when I arrive."

"You get a few weeks to settle in, right?"

Tessa nodded.

"Anything planned?"

"Oh, just a bunch of touristy things. Universal studios, the Hollywood Walk, Santa Monica Pier ... all the stuff that a newbie to the city should see."

"Sounds like fun. Wish I could take my vacation there."

Tessa smiled. "Me too. Particularly now that I know what fun clubbing-Min is like." She sighed. "But, Rome awaits."

Min nodded. "Yes, I have a lot of research ahead of me. Maybe next summer I could visit."

"That would be nice." Tessa frowned a little. "I am going to miss you."

Min grinned. "Hey, I'm not that easy to get rid of."

Tessa wished that were true, but the life of a hunter could be lonely. Trying to maintain even a tenuous connection would be difficult. Like Desange, however, she knew that Min was worth the effort. *I've made some good friends, people I can rely on. I'm not going to lose them.*

After breakfast, the women began their day of surveillance missions. Tessa took the first bar. It wasn't overly crowded, given how early it was in the day. *Most of the festival goers are still in bed from pulling all-nighters.* She unzipped her heavy parka. In contrast to Min's club attire, Tessa opted for warmth and comfort, wearing gray cargo pants, Doc Marten boots and a pale blue sweater. She found an open table and sat down. When the server came, she ordered a basket of fries and a coffee. *Caffeine and carbs. This will be another long day.*

Min waited in a nearby cafe, drinking a green smoothie. She wore a tiny earpiece microphone and speaker from Tessa's surveillance package. It was the size of a compact hearing aid. When in use, there was an annoying background hiss, but the unobtrusiveness was its key feature. After her first frigid night in Reykjavik, Min had decided to dress warmer. Her skirt ended just above the knee and was paired with neon leggings and fuzzy boots. Her tight T-shirt didn't show off her stomach, although it did flaunt her fit body.

Tessa put on her glasses and scanned the bar, detecting no demons. "All clear," she reported to Min through the earpiece. "I'll eat and check again in a bit."

"Take your time. I love these fancy juices. Think I'll order another, since the Curia's paying."

Tessa stuffed another greasy fry in her mouth. "Sure." *Would Marit sell Ecstasy this early? People may want to pregame or stock up for later.*

She sat for another thirty minutes, periodically taking her glasses on and off. Twice she wore them while walking through an adjoining room that contained a few tables, pretending she needed to use the restroom. Each time she tried, her vision became a blur with no spots of clarity. Satisfied there were no demons, she decided to head to the next site. "Moving out."

"Roger," said Min. She quickly slurped down her remaining juice.

The pattern continued for the rest of the day. The two women alternated their surveillance roles, moving from club to club. As the day wore on, the crowd sizes increased. By the time the sky grew dark, most of the bars were packed.

Tessa could handle crowded clubs in small doses, but after multiple days of nightclub reconnaissance, she sensed her anxiety increasing. At one bar, the crush of people triggered flashes of being packed inside a bunker in Iraq. She could remember the suffocating heat, how her clothing stuck to her skin under her armor, the smell of body odor, the shaking of the ground when a mortar round hit and the look of fear on the soldiers' faces.

I'm in Iceland, not Iraq. I'm not in a bunker. I'm never going to be in a bunker again.

Even with that affirmation in mind, she was still happy to trade off with Min. While her partner checked out the next bar – Tessa could hear the thudding music from across the street – she waited in a nearby coffee shop.

"Hey," Min's voice hissed out of the earpiece, "Can I stay a little longer? TekTek is spinning soon. He's a Korean DJ with some great songs and he's attracting a big crowd."

Tessa checked the time. *9pm. We still have the whole night ahead of us.* "Sure, enjoy the show. Do a scan and check in every twenty."

"Got it."

Give her some time to have fun. She deserves it. I know she's worried about being in the field and Arno ghosting on us is not helping. But she's handling the change well. She's smart and tough; she'll be a good hunter. Maybe I'll get lucky and she'll be assigned to LA. It would be nice to have a battle buddy when I'm hunting.

Tessa felt a little sad. She liked Min and wished she could stick around another year and see her fully develop into a hunter.

She'll be fine and there is no way this is the end of our friendship. I have too few of them to let a good one like her go.

As she finished her coffee, she saw Min emerge from the bar and make her way through a sudden burst of snow to the coffee shop. "I'm not sure if I like this weather or hate it," she said, brushing snow from her hair.

"I think I like it," Tessa said. "It's random enough to keep you on your toes."

Min ordered a croissant and then sat down across from Tessa.

"How's your head?"

Min grimaced. "Hurting. I wish the Curia could come up with a better method of detecting demons."

"You should invent it. I mean, you are the smart one."

Min smiled. "Thanks, but booksmarts only go so far in our world. I need to be able to kick ass too."

"Hey, you are in amazing shape. Most people couldn't pull off that tight shirt."

Min stuffed the warm flaky bread in her mouth. "So what's next on the list?"

Tessa pulled up the schedule on her phone. "Elektrobar. A DJ named Rue is playing."

Min's eyes grew wide. "DJ Rue is amazing. His album *Wet Dreams* got me through physics finals. Well, that and a lot of caffeine. Any chance I could take the next club too?"

Tessa shrugged. "If you think your head can handle it, knock yourself out. It's only a few blocks from here, so I'll stay put and get another round of coffee." She tapped her earpiece. "I'll be listening."

"Thanks." Min bundled into her coat and headed outside. The sun had set and the wind off the bay was ice cold. The venue was a walk down bar in an otherwise nondescript glass and steel box. A small neon sign next to a downward flight of stairs burned red – Elektrobar.

"Arrived." Min walked down the stairs and went inside. The door opened into a short corridor that was painted black and decorated with bumper stickers from various bands. She passed by a weary-looking bouncer who glanced down at her chest – the cold made the nipples of her perky breasts stand out prominently – and waved her past.

"Enjoy the show," Tessa said. She could hear the muffled sounds of a crowd and techno music in her ear. She signaled the waiter for more coffee.

Min checked her coat and headed for the bar. She had been good for the evening, drinking soda water and lemon. *I'll treat myself to one drink.*

"Vodka and Red Bull." *For the energy.*

The bartender nodded at her request and poured the drink. Glass in hand, she turned toward the stage, leaning her back against the bar. The club had a long, narrow dance floor, a small stage and two booths crammed into the far corners. It was over-packed, a sea of bodies decorated with neon paint and glow sticks. They were excited, ready for the music to start.

As DJ Rue entered his booth, the room darkened and strobe lights bathed the room in a kaleidoscope of colors. Min put on her glasses and did a sweep, the lights and people blurring around her.

"All clear." She removed her glasses a minute later and folded them back into her small purse. She finished her drink. Her head was throbbing, but she found the alcohol helped a little. She closed her eyes and listened to the sounds, trying to take her mind off the headache. *It will go away soon. It always does. Just need to give it another minute.*

"Are you a fan?"

Min opened her eyes. An attractive woman was standing in front of her and smiling. She was wearing a Deadmau5 T-shirt and black leggings. She sported a glow stick headband over her dark-haired pixie cut. Her short bangs were stuck to her forehead from perspiration.

Damn, she's cute. "Yes, I love *Wet Dreams*. Great album."

"Wanna dance?" asked the woman.

Min smiled. *I've got another 10 minutes before I need to do a scan.* "Sure, why not."

The woman took her hand and led her through the packed crowd into the center of the dance floor. Min started doing her typical vertical bouncing, but the woman pressed against her from behind, swaying rhythmically from side to side in a sensual, gyrating motion. She ran her hands down Min's chest, grazing over her stiff nipples. She then traced her hands lower onto Min's hips and thighs. When her hands reached Min's left inner thigh, she gripped tightly, feeling an object.

"What's this?" whispered the woman into Min's ear.

Min spun around, facing her. She put her arms on her shoulders and continued dancing. "Pepper spray. You never know what creeps are in these clubs."

The woman smiled and wrapped her arms around Min's waist, pulling her close. "Yes, all sorts of vile creatures lurk in the night."

Min felt a little uncomfortable. Although she found the woman hot, she didn't like her aggressiveness. She tried to pull away, but the woman's grip was firm. *I don't need her feeling me up like this. I need to stay focused on the mission.*

"Um, I have to use the bathroom, sorry." Min tried pulling free again, this time pushing on the woman's shoulder. The result was the same; the arms around her waist held her tight.

"My name's Marit. What's your name?"

Fuck. Tessa slammed down her coffee. "Min, get out of there."

Okay, stay calm. She doesn't know I'm a hunter. "Min ... my name's Min. I really have to go." *I should have given her a fake name.*

"Not yet. It's early and I haven't seen a hunter as cute as you for decades."

Min's eyes went wide. *How could she know? She can't. She's guessing.*

"Don't look so surprised. I saw you playing with your glasses." The smile that had been so enticing turned malevolent. "You missed a spot."

Still holding her tight with one hand, Marit's other drifted slowly down Min's hip and curved toward her inner thigh, eventually resting over her dagger. "I feel the energy of my realm as I touch you." Her icy blue eyes stared at Min. She forced Min to sway with the music, rubbing her hand against the dagger's sheath.

Min found Marit's touch both sensual and terrifying. *I have to get out of here. I could scream, but no one would hear me over the music. And who knows what Marit would do to me. Would she kill me in this crowded club? What would she do to these other people?*

"If you resist, before I kill you, I'll be forced to kill these nice people. But I'll let you watch. Going to be a good girl?"

Min nodded.

As she did, Marit noticed the earpiece. "Ah, party guests." She brought her lips to Min's ear. "Whoever is listening, I'm taking your friend to the Sundhollin Public Pool. You have an hour to meet me there. Otherwise, I play with her insides and leave what's left for you. Your choice."

A tear trickled down Min's cheek.

Marit pulled out Min's earpiece and dropped it on the floor. It was soon crushed by a nearby dancer.

Chapter 41

Tessa stood in the doorway of a dark rowhouse. It was across the street from her destination, the Sundhollin Public Pool. She thought about calling Ruth. *What can she do? There's no way the Curia can get personnel here in time. She'll just tell me to leave her. Collateral damage. I'm not going to do that. I promised Min I'd keep her safe. I have to try.*

The pool house was a sprawling three-story building with white brick walls. The windows were dark. She could see the entrance, but couldn't tell if the door was open or not. *Even if it is, it's because Marit is waiting in the dark, ready to kill me. She thinks by luring me here, she can kill at least two hunters. I need to find another way in.* She glanced at her phone. *And I have ten minutes to do it.*

The outdoor pools and hot tubs were surrounded by a wall. Tessa stealthily made her way around the perimeter, looking for a place where she could pull herself over.

Marit was waiting inside at the main Olympic-sized pool with Min. She had taken Min's dagger and forced the young hunter to climb to the top of a multilevel diving tower. She pushed Min to the edge of the diving board and stood close behind her. One hand was clamped on Min's shoulder, with a grip that could grind bones to dust. In the other was the dagger. Marit ran the needle tip across Min's throat and cheeks. She didn't draw blood, but the touch of the blade made her tremble.

Marit pressed her slender body against Min's and brought her lips to her ear. "I saw your aura swell at the club, yellow and orange. I know you are attracted to me. Should I play with your body?" She laughed. "I played with your friend's body. He didn't like the game, but he doesn't have to worry about that now."

Min gasped for breath, her body shaking as she stood at the edge of the diving board. "Just kill me."

Marit clucked her tongue. "Not yet. Once I kill your hunter friends, you'll be my after-dinner mint." She ran the tip of her tongue over Min's ear. "Sounds yummy, yes?"

"You're a sick bitch."

Marit laughed coldly. "I'm a demon. You're a hunter. That is the way of things." She pressed the tip of the dagger against the delicate skin of Min's neck, just hard enough to pierce it and draw a bead of blood.

Marit saw Min's aura grow red with anger and orange with fear, pushing out any yellow that had spiked at the bar. "I know you are angry that I've gotten the better of you, but you can't fight against your nature. Humans desire what we give them. We fill the void in each of you." She laid the edge of the blade along Min's trembling throat. "You want us to win."

I can't die here. Not like this. She pushed back tears. *Please, Tessa, help me.*

Tessa lifted herself over the wall. There were two outdoor pools, the heated water steaming in the icy air. The skies had cleared. Auroral sheets of green and blue writhed above. She lowered herself to the concrete walkway around the pools and crouched in the shadows by the wall. She pulled out her dagger and extended the blade. She saw a sign above a door with the figure of a man in a pool. *That must be it.* She gripped the knife tighter and pushed the door. It didn't budge. *Of course it's not that easy.*

She pulled the lockpick set from the surveillance package out of her purse. She had decided to bring it along on the mission, a suggestion she had learned in Tradecraft. *Thank you, Ivanov.*

As Tessa picked the lock, Marit told Min what she had done to Arno.

"I caved his face in. Literally. Then I pulled off his arm." She kissed Min on the neck. "Humans are fragile. You'll experience that soon."

Min clenched her teeth to keep from screaming. She forced her mind to fall back on her training and analyzed her current situation. *She's too strong. If I try to break free, she'll crush my shoulder and cut my throat. Tessa will come for me, I know her. Maybe she'll provide the opportunity I need to escape.*

"It's too bad I have to kill you. We could have had a lot of fun together." She ran the tip of the dagger over Min's breasts. "Now, the only one having fun is me."

Min didn't respond. She didn't see the point in conversing with a demon.

Marit sniffed Min's hair. "I can smell it on you. Pent-up desire. Unfulfilled wants and needs. It would have been nice to see your empty spaces filled, even for a night. So many lonely people out there. I relieve them of that loneliness. Why is that wrong?"

Tessa opened the door to the indoor pool. Min and Marit were standing on the diving board. She flinched when she saw the demon running the tip of the dagger over Min's neck and body. She looked around, but identified no cover. The only light came from within the water, lamps built into the floor, casting waving patterns on the ceiling. Although she didn't think she had been spotted, there was no way to approach Marit without being seen.

Fuck. It's a trap, but I have no other options. She stepped out. "I'm here."

Min looked down at her, face lighting up with hope.

Marit offered a wan smile. "Welcome. Any other party guests?"

Tessa shook her head. "I'm alone."

"You could be lying, but it doesn't matter. No one makes it out of here alive." She paused. "Except me."

"Let her go. She's not a hunter. It can be just you and me."

"I don't think so." Marit laughed. She pointed the blade at Tessa. "Your friend tried to kill me. He came apart, red and screaming. So will you." She kissed Min's neck. "And you."

Tessa held up her knife. She thought her only hope was to taunt the demon and give Min a chance to get free. "Don't you remember me, bitch? I almost killed you in Copenhagen. This time, I'm going to dust you with this knife and make glasses from your heart."

Marit grinned. "I thought you looked familiar. You ruined my top. Trying to use a gun on me, how amateur." Marit stabbed Min in the side with her dagger, just above her right hip. She twisted the blade as it hit the flesh.

Min's eyes went wide. The pain was intense, a burning spike that exploded in her abdomen. She had never felt anything like this. She let out a tiny cry.

The demon yanked Min's head back, kissed her roughly on the lips and then pushed her off the diving board.

Tessa watched her friend fall limply to the pool, smacking the water hard. She glared at Marit. "Fuck you!"

Marit laughed and leaped from the tower. She landed in front of Tessa with the grace of a jungle cat. She held up the blood slicked dagger and ran her tongue over her lips. "Shall we?"

Tessa knew she was at a disadvantage, more than the first time they fought. *In Copenhagen, Marit was outnumbered, surrounded and surprised. Now, I'm facing a straight-up fight with something tougher and stronger than me.*

She glanced over at the pool. The water around Min was cloudy with blood, but she was alive. She treaded water, trying to stay afloat while holding her injured side. *At least I don't have to worry about her for the moment.*

Tessa backpedaled a few meters, before settling into a fighting stance. She had limited space to work with – the walkway around the pool was only three-meters wide. She saw an entrance to the locker room and thought about taking the fight in there. But Marit was familiar with the pool house and she was not. *If I get cornered, I'm dead and so is Min.*

Marit span like a ballerina, holding the knife high, blade glinting in the pool lights. "You don't seem to be enjoying yourself? Isn't this what you people live for? The hunt, the kill. To see your prey fall to your blade." She pointed the dagger at Tessa, needle tip gleaming red. "Do you even understand the war you are fighting? Maybe you don't care. You have the dull, stupid features of a fanatic. Is that what you are?"

She's fucking with me. Don't let her get in your head. Block out what she's saying, watch what she's doing.

Although Marit kept talking, Tessa focused on the demon's hands, feet and eyes. She saw a pattern of motion, an opening that she could take. She waited for her moment and struck, a swift punch and thrust combination.

Marit was surprised; she had expected the hunter to wait for her to make the first move. The punch struck her in the arm, and the blade grazed her side. She leaped backward and touched the superficial injury.

"You ruined another top," she said, pouting. "For that, I'm going to pull out your ribs, one by one." She advanced on Tessa, a series of measured steps that ended with a kick that Tessa was able to roll with and a slash that opened up her left arm.

The pain was dull, but Tessa knew that it would become a serious problem soon. She held up her injured arm as a shield and tried to hit Marit with a flurry of knife thrusts.

Marit blocked the first few, while laughing, but missed one. The dagger sunk into her abdomen. The smile disappeared, replaced by a look of rage. She lashed out at Tessa, sweeping with her arm.

The blow connected with Tessa's injured arm and slammed her into the wall. She almost lost her grip on the dagger, but held on. Everything hurt, a mix of dull pain and spikes of agony. The focal point of the latter was her slashed arm. *Don't look, don't look, don't look.*

She looked.

The injury from the knife was bad, a cut from her wrist to her elbow that oozed blood. The damage from being struck was worse, a compound fracture of the humerus. The jagged edge of the bone had shredded her skin and her arm hung dead at her side.

"That looks unpleasant. You may need medical care." Marit picked Tessa up by her sweater and pressed her against the wall. She held up the dagger. "We can try amputation."

Tessa's vision was swimming. *Swimming.* She saw that Min had managed to cross the pool and pull herself out, her face contorted with pain, blood running down her leg.

Tessa threw her dagger away, toward Min. "If you let me live, I can give you information."

"There is no surrender." Marit sank her blade into the shoulder of Tessa's injured arm, a new pain mingling with what she already felt.

The dagger landed near Min's feet. She was shaking from blood loss and exertion. She crawled toward it, forcing herself to stay silent through the pain. Biting her tongue to keep from screaming, she reached out. She could taste blood in her mouth. She gripped Tessa's dagger and rose. She saw a black pool of blood at her feet. *Don't think about it. Just help Tessa. She needs you.* Min shuffled painfully toward Marit. *Not far. Meter. Less. One foot. Other foot.*

Marit was close to Tessa's face. "I think I'll bite off your nose and feed it to your friend." She opened her mouth and clacked her teeth together. She moved a little closer. "I'll let you watch that before I kill you." She opened and closed her mouth again.

She opened her mouth. Tessa's vision was a tunnel. At the end were narrow blue eyes and white teeth. *Not the way I thought I'd die.*

The blues eyes went wide, bulging. The white teeth turned red with blood. A slim spike of glass protruded from her mouth.

Marit screamed wetly. Min had stabbed her through the back of the head. She dropped Tessa and lashed out, striking Min hard enough to send her back into the pool. She batted madly at her head, trying to dislodge the blade.

Tessa reached up and grabbed the handle of the dagger in her shoulder. She pulled. Pain exploded through her chest. Her hand slipped from the hilt. She wanted to lay down and vomit. She saw Min clinging weakly to the side of the pool.

Marit grabbed the dagger's handle behind her head. She began to pull it out.

Tessa pulled again. The blade slipped out from her shoulder. Marit seemed so far away. Her arm felt like it was made of lead. She couldn't focus. *Fuck it.* She stabbed upwards, using her last reserves of strength. The blade sank into Marit's chest.

The demon let out a gasp. Her skin hardened and cracked. Her blue eyes were the last to go, drained of all menace, replaced by a look of pleading.

Tessa slumped over, coughing as the glassy dust of Marit's body coated her mouth and throat.

Min dragged herself out of the pool. She crawled over to Tessa. Her friend wasn't moving. "Don't die. Please don't die." She touched Tessa's face.

Tessa moaned. "Not dead. Not yet." Her eyes fluttered open. "Call the Curia. Get us out of here."

Min pulled Tessa's phone out of her pocket and hit the Curia's distress contact.

Tessa let out a weak chuckle. "I think we passed our field exercise."

Chapter 42

Tessa and Min were extracted from Iceland by private plane. Onboard, Ruth had used her healing powers. Although Tessa was unconscious during the process, Min was not.

"It was amazing," Min said when they got back to their room at the Academy. "She pushed the bone in, then used her power on you. I could see the skin sealing over and the bones popping back into place." She touched her own perfectly healed side. "And it was the same with me. I didn't feel anything, but I saw the skin heal in seconds. What she did was … unnatural."

"Well," Tessa said, "she is an angel."

"It shouldn't be possible. You don't just force cells to grow without some kind of input."

"I don't know, Min," Tessa said, feeling tired, but happy to be alive. "Add that to your list of things to further research."

Ruth gave them a few days to recover. Even with their injuries healed, she knew they had been through a psychological trauma and needed space. After three days of rest, she scheduled their debriefings. As the senior recruit, she called Tessa to her office first.

When Tessa entered her austere office, she was surprised to find Ruth alone. "Father McKenna isn't going to sit in?"

Ruth shook her head and motioned for her to take a seat. "Not for this one."

Tessa sat down anxiously, biting her cheek. No one had said anything to her about the fight with Marit since she returned. She had submitted her report and waited. *I disobeyed a direct order from Ruth, but how can I be faulted for rescuing Min? I couldn't let her die. She's an asset to the Curia. And she's my friend. Plus, we successfully completed the mission.*

"Why did you go after Marit?"

"You have my AAR. You have Min's too. We were following surveillance protocol and Min was taken by surprise. I had no choice; I had to go after her."

Ruth shook her head. "Of course you had a choice. You could have contacted me and asked for help. Or you could have left rather than engage the target, one that I explicitly told you not to fight."

Tessa shifted forward, sitting on the edge of the uncomfortable plastic seat. "Marit would have killed Min."

"And she could have killed you."

Tessa wanted to storm out. She counted to five and then said in the most even voice she could muster, "If you think I would abandon my friend to be murdered, you are out of your fucking mind. We went through this after Copenhagen. My personality hasn't changed."

Tessa and Ruth stared at each other, the tension like a thick cable connecting them.

"You're right," Ruth finally said. "The Curia would never expect you to leave a fellow hunter to be killed. You did the best you could in a difficult situation. You took charge after Arno went missing, performed your surveillance mission with admirable professionalism and reacted in the best way possible to Min's capture. However, it is my duty to point out that you could have been killed as well." Ruth paused, taking a moment to carefully choose her words. "Tessa, I worry about how much you value your own life. A dead hunter is of no use to the Curia."

Tessa nodded. "I faced death in Iraq and now I'm hunting demons. I don't want to die. I actually have people I care about. But there are so few of us and so many of them. And we only get lucky for so long. We take a bad hit or make a wrong call and we're gone. Like Arno."

"Does that frighten you?"

"No," Tessa said. "I accept it. If I become another mangled corpse in an unmarked grave, I'm okay with that, because I know why I'm fighting. I fight for Min and Desange and even guys like Arno. I'm fighting because killing creatures like Marit reduces the misery of the world, even if only a little. How many addicts like my brother did she create?" She settled in the chair, the hard plastic digging into her back. "If I can help the Curia rid the world of monsters like Marit, I will."

Ruth stared at Tessa, a smile slowly spreading across her face. "You are ready to be a hunter. If you ever have concerns, or doubts, and need someone to talk to, reach out to your fellow hunters. Sometimes hunts can be traumatic. If you find you need professional help once you're out in the field, we have resources for that. All you have to do is ask. I'll always be here for you, Tessa. Do you want to talk to a therapist about Iceland?"

She shook her head. "I'm fine, but you may want to check in on Min." Tessa had read her AAR, which went into excruciating details about what Marit had done, from the flirtation on the dance floor to the taunts and torments while they waited for Tessa in the pool house. She seemed to be handling it well, but Tessa wasn't certain. She had seen this behavior in Iraq, where a colleague acted fine after a traumatic event. It was only later – after substance abuse, violence toward others or suicide – that the deep-seated problems became clear.

"Iceland was a difficult assignment for you and Min." Ruth lightly drummed her fingers on the metal desktop. "I made it worse. I should never have teamed you with Arno."

Tessa was surprised at Ruth's admission of fallibility. *She must really feel bad about the position Min and I were put in.*

"My miscalculation started a chain of events that led to the incident in the pool house. And for that, I am sorry."

Tessa felt sympathy for Ruth. *She's been running the Curia for centuries, sending thousands of hunters to their deaths. If she makes a mistake, people die. Every demon we fail to stop corrupts more souls. The pressure must be enormous.*

"Another demon was destroyed. We've saved a lot of people from addiction and death." She nodded toward Ruth. "You're a part of that."

Ruth felt a swelling in her chest. She was used to people looking at her with awe, the angel leading the war against demons. But to hear Tessa's heartfelt words was something rare, even in the centuries of her existence.

"Thank you," she said, her impassive voice betraying none of her feelings. "You'll be heading to Los Angeles soon to join the North American cell, so we won't see each other as often. I've enjoyed our time together. I'm looking forward to following your career growth. You could become one of our top hunters in America." She held out her hand. "Congratulations, Hunter Sinclair."

Tessa shook the offered hand. "I'm excited to start."

Chapter 43

The sun was high, a pale white disk in a hazy sky. A light breeze blew off the crashing water, carrying the scent of salt. The decaying buildings creaked and groaned, a portent of their eventual fate. A pod of gray seals had beached on the bare gravel shore that separated the village from the ocean. Their grunts and groans echoed through the buildings, like the ghosts of long-dead villagers.

Tessa sat next to Min on the squat stone wall that surrounded the pile of boards and shingles where the village church once stood. A weathered cross stuck up through the jumble.

She shifted on the wall and took a drink from the thermos, feeling the warm hot chocolate chase away the December chill. "I'm going to miss you," Tessa said, passing the thermos to Min.

"I'm going to miss you too," Min replied. "The Academy won't be the same without you. The things we've done together..."

Tessa laughed. "I'll never get over how ready you were to fuck Marit."

Min laughed, almost spitting out her cocoa. "A girl has needs."

For a few moments, the two women sat listening to the moan of the wind and the grunts of the seals.

"It will be hard without you, Tessa." Min leaned into her.

Tessa wrapped an arm around Min's shoulders. "Hey, you'll be fine. Fuck that, you'll be amazing. You saved my life."

Min grinned. "Thanks. I owe you more than I can ever repay."

Tessa felt her eyes get misty. She gave Min a hug. "I've learned a lot from you too." She took the thermos back and sipped. "Deep friendships are hard for me, especially with women. I'm not sure I've ever had a female friend that gets me."

Min started to cry. "You better keep in touch. I'll always have your back. No matter where I end up in the world, you can count on me to come through."

Tessa felt a lump growing in her throat. *What if this is it? Then a life of text messages and missed calls. Each of us is going through our lives, but not together.*

The metal growling of Uri's Land Rover could be heard over the whistling wind and animal grunts. He was driving up to the helicopter pad, ready to take Tessa away.

"It's time." Tessa took off her gloves.

Min did the same. She gripped Tessa's hands tightly, the warm skin warding off the cold air around them.

"You're going to get through the Academy and become a great hunter. And stay curious. Your research is important."

Min looked sadly down. "I will."

Uri honked the horn of the Land Rover.

"I better go. I don't want to piss off Uri. He might toss me out of the bird."

"You can kick his ass," Min said.

The two women stood up and hugged. Neither wanted the moment to end.

Uri honked again and got out of his vehicle, walking decisively toward the helipad.

Tessa let out a sigh. "I'll contact you when I get to LA."

"Okay." Min released her hug. "I love you."

"I love you too."

Tessa felt a strong gust as the blades of the helicopter came alive. The overgrown grass on the turf roofs bent in the breeze. She gave Min one last hug and then turned and walked to the helipad. She didn't look back as she boarded.

The helicopter lifted off, the island rapidly receding. Tessa looked down, catching a glimpse of Min's bright yellow jacket among the gray buildings.

"Sad about leaving your friend?" Uri asked.

Tessa wiped her eyes with her gloved hands. "Yes."

"Get used to it."

Tessa wanted to tell Uri to go fuck himself, but instead she looked out the window, watching a gathering of puffins flying offshore. She thought of her relationships with Tyler, Min and Desange. They were complicated, forged by shared, broken experiences. *People like us, we can't lose each other. We are family.*